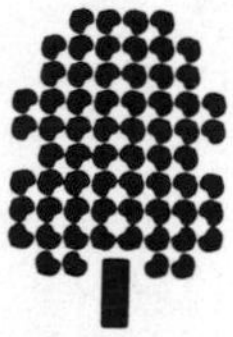

The
Sunset Bomber

D. KINCAID

THE LINDEN PRESS
SIMON & SCHUSTER
New York, 1986

LINDEN PRESS/SIMON & SCHUSTER and colophon are trademarks of
Simon & Schuster, Inc.

Designed by Levavi & Levavi

Manufactured in the United States of America

10 9 8 7 6 5 4 3 2 1

Library of Congress Cataloging in Publication Data
Kincaid, D.
   The sunset bomber.

   I. Title.
PS3561.I424S8   1986   813'.54   85-23712
ISBN: 0-671-60444-9

For L. 1-4-3-7 (and 16)

*J*ust at the corner, the light turned red. Fighting the big car to a stop, Harry glanced to his right. He saw a bronze Mercedes, a mass of honey-blond hair, a trim gray suit. Chanel?

She turned and fixed Harry with wide amber eyes. With a gloved hand, she motioned him to lower his window.

He did, fascinated.

Her voice was ladylike, serene, the large eyes frank, vulnerable, questioning.

"Would you like some head?"

Stunned, Harry tried not to show it. Nervously, he glanced at the still red light, his mind racing.

A hooker? Not likely. Too much style, refinement. A crazy? Maybe. But lovely. Christ! Once in a lifetime this happens, and I'm on my way to a funeral.

The light turned green. Harry tensed. He raised his left arm and pointed to his watch. "Late," he shouted over the noise of accelerating cars. "Meet me here at three?" A horn blasted behind them.

She smiled and slowly nodded, then pulled away into the flow of traffic. Harry accelerated too, moving behind her across the lanes. Her license plate was "CAA 1." CAA was a major talent agency. An agent's wife? . . . an agent?

Harry looked at his watch. Already one o'clock. How could he make Forest Lawn, sit through the service and get back to La Cienega and Sunset—all in two hours? Why hadn't he said four o'clock or, for that matter, six or seven? Two hours, for Christ's sake. What an idiot!

*H*arry swung the Bentley through the massive iron gates of the cemetery and followed the small road that wound through the beautifully landscaped grounds. At a crossing, a tall man in a black suit stepped from the guard house of English stone, motioning Harry to stop. He held a clipboard.

"The David Grant funeral, please." Harry found he was matching his tone to the occasion. It annoyed him.

"Chapel of the Pines, sir—keep bearing right."

Harry already knew where the funeral would be. As David Grant's attorney and executor, he'd been there the day before to make the "arrangements." The term itself was odd—all wrong. All the vitality, the electric energy that was David Grant was suddenly gone, shut off, leaving Harry to negotiate for the physical storage of the six-foot-three, two-hundred-pound thing that had been his friend.

"An oversized casket? We could bend Mr. Grant's legs if there's a financial problem." . . . "Bronze avoids seepage, you know." . . . "A dark business suit? He's not the same size now, you realize. He'll want a good fit." . . . "Why, of course, the coat has no back. Why would it need one?" . . . "A pillow?" . . . "A backrest?" Jesus!

For fifteen years Harry and his wife had been entertained, appalled, fascinated by David Grant, his heightened sense of drama, his brilliant, often cruel wit, his bizarre costumes, outrageous stunts and sybaritic life-style. Now, at forty-two, all that was over. David Grant, talented director, bodybuilder and art collector—cynical, romantic and proudly homosexual—had broken his neck in a fall from his Malibu terrace.

Harry felt a mixture of sorrow and anger. The Goddamn fool! Probably too much coke or too much pain. With David it was always too much something. But to fall off his terrace . . . ?

Harry drove up the narrow road, passing other mourners, still hurrying toward the chapel. Jane Fonda and Tom Hayden, old friends of David's, strode ahead looking grave, somber. Annella DeRe, the Brazilian actress, her black crepe dress clinging to her lush figure, stood under an olive tree, checking her makeup in a pocket mirror. Running a pink tongue around her lips, she put the mirror in her purse and stepped back into the road. Ray Stark, the producer who "discovered" David years before, turned to wave as Harry drove slowly by. Funny, Harry thought, I'm suing the bastard—we're not speaking—but here he waves. Where death is concerned, we're a band of brothers.

The bright sun reflected off the windshield and gave the entire scene a fragmented, dreamlike quality. The full hedges shielded those traveling the road from any feeling that this was a cemetery. And it *was* more than a cemetery. It was the dramatic setting for a gathering together of the Hollywood "family" in a time of bereavement, a happening, a ritual dance of kings, priests and commoners, as carefully prescribed and weighted with symbolism as anything that took place at Karnak, Stonehenge or Chichén Itzá.

Rounding a bend, Harry arrived before a stone chapel that belonged more in the Cotswolds than in Burbank. Its soft beige stone rose gently from the rolling green lawn to form a postcard picture against the bright-blue California sky.

Harry parked behind the chapel and made his way through the well-dressed mourners still milling on the steps, eyeing each other's outfits, moving from group to group, shaking hands, kissing cheeks, their voices low but discernible. "No great talent, but the son of a bitch knew how to live." . . . "He had Redford and Hoffman both thinking they were going to play the part." . . . "He put this ten-foot bronze cock in the swimming pool, underwater—at the deep end." . . . "If they give him a shroud, it better be basic black with pearls." . . . "Nine o'clock at Morton's . . . just the four of us, okay?"

Harry felt a vigorous slap on the back and turned to see Joe Miletti. A rival director and equally controversial, Miletti had feuded with David Grant for years. His concession to funereal custom was a black wool tie worn with his usual blue chambray workshirt. His broad, tan face was shielded by dark aviator glasses.

"I'm surprised David didn't leave orders barring me from his funeral, Harry. The gay D.W. Griffith sure knew I hated him; and, believe me, I wasn't the only one."

"Well, *someone* must have liked him, Joe. Lots of people are here."

"Come on, Harry, you know DeMille's great line 'Give the people what they want and they'll turn out every time.' Keep your pecker up, kid." He squeezed Harry's arm and moved away into the crowd.

Ray Stark arrived on the steps of the chapel out of breath. He embraced David Begelman emotionally, each patting the other's back the ritual three times.

Behind them, Karen Lloyd, tall, lovely and, in Harry's view, the brightest producer in town, stood talking with Mario Puzo. He was listening intently, chewing on his unlit cigar. She's undoubtedly out to buy his new book, Harry thought, and God help him if he's trying to negotiate with her. As Harry passed, Karen gave him a wistful smile. Harry knew she had been fond of David, tried to help him and must now feel the loss.

Now, those on the steps began drifting inside. Harry found himself walking beside Cary Grant, white-haired and splendid in a beautifully cut gray suit. He nodded to Harry as they both moved with the crowd into the chapel.

Coming inside from the bright sunshine, Harry caught the strong scent of flowers, the redolence of death. He identified himself and was directed to the first row. Moving down the aisle, he saw the aristocracy of Hollywood interspersed with David's friends from other worlds. Expensively tailored studio heads and grim-faced superstars sat among lady motorcyclists in black leather, professional wrestlers and David's black houseman, Achmed, wearing a turban and weeping uncontrollably.

Aaron Fernbach, the head of Consolidated Studios, was seated on an aisle. Politely, but firmly, he fended off those who would stop to shake hands, chat, demonstrate publicly their link to the source of power. Frank Price and Michael Eisner, both in dark suits and darker glasses, were quietly talking behind their programs like Venetian conspirators, while Lew Wasserman, his long face impassive, stared silently at the flower-bedecked casket at the front of the room. Each had the power of life and death over the careers and lives of thousands. Each could impose feelings, attitudes, ideas on hundreds of millions. Each in turn had to answer to stockholders and boards of directors . . . often questioning, sometimes dangerous.

Harry looked around the room for Paolo Monti, David Grant's assistant, roommate and lover. Not seeing Paolo, he took a seat next to Kevin Shaw, the Broadway choreographer. Years ago, Shaw too had lived with David, parting after a celebrated fistfight in Lutèce that had left the fashionable New York restaurant a shambles. Seeing him made Harry wonder once again what kind of crazy, uncontrollable rage would cause a man to start punching his dinner companion in such a place. Now, Shaw was ashen, greeting Harry quietly in a trembling voice.

Harry looked over to his right. At the end of the row was a wiry, deeply tanned woman in her sixties, her dyed blond hair framing a leathery, hawklike face—David's mother. "Florida Fannie," he called her, or "the author of my misery." Harry had last seen her sitting at the hospital, rocking back and forth, moaning "Buddy, forgive me. Oh Buddy, forgive me." That's what she called him, "Buddy." But "forgive me" for *what?* Harry wasn't sure.

Aside from the mourners, the setting was one of calm and solemnity. Soft light filtered through the stained glass windows, birds sang sweetly and, in the background, an organ softly played a hymn. The guests filing to their seats and those already seated were silent or spoke in funereal whispers.

Harry glanced around, nodding somberly to friends whose eyes he caught. The twinge of sorrow returned. Without real interest, he began to read the printed program, waiting for the ceremony to start.

Suddenly, the silence of the chapel was shattered by an enraged bellow, electrically amplified and resounding across the room at full volume, "Then there won't be a funeral, you fucking faggot!"

Harry thought for just a second and, amid a hundred simultaneous gasps, raced through a nearby door into the small room behind the altar.

Three people were in the room, each in a state of extreme agitation. A stocky red-faced Morrie Grant, David's brother, obviously the source of the thundering words, was attempting to pull a long Hebrew prayer shawl from the clutching grasp of Paolo Monti. Paolo, slight and blond, was muttering northern Italian curses with obvious rage. In the corner, pale beyond imagination, was a stammering representative of Forest Lawn Memorial Park.

Harry stepped between Morrie and Paolo. "Keep his hands off the tallith or I'll break his fuckin' neck," Morrie shouted.

Paolo literally spit his reply. "This hypocritical asshole wants to wrap David in that Goddamn rag—*David*, can you imagine?"

The cemetery official somehow made himself heard. "Gentlemen, the loudspeaker to the chapel is open. All of those present can hear you."

Harry spotted the amplifier and, moving swiftly across the room, managed to switch it off. He knew David hated the idea of religion, mocked it unmercifully. He guessed that the family had resented that for years and now, finally, wanted to bring him back into the fold.

The two antagonists glowered at each other... sputtering, ready to strike.

"Mr. Grant, let's talk for a minute" Harry said, nodding in the direction of the clergyman's robing room. David's brother angrily followed Harry into the anteroom.

"Look, Cain, you may be Hollywood's hottest lawyer, but this ain't your business or that fruit's. It's the family's business. It'll kill my mother if we don't bury Buddy in that tallith. So we're going to do it, no matter what anyone says."

Buddy, for Christ's sake, thought Harry. Morrie Grant hadn't seen his brother in twenty-five years, except to borrow money.

"Mr. Grant," Harry said, "your mother should be made as happy as possible and logically you're correct. You have the right to determine how David is dressed *if* you pay for the funeral. Now, if you're willing to assume the financial responsibility, we can tell Mr. Monti he cannot pay the costs and call the shots, that the family insists on it."

"You mean the guy who pays decides?"

Harry nodded.

Morrie Grant's aggression waned. "Well, I don't know—" His voice trailed off.

Harry knew he had him. "Look, Mr. Grant, suppose I get Monti to agree to put the tallith in the casket but not necessarily around

David. You could tell your mother you got it in there and just not be so specific about where . . . okay?"

Grant looked sore as hell, but he had no way out.

"Okay . . . but it's got to go in. No guinea fag's going to keep a tallith out of Buddy's coffin." He was already convincing himself he'd won. Harry nodded, led Grant into the other room and took Paolo into the anteroom.

"Okay, Paolo . . . we can make a deal that gives them nothing but gets the funeral on."

"What deal?"

"The tallith won't be around him, but it'll be in the coffin, so—"

"Nothing doing, Harry. Forget it! Don't make deals. David would shit at the idea of a Goddamn prayer shawl in there and you know it! That *giadrul* and his mother probably killed David. She was alone in the house with him when he died. You knew that, didn't you?"

"Paolo, listen to me, Goddamn it!" Harry interrupted. "If they push us, they've got a good case to wrap him in the tallith, not just fold it in there. Now talk sense. David doesn't know and doesn't care."

After a moment's thought, the young Italian took Harry's hands in his, smiling gravely. "Okay, Harry. That's okay. You're a good man to work it out. I'm sorry to cause you so much trouble. And, listen, I apologize for what I said about the prayer shawl. . . . I know it's your religion too. I meant no offense."

"No offense taken, Paolo. I understood."

And so the deal was done. Solemnly, they filed back into the chapel, the object of a hundred curious murmurs. Morrie bent over his mother, whispering assurances that David would have his prayer shawl after all. Harry and Paolo quietly took their seats, ready for the service to begin.

Harry thought how funny the whole thing would have seemed to David. He could see his friend, lounging barefoot, in one of his outrageous Hawaiian shirts, shaking his big head with laughter. "What a scene, Harry. Queen Mary of Mantua ready to scratch the eyes out of Morrie the Cretin. And what a headline. 'Grieving widow and foul-mouthed brother shock town.' Oh wow, Harry, oh wow!"

The image brought a smile, but another stab of sorrow—then, questions.

What had that last night been like? The coke, the booze, that harridan mother, making him crazy. Did he really fall or did she push him? Christ, they'd been battling enough and she was tough enough. Poor bastard, his last sight on earth was probably his own mother shoving him off a cliff. But then David would probably think that was funny too.

Halfway through the service, Harry grew bored and irritated. He'd heard lavish praise for David as an artist, a collector and a human being. But, no one had touched on what David Grant was really like. Many of those present must have known of David's neurotic need to torture and humiliate himself and everyone around him. Nobody was talking about that.

Harry's wife was an example. For years, Nancy had been in thrall to David's wit and dramatic flair. Yet she had not spoken to David the last six months of his life and refused to attend his funeral.

David, who loved what he called a "put-on," had invited Nancy to a "party" while Harry was out of town. When she arrived, Nancy found that the party was only David and an aging Western star. Soon after Nancy arrived, David left the house on what he said was an errand. The cowboy, already fairly drunk, jumped Nancy the moment David's car left the drive. After she wrestled her way free and fought him off for several minutes, the aging star told her angrily that David had assured him Nancy slept around widely and was aching to get him into bed.

David had just wanted to see what would happen. If Nancy fought the cowboy off, it would be a good joke. If she didn't ... well, that would be interesting too.

That was David, and describing him as "the cutting edge of the neo-surrealist movement" or "a loyal and loving friend" or "one of the nation's most distinguished and knowledgeable collectors of Oriental art" hardly captured the David Grant that Harry knew and the others must have seen as well.

Near the end of the service, Harry realized it was all a waste. It did nothing to make him feel any better and certainly couldn't help David. His thoughts returned to the blonde in the Mercedes. He glanced quickly at his watch. It was already two-thirty. If he skipped the interment, he could still make it back to La Cienega and Sunset by three, maybe three-fifteen at the latest. She might wait . . . if she ever came back at all.

The final hymn sounded and the mourners filed out onto the chapel steps blinking in the bright sunshine, adjusting clothing, patting each other, touching, consoling. Harry moved quickly through the crowd—a sea of Galanos, Armani and Blass. He smiled sadly to Barbra Streisand across the patio, nodded to Barry Diller and Warren Beatty, who gave him a conspiratorial wink, and stopped to shake hands with Mayor Bradley, whose quiet dignity always made Harry feel somehow better, calmer. Then, excusing himself, he hurried down the steps toward his car. Suddenly he found himself spun into a tearful hug by David's secretary, Lorna.

"Oh my God, Harry, how could he be gone? How? Oh God, how I'll miss him!"

"I know, Lorna, I know."

"I loved him, you know, Harry—adored him. There's no life without that man—none."

"I know, I know" was all Harry could manage. "We'll all miss him, Lorna. He was one in a million."

Some phrasemaker, thought Harry, stealing another glance at his watch. He was not fast enough for Lorna. "What are you looking at, Harry? You're coming back to the house, aren't you?"

"Lorna, I can't even stay for the interment. I'm supposed to be in court this afternoon. I've got an hour off and I'm late now. I've got to leave. I'll be over later."

"When?"

"Well, maybe five or six o'clock. But I'll be there."

This last was said as Harry had already begun to stride purposefully toward his car.

He'd be at least ten minutes late. She might still be there. But who knew what to expect from a blonde who blew men at traffic lights.

Harry started to pull out of his parking space when a huge man leaned in the window blocking out the sun. "Harry . . . Jesus, I hate to get you at David's funeral, but I got a tragedy on my hands—a fucking catastrophe, Harry, and I need your help."

"Hello, Ben. I didn't know you knew David."

"Yeah, I sold him that house in Malibu. It used to be mine, you know."

Ben Brody had made it big in the chain store business after the war. He'd lost it almost as big in the last ten years. Failure didn't suit his size and style, and he was depressing. But in the old days, he'd paid Harry's firm very big fees and Harry felt he owed him.

"Ben, I've got about one minute, then I've got to get to court. Can you call me?"

"Sure, but let me use the minute. I've only got one real asset left, Harry, that old store building up the coast in Gaynorville—worth maybe three hundred thousand dollars." Harry nodded. "Well, Maurice King tells me this morning that part of my building's on his property next door—where he's going to build a high rise. He says he wants me to move it."

"How much of your building's on his land?"

"He says an inch."

"An inch? Move the building for an inch? That's crazy." Harry looked at his watch, "He's conning you, Ben. He wants a payoff, the greedy bastard. I'll convince him you can't pay. Probably the survey is wrong anyway. . . . Look, Ben, I'm late as hell for court. I promise I'll fix it. Call me later."

Not waiting for an answer, Harry put the car in gear. Ben stepped away looking hurt, but relieved, and Harry pulled away with a noise and recklessness that he hoped would be attributed to his overpowering grief at David Grant's passing.

Two blocks before La Cienega and Sunset Harry saw flashing red lights in his rearview mirror. Christ, a cop! Harry pulled the Bentley over and waited what seemed an eternity while the officer got out of his car, studied Harry's rear plate and then sauntered leisurely to the front of Harry's car.

"What's the trouble officer?" said Harry, playing the sincere, solid citizen. It had no effect.

"Your license, sir." Harry handed it over and waited another eternity while the patrolman appeared to memorize the ten-line document.

"Did you know this expired last month, Mr. Cain?"

Harry did, but didn't say so.

"No, really? My secretary's supposed to see that doesn't happen. I'm very sorry about that, officer. I'll take care of it right away."

"Well sir, you don't have this year's license sticker either. That's why I stopped you."

"Well, it's here in the glove compartment, somewhere."

"Could I see it, sir?"

Harry's glove compartment was crammed with stereo tapes, old gasoline receipts and a brief he had taken home to study.

"I can't seem to lay my hands on it just now, but I've got one all right, and I'll see that it gets put on."

"Look, Mr. Cain, I've seen you in court. You're a well-known, responsible guy and I figure you own the Bentley. But you shouldn't be driving it. Not without a valid license. Where you heading?"

"Where?" Harry turned red. "Uh...to my office, nine thousand Sunset, right down the street."

"I'll follow you there, Mr. Cain. You get someone to drive you to the Department of Motor Vehicles and renew that license. Otherwise, don't drive."

The cop strolled back to his patrol car and waved to Harry to start.

Shit, what unbelievable luck! Harry pulled away from the curb theatrically, signaling and looking both ways. The cop pulled out after him.

Five frustrating minutes later, Harry pulled into the garage of his building, waving with a forced grin at the cop, who fortunately continued down Sunset away from Harry's rendezvous.

Harry counted to sixty, backed his car around and headed out of the garage. When he reached the street, he sped in the direction of La Cienega. It was three-thirty.

She was gone . . . or she'd never been there. Harry made three trips around the block. Maybe she was late too. He pulled up to the curb and tried to look nonchalant. Christ, what if the cop shows up again before she does? Ten minutes later, he knew he was fooling himself. She wasn't coming.

Harry drove back to his office, wondering what had gone through her mind. Had she waited, hoping and then giving up? More likely she found another guy at the next corner and took him home for incredible sex.

The thought depressed Harry immensely. No question, he thought, I blew it. Then he smiled. That's the trouble, *nobody* blew it. Then he had a thought. Not a bad thought. Maybe there was a way after all.

There were twelve phone messages, two labeled "urgent," when Harry finally reached his desk. He breathed deeply, enjoying the cool air and soft lights.

He surveyed the room, pleased as always. Deep-red Oriental rugs were thrown over a thick gray carpet that blended into soft-gray walls, accented by smoked mirrors and chrome lamps. The desk was a long, gray lacquer table, the chairs and sofas deco-opulent in gray velvet. Dominating everything were floor-to-ceiling windows that provided a dramatic view of the city.

Summbitch has style, Harry thought. He meant himself. Then he smiled, catching himself taking credit for his wife's superb taste. It was Nancy who redecorated his office the year before, replacing the English antiques and walnut paneling with the cool and soothing deco grays. She'd chosen the antiques too, years earlier. And before the antiques, he thought, there'd been what? Orange crates? Very nearly. But that was another story.

The phone rang with a muted warble. "Mr. Brody calling, Mr. Cain."

"I'll get back to him in a minute, Clara. Get me Skip Corrigan."

He read through the messages again until the intercom buzzed. "Skip Corrigan, Mr. Cain."

"Hello, Skip."

"Yeah, Mr. Cain."

"Skip, I want you to trace a California plate for me. Can you do it fast?"

"Sure, Mr. Cain, easy... what kind of a case?"

"Uh... confidential for a while, Skip... okay?"

"Sure, Mr. Cain"—Harry thought he could hear the hurt in his investigator's voice—"what's the number?"

"CAA 1."

"Twenty minutes max, Mr. Cain. You know the Skipper."

"I sure do, Skip... thanks."

The intercom buzzed again. "Carl Malone here to see you, Mr. Cain."

"Here, now?"

"Yes, sir, he has a four-o'clock appointment."

Harry had forgotten. The biggest divorce case in the state and he'd forgotten all about it.

"Send him in, Clara."

He reached for a file labeled "Malone Valuation," unread since it arrived the preceding day. His practiced eye swept down the columns to the bottom line, quickly absorbing the conclusions, leaving the details for further study.

A few seconds later, the gray paneled door opened, admitting the brighter hallway light and, with it, Carl Malone, one of the toughest and richest men Harry knew and, right now, the most worried.

Malone was a tall, athletic-looking man, with a thick head of white hair. Although he looked in his fifties, Harry knew from the file he was sixty-two. Wearing a well-tailored dark-blue suit, white shirt and light-blue tie, Malone radiated vigor and force. He gave Harry a firm handshake and eased his long body into a chair. Leaning forward, he fixed Harry with intense blue eyes.

"Trial's coming up fast, Harry. How's it look?"

"Same problems we talked about before, Carl—the Goddamn community property claim. Sixty million bucks. It's a big number, Carl."

"I don't see it, Harry. I had the steel company when I married her. How can it possibly be community property?"

"Carl, we've already gone through this. All she has to do is convince a judge you promised her it was half hers."

"With nothing in writing?"

"With nothing in writing, Carl. Usually, no judge will buy that kind of claim; but, with Fiona, I'm worried. She's one hell of a witness, beautiful, refined, Mayfair accent. A judge'll love her. He *could* believe her.

"That's why I'm worried, Carl. That's why I wanted you to come in today. We've got *you*. That's it. How do you prove you didn't say something? All you can do is deny you said it and try to show by the circumstances that it's improbable you did. That's what we've got to work on.

"Anyway, even though you had the steel company before you were married, you started Malone Electronics during the marriage and she's certainly going to get half of that."

Malone grinned. "I told you to forget that one, Harry. The electronics company's done nothing but lose money since I started it. It's worth a few hundred thousand at the most."

"You're being foolish, Carl." He patted the file on his desk. "Oh, the numbers back you up okay, but you don't realize what a so-called 'expert' can do to the valuation of a company. He can double it, triple it even; and sometimes a judge will buy his opinion as a way of giving a woman some money in a close case."

Malone shook his head, impatient at what he was hearing. "But Harry, for Christ's sake, she slept with eighteen guys in the three years we've been married, probably more. Dean says she can't get a dime." Dean was Carl's thirty-year-old son by his first marriage.

"Dean's wrong, Carl. I'm telling you that doesn't mean a thing in California. We've got 'no fault divorce.' She can fuck a gorilla and still get half your property. The only issue is how much property and how much support. Her sleeping around isn't even admissible in evidence."

"The support I don't mind, Harry. It's deductible and how much can it be? But half the property . . . thirty million dollars . . . for three years in which she fucked half the Bel Air Country Club. That's the most unfair thing I ever heard of."

Harry could see his telephone light flashing. He wondered if it was Skip Corrigan. He looked back at Malone.

"Well, those are the rules, Carl, and we've got to use those rules to win. There's no other way, so forget it."

"Okay, Harry, okay. Listen, I know you're the best. You'll do it. What can I do to help?"

"Get me every paper she ever signed or wrote, Carl. Everything you can find. Maybe we can come up with something helpful.

"I don't mean to discourage you. We'll find a way, but we can't take her claims lightly. . . . Look, Carl, I've got to rush down to court now—an emergency thing. . . . Can we finish this tomorrow?"

"Sure, Harry. How about Scandia for lunch?"

"That's great, Carl. Thanks."

Harry came around the desk to indicate that the meeting was over. Malone rose and made his way to the door. As he left, he tried again, "Still, Harry, Dean says she won't get a dime."

"Dean's full of shit, Carl, don't fool yourself. . . . And Carl—get me those papers. We really need 'em."

When Malone left the room, Harry turned to his two "urgent" messages. He found that, as so often occurred, each caller had used the word "urgent" just to get a quick response. One, a successful television producer, was suing his ex-business manager for fraud. Even though his case had been pending for over a year, he called just to find out if there was "anything new." Harry reminded the man that they were still waiting to come to trial and assured him that he would be told of any new developments. The other call was from an elderly novelist who felt that the federal government had been conspiring for thirty years to hinder the sales of his books. He wanted Harry to take the case on a contingency. Harry politely declined. Some "urgent," thought Harry. He was getting into a bad mood.

The intercom sounded again.

"Mrs. Cain calling."

"Okay, Clara."

"Hi ya, Nance . . . Jesus, what a day!"

"How'd the funeral go, Harry? I'm starting to feel guilty."

"No, you did what you thought was right. Anyway, it was mass hypocrisy with damn little real feeling."

"Well, in a way it's good I didn't go. We almost had nuclear war at the Art Council meeting. It started out peacefully enough but then . . ."

While he listened, Harry skimmed through his mail. A $3,000 bill from a court reporter who had been stiffed by the client and expected Harry to pay. The balance on his Air Travel Card was $7,200, I. Magnin's was $4,500, Greenblatt's Wine and Liquor $1,850, and American Express $3,800 for one month. Christ! Then a note from his accountant. His quarterly tax payment was $98,000. Harry sighed. The fees were big, and he was as well paid as anyone in the country, his income ranging between six hundred thousand to a million dollars a year. But the big fees came in irregularly; and although the money rolled in from time to time, oh God, how fast and how regularly it rolled out.

He turned his attention back to Nancy's problems over housing the museum's Oriental collection. She had handled things well. She usually did.

"Anyway, Harry, it ended up okay. But for a time there, wow!

"Listen, Harry, don't forget Arthur Abrahms is coming for dinner. Gail and her roommate are coming too; so come early if you can, maybe 6:00 or 6:30."

"Look, Nance, I'd just as soon miss an hour or two of Abrahms. He may be curator at the Metropolitan Museum, but he's a pompous ass. Anyway, I'm up to my ears in work. I can't be there until 8:30 or 9:00 o'clock at the earliest."

"Harry, that's not fair." He could hear the tension in her voice. "Gail treasures her time with you and we're lucky to have a daughter that feels that way. Besides, as long as Arthur is the governor's advisor on the arts, and I'm chairman of the Art Council, we've got to get along. He'll be coming at 7:30, Harry, and it's just plain rude if you don't show up till 8:30 or 9:00."

Harry could picture Nancy's intense, pained expression, the one that usually accompanied her lectures on his manners or behavior— lectures he often resented. Still, the Abrahms dinner *did* mean a lot to her, and there *was* Gail to consider. Harry's relationship with his daughter was a special one, his love for her a constant force in his life. And now, with his concern over her affair...

"Nancy, I don't really give a shit about Arthur Abrahms or what he thinks, but if it's important to you and Gail, I'll be there by 8:00 at the latest."

"Thanks, Harry, I'll tell Gail." He could hear the relief in her voice. "And Harry—I love you."

"Me too, hon. . . . See you later."

Harry hung up and gave his secretary his appointments for the following day. He had to be at Paramount at 11:00 o'clock and there was lunch with Carl Malone. At 3:00 he had to be out at UCLA to consult an expert in the economics department. He asked her to get him an appointment with Maurice King around 9:30 or 10:00 and to tell King's secretary that it was about Ben Brody. She called back to say that King would see him, but that it would have to be at 8:00 o'clock in the morning and at King's office. He agreed.

Then Harry used his private line to call Skip Corrigan. "Any luck?"

"Yes sir, just coming in right now . . . Carmel Ann Anderson . . . 1810 Starline Drive in Laurel Canyon."

"Thanks, Skip. You're great."

Harry smiled as he hung up. So that's "CAA." At least one mystery was solved.

He picked up the Malone valuation file and started to analyze the pages of factual data. His mind wandered. He slipped into his jacket, stepped into the outer office and left instructions that, because of David Grant's funeral, he'd be out the rest of the afternoon. He straightened his tie and, glancing nervously at his watch, walked to the elevator as quickly as dignity allowed.

Starline Drive was a rustic, winding road that twisted up into the hills from Laurel Canyon, one of the several passes between the city and the San Fernando Valley. Settled years before the others, and far less fashionable, Laurel Canyon was the home of artists, poets, musicians, young professionals, old ladies with numerous cats, starving Russian aristocrats, long-haired Jewish acupuncturists and others of independent spirit who loved its wooded, bohemian ambiance.

Architecturally, it was extraordinary. As Harry pulled the Bentley through the steep curves of Starline Drive, he passed log cabins, turreted Spanish castles, a Moorish mini-palace with minarets and a white onion-shaped dome, and, on a distant hillside, a glass saucer-shaped home resting on long steel columns, seemingly ready to soar over the canyon into space.

Eighteen ten Starline Drive was a tiny Cape Cod cottage set far back from the road and shielded from view by a thick growth of trees and shrubs.

Harry pulled up in front and walked toward the house. On the vine-covered porch was a large easel, heavily caked with paint. He could hear a Mozart symphony playing somewhere inside. He rang the bell.

"Who is it?" came a voice Harry thought he recognized as hers.

"Harry Cain. I wanted to see you."

The door opened an inch or two, the chain still attached. There was the face, even more striking than Harry remembered. The large amber eyes were set wide apart and radiated intelligence. The high cheekbones were framed by a softly flowing mass of honey-colored hair.

"Are you selling something, Mr. Cain?" That hurt. Harry was sure she'd remember his face as vividly as he remembered hers.

"No, I'm not selling anything. We met earlier today . . . at Sunset and La Cienega . . . I was late for a funeral. I wanted to see you again."

"Oh" was all she said, but she turned noticeably pale.

"I checked your license plate. I was anxious to see you, really. I went back to the corner but you'd gone."

"Oh." Still pale.

"Couldn't you take the chain off? I'm really not scary."

"Oh yeah, sure . . . it's not that you're scary . . . I just never . . . this place is different . . . it's where I work and live." The chain came down, the door opened.

She was not really what Harry expected at all. She was much taller, maybe five ten, and very slim. She wore paint-splattered jeans, sneakers and a white T-shirt that stretched tightly across the nipples of small, high breasts.

The room was brightly lit. On every wall and stacked in every corner were vividly colored paintings in various stages of completion.

"It's my studio and my living room too. Please come in and sit down. Would you like some wine?"

Harry nodded. She left the room and Harry looked around. Aside from the paintings, the furnishings were spare . . . a record player and three stacks of albums, a low Danish modern sofa; across the room, another easel, and a simple pine table bearing tubes of paint, linseed oil, thinner, a palette and ten or fifteen brushes. In a moment, the girl returned with a chilled bottle of Chardonnay and two glasses.

"Quitting time anyway, I guess," she said. She handed Harry his wine and filled her own glass.

"It's four-thirty. Is that when you usually quit?"

"No, not really ... I often work till two or three in the morning. I just said that because I'm nervous. I ... I've never had anyone here that I met on the street."

"Where do you take them?" Harry was nervous himself but fascinated.

"The car. Only the car. I park in a side street."

"Why do you do it?"

"I like it. It turns me on ... a lot."

"Only the car?" Harry asked, somewhat hoarsely.

"Yes, only there ... I don't know why I'm telling you this, Mr. Cain."

"Do you go out there every day ... I mean in the streets?"

"No, just every once in a while. It builds up. I think about it more and more and then I go out and do it. Then I come back here where nobody can get me ... except you, Mr. Cain."

Mozart's counterpoint filled the brief silence.

"I won't ask why you came. I guess it's obvious."

For a moment Harry thought of starting some line, but it was no use. She was right, it was obvious. "It was an exciting idea, a really beautiful girl at a traffic light. I mean, it's not your everyday experience." She smiled. "But it's more than that. Curiosity, fascination too."

"Well, you know my name, I guess, Carmel Anderson, and you've seen that I'm a painter and you know my hobby is fellatio with strange men. What else is there?" This last was said with a wry grin.

"Well, where are you from and why are you here?"

"I'm from Boston. ... I'm twenty-six and I came here because I was miserable in Boston and thought I might be less miserable here."

"Are you?"

"Yes, I suppose I am. I can work well here and when I want to be turned on, I can. It wasn't very easy on Beacon Hill."

"I can imagine."

"You know Boston?"

"Harvard Law School...but not much time on Beacon Hill. I worked my way through, waiting tables at the Wursthaus in Cambridge."

It crossed Harry's mind that, when he was at Harvard, she had not been born. He pushed the thought away.

"I'll bet you made the *Law Review,* didn't you?"

"Yeah. How'd you guess that?"

She refilled their glasses. "You seem bright as a new penny, Mr. Cain, and you've got an electric ego. It shoots sparks across the room. You'd have to be the best at everything."

"Yeah, I suppose so."

"I'll bet you're impossible at sports, gotta win, gotta kill 'em." She smiled. "Right?"

"Pretty much."

"Well, we each have our compulsions, Mr. Cain. I wonder which is more destructive?"

Harry shrugged and grinned. What could he say? He'd often admitted to himself and to Nancy that he had the compulsive drive of the superachiever, but never did he really consider it destructive. Well, he had no desire to argue now. He was getting just a bit high anyway, too high for verbal sparring with this obviously bright lady.

Mozart was replaced by Antonio Carlos Jobim. Carmel, standing, holding her glass, began to sway with the sensual Brazilian jazz.

"Would you like to dance, Mr. Cain?"

They came together and the moment their bodies touched end to end there was no pretense of dancing. Her lips were one inch from his, her eyes swimming into his. "Are you sure you want to kiss me, Mr. Cain? I mean it's sort of against tradition."

Harry was sure.

She led him shyly by the hand to a bedroom in the back. Slowly Harry undressed her, kissing her hair, her face, her body and then roughly tearing off his own clothes and throwing them to the floor.

She was a surprise, not angular and grinding as he had expected from her long, thin body. She enveloped him with a sweet, caressing warmth and softness. They moved slowly, very slowly together, savoring the rising joy-filled sensation, until, in a very short time, they led each other into a long, shuddering, overwhelming climax.

"Wow, Mr. Cain, wow!"

"Yeah, wow" was all Harry could manage, instinctively cuddling her in his arms.

She began to cry. "I didn't think I could any more. Not like that, not so good and not like that, no sir." She laughed at the same time the tears were rolling down her lovely cheekbones.

Harry began to kiss away the tears. "Well, you can. That's obvious. In fact, I'd say you're a superstar."

"You think so?" She brightened. "I can cook too."

Each wrapped in one of her kimonos, they sat on the bed eating liverwurst and bermuda onion sandwiches and drinking more of the white wine.

They talked easily together about many things—reminisced about places they'd both known in Boston. He told her about his cases and, warily, about his family.

She wanted to know if he loved his wife and, if so, why he did this kind of thing.

He didn't know for sure. He supposed, in part, he was seeking excitement, drama, heightened experience . . . and there were other complex reasons; but in this case, he said, it was mostly just that he wanted her, and loving his wife didn't stop that feeling one bit.

"In fact, I've got it right now. Or, more accurately, it's got me." He grinned. He slid his hand inside her kimono and felt her nipple harden instantly. He bent to kiss the erect nipple, moving his hand slowly down her body and up between her legs. He felt her moisten as she thrust upward against his caressing hand. He pulled her over on top of him, and once again felt her sweetness close down over and around him as they moved slowly, slightly, signaling internally, sending concentric ripples of feeling through each other until they were both moaning with the delicious sensation. They came almost immediately, clutching each other as the orgasm broke over them in undulating waves.

They held each other and swayed back and forth, savoring the joy.

Afterward, they talked again, the conversation flowing from subject to subject, without pattern. They spoke of Los Angeles, how it had changed and why Harry loved its raffish vitality. She described her family and how she, like her father and brother, had always lived on the income from a family trust, a fact that made her feel different, and, ironically, deprived. She told him of how she had become fascinated with painting and of her pride at finally selling some of her work, earning something for the first time. She speculated, with a self-deprecating smile, that painters, as a group, might have a tendency to sociopathic behavior. "It wasn't only Van Gogh," she said. "Take Forain. He painted like an angel, but was a vicious bigot, a leader in the campaign against Dreyfus." Harry argued that painters were no worse than any other creative group. He cited Shakespeare, who constantly squabbled over money and worked a devious scheme to corner the wool market, driving his neighbors into poverty. "And, of course, your friend Mozart. Unsurpassed music, but as a person . . . just dreadful; and Wagner was no bed of roses either. And how about Ezra Pound? That guy was a match for Forain any time."

"Pound for pound, the worst," she replied, grinning. He groaned and hugged her. They talked of everything that came into their minds, sometimes serious, sometimes laughing, reveling in the excitement of the new relationship.

At seven-thirty Harry showered, dressed and kissed her softly as he left. "I'll see you soon."

"I hope so."

Harry turned and walked down the path. As he reached the street she sang out, "I dig you, Mr. Cain."

Harry grinned and waved. He walked carefully down the path. Inside he was skipping.

*H*alf drunk and elated, Harry made his way home.

The large Mediterranean house, its lush gardens redolent with orange blossoms and jasmine, stood on a hill overlooking the city, sheltered from the road by a high wall.

From the house, its terraces and the dramatically lit pool, a million sparkling lights stretched for miles into the distance.

Harry was greeted at the door by Armando, his Guatemalan house-man. He could see a small group in the softly lit living room, a glowing fire casting their shadows on the stucco walls, the intricate

Florentine molding a realized dream of some long-dead former owner.

Arthur Abrahms had already been there some time. Heavy, bald and fiftyish, with a fringe of wispy black hair, Abrahms sat like a dark Buddha, a huge cigar clenched in his full lips, his faded denim shirt open four buttons to show his amazingly hairy chest.

He was already pontificating about modern art, stroking the hand of a slim, young girl dressed as a sixties hippy and certainly no more than eighteen. She was introduced just as "Sally."

Harry returned Abrahms's greeting, grinned at the situation and accepted an iced martini from Armando. Nancy sat across the room, looking darkly attractive, her slim figure beautifully draped in a white Holly Harp gown. Harry could see that she was nervous. He moved to her side and kissed her cheek, giving her arm an affectionate squeeze. She smiled up at him, grateful that he'd kept his promise.

"I'm surprised at you, Harry," Abrahms boomed. "How can one so obviously bright live here in Lalaland?" He did not wait for an answer but plunged ahead. "My God it's a cultural wasteland. Your so-called museum is sheer mediocrity, undiluted by charm. Your art galleries show either those dreadful children with the huge eyes or nudes painted on black velvet." Sally giggled and, encouraged, Abrahms continued. "Giant plaster angels and ceramic leopards pass as sculpture; and your architecture, my God!...a compendium of kitsch, from adobe to zolotone." Abrahms was gaining momentum, obviously relishing his own words and beginning to display his famous lack of tact.

At that point, however, his audience was distracted. Harry's daughter, Gail, arrived with her friend, Susan.

Gail's effect on Harry was always magic. He greeted her with a hug, grinning with love and pleasure at the delightful young woman he had produced. Willowy and dark like Nancy, she radiated intelligence and merriment. Her gamin haircut was a perfect frame for her piquant face and doe-like brown eyes. Her voice was musical, but her laugh was low, earthy. She was loving, funny and dear, and Harry basked in the sunshine of her presence.

Of late, however, Gail worried him immensely. A straight "A" journalism major in college, Gail, at twenty-four, was already an editor at *Time* magazine's West Coast bureau. She loved her job, was doing well at it; but, on a temporary assignment in England, she'd fallen hopelessly in love with Robin Milgrim, a middle-aged London gossip columnist married to a rich English socialite and widely known for his infidelity.

Harry had met Milgrim only once, during a libel suit. His column had reported that, for years, one of Harry's clients had been sleeping with his own sister. Working with a superb English barrister, Harry had forced Milgrim's paper to pay a heavy settlement.

Harry despised the man—considered him immoral, vicious, willing to write anything about anyone famous, totally without regard for the truth. Harry despised him all the more because most of the world considered him witty, charming and very attractive. He went to the best parties and talented, otherwise bright people enjoyed listing him among their friends. They excused his notorious womanizing . . . indeed, they followed it with interest and amusement like a spectator sport. They even excused his malevolent column, because it was entertaining, well written, even titillating. Secretly, they read it when they could, enjoying the thrill of seeing others laid open, violated by this man Harry considered scum. The son of a bitch is getting away with it, Harry often thought. And it seemed he was going to continue getting away with it.

But despite her father's often expressed feelings about Milgrim's ethics and his widely held reputation for multiple adultery, Gail seemed obsessed with him. When Milgrim was in L.A., Gail would move into his bungalow at the Beverly Hills Hotel. When he was in New York, she would take time off from work and fly there to stay with him at the Ritz Carlton.

When Harry voiced his feelings about Milgrim and their relationship, Gail's usual ability to face problems with balance and humor deserted her. She defended Milgrim fiercely, passionately, unable to concede any fault in the man. She was, she pointed out, an adult and capable of making her own choices, right or wrong. And in this instance, despite a lot of gossip and what she called Harry's "paranoid fears," she felt she was right . . . that Milgrim was an honest, loving man and that, ultimately, he would leave his wife and marry her. She was sure of it.

His daughter's involvement with Milgrim was a constant source of anguish to Harry. But tonight, with Gail radiant, laughing happily, Harry was determined not to let such thoughts spoil the evening.

He took another drink when Armando brought wine for Susan and Gail and let Abrahms's voice drone on in the background, while he grinned lovingly at Gail and tried to charm Susan.

Tanned, healthy and relaxed, the two girls turned Harry's evening into a delight. After two more rounds of drinks, they went in to dinner—Nancy's extraordinary lamb kidneys sautéed with mushrooms and minced green pepper, in a rich burgundy sauce. There was a crisp watercress and endive salad, and a marvelous Clos de Vougeot.

The arched dining room was bathed in the soft glow of two dozen candles, placed on the table, the sideboard and around the room. There was no other light, except for the tiny lights above Nancy's favorite paintings, Minartz's brilliant *Nuit de l'Opéra*, two anonymous but well-executed still lifes and her treasured Seurat. The candlelight was reflected in a hundred different surfaces, the heavy Georgian silver, the Baccarat crystal, the dark patina of the long trestle table. Armando moved quietly, filling the wine, seeing to the needs of every guest with calm discretion.

The meal was superb, but with more wine Abrahms became even more loquacious and overbearing. He was to testify the following afternoon before the state legislature in support of a bill to allow deaf people to sit on juries, with the testimony translated for them by a sign language interpreter. Waving his cigar, he spoke vehemently in favor of the bill.

"It's time every vestige of this cruel discrimination was wiped out. Last year, we succeeded in putting the blind on juries. This year, it'll be the deaf. Our handicapped citizens are not going to be second class . . . not while I can do anything about it."

"But Arthur," Harry said in the slow, serious tone that only Nancy knew meant he'd had a lot to drink, "the basic function of a jury is to observe the demeanor, the mannerisms, the speech of a witness, in order to decide if he's telling the truth. It's not a question of discrimination. Blind and deaf people are simply not physically able to do that particular job."

Abrahms glowered. "Spoken like a true reactionary, Harry. Stop living in the past. There's no reason why all of those perceptions can't be transmitted through the interpreter. You know, for a bright man, your ignorance of social change is appalling."

Sally looked down at her plate—embarrassed.

Harry was annoyed and a bit too drunk to ignore Abrahms's abrasiveness. He waded in, his words occasionally slurred, but only slightly. "Well, does your bill call for the interpreter to limit himself to actual words of the testimony or does it let him go further and tell the blind or deaf juror what he observes about the witness, the witness's appearance, tone of voice and manner of speech?"

Abrahms hesitated, "Well, I'm not sure about that actual text of the bill, but that might be a good subject for an amendment."

"You mean you'd have another person characterize the witness's manner of speech for the juror?" Harry asked. Nancy tried to signal him, hoping to avert what she thought was coming. He paid no attention.

"Is that what they do with a blind juror, Arthur—they have somebody else describe the witness's demeanor, his facial expressions, when he looks quickly over at his attorney, when his cheek begins to twitch . . . things like that?"

"Yes, that's right, another juror can do the job or—"

"Well then," Harry broke in, "you're not getting the handicapped juror's own independent judgment, are you?"

Nancy's expression was strained. The girls looked back and forth as at a tennis match.

"You certainly are," Abrahms responded. "The blind juror's simply being aided by the physical perceptions of someone else. His independent judgment is still there based on those physical perceptions."

"But that's impossible," Harry fired back. "The courtroom action involves hundreds of separate perceptions every minute, every one of them dependent on every other one. No one can accurately convey all of those perceptions to someone else who hasn't seen or heard them. What about jurors who are both blind and deaf, is that the next step?"

"Well, they may not be covered by this bill, but certainly the principle is the same, and I don't see why they should be excluded. They can get the testimony and the physical perceptions of the witnesses from someone else."

"Why do they have to be in court at all? How about paralyzed jurors who stay in their hospital beds and are simply told about the testimony, then asked to vote on the verdict? Doesn't the same principle apply to them too?"

Abrahms was growing angry, but before he could reply, Harry was at him again. Nancy discreetly held up her palm in the classic signal to stop. But nothing stopped Harry or even slowed his attack.

"What about blind or deaf soldiers?" Harry boomed in his best courtroom voice. "Don't we discriminate when we exclude blind and deaf men from the infantry?"

"That's stupid, Cain. They couldn't hear orders, they couldn't see to shoot, their lives would be jeopardized. So would the lives of their fellow soldiers. Don't be an ass!" Abrahms was seething, but Harry was enjoying himself.

"And your blind and deaf jurors don't jeopardize the lives of others? What about the defendant? Isn't requiring effective justice as important as requiring effective military service?"

Abrahms threw his napkin down on the table in disgust. "Look, Cain, I haven't the heart or the patience to play drunken semantic games with you. This is a very special day for me. I told your wife before you arrived, I just came from an all-night vigil at the Texas State Penitentiary . . . protesting the judicial murder of Ozzy Thomas. Unsuccessfully, I might add, because at dawn Ozzy Thomas was murdered."

Ozzy Thomas had been convicted of raping, torturing and killing two teenage girls. After four years of unsuccessful appeals, he had finally been hanged that morning.

"Why do you think a sadistic multiple killer like Ozzy Thomas shouldn't have been executed?" Harry asked innocently.

Abrahms replied in a tone of frozen anger, "No human being should, as you put it so coldly, be 'executed,' nor kept in fear of death for four years, and certainly not a potentially valuable citizen like Ozzy Thomas, a musician, a poet, a salvageable human being. The very wording of your question, the fact that you can even ask it, shows you have no feeling or concern whatsoever for Ozzy Thomas as a fellow human!"

Harry spread his arms out wide, palms up, in a gesture of mock surprise. "No concern for Ozzy Thomas?" his voice rang out across the now silent room. "You say I have no concern for Ozzy Thomas? Whose kidneys do you think we're eating?"

Sally let out a whoop and rocked back in her chair. Nancy spit her wine onto her plate. Gail and Susan roared with laughter.

Abrahms turned red, his black eyes burning with rage. Grimly he rose from his chair and left the table as the laughter rolled around him. At the door he turned, "Sally, we're leaving right now!" Chastened and sober, Sally rose and followed Abrahms from the room and, with a slam of the front door, from the house. Harry just sat there grinning. He felt fine.

An hour later, Gail and Susan had gone. Nancy and Harry were sharing a last drink, a dying fire the only light in the house.

The soothing voice of Nat Cole flowed around them—a mellifluous tide. "Annabelle," "Nature Boy," "I Like It" washed over them, the firelight flickering across the darkened room.

Nancy's head was on Harry's shoulder, his arm around her. She looked up, smiling affectionately. "Well, my friend, years ago you ruined me in the eyes of Philadelphia society. Tonight, you ruined me in the world of art and social protest. There's not much left."

"Nonsense. Abrahms won't tell a soul. It makes him look like a complete ass. And, besides, you had no part in it . . . it was your alcoholic, Neanderthal husband."

Nancy leaned closer and kissed him lightly on the cheek. "Neanderthal or not, I love you very much. Have from that very first day on Harvard Square."

"I've loved you too, Nance—from that first day."

They lapsed into a comfortable silence. Harry leaned farther back into the big cushions and gazed at the fire, thinking of what she'd said. "Philadelphia society?" . . . "ruined me?"—such stilted, old-fashioned words. Probably accurate though. She *was* the only child of a wealthy Bucks County family. She *was* expected to marry into "her own class." And Harry supposed you could call a girl like that "ruined" if she got knocked up by a starving Jewish law student— and then insisted on having his baby.

But they were in love. "Were?" Curious tense. Still, things *had* become different between them. Subtly so—but different. He tried not to think about it. He focused his thoughts on the good early years; but they kept drifting away; and as the stereo music shifted to Jobim, and he heard that soft Brazilian beat, he began to see Carmel—that sweet, graceful body swaying to the music—to feel her arms going around his body, to move closer and—

"A penny for your thoughts."

Harry looked over at Nancy, who sat smiling, awaiting his answer.

"Oh nothing really—just—"

"You were thinking about some lawsuit, weren't you?"

Relieved, he pulled her close. "Okay, Nancy, you got me dead to rights. But, you know, it's been such a hellish week, I..."

"Sure. Some romantic. Firelight, soft music and you're thinking of torts."

"Sorry kid," he said in his best Bogart imitation.

"It's all right...now that it's stopped."

He grinned, and stroked her hair. She made a faint purring sound and snuggled closer, lightly kissing his neck. Just for an instant, he tensed. Just for an instant, he saw Carmel again, framed in the light of her doorway, waving goodbye.

He sighed and patted Nancy's shoulder...twice, in soft syncopation.

"Christ, I'm beat. Got an eight o'clock meeting tomorrow."

Nancy's eyes darkened. Then she smiled. "I'm tired too...I guess."

Taking her hand, he gently pulled her to her feet. Arm in arm, they made their way upstairs, the dying fire throwing their shadows against the staircase wall.

*T*he telephone stabbed into the darkness. Harry struggled to consciousness, not sure where he was or what had aroused him from sleep. He groped for the alarm, thinking it the source of the irritating sound. The digital face read 3:15 A.M. Finally, he reached for the phone, which, insistently, kept ringing.

"Harry Cain?"

"Yeah, who's this?"

"Aaron Fernbach, Harry."

Fernbach was the heir to a Chicago banking fortune who had turned his back on the family business and come to California to pursue his dream of making movies. Through family connections, he was found a job as aide to a vice president at Consolidated Studios, then a tired, troubled company. He had enjoyed a meteoric rise to Chief Executive Officer of Consolidated and had turned it into the most active, successful studio in town. Still in his thirties, he had moved to the top faster than Thalberg and was generally considered better at his job.

Fernbach had never even called Harry at home before, much less at 3:15 A.M. Harry wondered how they found his unlisted number; but you could never underestimate the enormous power of a major studio.

"Harry, I'm sorry to reach you in the middle of the night like this, but we need your help . . . badly."

"My help . . . how? What's the problem?"

"The problem is they've got Sonny Ball downtown in jail. Our biggest romantic star, and they're claiming he stroked some guy in a skid row flick. I don't even want to talk about it on the phone. I don't want to talk about it at all. If you can't get him out of this, it'll cost us millions, Harry, fucking millions."

Harry knew who Sonny Ball was. The whole world did. Ball was an extraordinary actor whose softly curling blond hair and vivid blue eyes had made him an overnight box office sensation. Actually, he had worked hard for his success, and it had come only after years on the New York stage. Picked by Consolidated to do the film version of an off-Broadway play, Ball had gone on to rock the business with two back-to-back Academy Awards, each generating a hundred million gross. An intelligent man and Yale Drama School graduate, he had produced the second film himself and was now considered the hottest actor-producer in town.

Harry, wide awake now, turned on his bedside light and reached for a notepad. "Okay, Aaron, slow down. What have they charged him with?"

"It's what they call lewd conduct. It's crazy. I'll have someone there to tell you all about it. Can you get him out?"

"Aaron, I don't do a lot of criminal work these days—let me refer you to one of the guys who does."

"Harry, you've been kicking the shit out of the studio for years . . . three big cases, three big losses for us. The Goddamn criminal lawyers will take our money, get headlines and try to plea bargain. You'll win. Look, Harry, I know shit from shinola, and you're shinola. You're the guy we need."

"Well, first let's get Sonny out. Then we'll talk about it."

Two hours later, Harry was nestled in the blue velvet upholstery of a stretch limo, speeding down the Hollywood Freeway. Tired, but still buoyed by the excitement of a new challenge, he lay back in his seat, sipping a fluted glass of Roederer Krystal, watching through the one-way tinted windows as the lights of a thousand less fortunate drivers flashed by in the balmy California night.

Beside him was a slim, sensitive-looking man, neatly dressed in a Harris tweed jacket, open white shirt and designer jeans. He had the bluest eyes Harry had ever seen and the soft blond curls that had become famous. Sonny Ball had to be forty, but his boyish face and sparkling eyes made him seem thirty at the most.

Now Ball was in deep trouble. He'd been picked up at two A.M. for stroking a plainclothes cop in the men's room of a skid row theater. The charge was lewd conduct in a public place.

Harry looked over at the man sitting beside him. "Sonny, this is deadly serious to a guy in your position. You fight this and lose and you're dead with the public, at the studio, everywhere. A studio head can come back from embezzlement, forged checks, even outright theft . . . if he makes successful pictures. But nobody comes back from this kind of thing, especially a romantic lead."

"Tell me something I don't already know, Harry. *That*, I know. What I don't know is if I can win and what are the odds."

"Sonny, I couldn't give you odds if I knew more, and I don't know much. From the police report you've got very big trouble. First, there's an eyewitness . . . the so-called 'victim.' Second, this particular eyewitness is a cop. Third, what the hell were you doing in a Main Street movie at two in the morning? Don't they have urinals in Bel Air?"

"Very funny. What does the cop say?"

"His report says he was on felony detail working out of Central Division. He had to take a leak so he stopped in at the Climax Theater on Main Street. He was at the urinal when you came up and said something like 'Show got you worked up?' and he said something like 'Yeah,' and you said that you could take care of it for him if he'd come to your apartment, and then you started stroking his joint. He claims he said 'No thanks,' and walked away, that he let you go back to your seat and then came back with his partner to pick you up. The report shows a tube of Vaseline was in your pocket, and you had no I.D. End of their story. What's yours?"

"Okay . . . starting at the end. The I.D. was in the car. The Vaseline's for chapped lips . . . from the boat last weekend. As to the rest, I can't sleep, so I go for a drive. That's all. I get off the freeway downtown to see what it looks like that time of night. I drive around a while, kind of drifting, and then I see this open theater with pictures playing like 'Tillie's Night on the Aircraft Carrier' and 'She Lost It in Acapulco.' It seems like a big joke to me, you know, 'Let's see what the competition is doing,' so I park and go in.

"I watch the show for say twenty minutes . . . dismal, badly made. Then I go to the john. I'm standing at the urinal, and this guy comes and stands at the next one. He says something like 'Sexy show, huh? Got you excited?' I don't know what kind of creep he is in a place like that—and I want no trouble, so I just say 'Yeah, sure,' or something like that. Then I zip up and get the hell out of there. I go back to my seat, and about five minutes later, the same guy comes down the aisle with another guy who flashes a light on me and tells me I'm under arrest. Outside, I ask 'em what's the charge? They won't say. They handcuff me and keep whispering aside to themselves. Finally they search me and find the Vaseline and I got no I.D. That seems to do it for them. They push me in the car—none too gently, and off to the station. That's when I called Aaron."

Harry let out a sigh. "Okay, Sonny, I got the picture. It's a tough sale to a jury, but somehow we'll have to sell it. It means showing 'em why you were there and why the Vaseline, and—the hardest part of all—why the cop would lie. That's the key to this thing, Sonny. That's what I've got to come up with. There's a possibility . . . but, listen, let me work on it. Okay?" He paused and leaned forward. "You know, sometimes, in a case like this, they'll let you plead guilty to disturbing the peace. That way, you're not a sex offender and you don't have to register as one. Is that something you'd be interested in?"

Ball shook his head and gave Harry a wistful smile.

"Afraid not, Harry. Not in my line of work. No way. The whole world's going to be watching this one. I've got to beat it hands down, prove the cop's lying . . . or, let's face it, I'm finished."

Harry took a sip of champagne—using the moment to think.

"One other thing, Sonny. You've never married. Not that it makes you a sex offender, but to a jury a man-woman relationship would help. What can you do for me there?"

"Easy. My fiancée, Allison Fong. Eurasian, very sexy, very convincing."

"Will she be embarrassed to testify to a normal sex life with you?"

"Hell no! She'll give you just what you want. I promise."

"Okay, Sonny, that helps."

Harry knew he'd have to talk polygraph here, had to handle it tactfully. If Ball passed a private, confidential test, arranged by Harry, he'd keep the result quiet, then call the DA and offer to submit his client to a test by any independent polygraph operator and to stipulate that the result would be admissible in evidence. That might win the case all by itself.

There was no easy way to say it. He just took the plunge. "You know, Sonny, a favorable polygraph might help more than anything." He outlined his plan to trap the DA by taking a private test first. "It's not only a way to win the case, Sonny, it would help enormously with public relations. You know, 'Lie detector says Sonny Ball telling the truth.'"

"No, Harry, no polygraph. Forget it. I don't trust 'em, and if they gave us a bad result, even winning the case wouldn't make me safe. Somehow, sometime, somebody would get to that polygraph operator. Definitely not."

Harry shrunk a little inside. He thought he knew what Ball was really saying . . . that he wouldn't pass.

"Well, we'll talk about that later, Sonny. I'll speak to Allison Fong and you just wait. That's the hardest part, and, when the press starts calling in a couple of hours, it's 'No comment.' You'll have your day in court soon enough. If you win, we'll blast 'em. If you lose, no amount of denial beforehand is gonna help."

They sat for a moment in silence, the big limo slowing to make the Sunset off-ramp, the rose-colored dawn spreading across the sky to the east.

"You know what I don't get, Sonny? Why did the cop take a chance on so much heat? Christ, he had to recognize you and know he was getting into something very heavy."

"I don't think so, Harry." He patted the famous windswept curls. "I didn't have my piece on. It was back in the car. Without the piece and with my shades, I look just like any other slob out for an evening on the town. I go out like that quite often. Nobody recognizes me. And don't forget, I had no I.D. So they just didn't believe who I was, even when I told them. By the time they believed me, it was too late to back away."

He lifted a blond curl from his forehead, showing Harry the delicate, almost indiscernible netting of a five thousand dollar hairpiece. "See? Nothing on top since I was twenty-eight. But some terrific piece, huh?"

Harry just nodded, too surprised to speak. He'd never dreamed that the central figure of a billion female fantasies was as bald as a newborn baby.

"King Construction—Building Now for All Time." That's what it said on the door. Harry thought of Ozymandias and smiled through his early morning headache.

He was ushered into Maurice King's astrodome of an office and took a chair near the vast free-form desk. King, a small man with an Adolphe Menjou mustache, was on the phone to Milan, a fact he was trying to make obvious to Harry. He tossed a survey report across the desk and continued talking.

When he was finished reading, Harry knew the report was just as

Ben Brody had said. King hung up the phone and looked right at Harry, his small black eyes cold and hard. It occurred to Harry that this was the expression King must use to fire and foreclose.

"Mr. Cain, I'll be brief. I want no problems with you or your client. I feel compassion for Mr. Brody, but I need that land... my land that he's on. My building... the King Tower... is designed for the entire area and that's what I need, the entire area... not an inch less."

"Well, Mr. King, I appreciate your feelings and certainly Mr. Brody will want to compensate you for the—"

King cut in. "You don't understand, Cain; there's no question of compensation here. Mr. Brody's encroaching on my land, I've been paying the taxes on it and he's got no right to stay. He's got very limited alternatives. He can move the building or he can take it down. I will not, under any circumstances, sell him the land he wrongfully occupies."

"Moving the building's impossible, Mr. King. You know that. It's four stories of brick. And tearing it down would destroy the last asset Ben Brody has in the world."

"Well, Mr. Cain, there is one other alternative. . . ."

Harry knew.

"I'll buy his building, Mr. Cain. I'll solve the problem for Mr. Brody, but he can't expect any big price for a building that has to be demolished."

"I get the point, Mr. King. How much?" King leaned back, put his fingers together, building a steeple with his hands. "Oh, I'd say fifty thousand dollars, maybe fifty-five."

"Come on, King, that building's worth more than three hundred thousand dollars. The *land* is worth more than you're offering. We'll tear it down first."

"Mr. Cain, that land is worth seventy-five thousand dollars, maybe eighty thousand at the most, but it'll cost you thirty thousand to tear the building down and that's what you'll have to do if you don't sell to me. That leaves Brody only fifty thousand, at the most. I'll tell you what I'll do. I'll give him sixty thousand. But not a dollar more. Take it or leave it, Mr. Cain... I've no desire to haggle with you."

Harry could feel the anger rising. His voice was so dry it hardly came out. "I'll leave it, Mr. King, thank you." He slammed his case shut and started for the door.

"That building's going to hold up my construction, Mr. Cain. We'll be ready in three weeks. I want the building off my land within that period. After that, every week's delay'll cost me twenty-five thousand dollars and I'm going to hold Mr. Brody responsible for every penny of it. Maybe I can even hold you personally. I'll ask my lawyers. You'd better think some more about my offer, Mr. Cain."

Harry's head, dully aching when he arrived, was throbbing as he banged the door behind him. He was tired and angry but determined to find some way to take King's cute scheme and jam it down his devious throat.

"Skid row" was never what Harry called it. To him, it was "Main Street" and it always had been. He walked up Fourth from the dusty-windowed wholesalers of Los Angeles Street. Fourth was as dingy and scabrous as Harry remembered it from forty years before. Dumpy brick buildings, blistered, patched and peeling.

Harry rounded the corner of Fourth and Main into the bright morning sunshine and walked down Main to Winston. For just a moment, the hint of tears welled up. There was the store—years ago his father's tiny corner grocery—now a liquor store—and above it the two windows on Winston and two on Main that marked their home so many years before.

From the time Harry's mother died, just before the war, they'd lived in that one long room above the store. Two of them, Sam Cain, the gentle grocer, and his little kid. Frying fish in the bedroom, sleeping together with the comforting reflection of the red neon lights flashing on the wall.

Together they explored every inch of Main Street from First to Sixth, both sides of the street. They knew every occupant of that seedy stretch—talked with them endlessly . . . business, politics, religion, everything . . . little Harry shyly holding his father's hand, scuffing his shoes against the pavement, watching, always watching, taking in everything, saying nothing, unless they pushed him to.

They were all gone now, Angelo's Shoe Repair, Gus's Hot Dog place, Levine the pocketbook jobber, and the best of them, Harry's father... all gone now. The Follies Burlesque, the Penny Arcade, the Midnight Mission were still there, but the people were all gone, all dead or moved away to some nicer place.

Harry walked up Main toward Second. It was still early enough to see winos asleep in the doorways, ragged collars turned up against last night's cold, hands still clutching their muscatel bottle in the inevitable paper bag. So it was when Harry was there as a boy and so it was now. Even the faces seemed the same.

"Split Beaver, Frisco Style"... "Open 24 Hours" were what Harry could see advertised on the marquee of the Climax Theater on Second and Main. As he got closer, he could see that the feature attraction was "*Likkadisplit*—Secrets of the Italian Jet Set."

Harry bought a ticket and went into the darkened theater. Despite the flickering light from the screen, it was very, very dark. He took a seat in the rear. It was broken. He moved to another seat, crunching candy wrappers underfoot. Apparently the main feature was not yet on because the film playing seemed to be set in a western saloon. Several cowboys and cowgirls wearing only chaps, masks, guns and boots... no pants, shirts or skirts... seemed to be involved in a constantly changing combination of man-woman, man-man and woman-woman sexual encounters on the tables, on the bar and on the floor. One somewhat older woman in a bonnet and a ladylike western dress was tied to a chair making futile struggling motions to free herself while the others frolicked.

Now the limited dialogue made it clear that she was the preacher's wife, come to reprove the others for their sins. The others stopped playing and turned their attention to her. While she screamed in protest, her clothes were slowly removed and, when she was nude, four cowgirls began tickling her all over with huge soft feathers. Soon she began writhing, not so much in terror as in the excitement she was trying her best to avoid.

Next, two of the girls began to kiss her breasts and a third began slowly to kiss and lick at her inner thighs and between her legs. She began to moan and undulate her body in obvious pleasure.

At this point a tiny white pony, no larger than a Saint Bernard, was led right into the bar.

Harry sighed. He was sure of what was coming. His eyes had become accustomed to the dark, and he could see that there were three or four fellow customers for this morning's performance. Two were sound asleep, probably from the night before, and the third seemed very preoccupied with what was going on (or had now been completed) under his raincoat.

Even now, the theater was darker than most, and Harry wondered how the police had ever located Sonny Ball in his seat. On screen, the pony was being led toward his now hysterical victim. Harry stood and moved down the aisle toward the exit sign on the left of the screen. He parted the greasy curtain and entered a cement area, blinking at the glare of a bare bulb hanging from the ceiling. A metal stage door was on the left and a door marked "Men" on the right. Harry chose "Men" and went into the smallest and dirtiest restroom he'd seen in a long time. Two urinals, a sink and an open toilet were crammed together in an unbelievably small area that reeked with what must have been thirty years of unflushed urine. The floor was littered with paper towels, toilet paper and, surprisingly, watermelon rind. Once again, the room was brightly lit.

The walls were almost totally covered with graffiti . . . mostly phone numbers with elaborate sexual promises. Over the urinal someone had written in lipstick "Love it at 324A Hope Street. I'm eleven inches." Under this, someone else had written in green ink, "Amazing! How big's your cock?" On the paper towel dispenser was "Thirty billion flies can't be wrong—eat shit." There were no more towels.

Making mental note of what he could use in the physical layout of the men's room and the hall, Harry left quickly, made his way out of the theater and into the bright sunlight of Main Street. He walked a block deep in thought and, without knowing why, turned off Main at Third, going back to his car without passing Winston and his old home. One immersion in those memories was enough—maybe too much.

When Harry returned to his office, there were messages waiting from newspaper and television reporters all over the country. His secretary, Clara, had counted them. Tall, thin, angular and irreversibly unmarried, Clara, as well as Grace, the receptionist, and the entire office staff took pride in Harry's celebrity. It made them feel a part of something significant—something that made their jobs more colorful—more fun—more important. Now *People v. Ball* was set for trial on September 18, and they were beginning to realize that the whole world wanted the story.

The only message that puzzled Harry was that a Mr. Soto from the district attorney's office had called. Sonny Ball's case should have been assigned to someone on the city attorney's staff, not the district attorney. Why was the DA's office calling? The caller had given Grace no information at all.

Harry asked her to return Soto's call first. He could deal with the press later. A deep, businesslike voice came on the line, "Mr. Cain, I'm sorry to bother you at your office, but a rather serious matter has come up. Could you meet me at the Grant house tomorrow morning, say at ten o'clock?"

So it wasn't about the Ball case, after all. Now Harry was curious. But he was never surprised at anything David Grant would do. Probably dealing in young Chinese boys, Harry thought, smiling.

"Sure, Mr. Soto, I'll be there."

Harry knew he had to return the reporters' calls. Press relations were critical to him. But he decided that the best approach was to be guarded at this early stage. He'd have plenty of time later to beat the drums. Saying too much too soon could be damaging.

He leafed through the media calls and asked his receptionist to start the long list with Tom Musik at the L.A. *Times*. He thought he could get some reliable information from Musik instead of just giving it out. Besides, he could trust the man.

"Is it true you're going to represent Sonny Ball, Harry?"

"That's right, Tom."

"Any comment on the charges in the case?"

"Well, it's early in the game, but, in my view, the prosecution of Mr. Ball is a big mistake. I'm confident that, if the charges are not dropped beforehand, Sonny Ball will be acquitted."

"Funny. Bailey Scuneo at the city attorney's office says he's got your man nailed."

"Oh? B.J.'s going to try the case himself?"

"That's what he said. Unusual case for the chief deputy city attorney. But you know Scuneo."

"I sure do." Harry pictured the tall, bald pockmarked prosecutor—his dark guardsman's mustache, the inevitable tiny rose in his lapel.

Bailey J. Scuneo, or "B.J."—"Scumbag Scuneo" to many who dealt with him—was a driving, ambitious man, a man of strength, shrewdness and malice, who proudly announced that his English mother had named him after the "Old Bailey," London's criminal court, where, according to Scuneo, "They knew how to deal with criminals."

Harry despised the man. In their last case, Scuneo had announced repeatedly to the media that he would put Harry's client—a Beverly Hills stockbroker—behind bars. When Harry won the man an acquittal, he called a press conference at which he simply re-read all of Scuneo's pretrial boasts. The prosecutor's arrogant phrases echoed after him for weeks. He had sworn to get even. Now he might get his chance.

"Well, what else did the great man have to say?" Harry asked with more nonchalance than he felt.

"Just that they're going to start keeping the street free of marauding perverts, beginning with your client."

"Oh, is that all?"

"No, he also said Ball wasn't going to buy his way out of this with some overrated, overpriced Hollywood lawyer."

"That cocksucker."

"Is that a quote?"

"No, it's only 'background.' I'll give you a better quote when we win."

"Okay, Harry, talk to you later." The phone clicked off. Harry shook his head and sighed, then asked Grace to get him Ray Semple of *Variety*.

*H*arry loved the dim coolness of the Scandia bar. Eating in that softly lit, leathery room gave him a feeling of ease and well-being, just as the brightly lit main dining room made him unexplainably anxious.

Carl Malone hunched over his soup. "Fucking gazpacho, Harry. That's what's wrong with the world, gazpacho in a Goddamn Danish restaurant. We don't know where we're at now, Harry. Nobody sticks to his trade."

Harry downed the caraway-flavored aquavit for which the restaurant was famous and motioned the waiter to give them each another drink. "I don't notice you raising hell about the chili at Chasen's or the sauerbraten at Musso's."

"Not the same, Harry . . . Christ, you're slow for a smart lawyer. Chili's an American dish, strictly Tex not Mex, and Musso & Frank's always been an international restaurant, not French or Italian. They're entitled to serve sauerbraten. In fact, they've got to." Malone grinned wolfishly. He loved to debate anything and considered Harry an adequate opponent.

"If you want to make a point, Harry, you should ask me why an Austrian with a name like Wolfgang Puck opens a restaurant called "Chinoise," hands out chopsticks and then serves *foie gras chaud*. Doesn't fit. Anyway, enough of that. What's new on the case?"

"Not much of anything, really, but before we get into it I need your advice on a construction problem. I need to know if it's possible to shave a brick wall."

"Why shave it? Brick got no whiskers." Harry looked pained. "I'm sorry Harry, go ahead, you tell the joke."

"It's not a joke, Carl. I've got to take an inch off the side of a brick building." Carl's natural curiosity was piqued and Harry had his complete attention as he related Ben Brody's problem, telling Carl the dimensions of the building he had obtained that morning at King's office.

When Harry finished, Carl gave his sharklike grin. "That miserable son of a bitch King. I'd love to see you shove his building up his ass. Look, I'll check around. I think it's possible and I think I've got a guy who can do the job."

"What do you think it'll cost?"

"Four-story building, oh, ten, twelve thousand maybe, but you better talk to the contractor. I'll check it out and call you; then you and I can—" Carl stopped short. Coming through the bar, making every head turn, was a too familiar vision, almost six feet tall, with long, golden hair flowing across her slavic cheekbones, emerald green eyes and a wide, sensual mouth, her long, willowy body moving gracefully under smoke-gray chiffon. It was Fiona Malone.

Moving behind her on the balls of his feet, as though ready to strike wherever necessary, was Calvin "The Cat" Pierce, friend of the famous, expert in the martial arts and first-class trial lawyer.

Fiona saw them and showing not a trace of surprise at the coincidence, stopped by the table with Pierce in tow. She was magnificent, like the Eiffel Tower or the Sphinx; one of the wonders of the world. Harry could never get over her impact on men, any men. She moved with a feline grace, spoke with a husky-voiced English accent, and when she aimed her wide green eyes at an intended victim, he was finished.

"Well, Carl, how nice to see you."

"Yeah," Carl grunted. Three years of marriage had given him some immunity to Fiona, and he was very bitter over her claim to half of what he'd built with twenty-five years of sweat and brilliance, while she enjoyed herself with an army of tennis pros, ski instructors and traffic cops who were more than willing to overlook her regular violation of the vehicle code.

"Haven't lost the old charm, have you, Carl?" she laughed. "Relax, old pal, it's only money."

Carl took the full force of the green eyes and blasted back. "No, it's not only money, Fiona, it's a hell of a lot more than that. It's lies, cheating and things like that, things I used to think you couldn't possibly do, and then—" But he didn't finish. As Harry watched her movements with curiosity, Fiona picked up a glass of ice water, and, with a graceful gesture—smiling sweetly all the while—poured the entire glass slowly onto Carl's lap.

The moment was one of those that seems to be frozen in time, seconds feeling like hours. ... Fiona smiling at Carl, Carl turning purple, Pierce and Harry turning pale, no one else in the restaurant even noticing.

Then the spell was broken. Carl pushed the table away and jumped to his feet with a rush. "You Goddamn cooze, I'll—" But "The Cat" moved his compact body quickly and quietly between them, turning Carl's wrist smoothly behind him, so that Carl spun around and away from his target, sitting down again with a heavy thump.

Now everybody in the place was looking. Carl started up again, but Harry threw an arm across his chest. "Easy, Carl, cut it out right now." Harry was very firm. Pierce would disable Carl in fifteen seconds and relish the headlines, making Carl look like a wife beater that he had stopped from killing his lovely client.

Carl relaxed somewhat and sat back. Pierce followed Fiona to their own table.

"I'll get that English cunt, so help me God I will."

"Sure, Carl, sure you will. Now forget it, and have some more aquavit to celebrate. You probably just missed having your arm broken."

An hour later, Harry blinked in the glare of the bright afternoon sunshine as they left the dimness of the Scandia bar. He was feeling the aquavits and not feeling like work. His car came and he faced the choice—left to his office or right to the house in Laurel Canyon. He turned right.

Carmel came to the door in the briefest of bikinis, having been sunning herself on a blanket in the tiny yard behind the house. She beamed at Harry, plainly delighted that he'd come. She led him by the hand to the backyard, where, laughingly, she tormented him into stripping to his shorts and joining her on the blanket. When they lay side-by-side, shielded from the neighbors' view by a thick cedar hedge, she suggested that they both take off what they had on and "really" get the sun. While Harry pulled off his shorts, Carmel wriggled out of her scant bikini bottom and let the top fall away.

"Now," Carmel said, "let's lie on our backs and see how long we can think about making love without touching each other."

"Okay," Harry said, "let's see who weakens first."

Harry lay back and, almost at once, began to watch Carmel out of the corner of his eye. Her long legs were slightly apart and he could see the beads of moisture beside her silky, honey-colored mound. Gradually she began to breathe heavily and her lips parted. Her pink tongue slowly licked her lips. She arched her back.

"I lose," Harry mumbled, as he rolled over, delicately kissing her breasts, then sliding down her body, planting more tiny kisses on her belly and inner thighs, until, finally, with Carmel softly whispering "No," his mouth found her and his fricative tongue danced over her, grazing and caressing her, electrifying her with its touch, snaking into her. She began to thrust her hips upward, pressing against his mouth, using it, thrilling to it, making small, whimpering noises. She threw her head from side to side, biting at her lip, shuddering with pleasure. Finally, she reached for Harry, pulling him toward her, crying out for him. Answering her cries, Harry moved up and over her onto his knees. He entered her slowly, through the wet slickness, penetrating deep, feeling the honeyed warmth and softness close around him. Carmel moaned and, thrusting, rotating, moved with Harry until, almost in seconds, she cried, "Oh, sweet Jesus, I'm coming." "Me too," Harry groaned and together they came to a throbbing, shattering climax there on the blanket in the hot California sun.

Afterward they lay side by side, kissing and touching each other with tenderness and joy. Finally, Carmel sat up, leaning on her elbow, looking down at Harry, her eyes glowing with affection.

"I just want you to know, Harry Cain, that, if my life ended now . . . this very moment I'd feel—"

Suddenly, she jumped to her feet, screaming, frantically beating her hands at her head. Harry, seeing no reason for her strange and sudden behavior, rose quickly from the blanket. Carmel was shouting, "A bee! A bee! Oh, God, a bee—help me! Help me!" Her screams became louder and more hysterical, her arms windmilling about her.

Harry saw the bee land on the blanket and quickly killed it with a shoe. "He's dead, Carmel, he's dead. It's okay." He took her in his arms and she began to cry softly on his shoulder.

"I didn't want to you to see that, Harry, I certainly didn't want you to see that."

"Hey, it's okay," Harry said softly, holding her to him. "It's okay. Lots of people are afraid of bees."

Carmel was returning to normal now, wiping her eyes and nose. "It's not just bees, Harry. It's *all* bugs. It's my 'bug thing' and I guess it's abnormal. I wish I could help it, but I can't. Any kind of bug just drives me out of my mind with fear."

Harry smiled. "It's okay, Carmel, believe me. From now on, we'll have an indoor relationship." Then, taking her by the hand, he led her into the quiet and coolness of the house.

Later, after they'd showered and dressed and slowly enjoyed banana milk shakes straight from the blender, Carmel showed Harry her paintings and explained what it was she was trying to accomplish in this phase of her work.

"We all take color for granted; sky is blue, grass is green. By peeling that away, shocking the viewer with a different color world entirely, I think I can allow much more of what I'm trying to paint to get across." By radically altering the colors of what she painted, she hoped to convey the essence of the objects themselves, including human shapes and emotions. Stacked against the wall were men and women with haunting, agonized green faces, night skies of orange lit by blue streetlights and forests of black and purple trees. The work was vital and exciting to Harry, another intriguing facet of this strange, fascinating woman with whom he had become so enthralled.

It was close to five when Harry finally prepared to leave. He held Carmel tenderly; slowly, reluctantly moving away from the warmth of her body, the fresh smell of her hair and the compelling pull of her soft mouth and amber eyes. He knew he'd be back soon.

On his way to the office, Harry stopped to buy a paper. Sonny Ball's arrest had come too late for the *Times*'s regular deadline, but it made the headlines of the late afternoon final: "Sonny Ball Charged with Sex Offense." Fortunately, they had not used Bailey Scuneo's quote about Ball being a "marauding pervert," but the story was juicy enough even without that, setting the arrest in a "skid row porno house" and describing the charge as "making lewd advances to an undercover, male police officer."

The chairman of the board of Consolidated Studios was quoted as saying that he and his fellow board members had every confidence in the complete innocence of Mr. Ball and would support him with all the means at their disposal. The last paragraph said that the defense counsel would be the "well-known trial lawyer Harry Cain, often called the 'Sunset Bomber,' a reference to his lavish Sunset Boulevard offices and his unbroken string of courtroom victories." Harry was quoted as predicting an acquittal.

He folded the newspaper beside him on the seat with somewhat mixed emotions. He had never gotten over the thrill of notoriety, but he had serious doubts about how this case would turn out and about how long that firm studio support would last, with every newspaper and television station in the world carrying the lurid story.

There certainly would be no more Sonny Ball films until the case was over. There might never be.

At the end of the day, Carl Malone called to confirm that the brick on Ben Brody's Gaynorville building could indeed be shaved for around ten thousand dollars. He gave Harry the name of the contractor who would do the job. Harry called Brody, told him the idea and obtained Brody's delighted approval for Harry to make the deal and handle the whole thing.

Then Harry called Maurice King. "Going to take the sixty thousand, eh, Cain? Very sensible."

"No, Mr. King, it didn't work. Mr. Brody's not going to sell at all; he's going to shave his building. It'll be totally off your property long before you're ready to build."

"Shave it? That's crazy!"

"We'll see, Mr. King. Nice talking to you. Bye." Harry hung up. He'd enjoyed himself, but he expected to have much more fun with King before long.

All his life, Harry had loved the beach and the coastal mountain range, sweeping gray and purple back from the white sand and dark-blue California sea. Harry had awakened early the next day, packed his briefcase and headed out Sunset Boulevard toward Highway 101 twisting gracefully along the coast. As always, he relished every moment of his drive up 101, his sun roof open, brassy mariachi music on the Mexican radio station as the Bentley gracefully took the gentle curves of the coastal highway.

It was forty minutes before he drove up David Grant's winding, private road, the dusty brush giving off its pungent smell of creosote and sage in the warm morning sun.

That smell, the familiar road, brought back a flood of memories—and questions. How could David have accidentally fallen from the terrace? No amount of drink or drugs should disable him to *that* extent... or would it? God knows what he was capable of taking—or doing. Or was it the mother? She certainly had the motive—and the meanness, the raw guts to do it. And what was all that keening at the hospital about "Forgive me, Buddy. Forgive me." If he was drunk enough—if she felt enough rage, enough desperation...

Harry rounded the last turn and pulled up in front of David's hideaway and temple of pleasure. It was spectacular. Harry tried to think of other words to describe it, but "spectacular" was the effect David had sought, and it was really the only word that fit. Constructed of redwood and glass, its dramatic towers, levels and angles stood on a cliff above the sea commanding a view of thirty miles of coastline in each direction.

Gulls wheeled and dived just beyond the house as Harry used his key to open the front door. As always, David's huge Oriental gong, wired to the lock, sounded throughout the house.

A stocky deputy sheriff in a short-sleeved tan uniform strolled to meet Harry. "Mr. Cain?" Harry nodded. "Lieutenant Soto will see you in just a moment or two; please wait here." He turned abruptly and went out onto the terrace.

Left alone, Harry quickly looked around the room. It was undisturbed. Glass and sea in all directions, thick white carpets setting off the Oriental art and antiques. David had been fascinated with the Orient and over the years he had compiled a handsome and valuable collection.

Harry smiled at the tortoise shell shield and four-foot Samurai sword mounted over the white silk sofa. How David loved to play "dress up," oiling his body like Yukio Mishima, whom he idolized, and swinging the huge blade in what he claimed were ancient Samurai patterns of attack and defense . . . each accompanied by its own bellow or grunt.

Once, when he owed Harry a twenty-five thousand dollar fee for working out his contract at Columbia, David offered him the sword and jeweled scabbard, claiming that it had been the personal weapon of the last Tokugawa Shogun. Knowing David's propensity for colorful exaggeration, Harry took the cash. Now the sword and shield gave Harry a twinge of sorrow. It was hard to imagine David non-existent—just gone.

Harry walked across the room and saw himself reflected in the huge framed mirror. He looked lean and dark, well tailored in his gray flannel Mariani suit. He was pleased with what he saw, but was his hair just a bit too long?

The deputy coughed nervously to tell Harry he was back. "Lieutenant Soto can see you now, Mr. Cain. Please follow me."

He led Harry onto the terrace. A dark man in a light-blue suit was working at a card table, drinking coffee from a thermos. He continued to work without looking up.

There were chalk marks on the brick where David had gone over the loops of heavy black chain suspended between redwood posts, the only "railing" David would allow. It was about sixty feet to the rocks below, and, unfortunately, David had landed on his head.

Trying not to think about that cruel impact—to avoid the sick feeling that seemed to be overtaking him, Harry took a deep breath and turned his attention to the view. He could see the entire coast all the way south to Santa Monica, and off in the distance, Catalina Island with Mount Orizaba rising through the haze.

Finally, the dark man looked up. "So it's the Sunset Bomber?" he said without a smile. "Sit down, Mr. Cain. I'm Herman Soto."

Harry moved closer and settled into a chair. Soto was a hard-looking Latino in mirrored sunglasses that made him seem menacing—formidable.

For a long time he said nothing. Harry, uncharacteristically ill at ease, broke the silence.

"What's your thought, Lieutenant—an accident? David drank a lot and I suppose he could have fallen. Of course, there *was* the mother. I'm sure you've spoken to her."

"I'm not really sure of anything yet, Mr. Cain. I just need to get some facts. What about Grant's will? Does everything go to the family?"

"As it stood the night he died, his mother got the entire estate; but last week he told me he wanted to change that, to take his mother out completely. I was preparing the new will when he died."

"Why did he want to cut her out when she was staying with him?"

"Well, he found out she'd been remarried for three years to a man from New York. She'd been lying to David about it. Apparently, she thought David would stop sending her support money. David was mad as hell and he was going to tell her to go back to Florida; he was through with her. That's why he was going to take her out of his will."

"What day was that?"

Harry wondered why these questions couldn't have been asked over the phone. He answered anyway. "Let's see . . . that would be Friday."

"Oh? How long had she been staying here before that?"

"About a week."

"Did they get along before that?"

"Never . . . she's a dragon. You probably noticed. But David never missed a support check. Then, to find out she'd been conning him for years . . . he really blew up, cried in my office. I guess you know she was here with him when he fell?"

"Or was pushed." Soto smiled grimly.

"Or was pushed," Harry repeated without the smile.

"Have you questioned David's mother, Lieutenant?"

"We have, Mr. Cain, and she's left for Florida."

"She's *what?*" Harry was stunned.

"She's left for Florida, Mr. Cain. . . . But that's *our* concern, not yours."

Harry bristled but said nothing. Soto rose and began to pace the terrace. "How many people had keys to the house, Mr. Cain?"

"David told me there were just his, mine, Achmed's—that's his housekeeper—and the one he gave his mother."

"And that one had been Paolo Monti's, right?"

"Yes. David took it back from Paolo to give it to his mother when she arrived. Paolo moved to a hotel while David's mother was here."

"How long had Monti lived with Mr. Grant, so far as you know?"

"About a year."

"They were gay . . . right?" Harry hesitated. "You can level with me, Mr. Cain. You really should."

"Okay, they were, but they had a fairly stable, good relationship."

"Really? I suppose that's sometimes difficult to assess."

"Possibly."

"And before that, Mr. Grant lived with the choreographer Kevin Shaw, isn't that correct?"

"Right, for many years."

"Were there hard feelings at the split-up between Grant and Shaw?"

"I think very hard, but that was a long time ago. I doubt that Kevin's still sore. He was at the funeral and he seemed to take David's death very hard."

"Did he have a key to the house?"

"No, David said not. David was very careful about that. He always said there were only four keys—his, Achmed's, mine and, as he put it, 'the incumbent's.'"

Soto took his seat at the card table once again. He gestured to Harry to sit across from him.

"The incumbent's?"

"Yeah. He meant whoever was living with him at the time. It was Paolo's until he gave Paolo's key to his mother for the length of her stay. . . . Look, Achmed was off, the mother was here, no one else was. Why assume someone else got in?"

"Mrs. Grant said she heard someone come in and argue with her son downstairs."

"Well, that didn't take a key. David could have let any one of a hundred people in."

"No, the mother heard the Chinese gong ring. Grant had it rigged to go off only when the key turned in the front lock, right?"

—58—

"Yes, that's so, but you're assuming the mother's telling the truth."

"I'm not assuming anything, Mr. Cain; I told you, I'm just asking questions. By the way, where were *you* on Sunday night around midnight?"

Harry, surprised by the question, became wary.

"Home reading all that night. Why?"

Soto ignored the question.

"Anyone see you?"

"No . . . my wife was out of town that night and our housekeeper was on vacation."

"I see." Soto made the words sound ominous. "You're the executor of Mr. Grant's will, isn't that correct?"

"Yes," said Harry, his anger growing.

"That's two very sizable fees, right—one as lawyer and one as executor?"

"Possibly. But the way I feel about that family, I'll probably resign."

"Oh, really?"

"Look, if you're suggesting I pushed David Grant off that terrace to get some fees, you're out of your mind."

"I'm not suggesting anything, Mr. Grant; I'm just asking some questions. But now that you mention it, before we go any further, I should tell you that the Grant family has filed a formal complaint with our office, accusing you of murdering Mr. Grant. You're a suspect."

Harry just gaped.

"I know you're thoroughly aware of your rights, but I'll read them to you and, if you like, we can call this talk off or wait until you get an attorney here. I'll certainly understand."

"You've got to be kidding."

"I'm not kidding at all, Mr. Cain. You're a suspect, and I'm going to read you your rights." Soto pulled out a printed card and put it before him on the table.

Harry stood up and stared down at the man. "Firstly, Lieutenant, you questioned me in some depth *before* you told me I was a suspect and offered to read me my rights. So if you had any case at all, you'd have blown it.

"Secondly, you've got no Goddamn case at all; and if you understood your job, you'd know it."

Now Soto got to his feet and leaned menacingly toward Harry across the table. Harry glanced back. "What are you going to do, Lieutenant, punch me out?"

Soto hesitated and then leaned away slightly. Harry went on. "Did you ever hear of 'motive' and 'opportunity,' Lieutenant? Did you ever hear of a murder conviction without those two elements? What's the motive here—huh? You think I killed David Grant for the probate fees. Shit! If you'd done any home work at all, you'd know that, with David Grant alive, my fees would be twice as much—every single year.

"And where's the opportunity? You got a witness that can put me here that night? You do not! What a fucking joke! You let the mother leave town, a lady with all the motive and opportunity in the world, the lady who probably shoved him off that cliff and you make me your 'suspect.' Jesus, what a cretin."

Soto was leaning closer now, burning with anger. "I can book you right now, smartass—cuff you, run you downtown and book you for murder one."

"Why don't you do it then, asshole?" Harry stuck his arms out ready for the cuffs. "Go ahead and cuff me!" Soto stood unmoving.

"Listen, pal, you touch me, you 'run' me anywhere, you 'book' me for anything, and I'll sue your ass from here to Sunday. Better still, I'll have your badge, because you sure as shit don't deserve it."

The two men stood glaring at each other across the small table. After a tense moment, Harry turned and walked away.

"Don't leave town," Soto snapped.

"You either," Harry snapped back. And he left the patio.

At seven-thirty that evening Harry was alone in his office. Everyone else was gone. He leaned back in his desk chair listening in semi-darkness to a Brandenberg Concerto. Bach's contrapuntal magic soothed him, easing the anxiety of the day, the anger that he felt for hours after his confrontation with Soto.

Looking around the softly lit room, he felt the comfort of its lush decor. His eyes moved approvingly over the rounded gray surfaces, the smokey mirrors reflecting the city's lights.

He'd come a long way from the grimy walk-up office on Hollywood Boulevard. But even back then, he'd made the right decision—done the right thing—the right thing for Harry Cain anyway. With his Harvard *magna*, his *Law Review* credentials, all the major downtown firms had wanted him—made him fine offers. But he'd passed up the security, the prestige of an establishment firm to strike out on his own. Little divorces, petty landlord squabbles, small crimes— poor, desperate clients. Harry had thrown his intelligence and energy into every case, finding new ways to win—always win—had to win.

Slowly—over the years—the word had spread. Slowly the cases grew bigger, the causes more significant, the clients richer.

And now? Well, now, he supposed, he was there—just where he'd wanted to be during all those years of battling. Now Harry Cain was the guy, the main man—everyone's first choice . . . if he didn't have to defend himself against a murder charge.

The telephone rang, breaking the spell.

"Mr. Cain?"

"Speaking."

"Mr. Slutsky calling."

Yank Slutsky was the largest single stockholder of Consolidated Studios. Short, wide, and, a fringe of black hair curling down his neck, and rolls of fat bulging against his tightly, cut Bijan shirts, Slutsky was called "The Badger" by his friends and any number of worse names by those he had bullied, bluffed or lied to over the years. Famous for his superpatriotism and uncontrollable temper, Slutsky had little finesse, but vast power, which he exercised daily to help his friends, punish his enemies or just for the joy of wielding it. Yank Slutsky had "connections."

He came on the line, his high voice sweet, insinuating. "Hi ya, pal. How you doing?"

Harry thought he could smell the man's thousand-dollar cologne.

"Fine, Yank, how about you?"

"Okay, pal. I'm okay."

Harry said nothing.

"Listen," Slutsky went on, "you know I'm your biggest fan, don't you, Babe . . . your biggest fuckin' fan, okay?"

"Sure, Yank."

"Hey! Don't 'sure Yank' me, pal. I'm talkin' *emmis* here. Who got you Streisand, huh? Who sent you Pacino, okay?"

"Okay, Yank. Thanks. What's on your mind?"

"Well, I gotta keep the interest of the shareholders in mind, Babe, always. Am I right?"

"You're right, Yank."

"Okay then—it would help me ever so much if I could know the truth about Sonny Ball. You know, completely off the record of course. Like we never had this conversation. What I'd like to know is"—he paused—"is that cocksucker really a cocksucker or what? You know what I mean?"

Harry cut in. "Hey, Yank, you know I can't talk about that. He's my client."

"You're not listening to me, Babe. This is vital information. I *need* it, fershtay?"

"I hear you, Yank, but I just can't talk about it. I'm the man's lawyer."

An ominous silence followed. "Listen, you shyster fuck, don't give me that holier-than-thou shit. I know where you come from, you mealymouth turd wacker."

Harry found Slutsky's legendary temper amusing.

"What's a turd wacker, Yank?"

"Don't be funny, asshole. One thing I can't stomach is a guy who takes and don't pay back. I can have your fuckin' brains blown out, you know that; and I might just do it too. I can have you hanging by your balls on a fuckin' meat hook any time I want!"

Now, Harry was sore.

"Well, take your best shot, you fat creep. Come and try it if you've got the guts."

Harry slammed down the phone and sat trembling. He was making friends fast. First Lieutenant Soto and now Yank Slutsky. It was going to be a race to see whether he'd be arrested first or killed. He smiled to himself, but there was as strange feeling in the pit of his stomach. It was fear.

Despite Harry's concern, the next few days brought neither arrest nor assault. Soto called him, speaking coldly, formally. He had more questions about Kevin Shaw. He told Harry that David's houseman, Achmed, had disappeared and asked if Harry had any idea where the man might be. Harry did not, and felt somewhat guilty at the comfort he took in knowing that, now, someone else seemed to be the prime suspect, if there was really any "suspect" at all. With David's mother allowed to return to Florida, and no apparent move against anyone else, it seemed that Soto really thought David had fallen by accident or jumped. Perhaps that was right after all.

Meanwhile, Harry tried to deal with his practice and his life. He made the arrangements to get the brick work started on Ben Brody's building in Gaynorville, met with the accountants in the Malone case and handled his normal heavy caseload.

Although much of his practice involved litigation, Harry's reputation for shrewd intelligence, hard work and an obsessive drive to succeed had led to his being retained in matters as varied as motion picture contracts, cotton leases and corporate acquisitions.

With his practice growing and becoming diversified, Harry had come to depend more and more on his young partner, John Matsuoka, and their three even younger associates.

Tall, crew-cut, the oldest son of a well-know nisei family, Matsuoka had finished first in his class at Stanford Law School and, like Harry, had shunned the offers of the large downtown firms to become a deputy city attorney. He had established an outstanding record as a tough and successful prosecutor, before Harry lured him away.

John, like Harry, thrived on facing every kind of legal challenge; and every month he became more essential to handling Harry's burgeoning practice.

*D*uring that week, Harry made three more afternoon visits to Carmel's house in Laurel Canyon.

Harry had been involved in affairs before. He had given little thought to the reasons. But they were there. And they were complex. It wasn't only physical desire, although that was certainly a part of it. So was the need to prove himself—to compete and win. But there was also a yearning for adventure. Without realizing it, Harry tried to live a novel. Alone during much of his childhood, he found refuge in books. Haunting the public library he read everything he could, devouring stories of romance and high adventure, of tempestuous emotions and passionate conflict. As he grew older, he expected life to provide the color and drama his books had described.

At first, Harry found that with Nancy, in sharing the hazards of young love and early marriage. But as time passed, their relationship had grown "comfortable." Although they were "close," even loving, the romance, the quest, the challenge Harry expected—needed—had long ago waned. And for years, there had been other women—an actress, a fashion model, a divorce client, several more—all exciting at first, gradually fading, finally ending.

These relationships were never just sexual encounters. They were romantic adventures—voyages of peril and discovery. "Discovery" was a great part of it. Much of Harry's almost childlike enthusiasm and delight over women was the excitement, the exquisite delights of discovering a new and separate person—exploring, learning, coming to know her in a way others couldn't—knowing her desires, her physical and emotional needs, on the most intimate and intense level, knowing what she was like in moments of overwhelming passion . . . knowledge otherwise kept private, hidden from the world. To Harry, that old-fashioned phrase "carnal knowledge" had a special meaning, a particular truth.

But in all his earlier affairs, Harry had found nothing like Carmel—nothing like her intelligence, her perception, her wit—certainly nothing like the intense physical bond that had grown between them. Their physical relationship was like a powerful narcotic. It compelled him, pulled him like a magnet to the little house in the canyon. He came to know every inch of Carmel's body and how it would respond, when that heavy breathing would begin that meant her nipples would stand out erect and her silken, golden mound begin to flow with hunger for him, and he, in turn, hungered. She would massage him slowly, sensuously—covering his body with delicate maddening flicks of her tongue—the soles of his feet, his inner thighs, his testicles—until he shuddered with such intense jolts of erotic feeling that he could wait no longer to enter her, to drown in her.

Carmel seemed as obsessed as Harry, if not more so. She built her day around Harry's visits and wanted to know, to devour every detail about him, what he did and what he thought. For the first time in her life, she told Harry, she felt she was beginning what everyone else called a "normal" relationship with a man with no need to humiliate or degrade herself in order to be aroused. She was filled with gratitude and reveled in their time together.

Much of Harry's efforts in this period were devoted to preparation for the Ball trial, which was coming fast. Harry had covered the theater himself and had asked Skip Corrigan to get him a rundown on the arresting officer. He lined up a parade of character witnesses, started preparing Sonny Ball for his direct and cross-examination and met with Ball's fiancé, Allison Fong, who was all that Ball said she would be . . . an Oriental beauty, direct, intelligent, soft-spoken and ladylike, with just a hint of wanton sensuality below the surface, a quality Harry hoped would come across to the jury. She readily confirmed that she and Ball had an active and successful sex life and that they planned to get married and raise a large family.

Finally, Harry felt he was ready. He knew that Scuneo was good, but felt that, given any kind of break, his own skill and experience would win for him. He considered Allison Fong that break. Despite the serious problems of dealing with an eyewitness cop and explaining why Ball was in a Main Street movie at midnight in the first place with Vaseline in his pocket, Harry finally felt good about the case.

*T*hree days before the trial, Harry devoted the day to preparing Sonny Ball as a witness. To avoid interruptions, they worked at Ball's magnificent sea-view apartment on the Santa Monica Palisades.

Midway through the morning, Harry checked with his office for messages. Among them was a call from Gail. Harry returned the call from Sonny Ball's handsomely decorated bedroom. Sitting on the arm of a quilted suede chair, he admired the rich tones of tobacco, pumpkin and rust, the combination of chrome with soft leathers and rough, masculine fabrics.

Gazing out the large bowed window, Harry could see the coastline curving southward to Palos Verdes. The day was clear, and he could make out individual streets and buildings in Ocean Park and Venice.

Advised by a secretary that Gail was on another call, Harry agreed to wait on the line. He held the telephone in one hand and shielded his eyes with the other, in an effort to spot their old apartment building on Rose Avenue in Venice. What memories came at the thought of that first California home . . . the dampness of the place, the cracked linoleum floors, the red roses on the torn and faded wallpaper . . . Nancy, seven months pregnant, seeing him off for work in the early morning, waiting for him at night to share a late dinner when the law library closed . . . then the memory of that one terrifying night . . . Nancy screaming in pain, the doctor's worried voice, the race through deserted streets at three A.M. to St. John's . . . rushing along the hospital corridors, Nancy on a gurney, dead white, her face contorted with pain . . . then the long wait—alone, pacing— until, finally, the doctor came again, his voice still tense, cracking with fatigue . . . their hurried walk down the corridor to the pediatric I.C.U., and then, finally, the moment Harry would never forget as long as he lived . . . the first sight of that tiny figure, lying wired and intubated, breathing slowly, laboriously, but breathing . . . fighting for her life, just as Harry, himself, would have fought. His child, his girl. A fierce pride, an unbounded love filled him at the sight. Neither had left him, even now, twenty-four years later. His love for

Gail was something he could never fully explain. Perhaps it was linked to that night when he almost lost her, to seeing that tiny, courageous thing battling death. And it had been a very close thing. "Only five minutes to spare" the doctor had said. My God, what luck they had had to...

"Dad?" the familiar voice shook him from his memories.

"Oh, hi Gail, I got a message you called."

"Yeah... please do me a favor, will you?"

"Sure, I will... if I can."

"Have lunch with me today... at the Lobster?"

Harry looked at his watch. He could afford the time, and he'd certainly rather have lunch with Gail than Sonny Ball. "Okay, Gail. Is twelve-thirty all right?"

"Great. Thanks, Dad, I'll see you there."

*T*he Lobster was a tiny white shack at the entrance to the old Santa Monica Pier. Years earlier when the original owner died, the Portuguese chef had taken over. A genius with seafood, he had made the pocket-size restaurant prosper, and Harry always looked forward to lunch there when he tried cases in the West District Court only three blocks away.

Exactly at twelve-thirty, Harry pulled into the small parking lot. Gail was already waiting by the restaurant entrance. Like her father, she deplored being late, a trait Nancy called their mutual obsession with punctuality.

Over fried oyster sandwiches and ice-cold beer, they shared the events of the week. Gail said nothing about why she had wanted to meet, and Harry didn't ask.

As always, they delighted in each other's company and conversation, laughing, bantering, each finding the other funny and bright, loving the other, proud of the other.

Ever since Gail was a child, her relationship with Harry had been special. Harry's grueling schedule and long working hours left the day-to-day "eat your spinach" discipline to Nancy, while, almost like a divorced father, Harry appeared magically on weekends, a dashing figure who spirited his adoring little girl off to such places as Disney-land, the movies or the beach. As a result Harry had always seemed more like an exotic, treasured friend than an ordinary father.

When they'd finished their coffee, Gail asked Harry to walk with her on the pier. They strolled along arm-in-arm, like young lovers. It was a perfect September day. A light breeze swept the air clean, the clear blue of the sky was reflected in the sea, and the sweeping white crescent of sand was visible all the way to Point Dume, many miles to the north.

Gail stopped and they leaned on the railing, gazing out at the bay.

"Dad, I know how you feel about Robin. But you know how I feel too. I've got something to tell you, so have a seat."

She gestured toward a nearby bench overlooking the harbor. Harry's heart began to pound, but he joined her on the bench. Gail took Harry's hand. She paused and took a deep breath.

"Dad, I'm pregnant."

His mind reeled. For a moment, he continued looking blankly out to sea. Then he turned back to Gail.

"Milgrim?"

"Yes."

"Jesus!" He brought his fist down on the bench.

"Dad, listen, it's going to work out."

"*What's* going to work out? Certainly not marriage. He'll never leave his wife."

"He will, Dad, I'm sure."

"Come on, Gail, you're kidding yourself—leave the Honorable Diana Milgrim? leave that big estate? the parties with Prince Phillip?—no way. Anyway, it doesn't matter. We can easily take care of it. I'll set it up for you at Cedars."

"No, Dad. No abortion. I want the baby."

"You *want* it?"

"Yes, I do. I've thought a lot about it. I'm no kid any more, and I definitely want children, even if we don't get married. Besides, Robin's bright and healthy. His genes are good."

Harry interrupted. "Christ, Gail, this isn't a genetics class. This is life. This guy is married. He fools around everywhere. He'll never leave his wife, because she's loaded and gives him the social position

—68—

he wants. He'll never even *be* with you or the baby . . . Gail, honey, it just makes no sense."

"It does to me, Dad. Forget about the genes. I love him. That's the real point. Look, Dad, I know I can't sell you on Robin. I'm not even going to try. You'd have to know him . . . I mean know him on a personal level, not in some lawsuit. He's so much more than you think. He's a vulnerable, sensitive man with a depth of feeling that would surprise you."

Gail paused at Harry's skeptical expression. "I know it's difficult for you to accept, but it's true. Did you know he wrote a poem for me? 'The Moonlight Princess.' I would have loved it even if it were trash, but it's *very* good. That's what he calls me, by the way, 'Princess.' Oh Dad, he's such a tender, caring man. If only you could see it. And he's got nothing left with Diane . . . *nothing*. He's very open about leaving her. He doesn't care about the estate and all that nonsense. What he does care about is me, and someday we'll be married. I *know* it.

"Anyway, I want his child and I'm going to have it." She thrust out her jaw, her eyes blazing into his. He'd seen that look so many times. *"I'm going to the prom. I don't care if I have the flu."* . . . *"I'm going to sit in, police or not."* So many times. It was no good fighting her when she was like this.

He tried to smile. "Look, Gail, think about it some, will you? Keep an open mind. Consider all the elements here. Then, in a few days, let's talk again. Okay?"

Now Gail smiled. "Okay, Dad, that's fair. But don't expect me to change my mind."

"I understand. Just think about it, all right? Have you told your mother?"

"No. I'm going to tell her this afternoon."

Harry sighed and got to his feet. He helped Gail up, and, quietly, thoughtfully, they walked back up the pier. A large cloud had drifted across the sun and suddenly the breeze cooled, the day darkened, and Harry, leaving Gail at her car, drove back to Sonny Ball's apartment, his spirits matching the somber new quality of the afternoon.

"**D**id Gail tell you?"

They were sipping martinis before dinner. Nancy seemed so calm and serene that Harry wondered if Gail had reconsidered giving her the news.

"Yes, she told me; and, she's wrong—so *very* wrong. She's only a few weeks into her pregnancy. It would be safe and easy to terminate. But I don't think we'll change her mind. Remember, I felt the same way when I got pregnant with Gail."

"Sure, Nancy, but I wanted to marry you. This guy's married already—and forever. Besides, he's a miserable prick. Aside from his amoral, vicious column and his sponging off a rich wife, he's the worst philanderer in the world. Everyone knows it. He's always with some Goddamn starlet or model."

"This from Harry Cain?" she asked, just a hint of bitterness in her voice.

Harry reddened. Nancy had never raised the subject of "other women." Now, her ambiguous remark chilled him. There was no way she could know about Carmel, but how much did she know about his earlier affairs? Is that what her remark meant? Quickly, he changed the subject, not wanting to find out.

"Nancy, forget what Milgrim's like. Gail doesn't realize how a baby will change her life or her career. Her job requires freedom, mobility— she's throwing all that away. She's young, with so much to look forward to. This is no time to weigh herself down with the responsibility of a child . . . with no husband. Nancy, we've *got* to make her see."

Nancy sighed and ran her fingers through her hair. "I suppose you're right, Harry, but Gail's not easy to turn around when she's got the bit in her teeth and she's got it there now, with a vengeance."

"I know, I know. Still, we've got to try. I think I got her agreement to wait on any decision, to keep an open mind."

"You believe that?"

"Yeah, I do."

"Okay, Harry, good luck to you . . . to us, I should say . . . all three of us."

*T*he night before Sonny Ball's trial, Nancy was at a conference in San Francisco. Harry sat at his desk, with a cold roast beef sandwich and a bottle of beer, planning his cross-examination on a yellow legal pad. The news about Gail had upset him, thrown him off stride. But now that he was back concentrating, focusing all his energy on the case, he felt better.

At eleven o'clock Harry's telephone exchange told him he had an urgent call from a Miss Allison Fong. When he reached her at home, she was in a state of near hysteria. "Look, Mr. Cain, I don't know if I can do it. I never wanted to do it. I told him I couldn't do it."

"Hold on, Allison," Harry said. "Tell me what the problem is and we'll solve it. Get hold of yourself."

Harry could feel her tension through the wires, but he heard only breathing for several seconds. "Well . . . ?"

"Well, I just can't testify for Sonny tomorrow. At least I don't see how I can say anything that can help him."

"Let me be the judge of that, Allison. Just testify to what you told me in my office. You're his fiancée. You plan to be married and have a large family. Since your engagement you've had normal and regular sexual relations. That's basically it, Allison, and that's about all that can save him. So don't worry about whether it'll help. Let me be the judge of that."

"But you don't understand, Mr. Cain. It's just not true, none of it. We're not engaged. I just look good on his arm when he goes to parties, and, as for sex, he's never even kissed me."

"Jesus Christ, Allison, why did you feed me that line when you were in my office? You may have just destroyed him with this. I've been betting almost everything on you, on your testimony. There's damn little else. You just can't mean it. Did the two of you have a fight, what happened? Let me come over right now."

"Now hang on, Mr. Cain." Her voice was like he had never heard it. Hard and cold. "I need Sonny Ball—badly. He's my future, my only way in. If he's finished, I'm finished. It's as simple as that. Sure I lied. He asked me to and I didn't hesitate—not one minute. But now I'm facing a trial tomorrow and it's not as simple as I thought. A friend explained to me about perjury. You know, other people know the truth, lots of them. The whole thing could come out, even if they..." She paused again. "Look, Mr. Cain, if you tell me it's Sonny's only chance, I'll still testify to it, you know, jail or not. After all, prison probably beats going back to Hong Kong anyway. You just tell me what to do."

Harry sighed and took a long sip of beer.

"There's only one thing you *can* do, Allison, stay home."

"You mean it?" He could hear the relief in her voice.

"I mean it."

"You'll explain to Sonny that I was ready to do it, ready to testify but you told me not to? That's the truth, you know."

"Yeah, I'll tell him. Don't worry, just forget about it."

Harry hung up and slammed his fist into the desk lamp, knocking it to the floor. "Shit! Son of a bitch. Shit!" He could see the headlines, "Film Star Convicted, Sunset Bomber Bombed," with a picture of Bailey Scuneo, the winning prosecutor, smiling triumphantly at the news of the conviction he had predicted. "Shit on a stick." He kicked the fallen lamp across the room, snapping the cord from the plug and plunging the house into darkness.

He sat down at his desk in the dark and, after a moment, began to laugh. He reached for the scotch in the bottom drawer and took several long swallows from the bottle. Then, leaving the fuses to be changed in the morning by someone better qualified for the job, he stripped in the dark, groped his way between the sheets and, still smiling, drifted quickly into sleep.

The Los Angeles Criminal Courts building stands, in the undistinguished modern architecture of the fifties, along Temple Street, between Spring and Hill in downtown Los Angeles. Nearby are the old Plaza, where the huge city began; Olvera Street, with its quaint Mexican shops and stalls; Chinatown; Dodger Stadium and the thrusting power of the high-rise downtown business district. Two blocks to the south and east lies Little Tokyo, the world's largest concentration of Japanese outside Tokyo itself. Farther south along the freeway live half a million blacks, while east of downtown, in the sprawling Barrio, modern Latino life goes on. On the west and south, the Koreans, Thais and Vietnamese, more recent arrivals, are already struggling for their share of the American dream.

From the top floor of the Criminal Courts building the perspective is different. The vast, smokey industrial area, incongruously punctuated with towering palms, stretches east and south beyond the Civic Center for miles, all the way to the harbor. To the north are the mountains, Lake Arrowhead, Big Bear and Snow Valley; and far to the west lie the green expanse of Beverly Hills, Westwood and Bel Air and, on a clear day, even the Pacific, shimmering blue-purple in the distance.

But this was not a clear day. The smog was heavy, even in the early morning. The freeways and surface streets were crowded and the corridors of the Criminal Courts building teemed with hookers, pimps, harried prosecutors, seedy defense lawyers in polyester and boots, arresting officers looking out of place and, on the morning of the trial of Sonny Ball, an army of news photographers and television camera crews lusting after this latest and most titillating exposé of life among the handful of superstars who bring countless millions to the box office, are paid a fortune for every film and can be cast aside and forgotten almost as fast as they became famous.

The trial began with the long, careful process of picking a jury. The breaks went each way, resulting in a jury that was a mixed bag. Harry was boxed into keeping a construction worker—beer gut, tattoos and all—and a retired Swedish engineer who, unbelievably, wore a pince-nez and sat straight as a ramrod, apparently just waiting for the hanging. Bailey Scuneo was an experienced prosecutor who handled the jury selection with skill. Still, Harry was able to retain a Jewish housewife with warm, wrinkly eyes and a graduate student of music from UCLA. Both looked as though they'd be sympathetic and perhaps even forgiving. The rest of the jury seemed about average.

Judge Thomas Moran, a quiet black man, evenhanded and steady, nodded to Scuneo, indicating that the prosecution could begin its opening statement.

As always, Scuneo wore a tiny rose in the lapel of his blue pin-stripe suit. He was a bully—mean, but effective . . . and highly the-atrical. Before beginning his statement to the jury, he removed the rose from his lapel, sniffed it one last time and, with a gracious gesture, gave it to the court reporter.

As Scuneo stepped back to the counsel table to begin speaking, Harry took a look around the courtroom. Judge Moran sat on a raised platform flanked by the U.S. and California flags. He seemed alert and attentive, ready to begin the copious notes he would take through-out the case. To the judge's right was the witness stand with its chair raised almost to the judge's level. Beyond that the jury sat in a two-tiered enclosure along the side of the room. Quiet now, and serious, they were opening their notepads, reaching for pens, looking ex-pectantly toward Scuneo, for the moment charmed by his gesture with the rose.

Immediately in front of the jury was the prosecution table, at which Scuneo now stood to speak. A young associate was seated there ready to take notes. To their right, at the defense table, sat Harry, flanked by a tense Sonny Ball.

The bailiff, sitting at a small desk to Harry's right, was a heavyset man. His substantial gut hung over a tooled leather cartridge belt. He pushed his holstered .38 special back on his hip and eased himself farther back into his padded chair, pretending to listen.

The birdlike, nervous clerk sat at an oversized rolltop desk on the judge's left, guarding the entrance to his chambers. Between stamp-ing documents for filing and making entries on the court's calendar, she answered the muffled telephone bell with the hoarse whisper "Department 102 . . . Clerk."

As Scuneo began to speak, the court reporter concentrated, her fingers flying over the stenotype keys. She had blushed at Scuneo's gift of the rose, but she was a professional in a world of professionals. During recess, she might gossip with the clerk. But when court was in session, there was room for nothing but her job.

The gallery would normally have been sparsely occupied, mostly by retirees who spent their days trial-watching, moving from court to court, hoping to find an interesting case or one with a colorful lawyer. Today, this section was packed with reporters taking notes, sketching and whispering, until the bailiff stood heavily and raised a finger to his lips indicating the need for silence.

After his opening statement, Scuneo put the arresting officer on the stand, figuring that was all he'd need. Sergeant Dale Prindle was a stocky man with closely cropped blond hair. His uniform was freshly pressed and his black boots shined to a mirror finish. He sat erect in the witness chair, giving his answers in a firm, clear voice. He reminded Harry of a Marine drill sergeant.

Prindle told his story well and believably. The jury—even the housewife and the music student—seemed impressed. Harry saw the engineer look over at Sonny Ball with disgust; and the construction worker, his arms folded across his chest, wore an "I know these fags" expression.

Harry knew that, without Allison Fong, he had only one chance to win. He had to destroy the cop. Otherwise, no matter how well Ball did on the stand, the jury would figure he had all the reason in the world to lie, while this crisp, efficient-looking police officer had none. Either Harry would be able to get to Sergeant Prindle or the ball game was over.

Scuneo finished his direct examination and turned smiling at Harry with a theatrical "Your witness, counselor," meaning, "Let's see you do anything with *that* testimony, shyster."

Harry bounced out of his chair and came around in front of the counsel table, cutting off the witness's view of Scuneo, a tactic designed to unsettle him. It seemed to work. Just a bit of the military polish seemed to fade.

First Harry went to work on Prindle's motive to lie. He knew from Skip Corrigan's report that Prindle had been on felony detail the night of the arrest and had been transferred to the much safer vice squad after he nailed Ball. But he'd never admit what Harry suspected . . . that he made the arrest in order to get the transfer. Harry had to get that impression across to the jury by making Prindle believe he was going for something else—for the opposite of what he really wanted.

"Officer Prindle, at the time of your arrest of Mr. Ball you were on felony division, isn't that right?"

"Yes sir."

"That's the division that handles offenses like armed robbery and other important crimes, isn't that right?"

"Yes sir, that's correct."

"And isn't it a fact that after you arrested Mr. Ball you were demoted to the vice squad?"

The cop turned bright red. This smartass shyster was trying to make him look bad. Harry could see the anger and defensiveness just below the surface; maybe the jury could see it too.

"That's totally false."

"Are you telling me you were not demoted to the vice squad?"

The cop got redder. The crispness was gone. "That's no demotion, counselor, and you know it. Every man on felony division wants to get on vice duty. Anyone will tell you that's considered a big step up."

"I see."

Ten years before, Harry would have overdone it, asked a dramatic jury pleaser like "So, you were *trying* to get on the vice squad when you made this arrest?" But nine out of ten times, the witness would realize what had happened to him and change his testimony to explain it away, costing the inexperienced attorney everything he'd gained. Leaving it as is might not hit the jury on the head with the importance of what had been admitted, but it kept the point safer, so Harry could drive it home in final argument, when the witness had no chance to answer or explain.

Knowing he could do this, Harry moved on. "Was there anyone else in the restroom besides you and the defendant?"

"No." Prindle relaxed, feeling he'd won the first encounter, exposed the shyster's lie.

"Were there people in the hall outside the restroom any time that you noticed?"

"No."

"The back door to the theater was right next to the restroom, isn't that correct?"

"Yes."

"That's how you got into the theater, right?"

"Yes."

"You left your car there by the back door, isn't that correct?"

"That's right."

"Now, there's a light just outside the restroom and another just outside the theater's back door, isn't that right?"

"That's right, I think." The cop didn't know where Harry was going with these questions and he was getting edgy again.

"Those lights were both uncovered bulbs and they were very bright, weren't they?"

"I don't remember."

"You don't deny it, do you?"

"I don't deny it . . . but—"

Harry shifted to a new topic, leaving the old one hanging.

"Now, did the fact that Mr. Ball was a movie star lead you to make this arrest?"

"No sir. I had no idea *who* he was at the time of the arrest."

"You didn't recognize the defendant as Sonny Ball?"

"No sir."

Harry breathed a sigh of relief. That was the answer he wanted.

"In your experience, Sergeant, do many people use Vaseline or other lubricants for chapped lips?" This was obvious, but Harry couldn't lose on the question. If the cop said "Yes," Harry would say something like "Of course" and simply drop the subject. The jury might think that the cop had admitted something important, and the Vaseline evidence would be out of the case. Better still, if Sergeant Prindle argued with Harry about a question the answer to which seemed obvious to the jury, he might look biased and unfair and help build the impression that he was not just a city employee doing his job but a guy out to make a vice arrest stick at any cost for his own personal reasons.

The cop took the second route. "Sure they do, but they don't carry it around in their pockets."

"Oh? Where do they carry it, Sergeant?" That got a smile from the housewife and two other jurors. Harry was feeling a little better. There was really no answer the cop could make and he mumbled that he didn't know about things like that, but he looked a little bit unfair for mentioning it in the first place. His unbiased image was beginning to get a little tarnished.

Sergeant Prindle's patience was wearing thin now, and Harry decided to shorten things. He had another series of questions on which he couldn't lose. If he got lucky, they could win the case.

"Now, Sergeant, when Mr. Ball stood next to you at the urinal you claim he stroked you . . . in fact, sir, didn't he just brush by you?"

"Absolutely not."

"Come on now, Sergeant, wasn't it just a slight brush that could have been an accident?"

"It certainly was not, definitely not."

The cop was getting red again, the anger was boiling up beneath the surface. Harry thought he could use the anger.

"Well, Sergeant, just how long did this stroking last that you say was so deliberate?" Harry's voice was dripping with disbelief. The sergeant wanted to kill him.

"At least forty seconds."

Harry's heart began pounding with excitement. He smothered a grin, and resisting the temptation to trumpet, "Forty seconds!," he immediately moved to another subject. Any other subject would do, he didn't care.

"And how many people were in the theater that night, Sergeant?"

The cop was still back at the last point. He was waiting to argue about how long the stroking lasted.

"Pardon me, I didn't catch the question."

"How many people were in the theater that night?"

"Oh, I'd say fifteen to twenty, not many."

"Fifteen to twenty of them and two of you?"

Prindle liked the idea of his having shown bravery against the odds. "That's right," he said, becoming crisp and efficient once again.

"And you had to make the arrest in a dark theater. Wasn't that risky too?"

"Yes sir, it was."

Harry turned and walked back to the counsel table. "That's all I have of this witness."

As Harry sat down, Sonny Ball, looking very anxious, whispered to Harry, "I thought we had to destroy him to win?" Harry smiled, and putting his finger to his lips, wrote on a yellow pad where Ball could see it: "Relax, he's dead. He just doesn't know it yet."

Harry didn't really know it either, not by a long shot, but it was better to keep Ball's spirits up, especially since he was going to testify.

There was still half an hour until the lunch break. Harry decided to end the cross-examination with that much time left, so that Scuneo would not have the long noon recess in which to talk to the cop before taking him on redirect examination. He'd have to try to undo the points Harry had scored without going over the questions first.

That was always risky and could make things much worse. Harry guessed that a pro like Scuneo wouldn't try it. He was right. Scuneo, looking very confident, moved toward Ball, pointed at him and said, "Sergeant, is there any doubt in your mind, any doubt at all that this man approached you at the urinal, propositioned you and deliberately stroked you right there in that men's room on Main Street?"

"None."

"He did all of those things?"

"He did."

"That's all I have."

Harry took no chances. "No questions, your honor."

"Very well then"—the judge nodded to Scuneo—"call your next witness."

"The people rest, Your Honor."

That was a surprise. Harry was sure they'd use the second cop to fill in the background, if for nothing else than to give the jury a little breather after Sergeant Prindle. Scuneo must have a reason, Harry thought—probably figures we'd use the lunch break for preparation and wants to make us start our case right now.

That was fine with Harry. He wanted this case over fast while Sergeant Prindle's testimony was still fresh in the jurors' minds. He decided to waive his opening statement, forego the character witnesses and go with only Sonny Ball himself.

Before lunch, Harry questioned Ball about his work and his background. His responses were polite and earnest. The jury seemed to like him. He'd graduated from Yale Drama School, worked as a stagehand until he got his first acting parts, then acted both off and on Broadway for fifteen years before coming to work in films at Consolidated Studios. He'd acted in two films and produced one of them. He was developing a third, which he'd produce and in which he expected to act.

This kind of questioning carried Harry safely to the lunch break, and in the afternoon, he took Ball through his story just as they'd repeatedly gone over it: the sleeplessness that led him to drive downtown in the middle of the night, the whim that made him buy a ticket to the Climax Theater, the reason for the Vaseline, the fact that the approach at the urinal was initiated by the policeman rather than the other way around, Ball's reply, intended only to avoid trouble, his return to his seat and the arrest five minutes later in the darkened theater, followed by the whispered conversations and the handcuffs. It came out fine.

Then Harry took a long pause. "You're under oath, you know that, Mr. Ball?"

"Yes."

"Are you a homosexual?"

"No."

"Did you stroke that policeman?"

"No."

"Did you make an indecent proposal to him of any sort?"

"No."

"That's all I have."

Scuneo went after Ball fast and hard. He was forty-one and had never married. Scuneo looked meaningfully at the jury. He'd never been to a skid row movie before. He knew there were plenty of movies in Beverly Hills and Westwood; he knew it was much prettier and safer to drive to the beach, to the hills, almost anywhere but skid row.

Ball was holding his own, following Harry's advice to give short, direct answers, even when they seemed to hurt his case, and looking Scuneo right in the eyes as he answered.

Scuneo continued laying into him. Ball went to the men's room in the middle of the picture, not at the end. He didn't have a weak bladder. He did tell the stranger standing next to him that the show was getting him excited.

"Was it really getting you excited?" Scuneo asked with raised eyebrows.

"No, not at all." Ball gave a patronizing smile. Harry could feel him getting overconfident.

"Not even a hint of excitement throughout the whole film?"

"Not even a hint."

"What was the film about, Mr. Ball?"

"I don't really remember."

"Mr. Ball, wasn't it about men and women having intercourse? You remember that, don't you?"

"Yes, I remember that much."

"And sex between men and women just doesn't excite you at all, does it?"

"Not watching it."

"Not anything about it unless it's two men, isn't that right, Mr. Ball?" Scuneo looked at Ball as if he were beneath contempt.

"No, it's *not* right."

"Well, would you tell us if it were true?"

"Yes, I would."

"Oh sure, of course you would." Scuneo's words dripped with sarcasm. "That's all I *need* of this witness." He returned to the prosecutor's table.

"No questions, your honor." Harry smiled, trying to convey that Scuneo's examination had been so ineffective there was no need to ask anything at all. "The defense rests."

Now it was Scuneo's turn to be surprised. He must have expected a parade of character witnesses. He seemed bothered by the sudden close of the defense case.

"Any rebuttal?" The Judge looked at Scuneo.

The prosecutor whispered to his aide and then looked up. "No, your honor. The defense case speaks for itself. No rebuttal's necessary."

Harry grinned, trying to show the jury he considered this a joke.

"Very well, gentlemen, are you ready to argue?" They both were.

Scuneo got to his feet, paused for a long moment and then began to review the prosecution case, working in the points he'd made in cross-examining Ball. He did it neatly and efficiently, making it seem very improbable that Ball hadn't done just what Prindle said he did. He got some nods from the jury, especially when he talked about why the owner of a Bel Air mansion would be in the men's room of a skid row movie in the middle of the night. But it was impossible to guess what the jury was thinking, and Harry didn't try.

When Scuneo finished, Harry got to his feet. Standing at the counsel table, his hands clasped behind his back, he let his eyes move slowly along the rows of jurors. "Ladies and gentlemen, this is an unusual case in several respects. For one thing, it depends entirely on one man's word against another's. No other witnesses, just Officer Prindle and Mr. Ball.

"You have to decide which story to accept, but there are certain time-honored rules to apply in making your decision. The judge will tell you that you must believe Mr. Ball and find him not guilty unless you believe beyond a reasonable doubt that he is lying. If you have any reasonable doubt, if there is any reasonable possibility that it's Mr. Ball who is telling the truth and not Officer Prindle, then you must find Mr. Ball not guilty. Those are the rules and I know you'll apply them."

Moving out from behind the counsel table, Harry approached the jury box.

"Now, no one can say, really honestly say, that of these two men there is no reasonable possibility that it's Mr. Ball who's telling us the truth here today. Having heard the two men testify, you just can't say that. No one can.

"Mr. Ball describes an unusual chain of events, it's true, but again, no one can say that there's no reasonable possibility that that unusual chain of events didn't happen.

"Actually, the fact that it's so unusual makes it more likely to be true. If Mr. Ball wanted to make up a story, he could certainly have done a better job, come up with a story that was much less strange, much more believable. But we don't convict on strangeness or suspicion or anything else, except a belief in guilt beyond a reasonable doubt."

Then, pacing slowly before the jury, Harry summarized the defense position, explained away the Vaseline, the midnight drive, the movie and why, when questioned at a urinal by what seemed to be an aggressive and possibly dangerous stranger about whether the show had him excited, it was only natural and prudent to say "Yeah," and try to move away.

Harry stepped to the rail of the jury box, catching the eyes of the construction worker. "You don't argue with guys like that in a place like that. You agree pleasantly with *whatever* they might say and you get yourself out of there. That's what any sensible person would have done under the circumstances and that's just what Mr. Ball did. And it made good sense.

"But now, let's look at Officer Prindle's story and see if that makes sense. If you analyze it, you couldn't really accept that story, even if there were no reasonable doubt test. But there is; and here again, no one can say that beyond a reasonable doubt everything Officer Prindle told us was so.

"You might say, 'Why would a police officer make up a story like that. What's in it for him?' But I think we know the answer to that. He told us himself. He was on felony division. Very dangerous. You get shot, you can get killed. Everyone—that's what Officer Prindle himself said—'everyone' on felony division wants to make it to the vice squad. Officer Prindle certainly did. He *admitted* it right here on the stand. And why not? Prostitutes don't kill you, nobody ever got shot in a massage parlor or watching who comes out the back door of the Institute of Nude Wrestling."

Some of the jurors smiled at this. Harry went on, "So, Officer Prindle wants a transfer to the vice squad. And how do you get that? Simple. You make vice arrests while you're still on felony duty. Show 'em you've got the aptitude—got the right instincts. You find a guy in the men's room at a Main Street theater at two o'clock in the morning, you get him talking and maybe you tell yourself he's slim and well dressed and he might be a homosexual. You run him in, you say what you need to make the arrest stick, then they transfer you to the vice squad and you're safe. You've got what Officer Prindle admitted he wanted and everyone wanted.

"There's your reason for this arrest, ladies and gentlemen; there's your reason for Officer Prindle's testimony here today."

Harry moved back to the counsel table, the pause giving the point time to sink in. Then he turned and spoke from the greater distance.

"Now, as I said, Prindle's testimony won't hang together for two minutes, even without the reasonable doubt test. I'll just give you two examples. You know the rest yourselves.

"Officer Prindle tells us the offense happened in the men's room, but what did he do about it? He didn't arrest Mr. Ball in the men's room where it happened or in the brightly lit hall outside the restroom, or take him right out the back door, where his police car was parked and it was also brightly lit. No, sir, not Officer Prindle. He lets his man go back into the dark theater, he waits five minutes and then he arrests him there in the dark, where there are fifteen or twenty guys in the audience who might jump him any time. Does that make sense if there really was an offense committed five minutes earlier alone in the brightly lit restroom? It certainly does not.

"The answer is there was no offense committed in the restroom, and that's why there was no immediate arrest. Officer Prindle went back to the car to talk it over with his partner—decide what they should do. But I'll get back to that later.

"Let's examine what Officer Prindle said about the offense itself. That really is the best indication of all as to the truth. That really tells us something about Officer Prindle and about his story."

Harry walked back to the jury box.

"You remember I asked Officer Prindle how long Mr. Ball supposedly stroked him. Keep in mind this is no ordinary witness. This is an officer of the law, specially trained to observe and remember things like time and distance and to do it accurately. And what did he say? He said Mr. Ball stroked him for at least forty seconds. That's what he said, this officer of the law, 'at least forty seconds.' He didn't even say 'about half a minute.' He had no doubts, no need to be approximate. He said 'forty seconds.' He wanted you to believe he knew with precision.

"Now, I'd like you to look at your watch or your neighbor's watch, if you don't have one with you. If you would, take the watch right off your wrist and put it in front of you so you can watch it." The jury was stirring, looking at their wrists, opening purses, undoing watch bands. Harry took off his own watch and put it on the railing in front of the jury. "Now follow along with me and we'll just experience together what Officer Prindle wants us to believe he experienced with Mr. Ball.

"Now wait till I say go. Here we have two men standing side by side at the urinal. One slight stroke and that's enough to constitute the offense. That's enough to arrest and convict Mr. Ball. That's all Officer Prindle needs. Just one slight stroke and he can arrest Mr. Ball. Just one quick stroke is enough.

"But let's see what Officer Prindle tells us he did." Harry lifted the watch in the air with his left hand. "Okay, here we go." Looking at the dial, he started massaging the railing of the jury box with his right hand.

"Here's the offense right there, complete with the very first stroke. There's the stroke, and now Mr. Ball can be arrested. But is he arrested? Does Officer Prindle pull him in right there? No, not at all." Harry continued to massage the railing in front of the jury, rubbing back and forth as he spoke.

"No, Officer Prindle allows the stroking to continue on and on and on and on." Harry's voice rose. "It's still going on and on, do you know ladies and gentlemen, that's not even *five* seconds?

"Yet, here he is, this officer of the law, still standing there, still letting himself be stroked on his private parts—on and on and on, even though, long before this, he had that one stroke that would have been enough to make the arrest."

Now almost everybody in the jury was grinning. The old engineer had the biggest grin of all.

Harry kept at his regular stroking of the railing, talking to the jury all the while. "Okay, that's fifteen seconds. What do you suppose they're talking about standing there at the urinal with one fellow stroking the other like that, just stroking and stroking and stroking? Are they talking about how the Dodgers'll do this year? Have you seen any good movies lately? I guess they are, because it's sure a long time to stand there in silence."

Now Harry pulled the watch closer, stroking the jury box in small and loving circles. "Almost twenty-five seconds, folks, and it's still going on. The policeman is still standing there letting this stranger at the next urinal stroke him and stroke him, and continue to stroke him."

Chuckles were starting in the jury box now. The construction worker nudged the engineer with his elbow and winked. Harry continued to rub the railing in front of the jury. "Okay, they probably know each other fairly well by now, so they may be talking about politics or religion, or showing each other photos of their families, at least the policeman would be. The other fellow would be too busy stroking."

Open laughs were now coming from most of the jury. "That's thirty seconds, ladies and gentlemen, and you'd think that Mr. Ball's arm would be getting very tired by this time. I know I am." Harry looked weary as he continued to stroke the railing back and forth, back and forth in front of the jury. "And yet, all this time, after only one stroke could have done it . . . could have justified an arrest . . . this officer of the law, paid by you and by me, stood there letting himself be rubbed, stroke after stroke after stroke—probably five or six hundred strokes, just bravely doing his duty."

The housewife and two other ladies on the jury gave great whoops of laughter, the construction worker doubled over, the old engineer had his handkerchief to his face making snuffling noises and the music student, as well as the remaining jurors, all had big grins.

"That's it, forty seconds! That's just what this accurate, professional observer wants us to believe happened there in the men's room between Mr. Ball and himself. Well, hogwash, ladies and gentlemen, hogwash! It never happened. It never happened at all, and you know it as well as I do."

The laughter died down. Harry waited. "I'll tell you what *did* happen. This officer wanted to make a vice arrest to get himself on the vice squad. We've already established that. He stopped in at this Main Street theater maybe to find an arrest, maybe to use the bathroom, it doesn't matter. In any event, he found his man. There in the restroom he found a slim, nicely dressed man. What else could he be but a queer. That's what went through Officer Prindle's mind, I'm sure. Remember, he didn't recognize him as Sonny Ball. Well, he talked to the fellow, but couldn't get him to say much. Even when he said, 'Show got you worked up?' this man doesn't bite; he just says 'Yeah' and starts for the door. Well, no crime there and no arrest. Too bad. He's obviously gay, thinks Prindle, but he's too smart.

"So Prindle goes out to his car, kicking himself for not forcing the issue there in the men's room, somehow making the arrest. He tells his partner about it. They're facing a night of violence, possible death, on felony division. 'Look, if we pull him in, at least we can take an hour or so on the paperwork, have some coffee and maybe, just maybe, we'll make it stick and make the vice squad.' For five minutes they kick it around, standing there by the police car. Finally, they decide to do it. 'What difference does it make,' they say; 'he's a fag anyway; he should be off the streets. Just say he stroked you, that's all. After all, he *would* have stroked you if he had the chance.'

"What they didn't know, of course, was who they were arresting. Do you think they would have tried it if they knew Mr. Ball's real identity? Of course not!

"But they didn't know. So they made the arrest and they made up a story about stroking, and a man's life is nearly ruined because of it." Harry paused and looked squarely at the jury, letting his eyes move again from face to face. "Except for you, ladies and gentlemen. Except for you. That's where you come in.

"What you've seen here is something that you might see in a film. A man is on trial for his life, just like in a movie."

Harry walked over to Ball sitting attentively at the counsel table. He put his hand on Ball's shoulder. "Yes, in a very real sense, this man is on trial for his life, because, if he's convicted, his life, as he knows it, is over, ruined forever. Do you think he'll still be a motion picture star if he's convicted of stroking a policeman in a Main Street movie house? Of course not. No one will hire him, no one.

"So the situation is just like a movie you might see. This man sitting before you can be convicted, go to jail, be registered as a sex offender, in short, have his career, his entire life ruined. Or he can be acquitted, allowed to continue with his job, go back to his friends and his family."

There was no evidence that Ball even *had* a "family," but Harry hoped the jury would imagine one for him.

"Again, ladies and gentlemen, it's like a movie. But there's one big difference. *You* write the ending—each of you. *You* make the story one with a happy ending or you make it a tragedy, because, have no doubt, that's just what it would be—a tragedy for Mr. Ball, the end of his life, as he knows it.

"In making that choice, I beg you to look into your hearts, recall what you've seen and heard and find this man not guilty." There was a long silence and the jury looked very serious. It was so hard to know.

Ball grabbed Harry's arm and whispered. "The greatest thing I've ever heard in my life. What an actor you are, what—" Harry cut him off with a finger to his lips.

Scuneo was already up and beginning his reply. This time, he was more forceful. He reminded the jurors that this was a case brought by the people of the State of California and that the people included them, that Prindle was working for the people, working for them, that such cases were brought to protect them and the rest of the people and to keep the streets safe and clean, that they should ignore cheap dramatics and overlook what might be an exaggeration by Sergeant Prindle in the heat of cross-exmination when he was obviously made angry—and righteously so—by the stage tactics of the defense counsel. The facts were still there and it was still their duty to convict.

When he finished and the jury was instructed and retired to decide the case, Harry felt excited, impatient to hear the outcome. He told Ball it could be days, but Ball wanted to wait. Harry would wait too. He tried to do that in every important case, so when the jury came out to ask a question or even filed out for lunch, they'd see Harry sitting there, keeping a lonely vigil, caring. He felt that, in a close case, it could make a difference.

Ball went to have a cup of coffee and Harry went to make phone calls. Might as well find out what's been going on.

On his way to the phone, Harry parried questions from the reporters and camera crews that packed the hallway. This was no time to be making big claims or arrogant predictions of acquittal. There was nothing to gain; and if he was wrong, the press would make him look like an ass. Fifty flashbulbs popped as he said "no comment" and walked quickly down the hall.

He closed himself in a phone booth and called his office, jotting his messages on a yellow legal pad. A hearing had been set in a Nevada appeal he was to argue. The Raiders had finally accepted the terms he'd demanded for their new running back. Marvin Davis had asked to meet with him the next morning. Harry wondered why. The well-known billionaire was fascinating but always mysterious. The contractor had called from Gaynorville to say the brick work was completed on Brody's building, and Carl Malone wanted to see him about his case. Gail had called to wish him luck in the trial. Harry asked Clara to try for an appointment with Malone for five o'clock that day but to warn Malone that if the jury was still out he'd have to cancel.

Next he called Ben Brody. "Listen, Ben, the brick work's done on your building."

"That's great, Harry. I can't thank you enough, you know that. Where do I send the check again?"

"Ten thousand dollars to Patterson Masonry on Alameda Street, Ben; it's in the book. But that's not why I called. I want to give you some instructions and I want you to follow them exactly and without asking why. Okay? It's critical."

"Okay, Harry, whatever you say, but do we still have a problem with King?"

"We could, Ben, but we won't if you do exactly what I tell you."

"Okay, what is it?"

"King will be starting construction on his high rise this week. I want you to stay away from Gaynorville; just stay the hell out of there until after King's building is totally up."

"Sure, Harry, that's not hard, but why?"

"Never mind, Ben, I don't want you to know. Trust me. Okay?"

"Okay, Harry, you're about the only man I still trust."

"Thanks, Ben, but—" Someone was rattling the phone booth door; it was the court clerk. "Jury's coming in, Mr. Cain."

"Okay, be right there . . . thanks."

"Listen, Ben, I gotta run, I think we've got a verdict here. Don't go near Gaynorville . . . bye."

Harry hung up and walked quickly back to the courtroom. Some-one had already summoned Ball, and the two of them stood together at the counsel table like nervous schoolboys while the jury filed in. Harry thought they'd been fast—maybe too fast. The judge seemed surprised as well but tried to keep it out of his voice as he started the incantation that would determine the future of Sonny Ball.

"Has the jury reached a verdict?"

"We have, your honor."

"Please hand it to the bailiff." The clerk took the written verdict from the jury foreman and handed it to the judge, who read it to himself with no expression at all and handed it back. Turning slowly, the bailiff handed the verdict to the clerk.

Even after all these years, Harry knew no tension like this moment before a jury verdict was read. His heart pounded wildly, he clenched his sweaty palms behind his back to keep them from shaking. "Please read the verdict," intoned the judge. The brief delay was like an eternity.

"The jury finds the defendant, Sonny Ball, not guilty."

There was an excited buzz among the spectators, and the reporters scrambled for the doors. Ball turned to Harry with tears in his eyes, one hand gripping Harry's hand, the other his shoulder. "I can't ever tell you what this means, Harry. I can never thank you enough. I can never do enough to repay you."

The judge rapped for order, thanked the jury for their attention and diligence and dismissed them. One by one they filed by Harry, shaking his hand, congratulating him, some doing the same to Ball.

In the hallway outside the courtroom the flashbulbs popped and the television lights glared as Harry and Ball made their way slowly to the elevator. Three television reporters shoved microphones at Ball.

"Any comment, Sonny?"

"Sure." Ball squared his shoulders and turned the famous blue eyes directly into the cameras.

"*I* knew I was innocent. But sometimes innocence is not so easy to prove. Fortunately, I had the best lawyer in the country. The system works fine. But it's men like Harry Cain that make it work."

He put his arm around Harry and together they walked to the end of the corridor, the crowd of reporters running beside them, taking pictures, shouting questions.

As they neared the elevator, Tom Musik of the *Times* elbowed his way to the front of the group, his pad in hand.

"How about that quote you promised, Harry?"

Harry looked up and smiled.

"Today we sent a message to an overzealous public official who was so ready to condemn an innocent man, he forgot his job was justice, not just prosecution."

Now every reporter was writing.

"You mean Bailey Scuneo?"

"You bet I do. And I've got another message for him."

The elevator arrived. A deputy held back the crowd, while Harry and Ball stepped in.

Harry shouted to the waiting reporters. "Tell Mr. Scuneo the next time he brands a client of mine guilty before trial, he'll find himself on the wrong end of a libel suit. And he'll lose *that* too."

More cameras flashed.

"That's why he's called the Sunset Bomber," cried Ball with a grin as the elevator doors closed.

Two days after the Ball trial was Harry's fiftieth birthday. He was beginning to resent each year now, and they seemed to come more and more quickly. But this was a special occasion to which Harry looked forward. Gail was to join them for dinner, and the other guests would be Harry's favorites. During the day, he and Carmel would be together, away from the Laurel Canyon house for the very first time. They would swim, picnic and spend the afternoon at the beach north of Malibu. Harry had done that many times before; but, this time, the trip held an air of adventure and excitement, as well as risk.

The day was special from the start, the morning cool and fresh, the sky clear. Nancy was particularly warm. During the night she had secretly written "Happy Half-century" in soap on Harry's bathroom mirror. She rose early, made coffee and, pulling her beige silk robe around her, walked Harry to his car, her arm snuggly around his waist. She reminded him of the small party that evening, kissed him tenderly and told him how much she loved him on this landmark birthday. Harry felt a twinge of guilt as he pulled the Bentley from the garage.

Before he was to pick up Carmel, Harry had a breakfast meeting with Jay Kelly at the Polo Lounge of the Beverly Hills Hotel. At eight A.M. Harry walked up the palm-lined entrance to the famous old pink building, intrigued at the meeting to which Kelly had already given a note of mystery in his phone call the day before.

Harry had always liked Kelly, a big, handsome ex-cop who struggled through night law school, finally passed the bar and went on to build a fairly successful criminal law practice, while devoting much of his time to tennis, skiing and the race track. A confirmed bachelor with Irish charm, thick black hair and bright-blue eyes, Kelly was widely known as a devastating ladies' man. He called Harry to congratulate him on the Ball verdict and then said he wanted to turn a case over to him—one he cared about very much. Harry asked why he didn't handle the case himself, Kelly said he was reluctant to discuss it over the phone, and they arranged their breakfast meeting.

Sitting beside the lush patio over fresh raspberries, English muffins and coffee, Kelly began to tell Harry what was on his mind. Kelly's cousin was Lee Parlier, the television programming wizard who had actually doubled ABC's ratings and then left to do the same for another of the national networks, United Broadcasting Systems, better known as "UBS." Geting Parlier to switch from ABC to UBS, at the height of his success, had been the brilliant move of UBS's president, Alec Heath, himself a legend in the television industry. It had taken a contract with a built-in percentage of the profits of any series Parlier created, but Heath had done it—outmaneuvered his rivals at ABC, and landed Parlier.

In his first year at UBS, Parlier had created "High Rise," the most successful television series of the past ten years. The series focused on the lives of people working in a high-rise office building in Manhattan. The entire world identified with the characters and eagerly awaited each episode.

Kelly added that Parlier's share of the series profits was worth about ten million dollars. But as it became clear that "High Rise" was going to be such a massive success and that Parlier's contract would be worth millions, Heath suddenly fired him, claiming he had defrauded the network when he took the job by concealing that he had a criminal record.

"A criminal record?" Harry interrupted.

"Yeah, when Lee was younger he was a bad boy. He actually did two years in the joint."

"What for?"

"Fraud."

"Shit."

"Yeah. Anyway, Lee says he told Alec Heath all about his record before he was hired. Heath told him not to worry, it wouldn't make any difference, they'd keep it quiet, not tell anyone. After they fired Lee, Heath claimed he never knew about the criminal record. One good thing is Lee's FCC registration form shows his record right on its face. When I heard that, I thought we were okay—no problem; but Heath says Lee changed the form to show his record only *after* Heath signed it; and Heath...well, Heath's a well-known, clean-cut guy, even though he's a ladies' man; and Lee's an ex-con, so you can see the problem."

"And that's it—the case turns on whether a jury believes Lee told Heath about his record?"

"No, it's more complicated than that and worse than that. Lee tends to be a little paranoid, you know. I guess it's from his days in the joint. So when he starts to suspect Heath is out to get him, he sneaks into the network files on a Sunday afternoon and copies a bunch of documents for protection. But with Lee's luck, Heath catches him doing it and fires him on the spot. Claims Lee's sneaking in and copying records is a breach of contract. So they've got two grounds for firing him, fraud by concealing his criminal record, and breach of contract by sneaking in and copying the documents."

"And if you can get through those two, Lee gets ten million?"

"No, there's more. Do you know a guy named Neil Talbot at UBS?"

"Yeah, Heath's old buddy. Likes English suits and sixteen-year-old-girls—sometimes shares 'em with Heath . . . the girls I mean."

"That's the one. Well, after Lee was fired, Talbot claimed *he* was the one who had the idea for 'High Rise,' that he told it to Lee, and that Lee's just pretending to be the guy who created the show."

"Isn't there some written record of who actually created the idea—some treatment or outline, or something?"

"Not really. Lee says he came up with the idea and just put it in the works. Talbot says he came up with it. I took Talbot's deposition and he's very convincing. I almost believed him myself, and Lee's my cousin. Besides, like I said, Lee's an ex-con. Who's going to take his word against guys like Alec Heath and Neil Talbot?"

"Oh, I'm not so sure about that. You might pull it off. Heath's a bright guy okay, but he can be very arrogant and maybe overconfident. Who's representing the network?"

"A New York lawyer, a guy named Maynard Aldrich III, from Cavanaugh & Cutler. Real Wall Street type, kind of stuffy; but the firm's a good one, I hear."

"Yeah, Jay, it's real good and I've heard of Aldrich. He's probably their number-one litigator now."

"Well, as you've probably figured out, that's why I wanted to talk to you. I got into this because I was Lee's cousin and the only lawyer . . . maybe the only *person* . . . he trusts in the world. When he first got fired, Lee didn't know if he wanted to sue at all. You know, he'd

gotten used to being a well-respected guy . . . at least in the entertainment business, and he was sure that a lawsuit would let the whole
world know he was an ex-con. Even his kids don't know. They're
only six and eight, and Lee wanted to wait to tell them when they
were old enough to understand."

Harry put down his coffee cup. "That's probably just what Heath
was figuring, Jay. He hit on the perfect angle by claiming that Parlier
concealed his criminal record. A trial would necessarily make the
criminal record public knowledge, and Heath figured Parlier would
probably just go quietly without suing, and, even if he sued, no one
would believe him anyway. That's the way Alec Heath would figure
the situation and play it. I know him from way back. He doesn't just
play hardball, but very *dirty* ball—a real shark in Princeton clothing,
that guy."

"That I hadn't heard before, Harry. I've read about his romances—
all the actresses and socialites he's loved and left, but not much more
than that."

"He's a mean guy, Jay, mean, smart and completely unprincipled,
the kind of guy who likes hurting people—women, business rivals,
employees. He only plays to win—any way he can, whatever game
he's in and there are no rules."

"Well, I suppose that shows in the way he handled Lee's situation."
Kelly paused while he speared his last bite. "Anyway, at this point,
Harry, with the case coming to trial early next year, Lee needs something more than I can give him. I'll level with you, Harry, but if
you ever repeat this, I'll kick the shit out of you. I'm just not competent to try a case like this. Give me a drunk-driving case or even
armed robbery and I'll do the job effectively; but this thing, complicated financial stuff, no way. And I really like Lee. I think he got
royally fucked. But it takes a guy like you to do the job. It takes top
level brains as well as balls, and that's not an easy combination to
find. That's why I'm here, Harry. I'd be fucking Lee myself if I tried
to hang on to this case. Listen, Harry—as a personal favor to me,
take it on, will you?"

Harry put down his coffee and looked across the table at his long-
time Irish friend. "Jay, I'm flattered and it's an interesting case, but
I'm preparing the Malone divorce case for trial. John Matsuoka would

have to do most of the work on this, at least for the next few weeks."

"Listen," Kelly said grinning, "I'm not even sure John isn't better equipped to handle the case than I am, and if you repeat that, I'll really kill you. Sure, Harry, that's okay. But, seriously, you'll try the case yourself, right?"

"After the first of the year? Sure, I'll be able to do it by then. But, Jay, can this guy pay the fee?"

"Not in cash, Harry, but it's a hell of a contingency. After all, Lee can win ten million bucks and I've got it on a one-third basis. If you'll try it, I'll give you twenty-two percent and keep eleven and a third. That gives me about one-third of our share."

"Will Parlier advance the costs and recoup them out of his share?"

"That's what he's been doing all along and the costs have already amounted to over fifty thousand dollars, what with taking depositions all over the country."

"Okay, Jay, you got yourself a deal. I'll have John get right on it . . . and I'll want to meet Parlier as soon as possible."

*H*arry slid behind the wheel of the Bentley and drove ten blocks up Sunset Boulevard to his office. He was excited about the Parlier case. The battle with Cavanaugh & Cutler would be a challenge. The fee could be more than two million dollars. But mainly, he was looking forward to taking on Alec Heath. Harry had never really liked Heath, a man famous for his mistreatment of the numerous women who tended to be easy prey for his arrogant good looks and were particularly susceptible to the aphrodisiac of his power.

What Kelly didn't know—what no one knew—was that, for the past two years, Harry had nursed a bitter hatred for Heath, burned for a chance to go after the man, to hurt him any way he could. Without any advance notice, Heath had fired and humiliated Harry's oldest friend, Teddy Brenner, who had been executive vice president at the network for twenty years. When Teddy showed up for work one morning, the locks on his office had been changed. Someone handed him a newspaper carrying the story, previously released by Heath, that Teddy was fired for gross incompetence and was being "investigated." Teddy went home and three days later suffered a fatal heart attack. Harry had a big score to settle and this was his chance. The fact was, he would have tried the case for nothing.

The day continued its special quality. At the office, Harry's messages held only good news. A critical motion in a long-pending antitrust case had gone his way, and he was getting close to the settlement offer he wanted in a director's suit for breach of contract against Warner Brothers.

Harry called in John Matsuoka and outlined the facts of the Parlier case. He asked John to contact Kelly for the details.

By eleven o'clock, Harry had slipped a bathing suit under his pants and was ready to pick up Carmel. She was waiting in front of the house with an old-fashioned wicker hamper jammed with fried chicken, ham and cheese sandwiches and deviled eggs. Harry pointed to the two bottles of Dom Perignon in an ice chest in the back of the car and they were off for a beach north of Malibu that was usually deserted on weekdays.

After the long and lovely drive, they parked and followed a winding path through the brush, hearing the pounding surf as they got closer and closer to the beach.

They spread their blanket and, shedding their outer clothes, raced down to the water. Carmel stopped and probed tentatively at the icy tide with a reluctant foot. Harry continued his run without pause, diving under a huge breaker and swimming strongly out beyond the surf. He waved and shouted to Carmel, who finally made her way through the waves to join him. There, they dove to the bottom for handfuls of sand, playfully splashed each other, and floated lazily on their backs, watching a small cloud drift across the bright blue sky.

When they began to feel chilled, they returned to the beach and enjoyed a splendid lunch, growing slowly and pleasantly high on the champagne as they delighted in the feel of the warm sun drying the salt on their bodies.

Later, they walked hand in hand down the nearly deserted beach.

They were a handsome couple, Carmel tall and graceful in her brief white bikini, her hair blown by the light sea breeze—Harry tan and lean, his black Speedo suit molded to his narrow hips.

They watched the gulls wheeling and gliding above them and the baby terns hopping in the shallow water at the edge of the tide.

Throwing sidearm, Harry skipped a flat stone across the water. "Two bounces. That's a 'C minus.' I used to get three or four as a kid."

They walked farther down the beach, and, with his toe, Harry drew an enormous heart in the sand, placing "H.C." and "C.A." in the center. Carmel laughed. "Do that on Wilshire Boulevard, and I'll be impressed."

Harry grinned and turned away to run and plunge once again into the ocean. This time Carmel followed him eagerly. He taught her to body surf, patiently showing her how to time the break of the wave, to butterfly first at full strength, then adjust her speed to that of the breaking wave, and finally to hunch her shoulders as the power of the wave hurled her forward toward the beach, using her leg as a rudder to glide back and forth at an angle to the racing surf.

Back on their blanket, they lay on their backs in the sun, Carmel's fingers delicately tracing the muscles of Harry's shoulder and arm. She leaned over him, placing her face close to his chest—tan and beaded with salt water. "How I love the smell of your skin. You're my child of the sea, and I love everything about you. My God, you hold my heart in your hands. Do you know that?"

Harry could find no words to reply to her outpouring of emotion—nothing that could convey what he felt at that moment. He put his arm around Carmel and pulled her over on top of him, breathing the scent of her hair, feeling her sun-warmed body along the length of his own, his desire growing, throbbing, overwhelming him. He looked in the direction of the only other couple on the beach, an elderly pair some thirty yards away reading in canvas beach chairs. "Do you think they'd mind?" he asked hoarsely, moving his hips upward against Carmel's now responding body and reaching for the bottom of her suit.

She raised her head and glanced at the other couple, who were making an obvious attempt to divert their eyes. Carmel slid her body reluctantly from his. Lying beside him and taking his hand, she whispered in his ear.

"I may be depraved, my love, but I'm not that depraved." She sat up. "I think a cold hip bath is in order. That's what my brother's scout manual prescribed when a boy has disturbing thoughts. So how about a swim?" She stood and pulled Harry to his feet. Hand in hand they walked down to the water.

Later, as the late afternoon sun gave everything a rose-gold glow, they again lay side by side on the blanket, holding hands... silent. After a time, Carmel looked over at Harry and spoke in a quiet, serious tone. "Since it's your birthday... and maybe a watershed point in your life... it's a good day to tell me more about who you really are." She fixed him with her amber eyes. "I mean, who is Harry Cain, really?"

"I don't know what you mean."

"I mean, I want to know who you really are inside. I want to know everything that ever happened to you. I want to know who and what shaped you, what you felt about those people, what scared you, who you loved. Everything. I want to catch up on your whole life."

Harry was silent for a moment, then he started to speak, still looking up at the sky. "Well, I never really knew my mother. She died when I was a few months old. My dad raised me as a little kid—did everything. He was my mother, father, teacher, friend, everything. He came from the old country, got off the boat not even speaking English. Never could make much of a go at business, but maybe he didn't *care* after my mother died. I guess I'll never know.

"Anyway, he ran a tiny grocery store on Main Street. The thing he wanted most in life—had to have—was for me to have an education. College, law school, whatever. It *had* to be.

"His generation of Jews were like that, you know—sacrifice everything to get their kids a degree. You see the same thing in the Oriental immigrants settling here in L.A."

Carmel sat up, resting on her elbow. "Well, I think historically the Jews have always put education ahead of everything, haven't they?"

Harry nodded. "Sure, but keep in mind they had damn little to put it ahead of."

"Maybe so, Harry, but I have a kind of Darwinian theory about the Jews. I think centuries of persecution, of constant danger, of the need to flee one country and start life all over again in another—I think all that weeded out the stupid and the weak, leaving a gene pool that tends to produce not only survivors, but achievers... like you. ... But, I'm sorry. I interrupted you. Go on about your dad. I really want to hear."

Harry waited for a moment, letting the memories flood back in.

"Well, we lived over the store. Dad cooked, cleaned and worked very hard all day. He raised me and helped me at night with my school work and found time to know and, I guess, be loved by everybody in that crummy neighborhood... especially by me. We'd go out after dinner, after I finished my homework, and he'd make his rounds. For about an hour we'd walk up and down Main Street giving out comfort, sympathy, generally bad advice, but lots of love for everybody—and usually a buck or two for some, although God knows he had little enough to spare. In the end, the prize for me was Abe Cohen's penny arcade, nickelodeons, bombing machines, pinball, arrow kill—a dream world for a kid.

"We had only one big room. I slept on a surplus army cot. He used an old convertible sofa. Late at night I'd wake up and see the flashing neon lights from Main Street reflected on the wall. It made me feel good, comforted—lulled to sleep by the reflection of Lucas's Pawn Shop. In the morning, Dad was up making orange juice and eggs and seeing me off to school, and then all day in the store." Harry paused, grinning. "Well, you asked for everything."

Carmel leaned close and kissed him lightly. "I meant it. I love it. Tell me everything... everything."

"Well, we were always together, Dad and I, at least that's the way I remember it. I was only a little kid. On Sunday the store was closed and we'd take the old red street car all the way to the beach at Venice. How that man loved the beach. He loved the water, he loved the salt smell and he loved the feel of the sand between his toes. He taught me to swim when I was really only a baby. Later, we'd swim way out together, it seemed like miles, and then float on our backs. We'd buy candied apples on a stick and hot dogs. We'd sleep in the sun and then swim again. Then the long ride home, and I'd sleep all the way with my head on his shoulder. It was really a good life for a kid. You wouldn't think so, living over a Main Street store, but it was. It was a good life thanks to him.

"Then the war came and things changed fast. The street was choked with soldiers and sailors drunk, vomiting, fighting and, I suppose, spending. You couldn't even get in the penny arcade and most of the old faces began to disappear. Our friends' dusty old stores were replaced by bars, tattoo parlors and souvenir joints, all jammed with servicemen.

"Then one day, when I was eight, I came home from school, and my father hit me with a good one. 'Sit down, son,' he said, pulling at his long face. 'You know what Jews like us would have without this country?' I didn't say anything. 'Nothin, that's what we'd have. I'd be dead, or picking potatoes, or a cripple begging somewhere. No walks at night, no Sundays at the beach. No nothin! No nothin! You think in the old country you'd be in school getting "A's," heading someday for college? Not a chance. You'd be chopping wood or stealing—if you were alive at all, which you probably wouldn't be. Son, I . . . we owe this country everything, and it's time to pay. You read the papers. The war's going bad, really bad. I gotta go fight. I owe it.'

"And that's just what he did. Somehow he arranged for me to live with a family near Sawtelle; and within ten days, I saw him get on a bus for basic training, trying like crazy to hold back my tears. The people were okay, but it wasn't like having Dad. There was just a huge hole in my life these strangers couldn't fill, I guess no one ever filled. But I got by. My time was filled with school and sports and reading and, pretty soon, work. Always lots of work, even that young— to help pay my way.

"About every other letter from him, I'd go in the bathroom and cry. He'd been in the East for a while and then England. It was so cold and wet, he couldn't handle it after so long in California. Then, June 6, 1944—he landed on the beach in Normandy. The very first wave. They said he died on that beach in the first five minutes. I like to think he felt the sand in his fingers, smelled the ocean he loved so much, just that one last time before he died . . . a gentle forty-year-old private—just paying what he thought was his debt."

Tears were streaming down Carmel's cheeks. She grabbed Harry and began kissing his nose, his eyes, every inch of his face. He could taste the salt of her tears. Harry put his arms around her and they just held each other, rocking back and forth. Then Harry began to cry too. At first he wept softly. Then, with a bursting forth of long-held anguish, he buried his head in Carmel's shoulder and sobbed.

A few minutes later, Harry was feeling himself again ... back in control. He realized that the sun was already low on the horizon and glanced at his watch. "Jesus Christ, it's after six! We've got guests coming at seven-thirty for my birthday dinner, and we've got to stop by your place to change. Come on, let's go."

They scrambled to gather everything they'd brought, and soon were back in the Bentley speeding down the Coast Highway and making the long climb up Sunset Boulevard toward West Hollywood.

"Harry."

"Yeah."

"Do you know the story 'The Juggler of Our Lady'?"

"No."

"Well, once in medieval times a starving juggler was saved from a terrible blizzard by a few pious monks, who gave him shelter in the monastery. It was Christmas Eve, and the juggler saw each of the monks approach the statue of the virgin and put an object before her. One man carefully laid down a magnificent tapestry he'd woven over the entire year. Another gently set before the virgin an intricate carving of St. Jerome. There were paintings, handsomely inscribed manuscripts, candelabra, perfume and wine, all lovingly placed before the altar. The Abbot explained to the puzzled juggler that it was the tradition of their order that, on Christmas Eve, each of them made a gift to the virgin—the product of his own skill.

"The juggler was desolate. The virgin had saved him, given him warmth and comfort and he, who had so much to be grateful for, had no gift at all.

"The monks filed away to their cells, leading the tearful juggler to his own simple chamber, where they saw him kneel to pray.

"During the night, the Abbot was awakened by a banging shutter far down the hall from his cell. Sleepily, he went to fasten it and noticed a faint light coming from under the chapel door. Silently, he opened the door and looked into the chapel. There, in the glow of the candlelight, was the juggler. Standing before the virgin, he was juggling, first three, then four wooden balls, then those and two wooden clubs, beaming all the while with the joy of presenting his gift to the virgin."

"That's a beautiful story, Carmel. What made you think of it?"

"Well, it has a point, my darling. I'm going to give you my birthday gift."

And as they sped up Sunset Boulevard through Holmby Hills, Carmel slowly unzipped Harry's pants, deliberately bent in front of the steering wheel, pulled out Harry's penis, tongued it quickly in darting, tantalizing flicks, slowly ran her pointed tongue from the base to the tip of his now very erect organ and gave six fluttering kisses to the sensitive gland just below the tip. Then, while lightly tickling his testicles with her long fingernails, she took him into her mouth, sucking, working at him with her tongue, bobbing her head and moaning with her own pleasure, until finally, approaching the Beverly Hills Hotel, with Harry fighting to keep the car from wandering back and forth across the road, she brought him to a towering orgasm.

Carmel looked up at Harry from below the steering wheel, smiling like a depraved child. She swallowed long, slowly and with obvious pleasure. "Happy Birthday," she whispered.

*T*hat night, after the guests had left his birthday dinner, Harry, Gail and Nancy sat quietly by the fire, sipping brandy and watching the flames. Speaking softly, Harry broke the long silence. "Gail, honey, have you given any more thought to an abortion?"

The word "abortion" seemed to resound in the air, to remain awkwardly hanging between them in the moment before Gail replied. When she spoke, her voice was strained, tense.

"Funny, Dad, I knew you were going to get into that when you asked me to stay."

"Well?"

"Well, I did what I promised. I gave it a lot of thought from every angle. I'm glad I did, because now I know I'm not just acting out of emotion. I want that baby, Dad, want it badly. I'll never kill it, never give it up. So don't even try any more. Okay?"

"No, it's not okay, Gail." He looked over at Nancy, whose face looked white and drawn. "Your mother is out of her mind with concern over you, and so am I. We've got to keep trying to make you see that this thing makes no sense, not for your career, not for you as a person. You'll *have* children, Gail, but this isn't the time. And, damn it, this isn't the *man!*"

Gail got to her feet quickly. "Listen, Dad, I did what you asked. I gave it plenty of thought and I decided. Now please get off my case!" Her eyes welled up with tears and, pulling on her coat, she started for the door.

"Hey, hold on a minute. You're forgetting one thing."

She stopped and turned to face him, wiping at her eyes with her fingers.

"What's that?"

"This, you dummy." He moved across the room and hugged her to him tenderly, placing her head against his shoulder, patting her back, crooning to her softly. Finally, he spoke again. "Gail, this decision of yours is absolutely wacko. I hope you change your mind. But there's one thing you should never forget. We love you, always have, always will...whatever you do, whatever you decide." Then, putting his arm around her, he walked her to the door and out into the moonlit night.

When she had gone, he stood for a moment on the patio, breathing the scent of jasmine...looking at the lights of the city spread out below. He sighed. He was fifty now, and he felt it.

"*I* could play you," Dustin Hoffman cried, his dark, intelligent eyes fixed on Harry, shining with intensity. "Man, I could play you. Jesus, could I do it." He slammed his fist into his palm.

It was two A.M. at Sue Mengers's victory party for Sonny Ball. The Hollywood "A" list was flowing in and around the softly lit, high-ceilinged rooms of her strikingly dramatic home in the Bel Air hills. Sonny himself had just acted out Harry's closing argument for Hoffman, Towne, Karen Lloyd and several other guests, theatrically rubbing the coffee table and screaming, "Now he's rubbed him thirteen seconds. What's he doing this for? What are they talking about, the United Nations?" This was the third time Sonny had done it. Each time, the crowd roared with laughter. Harry had been cheered, backslapped, hugged and lionized for at least four hours. He loved it.

Now, Hoffman turned to Robert Towne, tall, gray-bearded and a prime source of Hollywood tribal wisdom. "Whatta ya think, Bob; are you man enough to direct me as Harry Cain?" Towne smiled but only slightly. "Well, you could play Harry—no question. In fact, I don't know who else has sufficient kinetic energy, enough dark force. Warren?... I think not, a different kind of magic. Redford? Not right either. Nicholson? Ridiculous. Only you; and now that Abel Gance is gone, I suppose only I can direct... and you, Karen, will you produce and protect us from the philistines?"

"You bet," said Karen Lloyd, smiling with good humor, "and, believe me, you'll need it."

"Well, you guys can produce and direct," Harry put in, grinning. "But with all respect to your 'dark force,' Dustin, I always thought of myself as played by Sonny Ball."

"You, a blond?" asked Hoffman.

"Why not?" Harry replied. "But if Sonny played me, then who'd play Sonny?"

Sue Mengers laughed. "Listen guys, nobody plays my client but my client. The only solution is we use a split screen and Sonny plays *both* parts—*if* the money's right." She put an arm affectionately around Harry. "I wish I was this one's agent too. I'd love ten percent of *his* action."

A few minutes later, Harry stood in the den quietly talking to Alan Nathan. A paraplegic, Nathan was a top screenwriter—the winner of two Academy Awards. As usual, his actress wife, May, a tall, pale blonde, stood beside his wheelchair, gently holding his hand as he spoke.

"I don't care what your client thinks, Harry. I know he and Paramount both *think* they've got a joint venture deal with Consolidated. But while they're sitting there happily counting the millions they haven't got yet, we cut to Yank Slutsky secretly making a deal with Metro and Vestron, leaving your guy way out in the cold."

"I can't believe it, Alan. I'd expect it of Slutsky, but Fernbach? Never. He's not that kind of guy."

"Come on, Harry. Don't talk like a kid. Who do you think's got the power at Consolidated? Fernbach? Shit! I can see him saying, 'Yank, we can't do this. It's not ethical' and, dissolve, Fernbach's on the street looking for a job; and we cut to Slutsky trying to hire Mike Eisner away from Disney. No, my friend, don't bet against the Badger."

"I'll sue the Badger's ass, along with the studio. They made a deal."

"Sure you will. They expect it. You think you're known as a cream puff? But fade in on Slutsky talking Paramount out of joining in your suit. Cut to a montage . . . calendar pages showing the passage of time . . . five years to trial, depositions, huge attorneys' fees, your guy settling for twenty cents on the dollar by the third year. Slutsky and Metro raking in billions . . . as we fade out. Has a ring of truth, doesn't it? Besides, I don't think Slutsky likes you."

At that point, Nathan stopped, embarrassed, as Aaron Fernbach entered the den, looking concerned. "Harry, don't you live over near Laurel Canyon?"

"West of there, Aaron, up in the hills."

"Well, there's a hell of a fire moving fast through the canyon. You can see it from the patio."

Harry went with Fernbach through the glass doors out onto the stone terrace, with its spectacular view of the city in every direction. To the northeast, the hills were outlined with an angry red glow, and just beyond the Mulholland ridge Harry could see the flames and sparks shooting high into the night sky.

"Christ," Harry said. "That looks bad. It's not near me, but I better make a call . . . excuse me."

"Sure, Harry, let me know if I can do anything to help."

"Thanks, Aaron," Harry said, moving quickly back to the house. He found a telephone closet, closed the door and dialed Carmel's number, praying the lines were not yet down. Three rings, four, five, then she answered.

"Hello."

"Carmel, it's Harry. How you doing there?"

"It's scary, Harry, it's not really close yet, but my neighbors evacuated—said it moves so fast there's no time to leave when it gets too close. What should I do?"

"Well, unless the fire department tells you to get out, stay where you are. I'm coming right now."

"You are? That's wonderful, but what about Nancy?"

"I'll take care of that. You stay safe. I'll be there in half an hour."

There was a pause. "Thanks, Harry. I'm really scared."

Putting down the phone, Harry began a hurried search for Nancy. He found her in the living room talking animatedly to Jane Fonda, her black Galanos dress, diamond earrings and silver and black Maud Frizon shoes a striking contrast to Jane's tan pants suit and the multicolored outfits swirling around them. As Harry approached, they were discussing whether female welfare recipients should be required to take job training. Seeing the tension in Harry's face, Nancy stopped the conversation.

"What's the matter? Is it the fire? It's not near us, is it?"

"No, it's farther east and way up the canyon. But I've got a problem. It's moving fast on Johnny Pell's house, and he's got his leg in a cast and is ... well, you know, he asked if I could help. I've got to do it, Nance."

"Of course, Harry, if you think you can help. I'll come along."

"No, Hon, that would only make me worry about you. I'd be less effective, and it could be very rough over there. I'm sure the Hoffmans will drop you home. Okay?"

"Sure, Harry, don't worry, you go help." Nancy knew John Pell had been a bright lawyer and a law school classmate of Harry's who had a severe drinking problem. Harry had always tried to help out by giving Pell part-time legal work and, occasionally, even loans. She knew Harry would want to help Pell out of a dangerous spot like this; but it frightened her. She wrapped her arms around Harry and held him for a moment, rubbing her cheek against his. "Be careful my love, will you?"

"Sure, Nance, I'll be okay."

Harry moved quickly through the crowd mumbling a few hurried goodbyes. He turned the corner into the entry hall, just as May Nathan emerged from the powder room, followed by a William Morris agent. Her face was flushed, her dress rumpled. The young agent was still zipping his fly.

Harry shook his head and went out into the warm night. Even this far from the fire, the air already carried the scent of burning brush.

Fifteen minutes later, Harry talked his way through the roadblock at the foot of Laurel Canyon, and drove up the winding road that led to Starline Drive. Carmel was out front playing a hose across her shingle roof. She ran to Harry and threw her arms around him. "I'm so glad you're here. Thanks so much."

He smiled tenderly and stroked her hair. "We'll be okay, but we may have to leave, and soon." The fire was beyond the next ridge, but they could see the red glow and the tops of the flames licking at the sky beyond the line of the brush covered hills. The air carried bits of ash. The smoke was acrid and unpleasant. The neighborhood seemed deserted.

"Is your stuff all packed?"

"No, just a suitcase. I really didn't think I'd have to leave."

"Well, you may have to. I've seen these canyon fires before, and they move a lot faster than you think."

As Harry spoke, the fire came sweeping over the ridge, less than a hundred yards away. Within seconds, the tall trees at the crest burst into flames, one after the other, the flames shooting from their upper branches fifty feet into the sky. With a *whoosh*, the fire caught the brush on the south side of the hill and roared down the slope toward the houses across the road from Carmel's.

A red fire marshal's car careened around the corner and pulled into the driveway with a screeching of brakes. A fireman leapt out shouting, "Christ! Didn't you get word to evacuate?" Without waiting for an answer he shouted again, "Get out now. I mean right now— follow me," and he was back in the red car, roaring down Starline Drive.

Harry picked up Carmel's suitcase and, putting his arm around her waist, hurried her into the car. He started the engine quickly and sped after the fireman.

Two blocks down the drive Carmel grabbed Harry's shoulder. "My paintings, Harry, I can't leave them. I've got to go back."

Harry stopped, keeping the motor running. "It's too late, Carmel, in five minutes your house'll be like a torch. We've gotta move out."

"I can't leave them, Harry. It's a year of my life, I can't. Please, Harry."

She looked into his eyes. Harry rolled his eyes toward heaven. "Jesus, I'm nuttier than you." He wrestled the car around in a tight U-turn and, leaving tire tracks in the road, raced back to the house. In the three minutes they had been gone, the fire had reached the area across the road, spreading first into the trees. Eucalyptus, cedars and pines, engulfed in the intense heat, burst into flames. Huge sparks and burning branches were falling on the shingled roofs and two houses were already beginning to catch fire. Harry jumped from the car.

"Where are they?"

"In the large bedroom mostly—what's not in the living room." The smoke was billowing from across the street and Harry began to cough as he and Carmel made their way into the house and turned on the lights, which, miraculously, were still working.

Harry began piling painting upon painting in the living room, while Carmel ran back and forth to the car carrying two or three paintings at a time. When Harry stepped out the front door carrying a stack of fifteen paintings, the smoke was so dense he could see nothing but a huge column of flames just a few feet across the street. The impact of the heat was staggering. The two-story log house directly opposite Carmel's was burning along with a row of giant eucalyptus trees that stood behind it. It was like facing a towering wall of flames a hundred feet high. Harry thought that his face was blistering and he could hardly breathe. He literally threw his pile of paintings in the back seat as Carmel came running up with two more, piled them on top and started to run back for more. Harry grabbed her arm. "No more! Let's get out of here." She looked sadly back at the house, its front door still open. Then she turned and jumped into the car.

Just then the corner of Carmel's garage began to flower with flame. Harry clambered into the driver's seat, started the car and, again, they raced down Starline Drive, winding through the smoke, down and around the twisting streets toward Laurel Canyon Boulevard. As Harry pulled around the fourth turn, he braked suddenly, throwing Carmel out of her seat. A large burning tree had fallen across the road, blocking their passage with its upper branches. The houses on both sides were in flames and Harry thought that, at any minute, the car upholstery would catch fire or, worse, the gas tank would blow.

He jumped from the car and ran to the fallen tree. On the left side of the road, the thick base of the tree lay across a stone wall and reached out into the street, creating an impassable barrier. On the right side, the burning upper branches blocked the street and stretched across a blackened lawn, almost to the door of a fiercely burning house.

The smaller upper branches at the right edge of the road presented a less formidable barrier than on the left; and, although they were burning rapidly, Harry thought there might be a chance if he drove right for that spot.

He ran back to the car. Carmel was looking dazed. A tear ran down her cheek. "Can we do anything, Harry?"

"We sure as shit can try. I'm not just going to sit here and burn."

He threw the car in reverse, raced backward for about twenty feet, then stopped. Revving the powerful Bentley engine, he shifted into low gear and jammed his foot on the accelerator. The big car surged forward, its engine screaming.

In less than a second, it smashed into the burning tree just at the right edge of the road. For an instant, it seemed the Bentley was caught in the burning branches, its tires spinning, fighting for traction. Then, with a crashing lurch, it burst free, scattering flaming branches in all directions.

Harry shifted into high gear and swept on down the road, still expecting the gas tank to explode at any moment. But the explosion never came; and after another three minutes of winding downhill through the billowing smoke and occasional flame, they reached Laurel Canyon Drive. The drive was clear except for a fire truck, its radio blaring, its red light flasing shadows on the nearby houses and trees. Harry turned right heading for Sunset.

In less than five minutes, he was checking a dazed Carmel into the Chateau Marmont Hotel. The charming, Spanish style lobby of the old hotel was crowded with refugees from the fire . . . sooty, exhausted, carrying pets and treasured belongings. Harry and Carmel stacked her paintings carefully in a corner and she stood beside him at the desk as he arranged for a room. Everything was taken but the penthouse, and he readily accepted that. An aged bellman went to gather the paintings while Harry and Carmel turned from the desk and walked hand in hand toward the elevator.

"Harry. Harry Cain!"

He turned. There, behind him, was Johnny Pell, in his stocking feet, wearing a bathrobe and carrying a bird cage. Harry's heart sank. With Pell was a thin, attractive woman in a powder-blue running suit. It was Liz Watterson, Nancy's college roommate, a fashion magazine editor who also had a home in Laurel Canyon.

Harry tried his best to brazen it out. "Hi, John . . . Liz. Glad you both got out okay." He turned to Carmel. "Carmel, this is John Pell and Liz Watterson, both old friends." He nodded toward Carmel. "This is Carmel Anderson, a client of our firm. We've been trying to rescue her paintings. We got most of them."

Noticing that he was still holding Carmel's hand, Harry quickly added, "I'm afraid Carmel's in a state of shock right now. It's been a long, rough night."

Liz Watterson's cynical grin was not lost on Harry. Pell smiled pleasantly and reached out to take Carmel's other hand. The ancient elevator arrived, and Harry and Carmel stepped in with the bellman. There was an exchange of "Nice meeting yous," as the doors closed on Harry's view of a still grinning Liz Watterson. "Shit," he said as they began their slow ascent to the top of the old hotel.

When they were alone in the penthouse, Carmel settled in a hot bath, while Harry, realizing he'd need his wits about him when he arrived home, stretched out on the bed to think.

Would Liz Watterson say something to Nancy? Maybe not. Many people believed they did their friends no favor by bringing them such unwelcome stories. He thought Liz might be one of them. Still he'd have to decide what to tell Nancy about whether he evacuated Johnny Pell. He didn't want to confide in Pell—that seemed especially disloyal to Nancy. Certainly he couldn't and wouldn't confide in Liz. Probably the best thing was just to say nothing and be prepared with an explanation if Nancy brought it up.

Later, Carmel cuddled in Harry's arms on the penthouse terrace, while they watched the sun rise deep red above the smoke and fire, silhouetting the tall buildings of downtown and the clean lines of the San Gabriel Mountains in the distance.

As the day broke over the city, Harry finally threw on his torn coat and headed for the door. Carmel put her arms around him, pulled him fiercely to her and covered his face and neck with kisses. "I love you, Harry Cain, I love you with all my heart and soul."

He looked down at the enormous amber eyes brimming with emotion. He felt his own eyes fill. "I love you too, Carmel," he said, quietly opening the door. Standing in the hallway, looking back at this beautiful, loving woman, her pale face and long graceful body, surrounded by vivid paintings, arms still outstretched toward him, Harry meant it—felt it. "I love you too," he repeated, closing the door softly behind him.

*T*he week before the Malone trial, Clara put a cardboard carton in the corner of Harry's office. It contained what appeared to be everything Fiona Malone had ever written or signed or doodled in the past five years. Perhaps a hundred separate pieces of paper were there. Harry wondered where Carl had dredged them up and where they had been kept all this time. But, no matter, they had to be read . . . every one.

For three weeks Harry had devoted hours each day to last-minute preparation for the trial. At the same time, he had been guiding John Matsuoka in the initial phases of their work on *Parlier v. UBS*, and trying to keep abreast of all his other cases. Despite the mounting pressure, he had spent two or three afternoons a week with Carmel at the bungalow she'd rented on Sweetzer after learning her Laurel Canyon place was a total loss.

At home, Nancy seemed unusually tense and strained. One evening Harry came home to find her sitting alone on the terrace, her eyes red and swollen, a balled up handkerchief beside her. She was reluctant to discuss why she'd been crying and when Harry put his hand on her shoulder, he felt her tighten and pull away.

"Is it Gail? Is that what it is?"

Nancy snuffled and put the handkerchief to her nose, continuing to look away from him, out toward the city.

"Yes, it's Gail," she finally said in a strained voice, as she rose to walk away to the edge of the terrace.

But Harry wasn't sure, and Nancy would say no more. When he took time to reflect on it, Harry felt Nancy had to be upset over Gail's situation and was probably also bothered by the long hours he was devoting to the Malone case and his preoccupation with it even in those brief periods when they were together.

At least Harry *hoped* that's what it was, hoped that Nancy's behavior was not a reaction to being told he was with another woman the night of the canyon fire. He decided not to press her to find out... at least not then. It was something he could deal with when the Malone trial was over.

The case itself remained as Harry had described it to Carl Malone. It involved enormous risks. First, the judge could believe Fiona's contention that Carl had orally promised her half of all his separate property... at least sixty million dollars. Second, the judge could feel enough sympathy for Fiona to put a high value on Malone Electronics, which was certainly community property, and, in that way, give her a sizable amount of cash for her one-half share of that losing venture.

The problem was Fiona. She came across as refined, intelligent and honest... a stylish lady. To Harry, Carl's gut reaction was right. Somehow it didn't seem fair that a woman could carry on as promiscuously as Fiona and, with the Judge totally ignorant of her behavior, receive an award of millions.

But that was what the legislature wanted when they enacted "no fault" divorce. The money was split fifty-fifty, no matter who did what. No evidence of adultery or cruelty was admissible. In a case like this, with no children, the only issue was money... what property would go to which party, what, if any, support would be paid and who would pay the lawyers. No one could show that the wife slept with her tennis pro or that her husband beat her black and blue.

Still, he'd find a way. He always did. He had to. The cardboard carton might help somehow. You never knew what seemingly innocent note, written years before, could turn a case around, destroy a well-constructed, subtly false story. Harry sighed and sat down beside the carton. Taking a fist full of notes from the box, he began to read.

An hour later, Clara announced that Carl Malone was in the reception room with no appointment but extremely anxious to see him. Malone appeared at Harry's office door, excited as a child with a new toy. Under his arm was a can of film.

"This is it, Harry, this'll show the judge what that cunt really is." Triumphantly, Carl put the film can on the desk in front of Harry. "Let Mr. Calvin Fucking Pierce take a look at this."

"Okay, Carl, hold it for a minute. Have a seat and tell me what this is all about." Carl settled into one of the chairs in front of Harry's desk. He paused and then gave Harry his wolfish grin. "Ten days ago, Harry, I got a call from Mr. Joe Don Sellers."

"You mean Rabbit Sellers, the all-pro split-end?"

"That's the man. Pride of the Dallas Cowboys. Best hands in the league." Carl got out of the chair and began to pace. "Mr. Sellers does more than just catch touchdown passes, Harry. He told me about his very interesting hobby. He takes films while he and his teammates fuck some very well-known ladies around Dallas and other places. He says that, contrary to what you'd think, the ladies find it very stimulating to know they're performing on film.

"Okay, here comes the interesting part. Two years ago, while I was in Brazil, the Cowboys played the Rams in Anaheim. I lost a thou on the game. Anyway, through Shirley Kelleher, a mutual friend, Rabbit and three other Cowboys met Fiona at a party. Everybody got very high, one thing led to another and four Cowboys ended up at our house.

"Apparently, Mr. Sellers never goes out without his camera. He told Fiona about his hobby and convinced her she should be immortalized on film. On my bed, that cunt. Anyway, he says she loved the idea, and the four of them had a high old time for about two hours. A good bit of it was captured on film.

"Rabbit said he just read about my divorce case and thought I just might like to buy a print. I did, for ten grand, and the result is right here." He slapped the can. "So, old buddy, whatta we do?"

Harry leaned back in the gray velvet desk chair and rubbed his eyes. "Carl, I just hope you haven't blown ten thousand bucks. I told you the rules weeks ago. Evidence of adultery just isn't admissible. You can't get it in front of the judge. Sure, it would be terrific if he could see what Fiona's really like. I can't deny the impact it would probably have on his decision, but I told you before, if it doesn't go to the financial issues, it doesn't get before the judge. He never sees it. Now why didn't you ask me before you committed the ten grand?"

"Harry, for Christ's sake, a guy calls me at night from Dallas offering me a porno film starring my own wife and you want me to tell him I've got to discuss it with my lawyer? Come on."

"Wait a minute, Carl," Harry cut in. "You just said something that gave me an idea." Harry's mind went back to the orgy film he'd seen at the theater on Main Street when he was investigating the Ball case. He drummed his fingers on the desk, thinking, running the possibilities through his mind. "We just may have a shot at it— a very long shot—and it's a hell of a risk—but . . . let me think about it some more. Leave the film with me and let me work on it."

"That's the way to talk, Harry. I knew you'd find a way. Fuck 'em, boy, take the risk. You've gotta get that judge to see the film."

"I haven't found the way yet, Carl, so don't get your hopes up. It's just that maybe, just maybe we can do it if Pierce makes a mistake and if you're a gambler."

"You're kidding. Am I a gambler? Is the Pope Catholic? Does a bear shit in the woods? Let'r rip, Harry, you've got my blessing."

Harry came from behind the desk. "Well, Carl, maybe. We'll see. Leave the film and we'll talk later."

Malone wrapped his big hand around Harry's. "Pal, this is the best I've felt in a year. Call me soon." As Carl turned and left the office, Harry was already on the intercom asking his secretary to line up a projector.

*H*arry had his first meeting with Lee Parlier later that day. He was appalled. Jay Kelly had told him nothing to prepare him for Parlier's appearance. Television's programming genius was a small, wiry man with bulging brown eyes. His dark hair was parted in the middle and slicked down with heavy grease in the patent leather style of the 1920s. He had an evil-looking pencil-line mustache and, to complete the picture of an art deco lounge lizard, he wore a tiny, closely fitted blue blazer with ballooning white flannel trousers and brown and white wing tip shoes. It was amazing. The man had done everything he could to create the impression that he was a cheap, sleazy con-man. A jury wouldn't believe anything he said—not even his name. No wonder Kelly thought he might not be up to this case.

Harry sighed, "Have a seat, Mr. Parlier." But the man moved forward, taking both of Harry's hands in his, focusing on Harry with the eyes of a King Charles spaniel.

"Mr. Cain . . . Harry, if I may . . . it's a privilege to meet one of the great legal minds of the country and an honor to be represented by him." He stepped back and bowed ever so slightly.

Harry's spirits sank even further. The man's manner went with his appearance. He'll be absolutely dead with a jury. Harry realized he had to deal with this quickly and brutally.

"Sit down, Mr. Parlier."

"Lee please, Harry."

"Yes. Anyway, sit down."

Parlier did. Harry looked at him without the slightest sign of friendliness.

"There are some things we've got to get straight right from the start or we can't make this work. Okay?"

Now Parlier looked serious, worried. "Okay, sure."

"I want no bullshit of any kind, ever. None. And you'll get none from me. Okay? I need you to give me straight, undiluted facts and that's what I want the jury to get. If they don't, they'll sense it. No matter how slick you may think you are, you can't charm me, and you can't charm them. Am I clear?"

Parlier was following, no doubt of that. "Yeah, sure, that's clear."

"Okay, charm won't get us anywhere. Neither will flattery. If the jury thinks you're trying to charm them, or, worse, flatter them, you'll hurt us badly. You're going to give them the facts politely, objectively and unadorned by any attempt to win points or help your case. I'll make the arguments and shape the facts you tell them into winning form. But you let me do that part."

"Okay, I'll do whatever you say, Harry."

"That's easy to say, Lee. So far I don't know if you can do it or if you *will* do it."

Parlier looked worried, obviously taken aback by Harry's brusk, unfriendly approach.

Harry went on. "Lee, it's going to take an enormous amount of hours of working together to make this go. We'll go through your direct testimony over and over again for hours, sharpening it, getting it in the most effective order and form. Then I'll actually cross-examine you, try to cover all the areas our opponents will cover, just the way they'll do it. It'll be hard work, Lee, but that's the way I do it and, if you can't do that or if you can't follow instructions, then I'm just not your guy. Okay?"

"Okay, Harry, you're my guy all right. I'll do it."

"Good. I'm also going to work with you on appearance and ward-robe. You're too"—Harry groped for a word—"stylish for a jury. They'll hate you. We have time for that, but I'm going to make you totally different. Let's talk about some preliminaries. I read in Mr. Heath's deposition that he claimed you signed a phony name to get into the UBS offices on Sunday so you could copy their records."

"Yeah, that's what he claims... you want the truth?"

"Lee, that's what I always want. If I don't get the truth, I really can't be ready to try your case. Besides, whatever you tell me is privileged. No one can make me disclose it."

"So we can always tell it differently at the trial, huh?"

"No, I don't mean that at all, Lee. I've never told a witness to lie and I'm not going to start with you. But if I know the truth, I can use it to your advantage. I can use it to try and avoid the harm from unfavorable things I know are going to come out, or maybe find a way to keep them from getting in evidence, or sometimes even use unfavorable facts to your advantage. But not by lying. So give me the whole truth about your using a phony name."

"The truth is I don't remember. I could've done it. I sure didn't want Heath to know I was there and maybe I did put down some other name. Listen, I've done it before. Not at UBS though." Harry raised an eyebrow. "Well, you wanted the whole truth, Harry."

"I know, I know. Go on."

"Nothing more to tell. I could've used a phony name, I just don't remember. It was a long time ago. But listen, Heath doesn't even have the sign-in book any more. There's no way that he can show what name I signed. I can just deny I used a phony name. It's not like I know I did it. I really don't remember."

"Christ, Lee, don't you listen at all? I don't want you to lie, ever. I want you to tell the jury just what you told me. You don't remember. Okay?"

"Okay, Harry, but it sure seems like it would be a lot better to deny it. It can't be good for me to look like I used a phony name to get into the building."

"Just let me decide that, Lee. This could be one of those cases where an unfavorable fact may turn out to be very helpful."

"I sure don't see how, Harry, but I said I'd follow your orders, and I will. I hope you believe me."

"I do, Lee." But Harry was by no means sure. They talked over other areas of the case for more than an hour and Harry told Parlier that, when the Malone trial was over, he wanted to go to New York and do some checking on his own with regard to the facts. It would cost a few thousand dollars, but it might turn up some helpful things. Parlier was agreeable. He wrote a check to cover Harry's expenses before the New York trip, gave him a hearty handshake and his most sincere look and, going out the door, said, "Harry, now I know why you're great."

Harry slumped in his desk chair. This one wasn't going to be easy.

*M*ajor civil litigation in Los Angeles County usually takes place in the main Superior Courthouse stretching along First Street between Hill and Grand. This vast, granite fortress stands only two blocks from the Criminal Courts building but light-years away in ambiance. Bordered by the Music Center and a landscaped mall, its well-tailored, better-paid occupants relax by the fountains and under the palms, conversing pleasantly, until, one-by-one, they stride away to argue complex legal matters before judges who are usually well prepared and occasionally even distinguished. Unlike the Criminal Courts, the concern here is not lives but money.

In that more refined atmosphere, Harry stood with Carl Malone outside the master calendar department, awaiting assignment to a trial court.

Today was the big day. Malone, tall and formidable in light-gray chalk-striped flannel, was uncharacteristically tense, constantly glancing about him at the throng moving down the courthouse hallways. He kept patting Harry's arm, as if to comfort him.

Once again, Harry wore his favorite navy suit and a rep striped tie he particularly favored for court. He looked crisp and efficient. Like Malone, he was nervous—always was at the start of a trial. But he'd learned long ago to conceal it, to radiate easygoing confidence.

At the other end of the corridor Fiona and her attorney sat huddled over a huge sheaf of papers with two other serious-looking men. Fiona's mother, a slender, white-haired Englishwoman stood beside them. Fiona was lovely in a rose-colored tweed suit, her silk blouse a darker shade of rose.

While both sides waited, countless photographs were snapped at each end of the hall. Harry was always a good source of news, even more so since his colorful defense of Sonny Ball; and, this time, his client was one of the richest and best-known men in the state and a man in the process of divorcing a beautiful woman who, for the past few years, had been the darling of the social pages.

Finally, the Malone case was assigned for trial to one of the many Superior Court judges, maybe the best of them from Harry's point of view. Judge Joe Kern was a big square-faced man. His gray hair had been kept in a crew cut all his life, or at least since the war, when he commanded a destroyer in the South Pacific. Before he was appointed to the bench, he'd served for fifteen years as a deputy district attorney, ending as the chief trial deputy. He was no great scholar, but he had good instincts, guts and a keen sense of humor. The tactics Harry had in mind might have a chance before Kern. With a pompous or prissy judge, there'd be no hope at all.

Standing at the counsel table, his muscular frame evident beneath his black pinstriped suit, Calvin Pierce made a brief but effective opening statement. The "cat" was good—one of the best. He was forceful, but courteous, speaking slowly, making his points with clarity and precision.

Pierce acknowledged that Mr. Malone had owned Cleveland Steel before the marriage, that, ordinarily, it would be his separate property. But Pierce would show that the steel company, like all of Mr. Malone's separate assets, had been voluntarily converted by him into community property. Under California law, a husband, just by saying so, could change his separate property into community; and, in those days, deeply in love with his charming new wife, that's just what Carl Malone did. Secondly, Pierce argued, Malone Electronics, a smaller, newer company, had been started during the marriage. Even if everything hadn't been converted into community property, then Mrs. Malone was at least entitled to half of the electronics company and Pierce would show by expert testimony how much it was now worth.

Pierce gracefully conceded that it would be unfair to divide the electronics company in half and jeopardize its skilled management by Mr. Malone. Malone, he said, should keep the company, and Mrs. Malone should be awarded a cash payment equal to the value of her one-half interest. As to the steel company, Malone was no longer active in management and the proper order was to give her one-half of the stock itself. It was an extremely valuable asset. The last annual report of Cleveland Steel showed its net worth at sixty-two million dollars, making Mrs. Malone's share worth over thirty million. "Indisputably, a lot of money." Pierce continued, "The kind of award that requires enormous courage by the court." "But," he said quietly, "it's the *correct* award in this case, and I'm confident that, when all the evidence is in, the court will so find."

Pierce knew his man. Kern loved to think of himself as a hard-nosed judge who would make a tough, courageous decision when it was right as a matter of law, even if it wasn't popular or pleasant.

Pierce also knew how to get the most out of his client. He introduced Fiona, who smiled shyly at the judge. Then he announced that she would testify later. This way, he gave her the benefit of watching the other witnesses and learning from their mistakes.

Pierce began with his expert on the value of the companies. He called Professor Byrd of the N.Y.U. Economics Department. Professor Byrd was tall and spare with wiry hair standing on end. He wore metal-rimmed glasses and a greasy-looking dark-gray suit. After establishing his academic credentials, he testified that he had served as a consultant to a number of large corporations in connection with their acquisition of other businesses and had, on many occasions, been called upon to evaluate privately owned companies for that purpose. At the request of Mr. Pierce, he had made a study of Malone

Electronics and had prepared a report setting out his conclusions as to the value of that company. Pierce had him identify a blue plastic-bound report as his work and handed copies to Harry and to Judge Kern.

Then Pierce took Byrd through the report page-by-page, showing the various statistical methods he used to arrive at his conclusion.

Harry hadn't been too concerned about Malone Electronics, because it had suffered losses in both years of its two-year history and, in the current year, was doing worse than ever. The company owed the bank a million dollars, which was almost all that its assets would bring if they were sold. So, without any earnings, its true net value was very little. If Fiona got fifty percent of that value in cash, she was looking at only a hundred or two hundred thousand maximum, or so Harry thought.

Now Pierce turned to the witness. "And Dr. Byrd, having described your various statistical methods, what, in fact, is your opinion as to the value of Malone Electronics?"

"Based on the gross asset to value formula and the loss reduction formula I've employed here, as explained at pages three to six of my report, the company's value is in the range of ten million dollars."

Harry looked up from his notes, stunned. He thought the professor would go high, but this was ridiculous. Malone snorted loudly, red with anger. Judge Kern glared angrily in Malone's direction. Harry decided to use the incident. "Your Honor, I apologize for Mr. Malone's noise there. He just lost control. No sincere man could make a valuation anywhere near ten million dollars, and it was just too much for—"

Pierce jumped to his feet. "Now that's improper, Your Honor, and Mr. Cain knows it. I intend to report Mr. Cain's conduct to the Bar Association and ask for appropriate sanctions."

Kern used his gavel hard. "All right, gentlemen, that's enough. I want none of that from either of you. Mr. Malone, this court will not tolerate outbursts or indications of any sort as to your feelings about the testimony. Do you understand?"

"Yes, Judge, I'm very sorry," Malone replied quietly.

"Okay, let's get on with the case. . . . Mr. Pierce?"

Pierce picked up the expert's report once again. "Would you explain the method of valuation by which you arrived at your ten million dollar figure, Dr. Byrd?"

"Yes, there are not yet any net earnings, a fact not surprising in a new scientifically oriented company. So, we cannot apply the usual price earnings ratio. Nevertheless, there are other standards that are accepted by the financial community in such cases. One is the gross asset to value relationship. On page four of my study I have analyzed comparable companies, showing the relationship between their gross assets and their actual market value as approximately three point five to one."

"Well, what were the gross assets here?"

"One million one hundred thousand dollars."

"Then wouldn't the value be only three point five million dollars, rather than ten million?" Pierce asked innocently.

Harry laughed to himself at the "only." Pierce would be thrilled to get a three point five million dollar valuation for that dog of a company, even though Professor Byrd had testified to ten million.

"No sir. The companies with which I have compared Malone Electronics were mature companies, so that their gross asset to value ratio could be taken unadjusted. Here we must adjust for the fact that the company is in its early, rapid-growth phase, and it's certainly a high-growth industry. This company's ratio should be far higher than three point five to one, and accordingly, I've adjusted the ratio by use of the declining loss formula."

"Would you explain that, please?"

"Yes. The company's loss in the first year was three hundred fifty thousand dollars. In the second year it was only two hundred seventy-five thousand dollars. The company's sales in the first year were three million dollars, and in the second year they were three point four million. Now mathematical answers can be extrapolated from both declining losses and expanding sales to tell us where the company will be when it reaches its maturity, its 'stability phase,' as Dr. Glover of MIT puts it in his very fine study of the subject."

"But Dr. Byrd, how does that affect the value of Malone Electronics?"

"Well, if we take the asset value ratio of three point five to one for mature companies and, applying this company's declining loss and sales expansion pattern, we adjust the ratio to reflect this company's anticipated position in its stability phase, we will get the correct answer."

Harry wondered if the judge was buying this pedantic double-talk.

"And what is that answer?" said Pierce with a dramatic gesture.

Byrd looked from Pierce over to the judge. Then he spoke with an air of great self-importance.

"As I said, Mr. Pierce, making the mathematical adjustments required to reflect this company's own predictable expansion, the value is approximately ten times its present gross asset position, or a total of ten million dollars."

Pierce smiled in Harry's direction. "Thank you, Doctor. I offer Professor Byrd's report in evidence. You may cross-examine, counsel."

Judge Kern, showing no signs of what he was thinking, accepted the report in evidence and nodded to Harry, who was seething at the complicated theoretical fraud Pierce and his "expert" were trying to pull on the court.

But Kern was no genius, and the figures and formulas were so complicated, he just might go for the ten million dollar figure. After all, Carl Malone would be left with plenty of money. Certainly, a three point five million dollar compromise valuation was a real danger.

Harry's job was to make it dramatically clear that the electronics business was really worth nothing like the huge figures provided by Professor Byrd, and that, for all his credentials, the professor was really nothing but a highly paid whore.

Harry stood, paused a moment and began his cross-examination. "Dr. Byrd, are you being paid by Mrs. Malone for your testimony?" Byrd hesitated, looked nervous. Seeing this, Pierce couldn't take the chance the professor would stupidly deny being paid, an answer the judge would know at once was a lie. He interrupted quickly, "We'll stipulate that Dr. Byrd is being paid a reasonable fee as an expert. Mr. Cain knows that."

Harry exploded: "Wait a minute. Don't you coach the witness. That's improper and you know it."

The gavel banged again. "Enough!" bellowed Kern.

But Harry crashed on: "Your Honor! That witness was about to deny it, about to perjure himself. You saw it. Mr. Pierce tried to save him, he knew—"

"Mr. Cain, sit down right now," thundered Judge Kern. Harry sat down, but he'd made the point.

"Now, Mr. Cain, continue with your cross-examination. Mr. Pierce, if you wish to offer any further stipulations, please ask to approach the bench and we'll discuss it. Proceed."

"Did Mr. Pierce tell you to come in with a high figure for Malone Electronics?"

"No, he did not."

"Did he tell you what side you were on?"

Pierce stood up. "I object, Your Honor. That assumes the witness is 'on a side' rather than giving his honest evaluation."

"Overruled."

"Doctor?"

"Mr. Pierce told me he represented Mrs. Malone, but I've made an honest evaluation here, not one favoring either side."

"Yes. Now, Doctor, have you inquired as to how the company did in the first three months of this year?"

"I didn't have those figures."

"Well, if the loss got progressively worse and sales got proportionately lower in that period, wouldn't that affect your adjusted ratio?"

"No, I would want to see the entire current year, not just three months."

"You wouldn't let any facts interfere with that ten million dollar number, would you?"

"Objection. Argumentative."

"Sustained."

For the next thirty minutes Harry took the witness through his "comparable" companies, in an attempt to show that they weren't comparable at all, that even three point five times gross assets was absurd for Malone Electronics and that the ten million dollar value was ridiculous. Harry scored some points, but it wasn't clear enough, not dramatic enough. He needed an ending that would leave no doubt in Judge Kern's direct, practical mind.

He put aside Professor Byrd's report and approached the witness, pausing for effect. "Dr. Byrd, you have testified that Malone Electronics was worth ten million dollars. You know its debts just about equal its assets, and you know it has a record of nothing but losses. Do you really want to stick to that opinion?"

"Yes sir." The professor was grim but stubborn. "That business is worth ten million dollars."

"You're certain?"

"Absolutely."

"You mean that's what a buyer would pay for it?"

"Yes, an informed buyer who understood its true value based on solid principles of mathematics and economics."

"And you could explain those principles convincingly to such a buyer?"

"I could, and any one of a hundred competent economists could make a similar, convincing demonstration, given an informed and intelligent buyer."

"Well, sir, this business being worth ten million dollars, I'm authorized by my client to sell it to you for half a million dollars. Will you buy it?"

Pierce screamed out, "Objection! That's not proper cross-examination, that's—"

"Overruled—he may answer."

Byrd looked back at Harry blankly. "You may answer, Professor," boomed Judge Kern.

"Well, Judge, I'm only a university professor. I don't have that kind of money."

Harry knew he had him. He pressed on. "Dr. Byrd, you testified to your many fine business consultantships and financial connections. I'll tell you what we'll do, we'll give you ninety days to raise the money—only five hundred thousand dollars, and you can easily resell the company for ten million dollars, as you just told us. Now, will you buy it?"

"Your honor!" Pierce shouted. "That's argumentative and absolutely improper."

"Overruled, Mr. Pierce. I want to hear his response."

Aware that the judge was awaiting his answer, Professor Byrd looked very tense. He put a finger in his collar to pull it away from his neck. He could see what was happening to him, and he didn't like it one bit. He could find no way out.

"Well, Your Honor, I'm not in the business of buying and selling companies. If I start doing that, I'll lose my reputation for objectivity. So I couldn't really entertain this proposal, even though I'd dearly love the profit."

Harry took a step nearer the witness and looked up at Kern. "Let's get this straight, Professor Byrd. You will not pay half a million dollars for this business you testified under oath can easily be sold for ten million dollars?"

"That's correct."

"That's all I have of this witness, Your Honor."

As Harry turned, he thought he saw just the trace of a smile at the corner of the judge's otherwise stern mouth.

On the way back from court, Harry stopped by Carmel's new cottage on Sweetzer. He needed soothing. Despite the success of his cross-examination of Fiona's expert, he remained very anxious about the case. And although he tried to put it out of his mind during the trial, he was becoming more and more concerned about Gail. Soon, it would be too late for an abortion. Yet, even though he'd raised the subject several times, she showed no sign of weakening in her resolve to have Milgrim's baby.

And things were still peculiar at home. Two days earlier, after a frustrating telephone conversation with Gail, he had phoned Nancy from his office, imploring her to talk sense to Gail before it was too late.

He had expected willing support, especially since he was about to start a trial, a time when Nancy always tried to make his life comfortable, to protect him from unnecessary strain. To Harry's surprise, his request for help with Gail was met with a long silence, in which he could hear Nancy's breathing. Finally, she had spoken coldly, uncharacteristically. "I think it's high time you exercised your responsibilities as a father, Harry, rather than always putting the burden on me. It'll be good for you. Besides, I'm busy now, and I think we've finished our discussion anyway."

He had heard the phone click and sat there looking at the instrument that buzzed annoyingly in his hand. He had replaced the receiver and turned back to his trial preparation, more concerned than ever about what was going on in Nancy's life. But with the trial beginning, there had been no time to find out, and Harry had not been certain he wanted to know.

In addition to the Malone case, the pressure of other work, other clients—all demanding his time—mounted with each trial day. Phone messages piled up, to be hurriedly answered during recess. Critical decisions had to be made in an instant before rushing back to the courtroom.

All these elements of stress, plus a rush hour trip on the freeway left Harry in a state of tension and fatigue as he pulled off Fountain Avenue into Sweetzer. His neck was stiff, his head beginning to throb. He felt his age.

When he arrived at Carmel's, everything changed. Harry felt he was entering a different world—a world of quiet and grace. A fire in the small Mexican fireplace was the only light, flickering in the rose dusk of the California evening. Schubert's Unfinished Symphony was playing softly on the record player. Harry's spirits rose. His normal buoyancy began to return.

Carmel greeted him in a short Japanese robe. She took his hand and led him into the softly lit room, then turned and pressed against him, kissing him hungrily. The stress of the day disappeared. Feeling the warmth of her body, the thrust of her breasts and loins against him, Harry was swept with such intense desire that, almost at once, they were together on the sofa, Harry's clothes strewn in a line from the front door. They clutched each other fiercely, rolling, holding and pressing together with abandon, until soon they were buried in each other, feeling each other's need—taking such pleasure from each other that, within seconds, each crying out, they came together, their climax rolling over them like a giant wave.

They lay talking softly, gently holding each other in the soft glow. With Carmel, Harry could open up, tell her everything he'd done, everything he'd felt—things he hadn't thought of for years. The nights he lay awake crying after his father died. The loneliness of growing up on his own, always in someone else's house, never his own. The constant need to work even as a kid. How it felt to rush to his job after college classes, when everyone else was drinking beer, hustling girls, enjoying life. He told her of pressing and repressing his one pair of slacks, afraid they were getting so shiny that people would notice. He described the heady excitement of arriving at Harvard Law School, the look of the place, the famous faculty, his awe at the caliber of his classmates, the brutal competition of that terrible first year, his soaring pride at making the *Law Review* and the unmatched joys of living in Cambridge as an academic hero... the winters, the drives, the Radcliffe girls—all of it. Then, the hard early years as a young lawyer. The Hollywood walk-up office. Not much joy and not much money. He told Carmel about his first big case, how he'd won it, the thrill of seeing his name that first time in the papers... quoted... becoming a well-known figure... a man on his way.

It came to him, as he described that turning point in his career, that just at that exhilarating moment, Nancy seemed—just a bit, only a bit—to slip away... to slide out of the center of his life, as if she had been there loving and caring, at the core of his existence, when she was so desperately needed, and then when she might no longer be needed quite so much, she had quietly, subtly changed, become slightly different—similar perhaps, but different.

Later, Harry showered and dressed. Hand-in-hand, they went to the door. As Harry was about to leave, Carmel pulled him back and looked at him with an expression at once so loving and so sad that Harry was immediately concerned. "What's the matter?"

"It's too much. You're too much. You're just too much."

"How do you mean?"

"I'm hopelessly in love with you. You know that. But now, I'm growing utterly dependent on you... I want you all the time. It worries me, it frightens me."

Harry took her face in his hands and looked down into her enormous amber eyes, beginning now to well up with tears. He pulled her close and held her, and they stood in the front door rocking together and kissing gently. Then he moved away and held her at arm's length. "Look, Carmel, what's happening to us is rare and marvelous. It's not something to be frightened of, it's something joyful, something to cling to. As the kids in my office say, 'Go with the flow, man.'" Carmel wiped her eyes and smiled. "Okay, man, I'll try."

*T*he next morning Calvin Pierce called Fiona Malone to the stand. As Harry expected, Fiona made a good first impression on Judge Kern, who was obviously taken with her extraordinary appearance and ladylike charm.

That appearance was not inexpensively arranged. She wore a soft-gray Chanel suit, the lapel and waist ribbon only slightly darker grosgrain. Her white silk blouse was Cocoon from the rue St. Honoré, her gray suede bag and shoes from Hermes. Her golden hair formed a perfect frame for her lovely, mobile face. At a nod from Pierce she moved gracefully to the stand and smiled—almost shyly—at the judge. When Pierce began to question her, she responded in a quiet, calm voice, her upper-class British accent connoting elegance and breeding.

From the night of their wedding, Carl had frequently told her that their love was the most extraordinary event in his life, that half of everything he had was hers, and that everything was theirs together. Once, he told her she should feel proud to be half owner of the biggest privately owned steel company in the West. Often, he said they were "partners" in everything and made many similar remarks. She testified that Carl said these things often until the last year they were together, and that he never said anything to the contrary until they separated. It sounded believable.

At lunch Harry sat beside Malone eating sushi at Omasa, a short walk down First Street from the courthouse.

Malone was intrigued at the variety of raw seafood Harry ordered for them, the names, the textures, the exotic tastes that Harry had enjoyed for years and that were a new experience for Malone.

Stuffing his mouth with hirame sushi, the delicately sliced halibut and vinegared rice disappearing rapidly, Malone asked if it was John Matsuoka who taught Harry about sushi and how to order it.

"Hell no. I think I taught John more about sushi than he taught me. I learned from my Japanese clients—especially on trips to Tokyo. What John did teach me was good Mexican cooking—mole poblano, chiles nogado, pollo con salsa verde. He's great at it. You know his dad's lifelong partner was Victor Alvarado. When the Matsuokas were interned during the war, Alvarado kept the business going. After the war, he not only gave old Akiro Matsuoka back his interest in the firm, he paid him his half of every penny earned while he was gone... with interest.

"Oh, John's told me a thousand stories about the Alvarados, but especially the Alvarado Sunday dinners where John's sisters Fumiko and Sashiko made the tortillas with the Alvarado women, and John himself, after sixteen years of apprenticeship, finally became the principal chef. Did you know they call him 'Juan' even today?"

Harry took the last piece of hirame sushi, and, turning his wrist, dipped the fish portion in soy sauce to which he added wasabi, a paste of hot green horseradish. "Listen, Carl, we've got to talk about the case." He went on to warn Malone that Fiona was doing very well and was probably winning back the judge's sympathy lost by Professor Byrd's obviously phony testimony.

"But, Harry," Malone protested, watching the sushi chef to see what was coming next, "the law's the law—he's gotta follow the law, doesn't he? He can't give her half of my separate property because she's good-looking, for Christ's sake, because she seems like a lady."

"It's not that simple, Carl." Harry was nervously wolfing the mirugai sashimi, slices of giant clam he ordered cut "usuzukeri," very thin. "The judge might just believe her—believe you promised her half of your property; and, if he does, she gets half. That is following the law, Carl, even though you and I know it's not the truth. Or, possibly, he'll decide that he'd like to see her get *something* and find the electronics company... which is community property, don't forget... is worth maybe two million dollars or so. Then he can give her a million. You've got much, much more, and he knows it."

"But that's not following the law, Harry; that's playing King Solomon, not being a judge."

"You're right Carl, but he's human. He's going to lean in the direction he thinks is fair, and if he likes her, thinks she's the fine, decent lady she seems to be, he may think it's fair to give her a lot of money."

"But, Harry, we've got the film. We've got to use it. We've got to show the judge what she's really like—cut through this ladylike bullshit. You said there might be a way. Christ, you were brilliant with that asshole professor. There must be a way with the film."

"I told you, Carl, there's only a wild outside chance I can get that film before the judge. Pierce has to get greedy, scared, ask for support payments. Then, we just might pull it off."

"Support payments? Shit. How can he ask me to give her thirty million dollars and still ask me to support her?"

"He won't, Carl, but if he doesn't put on evidence of what support Fiona needs, he can't get her any support order at all; and then if the judge doesn't give her thirty million or any substantial amount of property or cash, she'll be completely out of luck. Pierce may not take the chance."

"And if he puts on evidence of what she needs by way of support, that's good for us?"

"It could be."

"How?"

"Well, it opens the door to what income she can make and..."

"She's never worked, Harry; she's lived on her back. That's her trade, for Christ's sake."

"Let's wait and see, Carl. You want the rest of my tetaki?" Harry offered Carl the finely minced tuna mixed with green onions in the traditional "battleship" cup of seaweed and rice.

"No thanks, Harry. Hey, you didn't eat that much and it was great."

"Yeah, I never eat very much during trial. It's probably in my mind, but I think it slows me up. I used to though. When I was a kid, I'd go over to Olvera Street at noon, in the middle of a trial, and have two big burritos and a beer and then go back feeling fine. Now it's a few pieces of sushi and a cup of tea and I still feel heavy all afternoon."

They walked back to court in time to meet Calvin Pierce coming up the courthouse steps with Fiona. Pierce took Harry aside. "Look, Harry, you can see that Kern likes her. At the very least, he's going to go for my three point five million dollar theory, and maybe—just maybe—the whole enchilada, half the steel company plus five million or so. It's possible, you know."

"Sure, Cal. Anything's possible, but it won't happen. Anyway, we'll see soon enough...." Harry started to turn away.

"Wait. Look, Harry, I'll probably get killed for suggesting it, but suppose I could get her to take two million dollars plus a hundred thousand dollars a year permanent support. The support would be deductible, but it's got to be for life."

"No dice, Cal, I told you before my top is one million in deductible support payments—a hundred thousand dollars a year for ten years. You better grab that, 'cause it won't be around for long."

Pierce grinned. "Okay, Harry, I've heard your hard-nose act before. I know you've got balls. But they could sure get squeezed before this case is over." He turned and walked away to Fiona, who'd been waiting quietly a few feet away.

With Malone's approval, Harry had made the million dollar offer a number of times before the trial, but Pierce was never ready to take less than five million. Now he must be worried by what had happened to his professor; and even with Fiona coming across as well as she was, he was getting scared. He'd put on evidence of her need for support. Harry was sure.

And Harry was right.

As soon as court resumed, Pierce led Fiona slowly and carefully through a list of her "needs." They totaled two hundred fifty thousand dollars a year plus enough to pay her taxes. Fiona graciously apologized for her spending. She'd been raised that way, and Carl had generously spoiled her during the marriage, providing an even higher standard of living than before. Judge Kern seemed surprised at some of the figures but, generally, appeared to remain sympathetic.

When the list was over, Pierce moved back to the counsel table and, after a pause, put what was obviously a setup question. "Mrs. Malone, are these needs you've listed what your needs would be living separately from Mr. Malone, at least until you remarry?"

She picked it up beautifully. "Mr. Pierce, I'm not a Catholic, but I attended a convent school, and I live by the principles I learned there. I can't stop Mr. Malone from divorcing me; but in my heart he's my husband for life. I could never remarry, so that possibility has never entered my thinking."

Pierce did his best to look embarrassed, as if he hadn't deliberately planted the question and answer to appeal to the Judge's devout Catholicism. He mumbled, "Oh, I see," and fumbled with his notes as if confused. Then, he announced, "That's all I have."

Harry got up slowly. He'd have to draw some blood before he used his special play or he'd never get away with it.

"Mrs. Malone, you were married before, weren't you?"

"Yes, Mr. Cain, but not divorced. I was a widow."

She was dangerous. Before Harry could bring out that her first husband, a London doctor, had died, she made it look as though he were trying to create the false impression that she was divorced.

"Yes, I know. I'm getting at something else. Did your late husband leave you some property?"

"Yes, he did."

"Approximately how much?"

"What's the relevance of that?" Pierce exploded.

"I'll connect it up, Your Honor, it's preliminary."

"All right. If that was an objection you made, Mr. Pierce, it's overruled, subject to a later motion to strike if Mr. Cain fails to show its relevance."

Harry looked back at the witness. "How much, Mrs. Malone?"

"Approximately a million dollars in securities."

Harry worded the next question carefully to trigger fear in Fiona's calculating mind. "And whether or not the court believes Mr. Malone gave you half of his property, did you give him half of yours?"

She bit. "No, Mr. Cain, I did not. That money had come from my late husband . . . from his medical practice. He would not have wanted it divided with Carl Malone."

Harry was delighted. She'd been afraid that, somehow, the judge would reject her claim to half of Malone's property and still give Malone half of hers. So she tried to keep hers separate and, in doing that, made the whole idea of Malone dividing his property far less probable, which was what Harry was after.

"I see, so when he said that you were partners in everything, he meant you got half of everything *he* owned, but that you kept a hundred percent of what *you* owned, right?" Fiona was troubled now. There was a long silence.

"Well . . . yes. Ah, I suppose that's correct."

"And when he said that half of everything was yours, he meant that you would own half of what he had plus all of what you had?"

"Yes."

"He was making you richer than he was, right?"

"Well . . . maybe—"

Harry, sensing that she might be tempted to change her testimony, interrupted quickly. "You already said that you were to get half of his property, but you'd never offered half of yours to him. Are you changing that testimony now, going back on what you said?"

Pierce was on his feet shouting, "Don't interrupt, let her finish her answer. He's browbeating her, Your Honor, he's—"

Down came the gavel. "Mr. Cain, you know better. Mr. Pierce, if you've an objection to make, make it. I don't need a speech. Now, Mr. Cain, you will not cut a witness off in my court—ever! Mrs. Malone, do you want to add to your answer?"

Harry's outburst had worked, however. Now Fiona was afraid to change her testimony. "No," she said uncertainly.

Harry pressed on. "Then after Mr. Malone's promise, you actually had greater wealth than he did, isn't that right?"

"Oh, no."

"Well, didn't you have half of everything he had?"

"Yes."

"And you also had one million dollars of your own?"

"Yes."

"So if he only had the other half of his own assets, you were a million dollars richer. Isn't that right?"

"Yes, I suppose so, now that I think about it."

"And you said these promises from Mr. Malone came in the first year of your marriage?"

"Yes, from right after our wedding."

"So, by your first anniversary you were already richer than he was?"

"Asked and answered," Pierce objected.

"Overruled . . . you may answer."

"Yes." Fiona was unhappy with the sound of the answer, but she saw no way out. She was becoming a bit less ladylike; and not being able to figure out where Harry was going, she was growing far more nervous.

"I see. Well, then, by your second anniversary you were *definitely* more wealthy than Mr. Malone, isn't that correct?"

"Objection. Asked and answered again and argumentative."

Kern looked balefully over at Harry. "Mr. Cain, is the significance of these questions soon to be revealed?"

"Yes sir, very soon."

"Overruled. This is cross-examination. You may answer."

"I've forgotten the question, your honor."

"Read it back, Mr. Reporter."

The court reporter then read back the question as to whether Fiona had definitely been more wealthy than Carl on their second anniversary. "Yes, I suppose that's true."

"He didn't tell you again during the second year that you had half of everything?"

"He certainly did. He repeatedly said it during that year. That was a very good year for us."

Harry walked back to the counsel table and picked up a piece of paper. He handed Pierce a copy and moved slowly and deliberately back to Fiona.

"Mrs. Malone, I'm handing you this letter which appears to be signed by you. Will you look at it and tell us if that is, in fact, your signature." She took her time reading the letter. "Yes . . . but I didn't . . . yes, it's my signature all right."

"And is the letter in your handwriting?"

"Yes."

"Including the date?"

"Yes."

"Now that's the date of your second anniversary, isn't it Mrs. Malone?"

"Yes."

"And the letter was written that day, that is you didn't back date it or anything did you?"

"No . . . not that I can remember."

"Well, the letter refers to it being your second anniversary, doesn't it?" She read it again.

"Yes, yes it does."

"Mr. Malone gave you a ski lodge in Aspen, Colorado, for your anniversary, right?"

"If you call that giving."

"You mean it wasn't giving because he put it in his own name?"

"Yes. To me that's no gift, at least not the way a gentleman would give a gift."

Harry moved slowly back to the counsel table so that he didn't appear to be leaning over Fiona when she made her next answer.

"Mrs. Malone, would you read the letter aloud, please?" Fiona looked at the letter rather unhappily but began to read.

Dear Carl:

I cannot imagine your giving me a second anniversary gift and being mean enough to put it in your own name. I own tuppence hapenny compared to you and yet you seem to be threatened by the idea that my tiny holdings would be increased by owning a rustic mountain home. I'll be at the club when . . . or should I say "if" you care.

Fiona

"Now, you wrote that letter on your second anniversary protesting that you had a 'tuppence hapenny' compared to Mr. Malone. 'Tuppence hapenny' is an English expression meaning 'a tiny sum,' isn't that right?"

"Yes, that's correct."

"So, when you wrote that letter you just forgot that you already owned half of all of Mr. Malone's assets plus a million dollars of your own—right?"

Fiona saw the problem. Her eyes darted quickly to Pierce, who was looking at the judge. She took a deep breath.

"I didn't forget, I just didn't think of it at the time I wrote that note. I don't know why it didn't come to me then."

"And you ask the court to believe that during the two years preceding that note, the note in which you said that you owned only 'tuppence hapenny' compared to Mr. Malone, he had repeatedly told you, and you always believed him, that you had one-half of his sixty million dollar business and all the rest of his assets, plus a million dollars more of your own, so that you were really richer than he was."

"Objection. Compound and argumentative."

"I withdraw the question, Your Honor."

Once again, Fiona looked over at Pierce for help. Before it could come, Harry shifted ground. He'd tarnished Fiona's image, he was sure, maybe enough to get away with his plan for the film.

"Now, Mrs. Malone, you testified to your financial needs, but you did not testify as to your earning ability. You do have a million dollars of your own that's invested and produces income, isn't that correct?"

"Yes, but it only yields about seventy-five thousand dollars a year before taxes. I can't begin to live on that."

Judge Kern raised an eyebrow. Both Harry and Pierce knew that the judge himself made less than that and was supporting a family out of it. Pierce looked decidedly unhappy.

"Well, you do have the ability to earn money, don't you?"

"No, I have no marketable skill, Mr. Cain, not at all."

"Oh? Well, how did you support yourself in the five years before you met Mr. Malone?"

She knew she had a problem. Harry spotted the worry in her eyes. If she said she lived on her seventy-five thousand dollars income from her securities, she could do it again. If she admitted she'd lived on men, she'd mar that ladylike façade, perhaps beyond repair. Harry had her, but she was quick and game.

"Mr. Cain, I lived on a much lower standard in those days than the one to which Mr. Malone has made me accustomed. Besides, things were much cheaper then and I'm older now, my needs are greater."

"So, in the three years you've lived with Mr. Malone, you lost the ability to live on seventy-five thousand dollars?"

"Objection. Argumentative."

"Sustained."

Harry paused. Here it came. Very dangerous, but it might be an acceptable risk. Without taking that risk, a compromise judgment of a million or two million dollars was simply too likely. He plunged ahead.

"Now, early in your career you were an actress, isn't that correct, Mrs. Malone?"

"Yes, but that was many years ago. There'd be no work for me now in that field."

"Well, you could work in films, couldn't you, even now?"

"In films, Mr. Cain?"

"Yes, in films."

"Well, I never have . . . my only appearances were on the London stage when I was an actress, so I can't imagine who would possibly hire me in a film, especially at my age."

"Well, if you'll forgive me, Mrs. Malone, you are very beautiful and there are films in which you could be employed immediately without further training... so..."

"Are you asking me to make obscene films, Mr. Cain?" She was very quick.

"No, Mrs. Malone, obscenity is illegal, but there are films in which you might appear, in which you have already appeared and my—"

"What are you talking about, Mr. Cain? I've never appeared in any film." Slowly her eyes grew wide with panic. She suspected now what Harry knew. Malone too realized where Harry was going. He leaned forward with ill-concealed excitement.

"Well, if you could lawfully be employed in filmmaking, there's no reason why you would reject such employment is there?"

Fiona hesitated, but she could see no alternative. "No, I suppose not."

"And now that you've thought about it, isn't your recollection refreshed that you *have* actually appeared in a film, Mrs. Malone?"

"Objection, Your Honor, we're going far afield here. This has nothing to do with the case."

Harry jumped to his feet. "It goes to earning capacity, Your Honor— clearly a proper subject of inquiry. *Marriage of Swain* holds that the court will look not only to the actual earnings of a party but to his potential earning capacity as well."

Kern paused thoughtfully. "Mr. Cain, does your question go to recent events? I'm not concerned about any activity remote in time from this marriage. I don't care what she did years ago."

"No, Your Honor, I'll rephrase the question to limit it in time. ... Mrs. Malone, haven't you appeared in a film within the past two years?"

Malone sat back in his chair smiling wolfishly.

Fiona was deeply concerned, but she was still dangerous. "Do you include home movies, Mr. Cain?"

Harry was faster, subtler. "No, Mrs. Malone, I exclude movies made by your husband or family members. Have you made a film for other people than your husband or *family members?*"

"Do you mean for money?"

"Your Honor, it's obvious I can't get a straight answer from this witness." Harry quickly reached over to his second briefcase. "I offer this film, in which Mrs. Malone appeared last year, your honor. The court can judge for itself whether it's a film of commercial quality or only something that should be considered a home movie."

Pierce was on his feet. "Objection, Your Honor. Unless Mr. Cain can show that the witness received compensation for the film, it simply is irrelevant to this action."

"Not so, Your Honor. Suppose a wife has an obviously marketable skill like building houses and she's been building them free for her friends. Surely that's admissible to show she can support herself by selling those houses. The court must see the houses to decide if they are of salable quality. I offer this film for that limited purpose."

Pierce looked disgusted. "Your Honor, with all respect, this court is not a film critic, and this is a gross waste of the court's time."

"Your Honor," Harry shot back, "if we have to call experts on the marketability of Mrs. Malone's skills, we're prepared to, but I suggest the court take a look at the film before deciding its admissibility. Surely there can be no valid objection to that. Five minutes into the film the court can make its ruling."

Judge Kern's expression indicated that the approach seemed sensible to him. "Well, Mr. Pierce?" he asked. Pierce, surprised by Harry's seemingly reasonable suggestion, found himself unable to find a reason to object. "Well, Your Honor, it's a waste of the court's time and—"

"Surely we can spare five minutes, Mr. Pierce, in a case of this magnitude." Kern was going for it!

Fiona looked desperate. "Your Honor," she murmured, "could I confer with Mr. Pierce? I—"

Harry cut her off. "Your Honor, can we have a ruling and let them confer during the recess?"

"No, Mr. Cain, they can confer now, if Mrs. Malone believes she has information Mr. Pierce should have before the ruling." He turned to Fiona, who clobbered him with her green eyes.

"Yes, Your Honor, it's something he should know right now, and it will take just a minute." She didn't even wait for an answer but left the stand and gracefully moved to the counsel table, where she whispered frantically to a poker-faced Pierce.

When she was done, Pierce looked very angry. He waved her back to the stand and turned to the Judge. "Your Honor," Pierce thundered, pounding his fist on the pile of books at his side, "what we are seeing here is a piece of cheap, unethical trickery designed to prejudice this court, designed—" But Kern came down hard with the gavel, cutting him off.

"That's a very serious accusation against Mr. Cain, Mr. Pierce, and you better be ready to prove it. I'll hear an objection, if you have one, not a speech. Then I'll rule."

"Your Honor, I most strenuously object to this film being seen by the court. It is a personal matter, a film taken by stealth in violation of the law, designed solely—"

Harry leapt to his feet. "That's not true, Your Honor. I'm prepared to call witnesses not only that this film is of a quality shown in commercial theaters in this very city, but that it was made voluntarily and it was knowingly performed in by Mrs. Malone—that she knew what she was doing, that she did it willingly, even eagerly, and she knows that she can make money, lots of money, from it, any time she wants. Let me examine her as to the element of stealth and we'll see."

Kern looked very curious. Now he really wanted to see what this film was all about. He looked over at Fiona, who was white with anxiety. "Very well, Mr. Cain, I'll permit you to examine the witness on the voluntariness of her performance in the film you're offering."

"Mrs. Malone, you know the film I'm talking about, don't you?"

"I'm not sure..."

"Oh? Have you appeared in *several* such films?" Pierce was up again.

"Objection, Your Honor, that assumes she voluntarily appeared in any film."

"Sustained."

Harry started again. "Mrs. Malone, I'm prepared to call witnesses on the point, including Joe Don Sellers. Now you *did* appear voluntarily in a film made by Mr. Sellers, isn't that correct?" Fiona sat there speechless. She glanced quickly at two reporters sitting in the back of the courtroom.

As bright as she was, Fiona knew she had two choices. If she denied it, Harry was devil enough to have Sellers waiting outside the courtroom. The reporters would hear the whole bloody thing and the world would have the story within a few hours. If she admitted it, then she still had a chance, and the story might not get out, the damage might still be controlled. She chose.

"Yes, I knew I was in a film, but it's still a very personal matter."

Pierce tried again. "That's right, Your Honor, a personal film, even voluntarily made, has no bearing on this case."

Harry could see he was getting close. "Judge, that's the very issue. You can't rule on whether this film is merely of personal significance or is a salable asset until you've seen it, at least a few minutes of it. Then you can rule if it's admissible to show earning capacity. You could have seen it by now. We've been arguing for more than twenty minutes."

Pierce made a last desperate attempt. "Your Honor, voluntary or not, this is a calculated attempt to prejudice this court. If you see even five minutes—even one minute of this film, we will have a mistrial. The entire time spent on this case will be simply wasted, we will—"

The gavel banged down again. Pierce had taken the wrong tack with Judge Kern. "Don't threaten me, Mr. Pierce, and don't make a speech. You've objected and I'm going to rule without further colloquy. I'll see a portion of this film and then I'll rule on its overall admissibility. I've been around a long time and, if I exclude it from evidence, it will play no part in my decision."

Pierce had one more request. "Your Honor, may the film at least be viewed in chambers, rather than in open court?"

Harry smiled. "No objection, Your Honor."

"All right," said Kern. "We'll take a five-minute recess to set up the projector." He rose and started to leave the bench. Fiona left the stand, strode to the counsel table and, in a stage whisper even the judge must have heard, let Pierce have the full force of her anger. "You pompous ass, my poodle could have kept that film out of evidence—Jesus!" She stormed out of the courtroom, leaving Pierce red-faced with embarrassment. Malone turned to Harry with a wink.

Five minutes later in chambers, Harry was ready to start the film for the judge, the clerk, the court reporter and Calvin Pierce. Fiona elected to wait outside in the courtroom. "If necessary, Your Honor, we will prove that this film was made during the marriage and considerably before the parties separated."

"Just get on with it," growled Kern. The clerk and reporter looked anxious. Pierce looked white and drawn.

Harry turned off the lights and the film began. First all that could be seen was fuzzy, white film punctuated with black lines and specks. When a picture finally swam into focus, it was evident that the scene was a bedroom. Then, quickly, the camera moved to Fiona on her hands and knees—nude, her lovely breasts hanging down directly in front of the lens. She moved her shoulders from side to side, her breasts swaying with them.

Then the camera pulled back and Rabbit Sellers was on screen, also nude. His big hands began massaging Fiona's breasts from behind, while she wiggled her bottom and grimaced in what appeared to be ecstasy. Sellers moved out of the picture and, as if obeying an off-screen command, Fiona lay down on her back and began stroking herself, first rubbing, then cupping her breasts, then slowly moving her long fingers to her crotch as she began to writhe on the bed, her eyes closed and her legs gradually spreading, a lewd smile forming on her lips.

At that point, Butch Kemp, the Cowboys' middle linebacker, bulked into the scene . . . huge and muscular. He was also nude, except for cowboy boots. He climbed onto the bed, hunched over Fiona and slid his thick organ down and into her, as Fiona wrapped her legs around his back and began to grind in time to Kemp's thrusts.

Harry had almost forgotten just how good the film was, but he could see Kern staring in rapt attention in the flickering light of the screen. It was only a moment before Kemp obviously reached his climax and, without waiting a second, rolled off Fiona.

At almost the same moment Tube Tulley, the Cowboys' other split-end, came into view. This was the scene Harry remembered so vividly from the last time he'd seen the film. Tulley lay down on his back, his very erect penis even longer and blacker than Harry recalled. Fiona, her eyes staring glassily into the camera, squatted over Tulley, settling down on him, sliding that huge black shaft deep—ever so deep inside herself. Then, rotating her hips, at first slowly, then faster and faster, her golden hair flying about her head, she moved in ever more vigorous circles until finally her mouth gaped open and her head was thrown back in what was obviously a devastating orgasm.

Suddenly the lights went on. It was Kern himself who had moved to the wall switch.

"That's enough, Mr. Cain, I'm quite ready to rule. Let's return to the courtroom."

The court reporter was bright red. The clerk couldn't take his eyes off the screen, couldn't believe someone had actually stopped the action.

They all took their places in the courtroom, the lawyers standing at the counsel tables. Judge Kern rapped his gavel.

"The courtrooom will be cleared."

The bailiff stood and motioned for the onlookers to go. They gathered up their things and left the room.

Harry knew he was on thin ice. He had to make what he'd done look legitimate—to convince Kern that it wasn't just a cheap maneuver to create prejudice against Fiona.

"May I be heard, Your Honor," he said, "just briefly."

"Yes, Mr. Cain, but please be brief."

"Your Honor, I realize that Mr. Pierce will contend that because of the nature of this film, the court should not encourage Mrs. Malone to engage in such activities by charging her with the income that she could earn by making more films of that nature. But, Your Honor, the court of appeals has rejected a very similar contention in *Marriage of McBee*, 47 CA3d, 321 at page 324. In the McBee case, Your Honor, the husband had been regularly earning a hundred thousand dollars a year selling marijuana, and the trial court set spousal support for the wife based on that figure. On appeal, the husband argued that charging him with that income encouraged him to carry on an illegal activity, that, if he did not sell marijuana, there was no evidence that he could earn anything at all. The appellate court rejected that contention, holding that prior earnings, even if illegally obtained, could be considered in determining the husband's future earning capacity."

Malone looked up at Harry with pride and encouragement. Harry paused and continued, gesturing with his right hand.

"Our case is a fortiori, Your Honor . . . even stronger than McBee. The kind of films in which Mrs. Malone could appear are not even illegal, at least under the recent decisions of the Supreme Court.

Indeed, as I argued before, Your Honor, you'll find dozens of similar films playing all over the city."

"All right, Mr. Cain," interrupted the judge, "I've heard enough. I have the substance of your argument and I'm prepared to rule."

"Yes, Your Honor." Harry sat down.

"Mr. Cain, I'm going to take you at your word, that you meant this as a serious offer to prove earning capacity on the part of the petitioner. If I thought otherwise for one moment, Mr. Cain, I'd deal with you very strictly. I know films of this sort are marketed every day in the city and I recognize that this was voluntarily filmed by Mrs. Malone. She has so testified. Although, I must say, that aspect of the matter rather puzzles me. But I'm not prepared to rule that a person must market a product to the public because he or she enjoys making that product as a hobby, especially if the hobby is of a highly personal nature and of the sort condemned by most of society. The McBee case is a different thing—a proven commercial activity continuing over a number of years.

"In any event, I find, from just a few moments of this film, that it is essentially of a personal and noncommercial nature; and, as such, it will not be admitted in evidence."

The two reporters looked at each other knowingly, rapidly making notes. Harry tried to look beaten. "But, Your Honor, the duty to—"

"I've ruled, Mr. Cain," Kern thundered, "and I think you should consider yourself very lucky." Harry sat down.

But Pierce remained on his feet. "Your Honor, I have the unpleasant duty to move for a mistrial. You've seen a film that... and I say this respectfully... will no longer permit you, or any other human being in your position, to rule objectively on the financial issues in this case. This trial should begin anew before a new judge, and Mr. Cain should be severely reprimanded for his cheap tactics."

Harry jumped to his feet, but Kern waved him down. "Mr. Pierce, I've been on the bench for over twenty years, and I know how to disregard inadmissible evidence—which this is. It's excluded, Mr. Pierce—from the record and from my mind. As to Mr. Cain, I've already stated that I'm accepting his offer as being made in the sincere belief that the film showed earning ability by today's extremely liberal standards. While those standards proved too liberal for me to apply in this case, I'm not prepared to assume that Mr. Cain intended only to create prejudice, and I'm convinced that Mrs. Malone can continue to have the issues fairly tried before this court. Your motion is denied. Mr. Cain?"

"I have no further questions for Mrs. Malone, Your Honor."

"Mr. Pierce?"

"No redirect, your honor."

"Any further witnesses, Mr. Pierce?"

"No, Your Honor. The petitioner rests."

Over the next two days Harry put on his defense. Carl Malone denied that he ever told Fiona that half of his property was hers. He had three sons by his first marriage who were all in the steel business with him. Throughout his marriage, he wanted his boys to have the stock of the company, not Fiona. He testified that, in his opinion, as the owner of the company, Malone Electronics was worth under two hundred thousand dollars. Pierce confused Carl a bit on cross-examination, but Harry had spent two full days preparing him, and Pierce scored no major points.

Two of Carl's friends testified that Fiona had repeatedly complained that Carl kept everything in his own name and that "he thought of nothing but keeping his precious holdings separate." Pierce brought out on cross-examination that they were indeed close friends of Carl's; but beyond that, he was unable to shake their testimony.

Then Harry called Professor Lawrence Cable from Stanford Business School. Cable testified that, based on his analysis, Malone Electronics was worth at most two hundred fifty thousand dollars and probably less, and that there was no rational method of evaluation by which it could be assigned a value of ten million dollars, or even one million dollars or even half a million. Cable was well prepared and Pierce did little damage to him on cross-examination.

Harry decided to cut his case short and rested without calling his second expert.

After lunch, Pierce and Harry made their closing arguments. Harry was quiet and factual, saying nothing about the film. He emphasized the improbability of there having been any oral contract converting what Carl had worked so hard to build into community property, especially when Fiona was keeping her own property separate. He pointed out the gross inconsistency between Fiona believing she owned half of everything plus a million dollars . . . that is, being richer than Carl . . . and yet, at the same time, writing that she owned a "tuppence hapenny" compared to him. He laughed about Professor Byrd, whose complicated theory said Malone Electronics was worth ten million dollars but whose common sense told him not to buy it for half a million. He pointed out that, consistent with Professor Byrd's fear of buying the company at five hundred thousand dollars, Professor Cable had testified that, with its record of losses, the company was worth no more than a quarter of a million dollars, and that on cross-examination Pierce had made no dent whatsoever in that logical presentation. He reminded the judge that, so far as support was concerned, Mrs. Malone had lived for years on seventy-five thousand dollars per year and, despite a short three-year marriage, could do so again, especially since she would get some extra cash from her half share of Malone Electronics.

Pierce was more dramatic. He brought up the film and, pounding the table, bellowed that it was used only to prejudice the court, lead the judge to come in with a decision adverse to Mrs. Malone on the real issues. This, of course, was true, but Harry hoped Kern didn't think so or, having enjoyed the film, didn't care. Pierce shrugged off the "tuppence hapenny" note, as having been written in anger and without any real attempt to define the holdings of the parties. After all, even though he'd told her one-half of the steel company was hers, he was still running the company, she didn't have the stock in her name and certainly not in her hands, and it was natural to think of her own inheritance from her late husband as "tuppence hapenny."

Pierce was smart enough to poke fun at both professors. Like all academics, he said, each had his own theory. Probably the best thing to do, he smilingly suggested, was average their two conclusions at about five million dollars, a small enough sum to a man as rich as Carl Malone.

He urged the court to consider the lavish life-style to which Carl had accustomed Fiona, how all her current friends were people who lived at that very high standard and how hard and humiliating it would be now that Carl was tired of her that she should have to lose her friends and go back to her old poorer ways, especially when Carl was a man of staggering wealth to whom three or even four hundred thousand dollars a year support, all deductible, was simply a gnat, a tiny annoyance at most, while for her it was brutally, critically important.

He argued that if the court for some reason did not accept the oral transmutation of Carl Malone's property from separate to community, Mr. Malone, being by far the more wealthy, should pay his wife's attorney's fees, which, he added, would be in the area of three hundred thousand dollars, a very heavy burden for her to bear alone. In conclusion, Pierce asked the court to put whatever human faults Fiona might have out of his mind and to show that he had done so by awarding her a fair share of this vast, worldwide estate.

It was a good performance, and Harry was worried when he rose to make his reply. Despite his concern, he felt the best tactics were to be brief, to avoid repeating points he'd already made and not even to *hint* at sexual misconduct as an element to be considered.

He pointed out that when one "expert" is shown to be completely lacking in objectivity and off base by millions of dollars, while the other provides a fair and rational opinion, absolutely unshaken by cross-examination, you can't simply dismiss them both as air-headed "academics" and *average* their valuations. "One is right," Harry said, bringing his palm down on the stack of books before him, "and the other is wrong."

He paused and, with a slow smile, argued that there was nothing "humiliating" about living on seventy-five thousand a year without having to work for it and that the law did not require the court to take money from Mr. Malone and give it to his wife as support or fees, simply because he was richer or because it was "deductible." Giving Mrs. Malone more money because it would reduce her husband's taxes would simply shift the burden of financing her excessive spending to all the other American taxpayers, an economic policy, Harry added, that he was sure would not appeal to the court.

Seeing what he thought was a slight nod from the judge, Harry made the quick decision to stop. "At this point, Your Honor, since the court undoubtedly has the facts well in hand, I will not burden the record by further argument. Thank you."

Still standing, Harry began to gather up his papers, as did Pierce, both assuming the judge would take the case under submission for a week or so and then send out a written decision. Carl and Fiona, seeing their lawyers packing, rose and prepared to leave the court.

But Judge Kern was his usual, unpredictable self.

"Just a minute, gentlemen . . . and Mrs. Malone. I'm prepared to give my decision from the bench if you'll just sit down again. It's only three-thirty, and we easily can finish today, with no need for submission."

Harry, Pierce, Fiona and Carl all sat down at the same time and looked up at the judge. Fiona sat erect, her hands clasped in her lap. Pierce, beside her, looked tense but controlled. Judge Kern placed two pages of notes before him, smoothing them with his hands.

"I've followed the evidence each day and reviewed my notes each night. There are no serious problems of law here; and although I appreciate your excellent and thorough arguments, which I certainly considered, I can give you my decision right now, without dwelling upon it further."

Malone straightened his tie with an unconscious gesture.

Kern went on. "Firstly, on the issue of oral transmutation of Mr. Malone's separate assets into community property, I find that there was no such transmutation or promise to make his separate property into community.

"Accordingly, the Cleveland Steel Company, having been owned before the marriage and there being no evidence that Mrs. Malone's services increased its value during the marriage, is one hundred percent Mr. Malone's separate property."

Malone sat back, the beginning of a smile on his lips.

"Malone Electronics, on the other hand, is conceded to be community property, since it was formed during the marriage. I cannot accept the valuation testimony of the petitioner's expert which seemed wholly unrelated to any realistic concept of market value." Carl elbowed Harry in the ribs, the faint smile turning to a broad grin.

"On the other hand, I do not fully accept the position of respondent." Harry's heart sank. Malone leaned forward, once again fingering his tie. "I'm inclined to find some element of goodwill or going concern value over and above the value of the physical assets, even though we have a record of consistent and increasing losses."

As Judge Kern turned a page of his notes, Pierce began to smile, certain now that his five million dollar "averaging" argument had worked. Fiona looked at him and, seeing his smile, settled back in her chair, her tension easing.

The judge looked up and continued.

"I therefore find that the value of Malone Electronics Company is four hundred thousand dollars and, this being the only community property shown by the record, I award the company's stock to Mr. Malone and order him to pay two hundred thousand dollars in cash to Mrs. Malone forthwith."

Now Malone was beaming. He looked over at Harry and winked.

"On the question of support, I find Mrs. Malone's reasonable needs as a young woman without children to be seventy-five thousand dollars per year, and I find that she has sufficient income from her own separate securities to cover these needs, so that no additional spousal support is necessary at this time."

Pierce looked up in disbelief. Malone had clasped his hands behind his head and was leaning back in his chair.

"On the issue of attorney's fees, I recognize that Mr. Malone is by far the more wealthy party, but that is not necessarily the test if Mrs. Malone has the means to meet her own fees without impairing her separate capital. I find that, in light of the share of community property awarded to Mrs. Malone, she does, in fact, have sufficient means to cover her attorney's fees without invading her own separate assets; and, since Mr. Malone must pay his own fees, I make no fee award in Mrs. Malone's favor, leaving her to pay whatever may be a fair amount to Mr. Pierce."

Fiona looked pale, grim. Her fists were clenched, her knuckles white.

"Gentlemen, it's apparent that Mr. Cain is the victor here, and the burden of preparing a written statement of my decision is his. Thank you."

With that, the judge hastily gathered up his papers and left the bench. But not before Fiona blew. Just as Kern reached the door to his chambers, she whispered to Pierce, loud enough for the entire courtroom to hear. "You hopeless creep. You let him fuck me, fuck me blue." She burst into tears and, with her mother trailing in her wake, rushed from the courtroom, along with the reporters hurrying to find available phones.

*T*wo hours later, at La Golendrina in Olvera Street, Harry and Carl Malone were on their sixth margaritas. Malone, in a huge green and silver sombrero, was playing the trumpet with the mariachi band. When they finished "Guadalajara" for the third time, Malone staggered to the table. "Fucking world-beating genius. Harry, I'll never forget it, never forget what you've done for me. Fucking, stinking genius, the greatest fucking genius in the world. You can take your Ed fucking Williams and your Mel fucking Belli and shove 'em. Just office boys compared to the Sunset Bomber, Mr. Harry fucking whiz-bang Cain."

And on it went. At seven-thirty, with the sky darkening around the downtown buildings, Harry pulled himself away from the increasingly grateful Malone and, guided by the luck that somehow protects the innocent drunk, made his way home.

*H*arry put down the champagne, grinning, as he came to the end of the story. "... and there was nothing Pierce could do, nothing, Nance. Kern kept it out, of course. But you can't unring the bell. You can't unring the bell, Nance. Kern saw what she was. He didn't see all four guys lay her, but he saw the first two and that was enough. Christ, no sane man was going to give her millions of dollars for behaving like that, while she's living with her husband, taking his money. No man. That's what I counted on. That's why she got zilch. Not my great economic analysis or argument—which were pretty good though—pretty Goddamn good..." He ran down like a record after the player switched off. The excitement of winning was beginning to wear thin, and his head was just beginning to throb.

"Well, whatta you think, hon, we did it again, huh? Let's go out for dinner, let's celebrate. How about Le Dome or we'll drive out to

Seventy-two Market Street? Better still, let's just go down to Tony Roma's for some ribs."

Nancy, who had been silent through twenty minutes of Harry's stimulated talk, stared at him for a long moment. Then she spoke. "Celebrate? Celebrate what? My husband's lack of principles? His drunken gloating over a dishonest win?"

Harry looked up in amazement. He thought Nancy was enthralled with his story, but her focused attention during his long, triumphant narrative must have meant something quite different. Her anger astonished him.

"Aw, come on, hon, I—"

"Don't 'hon' me, you nattering hypocrite. You used to condemn Nixon for pretending to uphold the law while he secretly trampled it to gain his own ends. How many times have you said that not even the finest social purpose justified ignoring the law and violating someone else's rights? How many times have you given me Thomas More's speech from 'A Man for All Seasons' about the danger of knocking down the law to get at the devil? That's all hypocrisy—always was. You never believed it.

"Fiona Malone didn't lose because she was wrong under the law. You know that. She lost because of something the law says the judge never should have known—that she slept with other men and one of them was black. That's right—you even traded on closet racism." She pointed a finger at him. "You know damn well you did . . . and I know it too. The sad thing is you're proud of it, you arrant fool.

"You're fifty times worse than Nixon. At least he played dirty on a world stage for meaningful stakes—for raw unlimited power, on a grand scale. But you, you two-bit minor league horse-shitter, you sold out for what? To win some grubby divorce case.

"Did you ever consider *why* she was with those four men? Maybe she needs it, can't help it—like *you*." Harry sucked in his breath and started to speak. Nancy interrupted. "Don't try to deny it. Don't be even more of a hypocrite. You think I don't *know?* You think it's easy to live with the realization that your husband has to play around? *Has* to do it to satisfy some childish obsession?"

Harry said nothing. Despite her recent coolness and upset, he had continued to hope that Nancy didn't really know—to tell himself that his discretion had "protected" her from knowing in the past and that Liz Watterson had remained silent about seeing him with Carmel the night of the fire. Now he felt that was a vain hope. He stood silently as Nancy glared at him, her face suffused with anger.

"So who the hell are you to laugh at *Fiona's* needs, to use them like a filthy blackmailing pig to get some crummy win for that poor starved ego? You're worse than she in every way. You're betraying *us*. You're *destroying* me . . . and you don't even know—you don't even care." Nancy hurled her glass of champagne across the room, catching a still amazed Harry in the chest and drenching his gray tweed suit with 1964 Dom Perignon.

She raced up the stairs and slammed the bedroom door. Harry heard the lock turn and the sound of her sobbing. He sat there just shaking his head, still drunk, but not too drunk to recognize that the terrible thing . . . the really awful thing was that she was right.

*I*n the following days the atmosphere at home settled into a cold hostility. Nancy replied to Harry's comments with frigid politeness. Harry, for his part, would have liked things to return to normal. Usually a candid talk would end any fight between them. To do that here, however, would be to reopen the question of his infidelity; and Harry had no stomach for that. He remained silent.

For weeks Harry had promised Carmel that they would go away together, any place where they could be alone, away from the city, even for a short time. A week after the Malone trial, to keep his promise and because of the uncomfortable situation at home, Harry took Carmel to Las Vegas.

He also had business there. As "special counsel" to the Casablanca Hotel, Harry flew to Vegas approximately once a month for staff meetings and other hotel business. He hated the town, but generally enjoyed the drama of holding a key position with one of the affluent strip hotels.

Harry would put on his black pin-striped suit and dark glasses; and looking as darkly sinister as he could, would drift through the casino, playing Humphrey Bogart. Aside from the role playing, the legal and business problems were unusual and often intriguing. He was treated like visiting royalty and for two or three nights it was great fun. Beyond that point, however, the place depressed him immensely and, after a week, he began to feel like a resident of the city of the damned.

This time, however, Harry was working out a complicated financing arrangement for the construction of a high-rise tower on the hotel's extensive grounds. The problems were novel, an intriguing challenge, and he looked forward to sharing the feel, the experience of Las Vegas with Carmel. She, in turn, was thrilled, just at the idea of finally going away somewhere, anywhere with Harry.

Sipping champagne in the quiet luxury of the Casablanca's private jet, Harry told Carmel about his tactics in the Malone trial and about Nancy's surprising reaction to what he had done. He left out Nancy's comparing *him* to Fiona and the likelihood that, because of Liz Watterson, Nancy knew he was involved with Carmel.

When he finished by describing his own feeling that, at bottom, Nancy was probably right about his tactics in the case, Carmel sat forward. "No, damn it!" she cried. "Don't be so ready to accept the guilt she lays on you."

Harry put a calming hand on her arm. "I don't think it's that, Carmel. I think—"

"No," she broke in. "Let me finish. For a successful man in a highly competitive business you're amazingly ready to question your own conduct, to doubt your own motives. You don't need to, you know. You're kind and loving. You do nothing evil, nothing cruel. Without being really conscious of it, you live by a code that makes most men's morals look very shabby indeed.

"But you're so damn ready to accept that you're bad, because she says so and because you're guilty about other things."

Harry started to speak, but Carmel went on.

"You didn't break any rules. You *used* the rules to get the best result for your client. That's why you're so good at what you do. Maybe you used the rules in a way they were never intended to be used, but that's not the same as breaking them . . . not by a long shot.

"You told me it was proper to offer evidence of Fiona's ability to earn money. Well, damn it, she could make money from those films. Sure, a woman in her position wouldn't do it for money; but logically she *could* and logically you were entitled to offer that evidence . . .

even if you felt the judge wouldn't accept it. Other lawyers might be too 'nice' to have taken advantage of that logic. But you're not in there to conform to some country club standard of niceness, but to protect your client any way you can, so long as you don't break the rules.

"Your client *needed* your protection. Without you, Fiona Malone would have won millions of dollars she wasn't entitled to. You *couldn't* break the rules. You never did and never will. Don't you remember the Ball case? You told me you wouldn't use Allison Fong's perjured testimony even though you thought it would cost you the case. You would never break the rules, and you didn't in the Malone case.

"Why she has to take away all the natural joy you feel from a job well done I'll never know, but—"

"Hey!" Harry interrupted. "That's a long speech, and I love you for believing in me. But it's not Nancy's fault. Really. I question these things myself, Carmel; I always have. Nancy just knows when I'm so swollen with success that I need to be brought back to reality. That's not so bad for a guy with an ego like mine."

Carmel looked gravely into Harry's eyes, then spoke softly, tenderly.

"You poor naive bastard. You're like a sweet little boy. But how I love you. Jesus! I love you more than my life."

The sudden change in her mood gave him an uneasy sense of foreboding. After a moment of silence, Carmel took his face in her hands, continuing to look at him, her eyes brimming with love.

"Harry, I want to be with you every minute of the day—every day, forever. When will we be able to do that—be together always? I need you, Harry. Like a fix, I need you—but *all* the time. Harry, listen, tell me where I stand?"

Harry was startled. She'd never pressed him like that before. He was thoroughly caught up in their relationship physically and even emotionally. It swept him along like a surging wave, but there were strange, unsettling qualities about Carmel—not qualities he readily associated with words like "home," "wife" and "forever." Those words involved concepts, ideas, relationships Harry had never really explored with regard to Carmel. Perhaps he had avoided doing so. Now, confronted suddenly with her direct question, he had no desire to mislead her, but had no position prepared, no response ready. He decided to try the truth—or almost the truth.

"Carmel, I told you before, we've found something extraordinary together; devastating and very rare. I know I love you and I love being with you. I want to be with you all the time, but it's early to talk about commitments. We're just beginning as a unit. Let's allow whatever we are to develop for a while—see what happens. There's plenty of time for commitments."

For a fleeting second Carmel looked terrified. Then she turned on her golden smile. "I'm sorry, Harry, I feel so much more than I've ever felt before. I wanted to be reassured that it wasn't going away. But I don't want to pressure you into anything. You're right. Let's let things develop."

She leaned over and kissed him deeply, moving her tongue over and around his, pulling at it, drinking him in hungrily, running her fingers down his inner thigh, bringing him eagerly erect and driving from his mind any thought of being pressured.

The desert heat blasted them as they stepped off the jet at McCarren Field in Las Vegas. Carmel took Harry's arm in hers and leaned her head on his shoulder as they made their way to the Casablanca's air-conditioned limousine waiting for them on the runway.

As the big car moved down the exit ramp into the highway, Harry began to point out the massive strip hotels in the distance, the pink-purple hills rising from the desert behind them. Moving nearer, they could see the varied exotic architecture of the big pleasure palaces. Carmel pointed excitedly as they passed Caesar's Palace with its fountains and countless pseudo-Roman statues.

In what seemed a minute, they swept up the huge circular driveway of the Casablanca, a vast array of irregular Moorish buildings sweeping back and away from them in almost every direction. There were minarets, arches, domes and balconies, all stark white and surrounded by acres of palms, oleander and red, purple, pink and orange bougainvillea.

The car door opened and a seven-foot doorman in Arabic costume swiftly helped Harry and Carmel from the car. "Nice to have you back again, Mr. Cain." He signaled two hustling bellboys, similarly costumed, to move their luggage from the car to the even cooler entry hall of the giant hotel. Courteous greetings came from all sides. "Good morning, Mr. Cain." "Nice to see you again, Mr. Cain."

"You're pre-checked and comped, Mr. Cain. We'll take you right to your suite."

With the bellboys trotting along, bearing their luggage, they were guided by an assistant manager around the massive casino into a small but elegant elevator, down a beautifully landscaped ramp to huge double doors over which was written in bold pseudo-Arabic script "El Jadid."

With a flourish, the assistant manager opened the doors and showed them into one of the Casablanca's most opulent suites. While the bellboys quickly brought in their bags, Harry and Carmel explored. The suite was on two floors. The bedroom on the upper level over-looked a two-story-high living room, the ceiling of which appeared to be a vast desert tent of red and shocking pink that draped the entire suite. Piled along each wall of the living room were five-foot cushions in red, maroon and purple designs, artfully arranged around low coffee tables that appeared to have been covered with soft white goat's skin. A revolving multifaceted glass dome was suspended from the top of the tent and threw soft flickering tongues of multicolored light across every part of the suite.

As the others left, Harry and Carmel made their way up the white spiral staircase to the bedroom. The ceiling and three walls were mirrored, reflecting a hundred repeated images of the huge, round bed surrounded by billowing cushions and pink and purple drapes. Slowly they realized that a Muzak system was quietly playing an Americanized and romanticized version of Arabic music.

Off the bedroom was a bathroom dazzlingly decorated with Moor-ish tiles in blue, green and gold tones and centered around an eight-foot-square sunken tub. The tub and the spacious double sinks had ornate gold fixtures carved to represent birds, serpents and other mythical figures.

Each room of the suite had a small refrigerator-liquor chest fully stocked with champagne, French wines, all kinds of liqueurs and fine crystal glasses.

Carmel threw herself on the round bed and watched her image in each of the mirrors as she began to undulate her body in time to the Arabic music, while slowly, piece-by-piece, removing her cloth-ing. She beckoned with her arms to Harry, who moved beside her, unbuttoning his own things as he began, first slowly, then quickly and lightly, to kiss her ears, her eyes, her arms, her breasts and then to dissolve himself into her and the thousand mirror images of the pleasure they gave each other.

Much later, after luxuriating in the vast sunken tub, they dressed and slowly, with a warm feeling of contentment, made their way to dinner. Harry was in his black casino pin-stripe, a soft white shirt and dove-gray silk tie. Carmel was stunning in a simple white Grecian dress by Halston that clung to her graceful figure as she moved across the bustling lobby to the Tangier Room, a large and lavish dining room decorated in an even more extravagant version of their suite.

Here also, the light was provided by revolving, multicolored domes casting quickly moving rose and gold shadows over the candlelit tables in the center of the room. Along the sides of the huge room were private tables, each covered and separated from the rest of the room by its own desert tent, closed off by pink and purple draperies.

Voluptuous waitresses in see-through harem outfits moved quickly and quietly around the room, attending to the guests' every need. Every guest was a potential "player" and, given the consistent percentage relationship between the amount gambled (the "drop") and the amount won by the house (the "take"), every player meant greater profit for the hotel. And those profits could be very large indeed.

The maitre d' made a great fuss over Harry and led him to a large tent immediately to the right of the entrance to the room. He pulled aside the purple drapery to find, in the candlelit interior, a small private dining room, its table set for five with Buccellati silver, Baccarat crystal and ornate silver service plates.

A tall, slim man in a beautifully tailored dinner jacket rose from the table and moved toward them. His dark, wavy hair was combed to the side and he wore a carefully trimmed mustache. His brown eyes were lit with intelligence and humor. "Harry," he said, devouring Carmel with his eyes. "She's even more radiant than you said."

Harry took his hand and turned to Carmel. "This terminal lecher, Carmel, is Ian Nicholson. He owns the place. . . . Ian, this is Carmel Anderson."

The tall man took her hand in both of his. "Welcome, Carmel. You're my guest here any time you desire, with or without Harry. I mean any time, and I mean with or without notice."

Carmel warmed to Nicholson's gracious welcome. He gently moved her in the direction of the other two diners. "Carmel, this is Pat Tierney, my casino manager, and his friend Lola."

Tierney, a red-faced, white-haired Irishman in his fifties, wore a dark-blue suit with a pale-blue tie that matched his eyes. He had obviously once been very handsome, and he still had a boyish charm. He rose and took Carmel's hand. "Harry," he said, "she is far too beautiful and clearly too much a lady for the likes of you."

Lola, a statuesque brunette with a barely covered, incredible bust, said, "Hi, Carmel," without any real spirit.

They took their places at the table and were immediately served Dom Perignon from what seemed a never-ending series of bottles. As their glasses would reach the half empty level, one of the harem girls would appear to fill it immediately with more of the iced champagne.

Other girls, all young and beautiful, began to bring a series of dishes . . . individual eight-ounce pots of Iranian Caviar followed by lightly sautéed slices of goose liver in a superb sauce of white wine and grapes, a dish Nicholson had discovered at Lamazère's in Paris, where he had paid the chef five thousand dollars for the recipe.

Then, after a sorbet, they had a small but beautifully seasoned trennette al pesto, followed by an excellent rack of lamb, served rare, with a 1934 Chateau Margaux.

The dinner took over two hours. Nicholson was charming and witty, and his favorite subject seemed to be Harry's extraordinary triumphs on behalf of the hotel. He told how Harry had made his purchase of the hotel operation possible four years earlier, and how, by clever bluffing, Harry had won from the owners an option for Nicholson to buy for thirteen million dollars the ground under the hotel that was already worth fifty million; a transaction for which Nicholson graciously said he would never be able to pay Harry sufficiently.

Over brandy, Nicholson told his favorite Harry Cain story. Three years before, he said, he was about to pay a million in cash to an English group that represented a Saudi Arabian prince. After repeated calls to Riyadh, they assured Nicholson that their client would buy the hotel for a profit of twenty-five million dollars, provided that the representatives got their million dollar fee up front.

"They seemed a very reputable group," Nicholson said. "They

were led by a retired English admiral, who was the most distinguished-looking fellow I ever saw in my life. Tall, gray-haired, beautifully mannered. He even wore tiny medals on his dinner jacket.

"Well, Harry's hobby ... aside from the law ... is English history." Carmel looked up in surprise. "Oh yes, Harry's a man of many parts. You never know what subject will stimulate his curiosity. Anyway, the night the million was to be paid, Harry dined with the Englishman. He told the Admiral he was personally confused by Nelson's tactics at Trafalgar, which seemed to him so contrary to everything he'd heard about proper naval warfare. He asked the admiral to explain, if it wouldn't be too much of a bore."

Nicholson stopped and turned to Harry. "What else did you ask him? I've forgotten."

Harry smiled, enjoying the praise and attention. "Oh, some other stuff about Nelson ... I asked if he thought his last words were really 'Kiss me, Hardy' or could have been 'Kismet, Hardy,' which sounds much the same."

"Anyway," Nicholson continued, "an hour later, Harry came to my office grim as hell. 'Ian,' he said, 'if that's an admiral, I'm the Pope. He has no idea who Nelson was, much less what his last words were or even what Trafalgar might be. He's a frigging phony and you should boot his ass out of your hotel....' That's Harry, always timid about expressing his opinions."

"Well, I stalled the payment and spent more time checking these guys out. Naturally, Harry was right. They were the best con men in the business, they'd taken an aircraft manufacturer and a movie studio for a big bundle each and figured a hotel like ours would be easy pickings. They never figured on Professor Cain."

Nicholson rose and put his arm around Harry, looking over at Carmel. "He's the best, Carmel, the very best in the world. Would I have anything else?"

After another hour of drinking, everyone at the table but Tierney was very drunk—pleasantly so, but nevertheless very drunk. Tierney allowed himself a bit of scotch, but kept his mind sharp for the countless decisions he'd have to make throughout the night—extending or denying credit, raising a limit, closing a table or a game and, what seemed to take so much of his time as the hour grew later, directing his assistants to send girls to various rooms.

Harry had explained to Carmel that Vegas was the last bastion of total male chauvinism and that the thousands of available women who flocked to the town were treated like cattle. But Carmel could not imagine how startlingly true that was. There were, of course, the hookers and the show girls, who were permanent. And, on weekends, the town filled with eager amateurs—coeds up from USC and UCLA, secretaries, waitresses, teachers, even housewives, anxious to make some extra money and perhaps to have some fun in the bargain.

The most attractive of these were picked out by Tierney and his aides and allowed bar privileges at the Casablanca. Tierney knew them all by name, had tried most of them himself...in the line of duty, of course. When a big loser left the tables, he was sent a girl or whatever else he might prefer. There was no charge; the hotel paid the girls directly.

During the last part of the dinner, aides regularly contacted Tierney on his two table-side phones. He would reply gently, "Send Gilda up to Mr. Feigenbaum, Jack, along with a magnum of champagne." Then, after laughing with them for a few moments, he would take another call. "Ted, I think Joy and Alice both should go over to Mr. Takahashi's suite tonight. Tell them they're to make him feel very, very special. And give each of them an extra honeybee for me." "What's a 'honeybee'?" Carmel whispered. "A hundred dollar bill," Nicholson replied. "For some unknown reason we all talk about such things in code." Tierney picked up the other phone. "Jack, use Gloria for Mr. Sparks and tell her to wear the kind of outfit he likes. She knows."

All night long it continued. Like a general deploying his troops, Tierney dispatched his girls with detailed instructions on how to please the hotel's male guests and keep them gambling.

Finally, both Nicholson and Tierney excused themselves to attend to business, while Harry, Carmel and Lola strolled to the cavernous, ornate casino, where Lola soon left them to join a group of Japanese businessmen who seemed to be old and dear friends.

Carmel played craps happily and tipsily, while Harry watched. He disliked gambling and his management position at the Casablanca made it illegal for him to play there. Harry had no real technical knowledge of the game, and he was certainly loaded; but from what he could see, Carmel was being given a distinct edge by the stickman with whom Pat Tierney had quietly spoken only a few minutes before. Carmel had started with a self-limited fund of fifty dollars, and after an hour's play, during which waitresses brought them periodic glasses of champagne, she had won more than three thousand dollars. She was ecstatic and very drunk. They left the table and made their way arm-in-arm back to their suite.

The lights were low in the living room and Carmel switched the tape music to the channel labeled "romance." George Shearing's "Foggy Day" filled the room. They took off their shoes and, while Harry went to open a bottle of champagne, Carmel lounged back on a huge cushion spread in the corner of the room. There was a quiet knock at the door.

Harry looked questioningly at Carmel and moved to open it. There in the hall was a stunning redhead over six feet tall in black velvet track shorts, slit high to show her long, shapely legs. She wore black patent high heels and a man's white shirt, its tails tied in a knot above her midriff, its front barely covering her magnificent, outward-thrusting breasts. Her flame-colored hair was pulled back in a pony-tail. Her large green eyes were like two bright emeralds set in high ivory cheekbones.

If she's not a show girl, Harry thought, she sure as hell should be.

"Billy Frankenthal sent me, Mr. Cain. Okay to come in?"

"Sure," Harry said, stepping back and gesturing for her to enter.

Frankenthal was the casino manager at the Deauville, a mile down the strip. Harry had given him some free advice about his divorce; and, undoubtedly, he considered this "gift" only common courtesy, like a case of wine or a silver cigarette case.

The girl moved into the room swinging her hips to accentuate her extraordinary legs.

Seeing Carmel, she hesitated, resting her hand lightly on Harry's arm. "I'm sure Billy didn't know you had someone with you, Mr. Cain," she paused, looking over at Carmel. "But then, maybe your friend would get a kick outta me putting you to sleep my own way. If not, that's okay too. I'll just go on."

Harry glanced nervously over at Carmel, who was leaning on one elbow sizing up their exotic visitor. The girl stood in a dancer's pose, with one out-thrust hip, looking from one to the other of her hosts, waiting for a decision.

Finally Carmel smiled. "Well, I'll put Mr. Cain to sleep myself, but at least stay for a drink."

"Sure." Harry brought her a glass of champagne, took one himself and handed one to Carmel, who rose and came over to them.

"My name's Maya," the girl said with a strange distant smile. "Maya Ivanoff."

They stood talking as they drank—Maya with a kind of strange electric excitement about her, Harry nervous, asking questions, and Carmel quietly interested in what Maya had to say. As Harry thought, she was a dancer in the line at the Deauville. But surprisingly, she was working on her masters degree in psychology at the University of Nevada, living on the money she made dancing and through what she called her extracurricular activities for Billy Frankenthal.

Harry sat quietly while Carmel told Maya about her painting. Maya listened attentively, downing her champagne almost as fast as Harry filled her glass. Carmel and Harry were not far behind. Harry was relaxing now, finding himself getting more and more plastered. Carmel and Maya were obviously feeling much the same. The music had become Latin, a smoothly flowing bossa nova.

Maya did two or three graceful steps, kicked off her shoes and, barefoot, extending one long leg, undid the tie to her ponytail, allowing her massive carrot-colored hair to fall loosely swinging around her shoulders.

She smiled seductively. "Anyone want to dance?" Harry smiled too. Maybe after all, he thought, and moved toward Maya. But at the same moment, Maya put her arm around Carmel and swept her out into the center of the room, moving their bodies beautifully to the exotic Latin beat. After a few moments, Maya moved away from Carmel and, continuing to sway to the beat, untied her midriff and slipped out of her shirt. Harry could not take his eyes from her high, firm breasts. The nipples were rouged and were coming erect, as she moved to the hypnotic Brazilian music.

Then she stopped and slowly, sinuously wriggled out of her shorts, letting them gradually slide down her long legs to the floor, standing there absolutely magnificent, totally nude.

After a moment in which the music changed, Harry started to

move toward her. But she turned away, moving again toward Carmel.

Taking Carmel by the waist, Maya spun her around and, from the back, unzipped her Grecian gown, which slid to the floor of its own weight. Then Maya spun her again so that they faced each other. Carmel wore only tiny bikini pants. "Take them off" said Maya in a low, husky voice; and Carmel did, standing naked before Maya, magnificent herself, her tan body swaying to the music.

Harry was frozen, but erect with excitement. He watched as Maya placed one hand firmly on each of Carmel's shoulders, staring at her, mesmerizing her. Carmel's eyes were glazed over, her teeth clenched, her lower lip pulled down to her gum line as though she was feeling enormous pleasure or pain.

Gradually tightening her grip, Maya slowly forced Carmel down and in, along her own body, until Carmel's face was immediately opposite her rouged breasts. Then Maya moved her shoulders back and forth in time to the rhythm, sliding her taut nipples across Carmel's lips. As if by instinct, Carmel sought to nibble, to kiss, only to find Maya exerting more downward force, pressing Carmel farther and farther toward the floor until, finally, she slid to her knees, staring upward at the giant redhead.

Then, still moving slowly, as if in a dream, Maya removed her hands from Carmel's shoulders and, taking her thick golden hair in each hand, forced Carmel's head forward until her lips were close to Maya's undulating groin. Maya stood that way, barely swaying her hips to the Latin rhythm, tantalizing Carmel, holding her only a maddening inch away from the dancing ginger mound that seemed to so transfix her. Carmel's eyes grew wild now, rolling with excitement and desire. Finally, Maya thrust her hips forward, pressing herself out and up until she met Carmel's hungry mouth.

Throwing her arms around Maya's buttocks, Carmel buried her face in the carrot-colored bush, where she began to kiss and suck, as Maya slowly revolved her hips, hunching them forward at the end of each small circle to thrust herself harder and harder at Carmel's demanding mouth and probing pink tongue.

Pulling Carmel with her, Maya dropped to the nearby cushions, rolling her upper body so her head was above Carmel's thighs, her now wet vagina above Carmel's upthrust mouth, her long legs stretched out on each side of Carmel's head. Carmel lay on her back, her

—162—

mouth still buried in the carroty muff thrusting and revolving above her.

When she realized that Maya's face was now hovering over her own throbbing mound, Carmel spread her legs, pulling her knees back as far as she could and hunching upward toward Maya's wide, beckoning mouth.

Keeping her face just above Carmel, Maya began to plant tiny kisses and maddening flicks of her tongue on the sensitive places of Carmel's inner thighs, along the erotic line between her vagina and anus, then on the outer lips of her vagina, only to move teasingly away, up along her belly and then back and back again, over and over.

Carmel began to moan, while Maya licked at her lightly, tantalizingly, until, unable to stand it any longer, Carmel cried out, "Do it. Oh, do it," and seizing Maya's hair, pulled her face down to Carmel's steaming labia.

Now, using her skillful mouth and tongue, Maya began to work in earnest on Carmel, driving her into a frenzy of pleasure.

Each girl was sweating, writhing and twisting, groaning with sensation. Each had her hands on the other's bottom, pulling the other girl fiercely and hungrily to her own mouth.

Finally, Carmel began to scream with the onset of her orgasm, arching her back and digging at Maya's backside with her fingernails. Maya's moan became lower and deeper as she too reached climax, thrusting, pistoning her bottom to force all the pleasure she could from Carmel's eager mouth.

At first, Harry was achingly hard with excitement watching them, hearing their cries of joy, seeing their beautiful bodies intertwined, Carmel's thick, golden hair spread out on the cushion, a frame for Maya's thrusting ass. Maya's flaming hair, richly abundant, flowed over Carmel's tanned, spread thighs.

But as time passed and they continued delighting, transporting each other, wholly oblivious to Harry's presence, he realized he had no place in this. None at all. He paced the floor restlessly, then slid down onto one of the huge cushions, stretching his legs out before him. No one noticed. No one cared. He glanced nervously at his watch and idly reached for a copy of *Time* magazine lying on the coffee table. The cover story was on the California Supreme Court, a story Gail had worked on and had frequently discussed with Harry.

Looking at the magazine cover, not even conscious of the association, he found himself thinking of Gail, of what she was facing, of the hurt and disappointment that had to follow, of what that miserable son of a bitch Milgrim was doing to her life.

Angry and depressed now, feeling abandoned by the two women still entwined on the floor, he picked up an open bottle of champagne, turned and, silently closing the living room door behind him, went upstairs to bed.

In the morning Harry awoke to find Carmel in bed beside him, her blond hair flung out across the pillow, a peaceful smile on her sleeping face. His head throbbing, he showered, dressed and quietly left the room to attend the series of meetings that were to occupy the day.

He met Ian Nicholson in the hotel board room and they spun quickly into the round of conferences with mortgage bankers, accountants, title company officials and contractors that were essential to the high-level financing Harry was there to arrange. Sandwiched between these critical meetings were hurried conferences more characteristic of his Las Vegas trips... decisions on personnel, Gaming Commission problems and procedures to avoid theft in the casino. Soon, Harry was able to lose himself in dealing with the huge sums and complex legal and business problems that were involved in the operation of a first-class Vegas hotel.

By five o'clock, when he and Carmel left for the plane, Harry was exhausted and determined that, in the future, he would avoid hard-drinking nights before all-day meetings. He was getting too old for the process of making countless critical decisions all day long, under intense pressure, while suffering from a world-class hangover.

On the jet back to Los Angeles, Harry was quiet and Carmel was affectionate, holding his hand, resting her head on his shoulder, rubbing the back of his neck and generally trying to relax him.

Neither of them mentioned the night before until they were back inside the house on Sweetzer and Carmel had made them both martinis. Then she faced the subject head-on. "Harry, are you sore about last night—about Maya?"

"No," he said coldly, "I'm not sore."

She smiled, "Does your face know it?"

Now Harry smiled too. "Look," he said, "I don't really know how I feel about it. You're free to do what you like. No strings. That's what I've always said. But it was a surprise."

She came over and sat on the arm of his chair. "Harry, I think I know what happened."

"Yeah?"

"Yes, I think I can make it with no problem, make it with just my love for you, I mean, if I've got security with you. But if I don't, it's tough and I may backslide, drift into things like last night. What you said yesterday in the car about no commitments... that shook me, Harry, really scared me; and I think, subconsciously, I had to show myself I could find comfort elsewhere."

Harry nodded and Carmel went on. "Harry, we've got to face it. I'm not going to make it without some commitment from you. I get more and more dependent on you each day. I love you more than my life, Harry, and if I'm insecure with you, I'll backslide like last night, with the milkman or the plumber or someone—I know it. It'll kill you. You won't stay around. It'll kill me too, Harry. I'll end up a suicide, sure as hell, or in an institution.

"We've got so much going for us, we mustn't lose it, Harry. It's our only chance. All you have to do is tell me you'll always be there. Move in here. No marriage. Not now anyway. But if things work out after you've lived here a while, then who knows? Try it. Could you do it, do you think?"

Harry waited for a time before he replied, trying to get his conflicting thoughts in order. His physical need for Carmel was extraordinary. And there was more than that. He loved her. Respected her too... for her intelligence, her talent, her honesty, her humor. But always there, back in the dark recesses of his mind, was his intolerance... no, worse than that, revulsion... at her emotional weakness, her grotesque hysteria over insects, her old compulsion to be sexually degraded. At bottom, for all she was, she could never fit those rigid criteria Harry's environment had long ago conditioned him to demand in a "wife." She was, instead, one of the others...

needed, loved, even treasured; but not married.

Nor, despite the newly emerging hostility and coldness pervading his home, was he prepared to leave Nancy. Not now anyway. Probably not ever. Aside from her tirade of last week, Nancy was sound, loving—a fine lady; and whatever their problems, they'd been together too long, shared too many things, to cast her aside . . . at least for what he thought he'd find if he went into a permanent relationship with Carmel.

More than anything, Harry was totally exhausted and felt Carmel was unfairly pressuring him for a commitment at the worst possible time. He could stall, but despite his irritation, he really didn't want to mislead her.

Finally, he got up and began to pace. "Look, Carmel, I'm going to level with you. I love you, I adore being with you. You're right—we have something really rare and special. But I'm just not ready to leave Nancy and move in here. Maybe sometime later. I don't know. I know I'm exhausted tonight, and this really isn't the time to get into it . . . not yet. Couldn't we just see more and more of each other, be together without living together, without some kind of commitment?"

Her face fell. She put her drink down and replied slowly.

"I can't make it that way, Harry. Can you honestly say you'd put up with what happened last night . . . time after time?"

"I don't know, I just don't know."

"Well, I know. Someday . . . after I got even more dependent on you, after I really couldn't live without you, you'd bolt, and it would be ugly and final, and I'd be destroyed, finished forever. I can't do that, Harry, I can't—"

Suddenly Carmel began to scream at the top of her lungs, waving her arms wildly. Harry was stunned and then saw that a huge gray moth was battering itself against the lamp shade, just beside Carmel, and that this had thrown her into a hysterical fit. "Jesus, Carmel," he shouted, "it's only a Goddamn moth. Now stop it!"

His voice affected her like a slap in the face. She stood still and white, trembling. "You're disgusted with me," she sobbed. "Bugs terrify me, you know that, but this time, I disgust you. And I love you so, Harry, I love you so. I don't ever want to disgust you."

She moved forward toward the moth. "I'll prove I love you, Harry," she said, her eyes glassily fixed on the fluttering moth. "I'll show you. I'll make you know how much I love you."

Slowly, moving like a sleepwalker, she reached out and closed her hand over the huge gray insect. With trembling hands, she held it up by the wings, tears running down her pale cheeks. "See him, Harry, see him. Do you want me to eat him, Harry? That's how much I love you, Harry. You know how I feel about bugs, Harry. It's killing me to touch this thing. But I'll eat him, Harry—eat this bug—*for you*, I'll eat him right now—eat him alive."

As in a trance, she brought the big moth to her lips and took a small bite from his pounding gray wing. Weeping now, she chewed and chewed at the bit of insect, looking straight at Harry the entire time.

Harry could take no more. Moving quickly, he smashed the moth from her hand and crushed it with his foot. Holding her by the waist, he put his finger into her mouth, pulled out what he could find of the chewed wing tip and threw it to the floor. Then he pulled her to him, comforting her in his arms as she wept long and bitterly, until Harry too began to cry.

He held her there, standing and swaying together until their tears had stopped and she no longer trembled. Then he led her to the bedroom and helped her undress and slip into a night gown and robe. He did this tenderly, lovingly—as he had with Gail when she was a child.

They were silent now, knowing he would leave. Hand in hand they moved to the front door.

There Carmel stopped and looked up at him, her face pale, drawn, chewing on her lower lip—a desolate child. "You mean it, don't you? You're not going to do it, are you... ever?"

Harry knew he could deny it—could persuade her they'd be together someday. He knew she wanted to hear that—would accept it. Yet he said nothing. After a moment, she opened the door and, standing with him on the porch, looked up at the millions of stars in the black California sky. "I love you, Harry, I'll always love you, always to the day I die. Remember that, Harry, remember it." Harry was silent. He hugged her tightly and buried his face in her golden hair, smelling that marvelous scent that was hers. Then, in a moment, she was gone and the door closed behind her.

*T*he next week began with an announcement in the trade papers that Consolidated Studios had reluctantly decided not to renew Sonny Ball's contract. No reason was given, but it was plain that the publicity from the case had taken its toll. Even winning, Sonny had lost.

During that same week, Harry was caught up in the regular press of his business, plus preparation of an important motion for summary judgment in a plagiarism case. At the same time, he was trying to complete the Casablanca's financing arrangement, and it was proving more complex than his clients had expected. When his thoughts went to Carmel, he was generally able to push them away and concentrate on the business at hand. He told himself it wasn't really *over* with Carmel, that neither of them would do without—*could* do without—their shattering physical union, but that it was best to let things cool off for a time.

Meanwhile, the coldness and hostility at home began to dissipate. Nancy was friendly for the most part, sometimes even affectionate. But still there was a reserve, a residue of tension that prevented any attempt to dismiss her outburst over the Malone case as the result of too much alcohol or accumulated resentment over his virtually abandoning her during the long period of trial preparation. Nor could he tell himself she didn't really know about Carmel (and the others) or didn't really care. He knew better—knew that Nancy felt real and deep-seated anger over the way their lives had gone, over the things he'd done, and was doing—knew that with her anger now spoken, openly acknowledged, it could never quite be the same between them.

With the Parlier trial approaching, Harry was deeply concerned about Lee Parlier, and whether he could effectively try the case, given his personal distaste for the man. One thing he had to do— he had to speak frankly about the situation with Jay Kelly—and soon, before it was too late to make a change.

The afternoon light was fading as Harry sat across from Kelly at El Jardin, in the old section of town near Echo Park. They'd met after court and, unable to resist the freshly heated wheat tortillas with guacamole and carne al pastor, they'd eaten far too much and washed it down with an abundance of Corona Extra. Harry pushed back from the table and covered his glass with his hand. *"Nada más, Luis,"* he groaned to the smiling owner. *"Muy rico, pero nada más, por favor."*

While they ate, Harry had briefed Kelly on the Parlier case, making it clear that, given Parlier's smarminess, his gross and obvious insincerity and his absurd dress and appearance, Harry doubted the case could be won and was not at all sure he even wanted to try it.

Kelly had listened to it all without response. Now he put his glass down and leaned back in his chair. "I know he's hard to take, Harry. He's just his own worst enemy—like a stupid clumsy kid trying to pretend he's something else—and doing it badly.

"But you know, Harry, sometimes I think we're all kids—always. That all men are. We start out that first day in the school yard, lower lip stuck out, arms folded, fists clenched, trying to seem so tough. Can't cry, can't seem scared, even though we're fucking terrified. And we start competing, trying right away to beat the other guy, to be first, to be toughest, to be best. And we keep up that corrosive process until it warps us, rots us—until we're never real, never unaware for a moment of how we look, whether we're ahead or behind.

"Then we reach the point where we never draw a relaxed breath, never escape anxiety over the effect we're having on everyone else— and, always, there's that constant, unquenchable thirst to prove ourselves—to beat somebody."

Kelly paused and smiled. "You know, if I weren't blasted on this Mexican beer, I'd never be going on like this. But Goddamn it, Harry, you point out the artificiality in Lee . . . and I know it's there . . . but sometimes I could weep for *all of us* having to go through life like we do, scared, posturing, baring our fangs like frightened monkeys trying to outbluff a bigger, stronger animal."

The waiter filled Kelly's glass. Harry put his hand over his own glass to avoid the refill. Kelly drank half the beer and continued.

"You know, Harry, sometimes I think the only mature people in the world are women. You may think that's crazy, but consider it. Women never have to go through the horseshit we do. They get the chance to grow, to develop, to be sound. God, I envy them that. Maybe they ought to be running the Goddamn world, Harry. They'd do a damn-sight better job, and they deserve the chance too. But we poor men, poor stunted bastards, God help us."

He finished his beer, wiped his mouth with the back of his hand, then leaned forward, looking directly into Harry's eyes. "Listen—all this wasn't just a drunken Irish lecture. It had a point. The point is—don't come down too hard on poor Lee. Please. Think about all of us—all of our miserable frightened posturings. Lee's just had to scramble a little more than most of us, and he's probably gone just a little more off-kilter than we have, and is a hell of a lot more scared. So give him a break, will ya?" Kelly flashed his infectious Irish grin.

Harry smiled back, moved by the big Irishman's words. "Okay, Jay, I'll hang in. Don't worry."

He meant it. But, even as he spoke, he still had major doubts about ever working successfully with Lee Parlier.

*T*wo weeks later, driving back from federal court, his adrenaline still flowing from the give-and-take of oral argument, Harry began to feel the old hunger for Carmel, an overpowering desire he could not recall feeling for anyone else, ever. He remained painfully aware of what seemed real instability in Carmel . . . an out-of-control quality he felt unequipped and unwilling to handle. He knew now that his inability to deal with that side of her nature would rule out any kind of permanent relationship. But none of that overcame the compelling excitement he felt at thinking of her, imagining them together, arms and legs intertwined, giving each other joy and pleasure beyond anything he had experienced before. Almost without willing it, he found himself driving along Fountain Avenue, turning into Sweetzer and pulling up near Carmel's small cottage.

He was smiling as he walked up the path. Ringing the bell, he thought of what he'd say to put her at ease, to explain why he'd stayed away so long.

There was no answer. The bell was working. Harry could hear it ringing inside the house. He went around the house and found a spare, elderly man in overalls pulling weeds from the lawn.

"Hello. I'm looking for Miss Anderson. Do you know if she'll be back soon?"

The man raised himself stiffly, shielding his eyes from the afternoon sun. "She's moved out, mister. Left several days ago."

Harry felt his heart stop. His mouth was suddenly almost too dry to speak. "Where did she go? Did she leave a forwarding address?"

"No . . . just up and left. Wasn't no lease, you know. Don't know where she's gone."

Harry just stood there, not knowing what else to say, not wanting to leave, to end it. Finally he could see the man looking anxiously down at the weeding that remained to be done. "Well, okay then, thanks; and listen . . . if you hear from her will you have her call me, please?" Harry handed him a card. The man peered at it and put it in his shirt pocket.

"Sure thing, Mr. Cain. Sorry you missed her." He bent to continue his gardening. Harry turned away and went out to the street, back to his car. He was numb, his mind sliding for the moment away from the realization that Carmel might be finally, permanently gone.

That night it hit him. Alone at his desk, he was suddenly overwhelmed by a stunning sense of loss, and found himself completely unable to work. This would pass, he knew. Or would it?

Two days later, Harry got a call at the office from Pat Tierney in Vegas. "Harry, I thought you ought to know something—and tell me to butt out if you like, okay?"

"Sure, Pat, what is it?"

"Your girl, Carmel, she's up here."

"Up there?"

"Yeah, She's been up here a couple of weeks. I ran into her last Friday and she said she was staying temporarily with a dancer friend of hers, that she didn't have a job. But I heard today she got fixed up with Billy Frankenthal at the Deauville."

"You mean he's sending her out to rooms?"

"Yeah, that's what I figure, Harry. I'm sorry I had to be the one to tell you. I just thought you'd want to know."

"No, that's okay, Pat, you did the right thing. Thanks."

"Yeah, for nothing. Anything I should tell her, Harry?"

"No, that's all over, Pat. Nothing more to say."

"Okay, Harry. Sorry."

"Sure, Pat . . . talk to you later." Harry put down the phone, with a sick feeling deep in the pit of his stomach. He turned to the work on his desk, but no thoughts would come, only pictures he didn't want to see. Fat Billy Frankenthal sending Carmel out to satisfy kinky Arabs, drunken Japanese and slavering Turks. God knows what else. Sent out to spread her legs for the high rollers, and, worse than that, loving it. You bet that was worse. Goddamn fucked-up nympho, he thought, I really loved her. Why did we have to blow it? Why? No answer came.

*D*uring the next few weeks Harry was able to keep his mind off Carmel only by immersing himself totally in his work. The Casablanca financing deal had closed, but other cases, other matters, kept piling up. His days were filled with an over-demanding schedule plus the rigorous preparation for the Parlier case.

Harry tried to learn everything he could about Alec Heath and Neil Talbot. He asked everyone he thought might know something and followed every lead. He asked ex-girlfriends, interviewed Talbot's former houseman. He studied UBS's reports to the Securities and Exchange Commission seeking information about the network and its principal executives. He had a difficult client, okay, but damn it, he'd be prepared.

He planned a trip to New York after the first of the year, intending to use every contact he had that might be helpful in developing information about the case. He retained a good handwriting expert . . . or, as the man described himself, "a questioned-documents examiner," and he began the endless process of working with Lee Parlier himself.

Gradually, battling Parlier all the way, he worked toward his goal of presenting the irritating little man as a likable, believable witness and someone to whom the jury would be willing to award ten million dollars.

At the same time, Harry began working on Parlier's appearance. After weeks of argument, he persuaded the man to stop plastering his hair with grease, and took him to Novello's in Beverly Hills, where, as if by magic, Tony Novello gave him a fluffy, boyish hair style that completely changed his appearance. Then Harry persuaded Parlier to put aside the tight-fitting jackets and balloon slacks. The day before Christmas, Harry took him to Carroll's and found him three very plain, trim suits in gray, blue and brown.

The change was extraordinary. The slippery 1920s con-man was gone, replaced by a somewhat nondescript but honest-looking little man—not handsome, but certainly neat and respectable.

On Christmas morning, Harry and Nancy visited Gail's apartment to leave their gifts and share an eggnog. Gail was warm and loving and, to Harry, seemed to have that special translucent beauty that comes with pregnancy. It was clear now that she was going to have the baby. She had bought everything she'd need and set it up in what had been her spare bedroom and was now called the "nursery." Gail proudly showed them the hand-carved Norwegian crib, the tiny pink and blue knitted outfits she and her friends had made, the colorful plastic mobile that would hang over the baby, encouraging hand and eye coordination.

While Harry watched a football game on television, Gail and Nancy talked alone in the nursery. Occasionally, Harry could over-hear snatches of Gail's conversation about disposable diapers and good local schools.

Harry had intended to convince her that, even though it was late for an abortion, putting the baby up for adoption was the only sensible course. He left without raising the subject.

In the car on the way home, Nancy suddenly began to cry. Softly sobbing, she told Harry how she ached for Gail, how worried she was about how Gail's life would now develop. Harry put his arm around her and, pulling her over next to him, tried to give her what comfort he could. Grimly, miserably, he got them home.

Later, they opened their gifts and ate Nancy's traditional Christmas cassoulet. They did the normal things, but Harry felt far from normal.

Silently, he resolved that he would find a way to convince Gail, to solve the problem. He had no idea how.

*B*efore trial, most cases in the California court system are assigned to a judge whose job is to see whether the case can be settled through a mandatory but informal conference in the judge's chambers.

In mid-January, Harry appeared at the mandatory settlement conference in the Parlier case. He was still carrying a grudge over what UBS had done to his friend Teddy Brenner. But a good settlement was far better for his client than a trial, and Harry wanted no hint of his personal feelings to interfere with the settlement process.

In the courtroom, before the start of the settlement conference, Harry politely introduced himself to the UBS lawyer, Maynard Aldrich, who had flown out from New York.

Aldrich was a large man, well over two hundred pounds, at least six feet two. He had straight gray hair, a florid complexion and pale-blue eyes that were extremely small for his large, round face. He was the very picture of the eastern establishment in his double-breasted oxford-gray suit, white-collared, light-blue shirt and navy silk tie.

"Oh yes, Cain, I've seen your picture in the papers," he said coldly, turning away to confer with a young attorney carrying two huge Mark Cross briefcases initialed "C&C" . . . Cavanaugh & Cutler.

Harry seethed but tried not to show it. He was not surprised by the man's patent hostility. Harry read him as a bigot and a prig. A background check showed that Aldrich was old-line New York society, Groton, Porcellian at Harvard and, later, that exotic addition to the background of so many similar men, the CIA. Aldrich had been deputy director for some four years, having taken a leave of absence from his law firm. Harry's grades at Harvard would have put him at least a hundred places ahead of Aldrich in the class, had they been in the same year at the law school. But if they had been, Aldrich would still have said, "No *gentleman* finished ahead of me."

Nothing further was said between Harry and Aldrich until they were ushered into the judge's chambers. Judge Peter DeMarco had been assigned to handle the settlement conference. His father had been a judge before him, and he had known Harry well when they were both practicing attorneys. No genius, he was nevertheless a popular judge, hard-working, courteous and scrupulously fair.

DeMarco wore neither his robes nor his suit jacket. Instead, he had pulled a beige cardigan sweater over his shirt, which was unbuttoned at the collar, his tie loosened and pulled somewhat askew. The conference being in chambers, such informality was customary.

He told the lawyers he had read the file and felt strongly that this was a case that should be settled, not tried. He asked if any offers had been made. Both sides replied that there had not been. Aldrich added that he was prepared to make an offer, but that it would be his best and only offer. Harry could either say "Yes" or "No." Aldrich was not interested in any counteroffer.

"Okay, Mr. Aldrich," the judge said, lighting a cigarette, "let's hear your offer."

Aldrich leaned back and focused his tiny blue eyes on the judge. "First, Your Honor, I'd like to make a brief explanation of how my clients view the case. To begin with, we have the plainest kind of fraud here by Mr. Parlier in concealing and lying about his criminal record. That makes the contract voidable by the network, so Mr. Parlier gets nothing. But let's suppose a jury were to feel that there was no fraud. This man, Parlier, still committed the most flagrant and material breach of contract imaginable. He broke into the network offices to steal their secrets. Even without the fraud, he was correctly and properly fired and is still entitled to nothing. But even if there had been no fraud and no breach of contract either, the only item that could possibly generate any substantial sum of money for Mr. Parlier would be his claimed share of the 'High Rise' television series, and he could only receive that if he could prove he was the creator of the series. The evidence is quite clear, Your Honor, that he was *not*. Mr. Neil Talbot, a senior network executive, created the series and Mr. Parlier attempted—again fraudulently—to take credit for that outstanding contribution of his fellow worker. Accordingly, Your Honor, we are not prepared to make an offer in the area that someone like Mr. Cain will undoubtedly suggest."

Aldrich paused and took a small notebook from his suit pocket. He put on rimless glasses and read from his notes "The plaintiff is prepared to offer Mr. Parlier one hundred thousand dollars, payable at twenty thousand dollars per year for five years. This would be offered, Your Honor, only on the condition that Mr. Parlier acknowledge publicly, in a statement to the media prepared by us, that he was not the creator of 'High Rise.'"

Judge DeMarco, looking somewhat amused, turned to Harry for comment.

Harry was angry but remained determined not to show it. He sat back, seemingly relaxed, and replied with a smile.

"Judge, since you've read the file, I don't have to tell you that's ridiculous. We'll show there was no fraud and no breach either, and that Mr. Parlier very certainly was the creator of 'High Rise.' Mr. Parlier's damages on the cross-complaint amount to ten million dollars. No rational, sincere person could evaluate his chances at less than fifty-fifty, and that makes the settlement value of the case, as I see it, at least five million."

DeMarco smiled again, "I thought you'd feel that way, Mr. Cain. I would guess Mr. Aldrich thinks you've got considerably less than a fifty-fifty chance here, and my own view is that he's probably right. But I'm inclined to agree that a hundred thousand dollars, even paid in cash, is much too low to have any prayer of being accepted. Mr. Aldrich, shall we confer alone to discuss whether there is any flexibility in that offer?"

"No, Your Honor, there's no need for that. I can tell you here and now we'll never offer more than one hundred thousand, not to a man like Parlier."

The judge looked a little bit annoyed and turned to Harry. "Well, let's try a different tack. I doubt, Mr. Cain, that with numbers this size, you're firm at five million. Why not give me your best offer. What's the lowest you'll go?"

"The lowest I'd recommend, Your Honor, would be the five million, paid right now in cash, and that's only because settlement is in my client's best interest. Frankly, I'd rather try the case, and Mr. Aldrich is making me feel more and more like trying it every minute we spend here."

There was a trace of humor in DeMarco's eyes as he crushed out his cigarette. He sat back, looking at them both, before he spoke. "Gentlemen, in my own view, five million dollars is still too high for this case. I could see it settling in the range of one and a half to two million dollars, but there's really no point in my leaning on Mr. Cain if you're really firm at one hundred thousand, Mr. Aldrich; a figure I must tell you I consider totally unreasonable, especially on the part of a large corporation toward what appears to have been a generally productive employee."

Aldrich reddened. He spoke with feeling. "Lee Parlier was no productive employee, Your Honor. He was a crook, a convicted swindler who continued his pattern of dishonesty while taking my clients' money. He deserves nothing... except possibly another trip to prison, and only Mr. Cain's kind would take on such a case."

Harry felt a surge of anger, but before he could speak, Judge DeMarco leaned forward across his desk, the humor gone from his eyes. "Mr. Aldrich, I don't know what you mean by 'Mr. Cain's kind,' but I don't like the sound of it. Mr. Cain is an honorable practitioner before this bar and you don't help your cause with that kind of personal attack."

Aldrich looked back at the judge and spoke with equal force. "Judge, I have my own opinions about people and about lawyers I deal with, and I don't hide them very well. We're in chambers, not before a jury, and we're all grown-ups, so I see no harm in being frank. However, I'll put aside my feelings about Mr. Cain in deference to the court. There is an important matter I think he's overlooking in his haste to collect his fee."

"Hey!" Harry bellowed.

"That's enough, Mr. Aldrich," the judge warned.

"Of course, Your Honor. I'm sorry. What Mr. Cain should remember is that Mr. Parlier has been lucky enough to get no news coverage of this case that disclosed his criminal record. We deliberately tried to keep his record away from the press, and I was amazed that it hasn't come out... yet. At the trial, of course, it must come out. The press will be there. There will be television news coverage as well, and the world will soon learn that Mr. Parlier is an ex-convict, convicted of fraud. Unfortunately, so will Mr. Parlier's children. So I think, Your Honor, that Mr. Cain will best serve his client's interest by grabbing that hundred thousand."

Now, Harry spoke up. "Judge, there's a word for that. It's called blackmail. It's just as much blackmail when practiced by a distinguished New York law firm as by a common criminal. And I'll tell

—177—

you right now we're not paying. We'll try this case and I want to make it clear that, in light of Mr. Aldrich's conduct here today, I will not recommend five million or seven million or any settlement at all, *ever*.

"Gentlemen," the judge said, rising from his chair, "I think you'll agree with me that this is a waste of time. If either of you changes his view in the future, I'm available at any time to try and facilitate a settlement. But for now, it's obvious there's nothing to be done here."

"Thank you, Your Honor," said Harry.

"Thank you, Your Honor," said Aldrich.

Both left the judge's chambers without further word to the other, each determined to bring the case to trial and win it decisively.

*I*n the car, driving back to his office, Harry felt the resentment, the anger at the pit of his stomach. After all these years, all the visible success—even adulation, he was still deeply aware that he was unacceptable to people like Maynard Aldrich. He'd felt it at Harvard. His intelligence and exceptional grades, his knowledge of history and literature, his looks, spirit and wit . . . none of it meant a thing. *To them* he was nobody. He'd tried to adopt their clothing—the shapeless tweed jacket, frayed Brooks button-down— protective coloration. Only it didn't protect. He could see it in their eyes, growing cold, glazing over. He could hear it in their voices, feel it . . . a palpable thing there in the room.

Oh, there were many people from the same background as Aldrich who were not like that. It was rarely that way with the women. With women, Harry seemed able to break through any barrier, to form relationships that transcended things like background, religion and class.

And he had male friends as well, who were bright, broad-minded, easy to be with, ready to accept Harry for what he was, even though they were from the oldest of New York or New England families.

But, so often, to men like Aldrich, Harry was an outsider—not a "gentleman"—no family, no background, no acceptable school, no club—and his religious affiliation? No need even to discuss *that*.

That was years ago. But he'd felt it ever since, each time he'd encountered an Aldrich, that sick feeling that no matter what he did, what battles he won, what fame he achieved, he was less than a person in their eyes. He tried to ignore it, to dismiss such people as silly, shallow bigots. But it hurt. It angered. And it was there— every time.

The remedy for that, Harry thought, switching lanes and angrily flooring the gas pedal, was to beat the cocksuckers. He looked over at the hills flying by, the silly "Hollywood" sign, glaring white in the sunshine. He smiled and relaxed a bit. That's right, he thought, that's always been the remedy—always—you've got to beat 'em.

As the weeks passed, Harry began to think more and more of Carmel. He felt it wasn't really *over* between them. Somehow, somewhere, they'd come together again. He felt he was even ready to accept what she'd done up in Vegas. He knew *why* she'd done it, and once it was behind her, he could put it behind himself as well. He thought that most probably she'd return to L.A., a place she loved, a place they'd shared—could share again.

Meanwhile, in many ways, Nancy seemed close to her old self again. She was generally warm and friendly with Harry and he felt no trace of hostility. They shared a growing anxiety over Gail's pregnancy, realizing, now, that the baby was really going to come, to stay, to be a permanent part of their lives. Still there was a distance between them, a distance Harry hadn't felt before the night of the fire. It was manifested in many ways. For years, at the end of the evening, they'd lain side by side in bed, sharing their thoughts, having rambling, personal talks about their friends, themselves, everything. Now it was different. Nancy would smile tenderly, touch Harry's shoulder lightly, and, with a quiet "good night darling," turn out the light. The problem was still there—an undefinable thing between them. Harry felt it often and wondered if it would ever be gone.

*H*arry took the red-eye to New York, where he had only two days to discover the facts he needed for the Parlier trial. He loved New York and flew there often, but this was not a trip on which he could enjoy the city. He crammed dozens of meetings and interviews into his brief visit, crisscrossing midtown Manhattan at a blistering pace. Even dinner at Christ Cella's was devoted to an attempt to wheedle, pressure and charm inside information from a former UBS executive.

Riding to the airport the next afternoon, Harry slumped back into the plush velvet seat of the limo, reviewing his notes. He'd gathered considerable information about UBS, Heath and other aspects of the case. Much of this could be helpful at the trial. Other things he'd learned seemed unrelated to the issues in the case as he saw them now. But you never knew. Cases changed as the testimony started to come in. New claims, new issues developed. Yesterday's plan had to be revised, sometimes abandoned; and facts that had seemed irrelevant before the trial started could ultimately win or lose a case. In trials, flexibility was often the key to success. Maybe in life too, Harry thought. With a sigh he stuffed his notes back into his jacket pocket and gazed out at the gray, boring sprawl of Queens Boulevard.

*W*hen he returned to Los Angeles, Harry worked almost daily with Parlier, cross-examining him, helping him to anticipate the kinds of questions he'd face from Aldrich, setting traps for the New York lawyer, things Parlier would say and do that would lead their opponent into mistakes, perhaps into bringing out damaging testimony about Alec Heath or the network that otherwise would never come out. Harry was never completely satisfied with his preparation in any case, but gradually he and Parlier were approaching a state of readiness with which Harry could at least feel relatively comfortable.

It was a good thing. Harry's share of the potential recovery in the Parlier case began to look more and more significant. As in most years, Harry's income was large but irregular, while the expenses . . . the house, the help, Nancy's clothes, the trips, the cars . . . all continued relentlessly crossing his desk, even in those periods when no income arrived. And the taxes! My God, they were enormous. Like a number of other high-earning, high-living lawyers, there were times when Harry had to borrow from the bank just to meet his payroll.

By February, with Carl Malone's large bill still unaccountably unpaid, Harry's bank loan was coming due, and the trickle of incoming fees was agonizingly slow. Malone's bill was three hundred thousand dollars, a figure Harry considered more than fair, in light of the months he had put in on the case and the enormous amount of money he had saved his client. The bill had been sent out three times; and it was now long past due. Finally, Harry had sent Malone a courteous note suggesting that he'd probably mislaid it. Still no payment had come. There was no concern about Carl's ability to pay, and no doubt about his having been pleased with the result; but, soon, Harry would have to speak to him.

With Parlier, he could win big—solve the immediate problem. He always wanted to win and he particularly wanted to beat Maynard Aldrich and get those bastards for what they'd done to Teddy Brenner. But he had to face the fact that this time he also *needed* to win . . . for the money.

*U*nited Broadcasting Systems v. Parlier finally came to trial on a Friday in late February. It supplanted Harry's worries about money, his concern about Gail and the surprising need he still felt for Carmel. It supplanted everything. As always, he was completely absorbed in the trial, totally focused, totally concentrating on the case.

The courtroom, Department 47 of the Superior Court, was one that Harry recalled with fondness. Two years before he'd tried and won a hard-fought paternity case there, and the familiar surroundings gave him a feeling of luck and confidence.

Between the network's house attorneys and the Cavanaugh & Cutler personnel, there were six lawyers crowded around the UBS counsel table as the case started. Harry and John Matsuoka sat alone, flanked by a nervous Lee Parlier. As in many of Harry's cases, the press was well represented in the gallery. Alec Heath was, after all, one of the glamour figures of the television business, and the whole world loved "High Rise," the series that would play such a major role in the trial.

Harry worried about the judge. Elizabeth Hailey was a straightlaced patrician. Plain, horsey and highly intelligent, she came from an old-line San Marino family. She might consider Maynard Aldrich "her kind." Harry—with his flamboyant reputation and Hollywood connections—definitely was not.

Observing Judge Hailey's pale, angular face, thin lips and tightly knotted bun, Harry made a mental note that, for the rest of the trial, his Gucci loafers should be the ones without the big gold buckles.

Picking a jury, opening statements and the testimony of three preliminary witnesses for the network occupied the first two weeks of trial. The network's side of the case was presented first, since, technically, UBS was suing to declare Parlier's contract canceled and it was, therefore, the plaintiff. Parlier was the defendant and had also cross-complained for the ten million dollars he claimed was due him under the contract for "High Rise."

The first critical point in the case was the testimony of Alec Heath. As Harry had feared, the network president made a fine impression on the jury. Heath was a slim, athletic-looking man in his late forties, with black hair graying at the temples and startlingly bright blue eyes. He was beautifully tailored and through the initial phases of the case sat at the counsel table with Aldrich and the others, always dignified, polite, even courtly... the clean-cut, urbane executive, physically and mentally fit.

Heath's direct testimony bolstered that impression. He avoided the temptation to criticize Parlier. He was above that. He told of his background and how he had "contributed" in his own way to bringing UBS to its present position of success. He told how impressed he had been with Lee Parlier's record at ABC and how he was willing to give him the richest contract in television history to come over to UBS. He described their initial conversation in detail, bringing out almost reluctantly that, each time he thought they'd reached a deal, Parlier would ask for more. Finally, however, they'd reached a formal agreement, and Parlier went to work.

Aldrich stopped and walked to the jury box. He slowly took off his rimless glasses and there was a long moment of silence. "Now, Mr. Heath, I want you to be absolutely sure of your next answer, because it is critical to this case. At any time prior to your hiring Mr. Lee Parlier did he tell you of his criminal record?"

"Absolutely not."

"Did you ask him?"

"No, I never suspected that there was any possibility of such a thing."

"Did you ask about any problems in his background?"

"Yes, I asked if there was anything at all adverse in his background."

"Did you tell him why you were asking?"

"Yes, I told him that network television was probably the most regulated and sensitive industry, that if there was even the slightest thing that was embarrassing in his background it could seriously hurt us with the FCC and do us permanent damage with the sponsors and advertising agencies."

"And what did he answer?"

"He said there was nothing."

"And on that basis you hired him?'

"Yes."

"Would you have hired him if you had known he had a criminal record?"

"Certainly not."

"Why?"

"For the reasons I told him. The commission would be very concerned and could take a much more critical approach to our company, even if they approved Parlier at all. And perhaps more importantly, the advertising agencies are constantly afraid of anything that might affect their clients, the program sponsors; and the sponsors in turn are constantly afraid of anything that could make them look bad in the eyes of the public. If our vice president in charge of programming was a convicted felon, a man who'd committed fraud, they would simply take their business elsewhere. We could never, never, take on such a man . . . never."

Aldrich then wisely introduced Parlier's FCC application showing his criminal record. He did this rather than leaving it to Harry to bring out. In this way he could treat the application as a part of his attack on Parlier, rather than something he had to defend against when it would be brought out by Harry.

"Now, Mr. Heath, when did you first see this application listing and including Mr. Parlier's criminal record?"

"After he was fired, Mr. Aldrich. Never before."

"But it has your signature on it. . . . Can you explain that?"

"I certainly can. When Parlier brought it to me to countersign, it did not show anything about a criminal record. Question eleven, 'Do you have a criminal record?,' was answered 'No' on the form I signed. He changed it after I signed it. Then he attached his criminal record and sent it on to the FCC without my knowledge."

"When did you last see the form as you signed it, that is, the form saying 'no criminal record'?"

"After I signed it. I gave it to Parlier to mail to the commission. That's the last time I saw it."

"And then, as you've told us, you first saw the changed version showing the criminal record two years later, after Mr. Parlier was fired?"

"Correct."

"And that changed version you received from the FCC itself, right?"

"Right."

Aldrich stopped and returned to the counsel table. Every eye in the jury had been on Heath absorbing the impact of his crisp, confident and very effective testimony.

Aldrich looked up from his papers. "Your Honor, I see that it's four twenty-five. This might be a good time to stop for the day."

"Very well, Mr. Aldrich. We'll stand adjourned until nine-thirty Monday morning. Have a good weekend, gentlemen."

Utterly exhausted just from the concentration required to listen, Harry made his way out of the courthouse and down North Main to the old Plaza. A favorite of Harry's, the small tree-lined square had been the center of the little settlement known as El Pueblo de Nuestra Señora la Reina de Los Angeles de Porciuncula, when no one could have guessed that the quiet Mexican village would someday sprawl for sixty miles in every direction, encompassing millions of highly diverse people riding the freeways to high-rise offices, factories and sound stages, racing on weekends to the mountains and beaches, basking in the sun and complaining of the smog.

Harry sat on a bench near the deserted bandstand, lost in thought. The wind swept the fallen sycamore leaves across the path and blew lightly at Harry's dark hair. He was worried, deeply worried about how effective Heath had been and how much success he'd have in getting to him on cross-examination. The jury was obviously impressed with Heath, and unless Harry could thoroughly discredit the man, the case was lost. Certainly the balance of Heath's testimony, which would be about the day Parlier was fired, wouldn't help.

Thanks to Harry's pre-trial investigation, however, there were some things that might be of assistance. Harry felt he had the material to nail Heath, but the trick was to use that material properly, and he had to assume that Aldrich would have worked with Heath for days to prepare him for cross-examination just as Harry would have done in Aldrich's place.

Harry knew that, even aside from Parlier's testimony, he had to make it seem probable to the jury that the FCC application contained Parlier's criminal record when Heath first saw it and completely improbable that, as Heath claimed, it was changed by Parlier later and before the application was mailed. He had to anticipate how Heath would try to explain away the information Harry's investigation had turned up, and, by careful questioning, he had to cut off in advance Heath's ability to come up with any credible explanation. He thought he could bring it off, but it would be a very close thing.

Harry slowly rose from the bench and made his way back to the courthouse parking lot. What a way to make a living, he thought as he pulled into the bumper-to-bumper crush choking the westbound lane of the Hollywood Freeway. He wouldn't have changed it for the world.

*T*hat Saturday it rained. Nancy and Harry sat reading by a low fire, its crackling a pleasant counterpoint to the rain drops falling on the tile roof, splashing in the copper gutters and dripping softly from the trees to the shrubs and flowers below.

After an hour or more, Nancy rose and walked over to the massive arched window that looked out over the city. She watched the falling rain for a time and then turned back to face Harry, still reading on the couch.

"Can we talk for a while?"

"Sure, hon," he said, putting his book aside with just a hint of reluctance. "What's up?"

"I want to give you some understanding of what's been happening."

"Happening?"

"I mean with me."

"Oh?"

"Yes. I'm sure it's no surprise to you that I've been under quite a bit of stress lately and I don't mean just Gail . . . although that certainly upsets me. I've been trying to work through some things, basic things, like you and me and where our lives have gone and where they're going . . . things like that."

Harry sat back, feeling anxiety over what might be coming.

"I'd gone along for years, Harry, closing my eyes to what you might or might not be doing. You know what I mean," she said, pausing, "with other women."

Harry started to speak, but Nancy held up her hand to stop him.

"No, let me go on. I don't want to get into all that. I don't need to, at least not yet. Anyway, I put the whole thing out of my mind. I could do that because nothing forced me to face it.

"Then two things happened. For one, I began to think I wasn't really doing the right thing for us . . . well, for myself anyway . . . by keeping my head in the sand. I began to let the questions creep into my mind—questions I'd never wanted to face before. Then, soon after that, I was suddenly confronted with the reality, slapped with it, forced to face it squarely."

Harry's thoughts flashed to Liz Watterson and the Marmont lobby. Again he started to speak. Again Nancy cut him off.

"No, *please* let me finish. I'm not going to go into the facts or explanations. I just want you to know what's been happening." She paused and walked over to sit beside Harry on the couch. "Look, Harry, who told me or what they said or what you were doing or why isn't important . . . not right now. What is important is that I'm more open with myself about the whole thing and that you understand what I've been going through."

"Okay, Nance," he said, "go ahead."

"Well, as I said, I was squarely confronted with it, and when I had to face up to the situation, I found I couldn't do it very well, if I could do it at all. I felt a lot of anger. Still do . . . you've seen some of it . . . and fear too. I felt fear. I'm trying my best to work it all out, to get a new focus on things, a new approach, one that will help me deal with our lives and try to keep them together. I'd like that, Harry. I don't know if I can do it, but I'd like it. You don't really need to answer. I'm not even sure I want you to . . . at least not yet."

From Harry's point of view, that was a good thing. He had no idea how he might respond. Instead, he put his arms around Nancy and drew her toward him. He kissed her tenderly, and with her head on his shoulder, they sat in silence before the fire, listening to the rain, each lost in private thought.

*H*arry had been right about the next court session. Alec Heath was still on the stand, and from Aldrich's opening question, things got worse for Lee Parlier.

"Now you told us Friday you would never have hired Mr. Parlier in the first place if you had known he had a criminal record?"

"That's right."

"Well, would you tell us please the circumstances under which Mr. Parlier was fired?"

"Yes. I happened to come to the office on a Sunday, and there was Mr. Parlier in the Xerox room copying our documents, hundreds of them, many of them very sensitive."

"What do you mean by sensitive?"

"Well, things our rival networks would give their eyeteeth to see, like our revenues, our deals with sponsors, our operating costs, what we're paying talent and the like. He had copied them all for a two- or three-year period."

"I see." Aldrich bent to pick up a note from the counsel table.

Parlier was glaring at Heath with obvious hatred. Harry made a mental note to tell him during recess to try harder to mask his feelings. It would be difficult, but it would make a better impression on the jury.

Aldrich turned again to the witness.

"Now, did you have any conversation with Mr. Parlier on this occasion?"

"Yes. I said, 'What the hell are you doing?' He said, 'I'm Xeroxing.' I said, 'You're copying our top secret documents and I want to know why.'"

Heath paused. Aldrich moved over to the end of the jury box. "Yes, Mr. Heath, what then?"

"He told me it was none of my Goddamn business."

"And what did you say?"

"I said, 'Get out of here right now, you're fired.' I'm afraid I lost my temper. Anyway, those are the last words we ever exchanged."

"Now after this conversation did you examine the sign-in book that records who entered the building?"

"Yes."

"And what did you observe in that sign-in book?"

Harry was on his feet, "Objection, Your Honor, the book itself is the best evidence of what it says."

"Sustained."

Aldrich smiled. "May I examine the witness to lay a foundation for the admissibility of secondary evidence, Your Honor?"

"Certainly."

"Mr. Heath, where is the sign-in book now?"

"It's been destroyed."

"How did that happen?"

"It's routine. At the end of each year the books are destroyed. It was my own carelessness not to order someone to make an exception for this particular book."

"Why do you say that?"

"Because the book showed that Parlier had signed in with a fraudulent name."

"A what?"

"A phony name. He had written, 'Barley,' or something like that, so that no one could tell whether it was Parlier and know that he had been in there on Sunday copying our records."

"Thank you, that's all," Aldrich snapped, glaring in Harry's direction."

The judge looked over at Harry. "Mr. Cain, cross-examination?"

This was it. Much of the result of the case would turn on the next hour. Harry stood and paused for a moment, looking straight at Heath. Sometimes a witness would look down or away, starting the cross-examination off with a psychological edge to Harry. Not Heath. He stared right back at Harry, confident, quietly defiant. This was going to be a tough one.

"Mr. Heath, you know that Mr. Parlier claims his criminal record was on the FCC form when you signed it, isn't that correct?"

"It's correct that he claims that, but he knows it's a lie."

"Are you aware, sir, that he claims you mailed in his registration form yourself?"

"I know he claims that now, but again, he knows it's not so. I gave him the application to mail after I signed it."

"Did you read it before you signed it?"

"Certainly."

Harry was ready to start cutting off Heath's possible ways of escaping from the traps Harry planned. But he wanted Heath to believe he was after something totally different.

"There's no possibility you just signed Mr. Parlier's application without checking to see if a criminal record was attached, is there?"

Heath was already growing impatient with what he considered a bumbling performance by Harry. It was just wasting his time.

"Mr. Cain, I've already testified that I read the application and read it carefully. It did not... I repeat, it did not contain any indication of a criminal record. It said, as I signed it, 'no criminal record.'"

"Well, Mr. Heath, don't you often sign documents without reading them or knowing their contents?"

"I do not, sir."

"Oh? Weren't you generally . . . as a matter of practice . . . careless or at least unconcerned about the contents of documents you signed?"

"I was not, sir; I took my responsibility seriously and that included knowing just what I was signing . . . always, on *every* occasion."

"Mr. Heath, didn't you sometimes sign letters and other documents in blank, leaving Mr. Parlier to fill in the contents after you signed them?"

"Never! I have never signed a letter, form, contract or any other document in blank to be filled in by Mr. Parlier or by anyone else."

Harry breathed a sigh of relief. He had what he wanted. He'd use it later. He was tempted to nail the point down further, right now; but he decided not to take the risk, not to ask that one question too many, that could warn the witness that he'd hurt himself and lead him to change or dilute the answer he'd previously given.

Heath was too bright for risk-taking, and Harry quickly moved to an entirely new topic. "You say that you didn't see the form showing Mr. Parlier's criminal record until after he was fired. But did you know from any other source that he had a criminal record before that time?"

"No."

"Didn't Mr. Parlier tell you he had a record?"

"Absolutely not."

"Mr. Heath, what was it that you said to Mr. Parlier when you found him Xeroxing documents on a Sunday?"

"Well, it was quite brief. I asked him what he was doing; he said he was Xeroxing. I asked why. He said it was none of my business. I said, 'Get out, you're fired.' I probably called him a name or two. That was about it."

"Well, did either of you say anything else on the occasion you fired him that you haven't told us about?"

"No, not that I can think of."

"And when you told him he was fired, he left?"

"Yes."

"Immediately, without doing anything further?"

"Yes, that's right."

"And then you went downstairs to look at the sign-in book?"

"Yes."

"And you left as well?"

"Yes, that's right also."

Harry had the foundation for another good argument. He'd make it later. He switched subjects again.

"Mr. Heath, whether you mailed in Mr. Parlier's application or he did, the normal practice of the company was not followed in the case of his application, isn't that correct?"

"I'm not sure what you mean."

"Well, isn't the normal practice that the network compliance officer prepares such applications with information supplied by the applicant, and then the compliance officer sees that the application is signed by the applicant and by you and then mails it in?"

"Yes, that's true, that's the regular practice."

"And in Mr. Parlier's case, he filled out the form himself, isn't that right?"

"That's right."

"So as far as you know, the network compliance officer never even saw the form, isn't that correct?"

"Yes, that's correct."

"Normally the form is mailed to the FCC by the network compliance officer, isn't that also correct?"

"Yes."

"And normally there is a copy of the FCC application form kept right in the applicant's personnel file at the network, isn't that right?"

"Yes, that's our usual practice."

"Was there any copy of Mr. Parlier's registration form kept at the network?"

"No."

"Who was the compliance officer when Mr. Parlier's registration form was completed?"

"Mr. Jordon Alcott."

Harry very deliberately consulted a document in his file. He wanted Heath to think he had a statement from Alcott. The fact is he did not. He was looking at a totally unrelated piece of paper. He looked up from what he appeared to be reading.

"And did you personally give Mr. Alcott instructions that Mr. Parlier's registration form was to receive special treatment?"

Heath paused, becoming wary. He didn't want to be in the position of contradicting what appeared to be something Alcott had said. "Well, yes, I think those instructions came directly from me."

"And you told Mr. Alcott that Mr. Parlier would process his own application?"

"I said I would handle it myself."

"Including mailing it directly to the FCC?"

Heath flushed but kept his head. "I didn't specify who would mail it or who would type it. I just said I'd handle it and Mr. Alcott would not need to be involved."

"Did you tell Mr. Alcott there would be no file copy kept?"

"Probably I did."

Harry consulted the paper in his file again. "And did you tell Mr. Alcott"—(now Harry pretended actually to read from the paper)— "that no one in the company was to see Mr. Parlier's application but you and Mr. Parlier?"

"Probably I did."

"Do you know of any other registration form that has ever been handled in this manner at UBS?"

"No, I suppose not."

"Actually, the information in Mr. Parlier's registration form was to be kept a secret from everyone but the FCC, you and Mr. Parlier. Isn't that right, Mr. Heath?"

"He insisted that the information about him be kept totally confidential."

"And that's why no one else saw it and why no file copy was kept and why it was mailed in directly by you or by Mr. Parlier, isn't that right?"

"By him, not by me."

"Well, that's why it wasn't mailed in by Mr. Alcott as in every other case, right?"

"Yes. Parlier wanted it that way."

"He wanted it confidential?"

"Yes."

Harry moved back to the counsel table. He made a hand signal to John Matsuoka, who quickly unrolled a giant blow-up of Parlier's FCC registration form that had been standing, mysteriously rolled and tied at the end of the counsel table. Together, they tacked it to the cork board near the witness stand. Harry approached Heath again.

"Now, you say that when you signed this document, question eleven, which reads 'Do you have a criminal record? (if so, please attach),' was answered 'No,' rather than 'Yes,' as it now appears on this exhibit?"

"That's correct."

"And no criminal record was attached, like the record now attached to this exhibit, is that correct?"

"Yes, that's right too."

"Well, Mr. Heath, as the application stood when you signed it showing, as you claim, no criminal record, what information was it that Mr. Parlier wanted so badly to be kept secret?"

"I don't recall."

"You don't recall?"

"No."

"Well, look at the form here in blown-up size, read it over thoroughly and tell us what there is on that form *other than a criminal record* that Mr. Parlier could possibly want to keep confidential?"

Heath looked at the chart at some length. It was no help to him. "I just can't recall, Mr. Cain, if I ever knew."

Harry slapped the form with his palm and let a heavy note of sarcasm fill his voice. "You ordered secret, special treatment for this form, different from any other case in the history of the network, and yet you have no idea what there was in this form that was supposed to be kept secret?"

Now the jury were beginning to get the idea, and Heath was getting flustered for the first time. "Who knows, maybe it was his name."

"He wanted *his name* kept secret?" Harry shouted the question.

"I was just joking. He was a very secretive man. It was an attempt at humor, Mr. Cain."

Harry looked at the jury. They were rapidly losing their faith in Heath and beginning to follow Harry's theory. Harry saw no risk in emphasizing the point just in case some of the jury members missed it. "Wasn't it Mr. Parlier's criminal record that he and you wanted to keep from the others?"

"No. Absolutely not. That was not in the application when I signed it."

"Of course." This time it was Harry who was sarcastic.

"Now, Mr. Heath, tell us how you first found out Mr. Parlier had a criminal record."

Harry already knew the answer from the pre-trial depositions. He was taking no risk with the question.

Heath seemed relieved at the change of subject. "I wrote to the commissioner for a copy of the registration form because we had no copy in our own files. We were closing out the Parlier file and wanted it to be complete."

"When did you do this?"

"Shortly after he was fired."

"And that's when you first wrote the FCC for a copy from their files?"

"Yes."

Harry's plan on this point depended on the dates. He wanted to show considerable time elapsed between Parlier's being fired and the receipt of the application.

"Mr. Heath, I'm going to hand you two documents from your own file, one, your letter to the FCC asking for a copy of Mr. Parlier's registration form and, second, the FCC's letter sending you the form on April twenty-fourth."

"Yes."

"Now, does that refresh your recollection as to when you first got the application from the FCC?"

"Yes, sometime after April twenty-fourth."

"And Mr. Parlier was fired on Sunday, April tenth, isn't that right?"

"Yes."

"So your first knowledge of his criminal record came after April twenty-fourth, at least two weeks after he was fired, isn't that correct?"

"Yes."

"No anonymous caller tipped you off before that time?"

"No."

"You just had no idea that Mr. Parlier had any criminal record when you fired him or any time in the next two weeks, right?"

"That's right, Mr. Cain, I've told you that three times."

Harry turned to the judge. "I see it's almost eleven o'clock, Your Honor. Might this be a convenient time for the morning recess?"

"Gentlemen, please approach the bench." Harry and Aldrich moved forward to within whispering distance of Judge Hailey, whose words were inaudible to the jury.

"How much longer do you think you'll be, Mr. Cain?"

"Oh, it's hard to say, Judge, it could go on all day or things could switch around and end up quickly. Probably it'll take some time, but I doubt it'll be more than the rest of the day."

"All right," the Judge announced, "we will stand in recess until eleven-fifteen."

Harry was a bit uncomfortable about his evasive answer to Judge Hailey. But he was playing the "recess game," and he thought the result was worth it. Barring surprises, he probably had less than ten minutes of cross-examination left. But if he said that, the judge would make him finish before the break and Aldrich would use the recess to work with Heath preparing him for redirect examination.

With an intelligent witness like Heath, Aldrich could make considerable progress, even in ten or fifteen minutes, preparing him for redirect examination. He could then explain away much of the damage Harry had done to Heath on cross-examination.

But redirect examination to repair such damage was very dangerous without adequate preparation; and if Aldrich was handed the witness in the middle of the court session and forced to begin redirect examination with no time to prepare his witness, he might just pass up the opportunity altogether. What Harry wanted was to start on Heath right after the break. Throw his biggest punch and then, suddenly, quit. That way Aldrich could get stuck. The rest of the morning was available for testimony and he could hardly beg for another recess to prepare his client. He'd have to start redirect examination without adequate preparation, at least on Harry's last set of questions. He might hang on until the noon recess, asking only meaningless, unimportant questions in order to stall; but if he went the whole hour without explaining away the damage Harry had done to his client, he'd look very weak indeed, and the jury could become hard to sell on any explanation he trotted out after having lunch with his client.

Also, Harry could comment very pointedly in argument on the failure to give an explanation until Mr. Aldrich and Mr. Heath had spent an hour together over lunch getting their story straight.

The other horn of Aldrich's dilemma would be that if he tried to repair the damage without adequate preparation, it could get much, much worse. Harry's guess was that Aldrich, experienced and conservative, would never take the risk.

When the recess was over, Heath returned to the stand, looking not nearly so fresh as when he'd started. Harry pulled another paper from his file, laid a copy in front of Aldrich and handed one to the witness. He paused while both Heath and Aldrich read what he had given them. Then he began.

"Mr. Heath, you testified that you always knew what you signed and you gave it careful consideration before you signed it. Is that your signature on the letter there before you?"

"Just a minute, Your Honor," Aldrich bellowed. "May we approach the bench?"

"Certainly."

Aldrich's face was suffused with anger as he spoke in low but furious tones to the judge. "Your Honor, we served written interrogatories asking in detail for a description of every document that supported Mr. Parlier's contentions on every issue in this case. At no point did Mr. Cain give us this letter he's trying to get before the jury. Under the law, Your Honor, he cannot use that letter, because he did not disclose it to us. That, of course, is just the kind of tactic that I'd expect from Mr. Cain; conceal a letter and then try to use it at trial as a surprise. He—"

The judge cut him off, her voice cold and stern. "We don't need that kind of comment, Mr. Aldrich. May I see the letter?"

Harry handed his copy of the letter to Judge Hailey. Her thin lips tightened as she read it. "Mr. Cain, I can see the significance of the letter, of course. But Mr. Aldrich is correct. It seems to me that he's entitled to have it excluded. Do you concede that the interrogatories called for a disclosure of this letter?"

"Not at all, Judge. The interrogatories were served and answered three months before I got into the case. This letter was turned up in the FCC file only by my own investigation after the interrogatories were answered. It was an 'after discovered document' within the meaning of *Kaplan v. Bond*; and, as such, we had no duty to notify counsel of its existence.

"Had Mr. Aldrich submitted a second set of interrogatories to pick up documents or witnesses discovered between his first interrogatories and the time of trial, we would, of course, have listed this letter. But he did not do so, and, of course, it's proper evidence right now."

Judge Hailey turned to Aldrich. "Any comment?"

Aldrich looked extremely uncomfortable. "Well, Your Honor, under the federal rules—"

"We're not in federal court, Mr. Aldrich. The federal rules have no application here. Mr. Cain has correctly stated the applicable California rule; and unless you have anything further, I'll allow his examination to proceed."

"Nothing further, Your Honor."

Harry moved over to the far side of the jury box, trying with body language to create the impression that his questions were coming from the jury itself, that they were one with him in asking them.

"Mr. Heath, while we were talking with the judge, did you have the opportunity to read that letter there in front of you?"

"I did." Heath's voice was dry and difficult to hear.

Harry heard it but put his hand to his ear as though he had not. "I'm sorry, I didn't hear you, Mr. Heath. Have you read the letter there before you?"

"Yes."

This time the answer was more audible, but Heath's voice was strained with tension. He looked like a fighter on the ropes, waiting, not knowing for sure what was coming next. The jury's attention was now riveted on him. They sensed that the letter was something vital.

"Well, Mr. Heath, that is your signature there on the letter, isn't it?"

Heath looked at it again and slowly looked up.

"I'm not sure."

"You're not *sure*," Harry shouted. "Doesn't it look like your signature?"

"Yes, it does."

"We have Mr. Alexander Norton here in court, right there in the back of the courtroom." Harry pointed out a tall, cadaverous man in a black suit. "You know, the famous handwriting expert. He's prepared to testify..." Aldrich was on his feet to object.

Before he could speak Heath went on. "No, no that's not necessary. I think that it's my signature." Aldrich sat down.

"You *think* it's your signature?" Harry boomed.

"It *is* mine, I'm sure," said Heath softly.

"What's the date of the letter, Mr. Heath?"

"January 23, 1981."

"That's just about when Mr. Parlier was hired, isn't it?"

"Yes it is."

"And this letter is on your own stationery as president of the network?"

"Yes."

"And it's addressed to the Federal Communications Commission in Washington, is that correct?"

"Yes."

Now Harry backed up to the far end of the jury box and paused. There was total silence in the courtroom. "Okay, Mr. Heath, please read to the jury what you wrote to the FCC at the time that Mr. Parlier was hired."

"Read it yourself, counselor," Heath spat with grim hostility.

Harry turned to the judge with a questioning look. "Your Honor?" he asked, as if to say, "Will you let him get away with that?"

Judge Hailey looked balefully at Heath. She spoke slowly, in a steely tone. "Mr. Heath, you are instructed to read the letter aloud."

Heath was so pale you could feel, if not see, the blood coursing through his veins. There was another long moment of silence.

"As you say, it's addressed to the Communications Commission. It says, 'Gentlemen: In response to your inquiry, we have indeed investigated the facts of Mr. Parlier's criminal record and are satisfied that it should not be an impediment to his becoming an officer of this company.'"

"And how is the letter signed?"

"'Very truly yours, Alec Heath.'" Now the blood came slowly back into Heath's face. "But I never saw that letter."

"Of course you didn't, Mr. Heath." Harry intoned sarcastically. "It's your signature there on the letter. It's only five lines long; and you told us you never signed anything without knowing its contents. But in this one case, you want the jury to believe you never saw it. Is that right?"

"Objection," Aldrich shouted. "Argumentative, harrassing the witness."

"Sustained."

Harry walked slowly back to the counsel table, making a rapid calculation. Normally he would never give a hostile witness the chance to explain away an incriminating document. But here he wanted to commit Heath to an explanation before he had the chance to think it out and to confer with Aldrich. There was still a way out for Heath. He could claim the letter refreshed his recollection, that he did know Parlier had *some* criminal record, but thought it was only some minor offense, not involving anything serious, that Parlier had lied about the *extent* of his record, which would still be a fraud.

That was why Harry had carefully phrased all his earlier questions in terms of Heath not knowing that Parlier had "any" criminal record. Heath had given him the answers he wanted, but seeing the letter might change his story. Harry wanted Heath to stick to his denial that he knew about the letter at all, something the jury would never buy. His answers already said that, but he could still back away from it if not pinned down now.

Harry decided to take the plunge. "Mr. Heath, in light of this letter you wrote to the FCC, your earlier sworn testimony that you did not know Mr. Parlier had a criminal record was untrue, wasn't it?" Harry phrased the question in a way that almost forced Heath to deny the existence of the letter or admit that his "sworn testimony" had been false. He gambled that Heath, under the emotional pressure of that kind of question, would never see the way out of his dilemma.

Heath looked once again at the letter, not knowing which way to go. Then he decided. "Mr. Cain, I've never seen this letter before in my life. I don't know how Mr. Parlier did it, but somehow he got my signature on this letter without my even knowing it."

Harry breathed an inner sigh of relief. Now it would be next to impossible for Heath to revise his position. He decided to wind up his cross-examination without using up any further time. "Mr. Heath, before you saw this letter, you testified that you *never* signed anything in blank, that you *never* signed anything without knowing its contents. Are you telling us now that *that* testimony was untrue?"

"No, but somehow he did it. . . . Parlier, that is. I simply have never seen that letter before. I can't explain it, but I know I've never seen it before."

"Even though you signed it?"

"Even though I signed it," Heath said in a voice that could barely be heard.

"That's all I have of this witness, Your Honor."

Harry sat down. It was eleven-twenty-five. Aldrich was in the spot Harry had planned. He had thirty-five minutes until noon and no time to prepare his client at all for an attempt to explain away the heavy damage he'd suffered on cross-examination.

Aldrich rose slowly and took off his glasses, thinking, weighing all the possibilities. Harry could see his mind working. "Your Honor, in light of this last development, I respectfully request that we take the noon recess early."

Harry was on his feet, "Your Honor, I object. If Mr. Heath has still another explanation of his own letter, let him make it right now, not after he eats lunch with his lawyer."

The gavel came down. "Gentlemen, approach the bench." Both attorneys moved forward again. Judge Hailey looked down at Harry as if he were some sort of bug about to be squashed. "I want no more of that, Mr. Cain. Do you understand? You could wind up with a mistrial if I hear anything like that again, plus a contempt charge. Do you hear me, Mr. Cain?"

"Yes, Your Honor. I was carried away in the heat of combat. I apologize."

Aldrich thought he saw a way out. "In light of Mr. Cain's outburst, the only fair thing to my client would be a mistrial, and I think that Your Honor might..."

Now the judge's iron gaze turned on Aldrich. "Mr. Aldrich, I don't mind telling you that I am most unimpressed with your client's veracity. You're fortunate that you have a jury here and that I'm not deciding the facts. I'm satisfied that the jury followed the cross-examination quite well and were not prejudiced by anything Mr. Cain said . . . so far." She gave Harry an ominous look. "So far, Mr. Cain. Do you read me?"

"Yes, Your Honor."

"Now, gentlemen, it's eleven-twenty-eight. This trial must move along. You will proceed, Mr. Aldrich, and we will take the noon break at twelve-thirty."

Harry was delighted. The judge knew just what she was doing. She thought Heath was lying, and she wasn't going to let Aldrich use the time to prepare another explanation for him. With an hour to go until lunchtime, longer than either Harry or Aldrich had expected, there was simply no way for Aldrich to stall without totally antagonizing the jury. He had to face the hard choice right now, plunge in and try to explain away the letter without any time to prepare Heath, or give up at least this part of the case, hoping to turn things around in cross-examining Parlier or to win the practical victory by showing that Neil Talbot, rather than Parlier, had created "High Rise," so that, even if Parlier's contract remained in force, he would be awarded nothing.

Aldrich, a conservative if nothing else, chose the safe course. "Your Honor, we have no redirect at this time."

"All right, Mr. Aldrich, please call your next witness."

Aldrich used up the rest of the morning, reading a stipulation as to Parlier's criminal record and presenting an expert as to the sensitivity of the television business and how a network could not afford to hire a man with a serious criminal record.

When the "expert," a self-important president of a rival network, finished his direct testimony, Harry was sorely tempted to take him on. But he had done Harry no real damage, and it made sense to end the morning ahead, tacitly telling the jury that the expert's testimony was meaningless in light of Heath's obvious lie on the fundamental point in the case.

Harry looked as bored as he could. "No questions, Your Honor."

Aldrich got slowly to his feet.

"It's twelve-twenty, Your Honor. Perhaps we could take the noon recess now, rather than begin with a new witness?"

"Very well, we'll adjourn until two o'clock."

*J*ay Kelly joined Harry, Parlier and Matsuoka for lunch at the Music Center. Harry explained that while they'd scored heavily on Heath during cross-examination, the case wasn't over yet—not by a long shot. Harry laid into his Boeuf à la mode with vigor, gesturing with his fork between bites of the cold jellied beef.

"Sure, I think we've probably got 'em on the fraud claim. That jury's not going for the story that Parlier somehow got Heath's name on that letter to the FCC. But we still have to get over the hurdle of whether he was in breach of his contract when he came in to Xerox the records on Sunday."

"Of course," said Kelly, smearing a piece of veal sausage with dark mustard. "But, Harry, it does seem like the fraud claim is behind us—and that's a big one."

"You're probably right, Jay," Harry replied, "but remember, even winning the fraud issue *and* the breach of contract issue doesn't get Lee any real money."

Harry turned to Lee Parlier, jabbing the fork in his direction. "We've still got to sell them on your having created 'High Rise,' Lee. That's the ten million dollar question, and, to get that, we not only have to sell them on the facts, but to make them want to give you that kind of money. They're only going to do that if they like you and are really outraged at Heath. Otherwise, they can easily come in with a compromise verdict—that you didn't commit fraud and didn't commit any breach of contract, but that you didn't create 'High Rise' either, so all you get is one year of salary, less the money you earned from your new job.

"If they do that, we 'win'... theoretically... but you end up with barely enough to cover your expenses and the whole thing is really a loss. Our big job from here on is to keep the jury steamed at Heath, and, of course, at Talbot too."

Harry paused for a swallow of iced tea. Then he turned again to Kelly. "Even on the fraud claim, Jay, we could still lose. Christ knows we've worked long enough to get Lee ready for his testimony, but if they hurt him badly, they could even turn things around on that issue. It'll be a long time between our nailing Heath with that letter to the FCC and the jury verdict. Their dislike of Heath can fade before that time, especially if they start disliking Lee even more.

"Anyway, Lee, let's use the rest of the lunch to go over your testimony again. I'll cross-examine you and—"

Parlier rolled his eyes in mock anguish. "Harry, for Christ sake, let's relax. We've already worked on cross-examination for at least twenty hours."

"I know, Lee, but when you're up there all alone with Aldrich coming after you, you'll be glad we prepared." And Harry would not be dissuaded. For the balance of their lunch, he fired question after question at Parlier, trying to anticipate the tactics Aldrich would use and to help Parlier develop effective answers.

When they returned to court, Harry encountered a seething Maynard Aldrich. "Your cheap shot with that letter will backfire like you've never seen, Cain. Mr. Parlier will be very sorry he ever pulled that one and so will you and I mean personally. I don't like phony documents, and lawyers who use them shouldn't be practicing law."

Harry grinned. He was certain Aldrich would have a team of experts work over the letter, but they'd find nothing. Harry had consulted his own expert to make sure before he used the letter. He tended to trust Parlier, but it paid to be safe. Now he was delighted that UBS was going to waste all that time, effort and money on a dead end.

Still, he couldn't resist upsetting Aldrich. "Mr. Aldrich, I haven't forgotten your attempt at blackmail at the settlement conference and I think that, if we see any bar association proceedings in this matter, they'll be in New York. Any partners in your firm been disbarred before?"

He turned away to speak to Parlier before Aldrich could answer.

*P*romptly at two o'clock, Judge Hailey took the bench.

"All right, Mr. Aldrich, you may call your next witness."

But Aldrich had a game of his own. "The plaintiff rests, Your Honor."

"Mr. Cain?" The judge peered over at Harry.

Harry realized now that Aldrich had probably never intended to call any witnesses after the lunch hour, that he planned to save Neil Talbot for rebuttal after Harry had put on his case, and that he had tried to throw Harry off balance and keep him from being prepared with his own first witness. Fortunately, it hadn't worked.

Harry rose slowly and paused, seeking to make the moment a dramatic one for the jury, always trying to hold their attention. "Our first witness is the defendant himself, Mr. Lee Parlier."

And so Parlier took the stand and, in the next few hours, the value of the long weeks of work, the repeated sessions of practice examination would be tested.

Parlier answered Harry's initial background questions firmly and in a polite and pleasant tone. He avoided going beyond the questions to engage in self-praise or self-vindication, as he had in their early practice sessions. He made just the points Harry wanted to make, in crisp and logical response to the questions he knew were coming from long hours of preparation.

He described growing up in a ghetto area of Philadelphia. His companions had all been gang members and he had foolishly become involved in early criminal activities. Always a coward, he said, he tended to become involved in nonviolent financial schemes rather than armed robbery like his friends from those days. At seventeen, not knowing any better, he'd been caught selling phony lottery tickets and was sent to juvenile hall. At twenty-three he was convicted of fraud for selling nonexistent Arizona lots to gullible Philadelphians. The fraud conviction led to his serving two years in the state penitentiary. He never wanted to go back; and, with the help of an unusually effective parole officer, he never had.

He told how he worked his way up in the entertainment business from a theater usher to the owner of four movie houses. He'd become fascinated by television early in the game and gambled by hiring a writer to do a treatment of an idea he had for a television special that actually got produced. This led to his career as an independent television producer. He described the three series he had created and produced, two of which had become top-rated shows, even though most of the money from them went to the network and to the studio that financed the production.

He described how ABC asked him to join its programming department. He'd refused because he knew he'd have to disclose his criminal record. He agreed, instead, to become an outside consultant for ABC, a situation that resulted in no such disclosure because no application to the FCC was required. While he was advising ABC on programming, their ratings almost doubled. He added (as Harry had planned) that, although he got the credit for this, most of it was really the work of ABC's excellent programming department.

Following the afternoon recess, Parlier went on to describe how he'd been approached by Alec Heath, who promised him the moon to come over to UBS as vice president in charge of programming. Heath offered an unprecedented contract that gave Parlier, as a bonus over his six hundred thousand dollar yearly salary, a percentage of the network's profits from any new series he personally created.

He told Heath in confidence about his criminal record, asking him if it would prevent his becoming an officer of UBS. Heath said "No," not if it was handled right, that they'd have to disclose the record to the FCC but that no one else at the network would need to know about it at all.

Heath said that there would have to be an FCC registration form, but it would be kept in the strictest confidence, handled and seen only by Parlier and Heath, with no copies kept in the network files. Heath gave blank copies of the FCC registration form to Parlier, who prepared the form himself. He answered question eleven "Yes" . . . that he did have a criminal record, and then, as the form directed, he attached a copy of that record. Then, with the registration form just as it was in court, he presented it to Heath, who signed it and said he'd mail it himself.

Through Harry's questions, Parlier described his success as the programmer for UBS, although again volunteering as Harry had advised, that much of his credit was due to his staff and that Heath himself had been an enormous help.

At first, Parlier had been so enthusiastic about his new job, he'd even gone out and bought a few thousand dollars' worth of UBS stock. It seemed the perfect situation.

Then he described how he had worked out the idea for "High Rise" in early 1982, shaping and refining the concept until on May 15, 1982, at a lunch meeting in New York, with Heath's right-hand man, Neil Talbot, and Teddy Brenner, the senior vice president of the network, he presented the series idea. Talbot and Brenner were both immediately enthusiastic. Then Parlier identified his memorandum of the May 15, 1982, meeting and of seven later meetings at which the "High Rise" series had been discussed and developed. He told about the countless hours he'd expended on the series and finally about its enormous success in its first season, during which it had been the number-one-rated show eighteen times and in the top five every single week of the season.

Toward the end of the day, Parlier described his growing suspicion that Alec Heath would try to prevent his receiving the huge sum his contract called for in light of the unprecedented success of "High Rise." He heard rumors that Heath was out to get him, that Heath's henchman, Neil Talbot, was now claiming to have created "High Rise" himself and that, at the very least, the figures would be faked.

He was sure he'd never get a fair shake in court because of his criminal record; and to protect himself as much as he could, he came in on a Sunday afternoon to Xerox the sponsors' contracts on "High Rise" and his own memos relating to the series; nothing else. Heath had caught him doing this and fired him, telling him to leave immediately. Parlier had packed up his documents and left within two or three minutes, and that was the last time the two men had spoken.

"Your witness," Harry said, pleased with Parlier's handling of his direct testimony but terrified of what could happen to him on cross-examination.

Aldrich rose slowly. "Your Honor, I see that it's approaching the end of the day and I would suggest that rather than begin now we start with Mr. Parlier's cross-examination first thing in the morning."

Judge Hailey turned to Harry. "Any objection, Mr. Cain?"

"No, Your Honor."

"All right then, but I want to move this case along. We'll resume again at eight-thirty in the morning, and see if we can go through the morning without a recess, unless Mr. Parlier feels one is necessary."

*T*he next morning began early as scheduled. Harry had worked with Parlier for two more hours the night before and had left feeling relatively confident over the state of his client's readiness. Still, as they took their places for the morning session, Parlier looked pale and drawn, and Harry began to worry.

Aldrich plunged into his cross-examination without hesitation. He was neither subtle nor courteous. To him Parlier was a crook, and he went after him hammer and tongs, shouting, badgering, suggesting with each question that Parlier was not giving straight answers.

He repeatedly referred to Parlier as a "convicted felon" and sneered at his insistence that he'd disclosed his criminal record, particularly his conviction of fraud.

He brought out that Parlier's May fifteenth memo concerning "High Rise" did not specifically say that it was Parlier who had "created" the series or had "presented" the idea at the lunch meeting that day, but said only that the idea had been "discussed" with Talbot and Brenner, which was equally consistent with Talbot's having created the series.

Aldrich treated with sarcastic derision Parlier's answer that he was just recording the meeting, not trying to create a record to protect himself. "Sure," thundered Aldrich. "That's why you sneaked into the office to steal records on a Sunday."

But, generally, Parlier gave calm, straight, short replies, and he wasn't being seriously hurt. After a few minutes Harry began to breathe more easily. It was becoming apparent that, for the most part, Aldrich was asking questions Harry had anticipated and had covered with Parlier, although he was asking them with more nastiness and sarcasm than Harry had used in practice.

Parlier seemed able to recognize the moves about which Harry had warned him. He was slowly gaining confidence and successfully maintaining the calm demeanor that Harry had told him was the best defense against Aldrich's slamming, swarming kind of attack.

Skipping back and forth between 1982 and 1983, in an attempt to keep Parlier off balance, Aldrich began to question Parlier about the day he was fired. This was the area in which Harry had encountered the most difficulty in convincing Parlier to follow his advice. But now, when it counted, Parlier did just what Harry had asked.

"And so you went into the office on Sunday the ninth?" "Yes, sir." "And didn't you obtain entry by signing a false name in the sign-in book?"

This was what Harry considered the critical question. He mentally crossed his fingers, hoping that Parlier would follow Harry's plan and not his own tendency to deny everything he thought would make him look bad.

"I don't know," said Parlier in a firm voice, looking directly at Aldrich.

"You don't *know?*" Aldrich bellowed.

"No sir."

"What do you mean by that?"

"Well, I heard Mr. Heath testify that he saw a false name in the book, but I really don't remember. I certainly didn't want Mr. Heath to find out I was there until I was finished. Maybe I did sign a false name. I simply don't remember doing it or planning to do it. But I suppose it's possible I did."

It all seemed very reasonable to the jury. They were nodding as Parlier spoke. But Aldrich was convinced that he'd won a critical admission from Parlier, one that hurt him badly. "In fact, Mr. Parlier, you *did* sign a phony, a fraudulent name in that book, isn't that so?"

"I just don't remember, Mr. Aldrich. Maybe I did."

Aldrich looked at Parlier as if he were an insect. "Yes, Mr. Parlier, maybe you did," he said, turning dramatically from the witness in obvious disgust.

Then Aldrich moved to another area on which Harry had repeatedly drilled Parlier, one that could catch Aldrich in a damaging trap but, if not done correctly, could boomerang.

Here again, Parlier followed Harry's guidance perfectly. Aldrich began to ask about Parlier's first conversation with Heath after he'd agreed to join UBS. "Well then, after Mr. Heath shook your hand and welcomed you, didn't he brief you on the sensitive public position of UBS and how essential it was to preserve the network's image?"

"Do you mean was that the next thing he said?"

"Yes."

"That wasn't the next thing he said, no sir."

"Well, Mr. Parlier, what *was* the next thing he said?"

Harry fought to keep his delight from showing. Aldrich was taking the bait. Parlier looked down at his hands as if embarrassed.

"I'd rather not get into the next thing he said, Mr. Aldrich."

Aldrich began to get the scent of blood. "Well, sir, I'm afraid that you *must* get into that. What is it that Mr. Heath said next?"

"It had nothing to do with my job or this case," Parlier said in a pleading tone, begging Aldrich with his expression not to make him go on.

Now Aldrich was sure he was on to something big. "Well, sir, I'm afraid you must tell us."

"No sir, I won't," Parlier said gently but firmly, exactly as Harry had told him to do it.

Aldrich leered. "Mr. Parlier, the court will instruct you that no matter how harmful it may be to your case you must tell us what was the next thing that was said."

Parlier hesitated for several seconds, indicating by his expression that he and his case were in deep trouble if he was forced to go on. "No, Mr. Aldrich, I prefer not to say."

Aldrich turned to the judge with a shrug. "Your Honor?"

The judge looked gravely at Parlier. She spoke in a firm, even tone, "Mr. Witness, you will answer the question."

"Your Honor, I really prefer not to answer and I promise you it has nothing to do with the case."

At this, the gavel came down hard. "Mr. Parlier, you will answer that question or you will be held in contempt. And I mean right now!" Judge Hailey glared at Parlier with growing impatience. The jury thought he was about to confess to murder.

"Well, Your Honor, must I do it verbatim?"

"Mr. Aldrich, what is your request?"

"Verbatim, Your Honor, or as near to verbatim as the witness can come."

"All right, Mr. Parlier, as close to verbatim as you can come."

Parlier gulped, "Well, I know it's wrong."

Down came the gavel again. "That's it, Mr. Parlier. You're in contempt of this court. I'll allow you to purge yourself of that contempt and avoid punishment if you give us the verbatim answer or as close as you can come to a verbatim answer, right now. One more delay and you will be punished."

Again Parlier gulped, "Well, okay," he said, still seeming reluctant to speak. "What Mr. Heath said was, now I was aboard . . . that's the word he used, 'aboard' . . . I could participate in what he called 'fringe benefits.' He said that he and Neil Talbot were 'fucking' . . . I'm sorry," he said, looking down and very embarrassed. "He said they were fucking a fourteen-year-old runaway girl they'd set up in a Hollywood apartment. He said they'd trained her to give the greatest head in the world. . . . Listen, I'm sorry, but that's what he said. And he asked would I like to get in on it. I said I wouldn't, and he said something like, 'I didn't know what I was missing.' That's about it."

—209—

Harry fought to suppress a smile. He heard gasps from the jury box and murmuring from the spectators.

Judge Hailey stared at Heath. Aldrich stood as if transfixed, realizing how he'd been led into a terrible trap but unable to react in any helpful way.

The gavel came down again. "The witness's last answer is stricken on the court's own motion. The jury will disregard it as wholly irrelevant. However, I want to point this out, the jury will not draw any conclusion from Mr. Parlier's answer or from my remarks that are adverse to Mr. Parlier in any way, since he was ordered to state what was said in the conversation and so testified only when ordered to do so."

Approaching the bench, Aldrich moved again for a mistrial. It was denied. His face reddened with frustration, his small eyes glaring with ill-concealed anger that Harry had used him to bring out these very unsavory facts about Heath, facts he couldn't even seek to refute, since they were not even "in evidence." But Aldrich knew the jury wouldn't forget them.

He went after Parlier for the balance of the morning, shouting and bullying, determined to break him with the force of his questions. But the long hours of preparation paid off; and when Aldrich finally announced the end of his cross-examination at twelve-thirty, Harry's appraisal was that Aldrich and Heath had been hurt substantially more than Parlier, who had generally held the jury's sympathy.

Harry had planned to go over a number of the areas Aldrich covered to make them clear to the jury, but Parlier had come through the cross-examination so well he abandoned the idea.

"No questions, Your Honor," he said, putting his files into his briefcase.

"Very well then, we'll take the noon recess."

*E*ntering the Restaurant Rex in downtown Los Angeles was like stepping out of time and place, from the press of the bustling downtown streets, into the art deco dining saloon of a 1920s luxury liner. The fluted walls, rising to the balcony in modular rings and leaf trimmed edges, were softened and graced with rounded mirrors and frosted glass. The soft beige walls and upholstery, the opulent fan-shaped sofas and the heavy tan carpeting added to the feeling of quiet elegance.

Gail had called Harry the evening before, asking if they could meet for lunch. Although she said only that she was looking forward to seeing him, he suspected she had something on her mind.

When he arrived at the restaurant, Harry saw Gail was already seated at a table in the back. He crossed the room to join her.

Gail looked pale but beautiful in a tan silk maternity dress that seemed chosen to complement the room. Harry noted the half-finished martini as she rose to give him a hug that seemed a bit too urgent and a shade too long. Danger signals.

He seated her, the triangular table allowing them to sit close to each other without being crowded, enhancing the feeling of intimacy that somehow pervaded the large room. Ordering a glass of wine, he began to answer her questions about the trial. She was amused and delighted at his remaking of Parlier's appearance and on hearing how Aldrich had been lured into demanding that Parlier testify to what Heath said when he was hired, her low, musical laugh spilled across the room, filling Harry with pleasure and pride.

They ordered . . . poached oysters with matchstick vegetables and grilled swordfish with anchovy butter. When the waiter left, Harry saw Gail's expression change. The dark eyes grew soft and serious, their merry impishness suddenly gone.

There was a moment of silence, and Harry decided to take the lead. "Gail—listen, hon, maybe I'm imagining things, but I get the strongest feeling there's something you'd like to tell me . . . am I right?"

Gail looked relieved. "You're right, Dad. There is something. I've been sort of putting it off."

Trying to keep things light, he did Bogart. "Okay then, kid, what's it all about? I can take anything."

She continued to look serious and went directly to the point, speaking quickly. "Dad . . . I know you're not going to be happy about this. I'm moving to London."

Harry was stunned. He put down his fork and, for a second, they simply looked at each other.

"What do you mean moving? How long will you be there?"

She paused and then replied softly. "Permanently, Dad, I've got a job there. It's where I want to live."

Harry felt the blood drain from his face. His hands were icy. The moment seemed suspended interminably. He toyed with his wine glass. "You're going to live there permanently?"

"Yes."

"But why? When did you decide?"

She sipped her drink and slowly put it down. "I love London, Dad. You know that. And I'll have a fine job there—assistant to the magazine's London bureau chief. But mostly, I want to be near Robin. I want the baby . . . his baby . . . to be near him too, to grow up where he and his father can be close."

"Gail, honey, that makes no sense at all. The man is married. She's very rich, very social. I've told you before, he'll never leave her—never give that up. With the baby, you'll be an annoyance, an embarrassment. He won't even want to see you. You'll hang around London with your baby, lonely, miserable, waiting for some odd afternoon when he might decide to get away from the office and stop by. And, of course, there'll be other girls too. He—"

"Okay, Dad, that's all I can take right now." Her tone was sharp. Then, as if sorry for that, she leaned forward and took her father's hand. "I know you want what's best for me. But just at this point I don't want to hear anything more like that about Robin. I love him . . . very much, and I want to be near him. You don't really know him and I do. I'm sure I can make it work out. So please don't root against me."

"You know I'm not 'rooting' against you, Gail. I'd never do that. I can't say I'm for it. You know I'm not, and I don't think it'll work

... ever. But if you go, and I hope you won't, I'll be pulling for you all the way."

She smiled. "I know, Dad, and I appreciate it. I also know how sudden this is. But it all came together quickly. I only heard about the job opening up last week and found out yesterday that a friend's flat in Chelsea will be available. She's been shifted to Berlin and leaves in a couple of months. It's a terrific flat and just perfect for us—me and the baby, that is. You'll see it when you come. After all, you get to England two or three times a year."

She was selling him now. She could sell him on almost anything, ever since she was a child. This time though, he felt empty, still icy cold, still unbelieving.

"Look, Dad, it's months before I go. I want the baby born here, and the job won't start until summer. So don't look so miserable."

Their food arrived and Harry toyed with his oysters and then his fish as Gail tried unsuccessfully to make him feel better.

They finished their lunch with long stretches of silence. Finally Harry reached across the table for her hand again and brought it to his lips.

"I love you, Gail."

"I know."

He saw a tear begin in the corner of her eye.

Harry tried to find himself again as they rose to leave. "Okay," he smiled, "I'll learn to live with it." He slipped his arm around her waist as they stepped into the glare and noise of the downtown street.

*H*arry was still upset when he returned to court. He rudely shrugged off a question from Parlier, who was sitting at the counsel table. Unpacking his papers, he fought for control—for the concentration he'd need to get through the afternoon. It would not be easy.

He announced that his next witness was Alden James, formerly financial vice president of UBS.

Harry could feel the tension in his own voice as he spoke. He hoped the jury couldn't discern the change.

After establishing James's background and his position with the network in 1983, Harry got to the point.

"How did you first hear that Mr. Parlier had been fired?"

"Alec Heath called and asked me to attend a meeting to discuss it."

"Did you do that?"

"Yes."

"Are you able to fix the date of that meeting?"

"Yes. It was the Monday after Parlier was fired. It's entered in my date book."

"And have you brought your date book with you?"

"Yes."

The book was marked for identification and returned to the witness.

"What was the date of the meeting at which Mr. Parlier's discharge was discussed with Mr. Heath?"

"Monday, April 11, 1983. It was in Mr. Heath's office."

"And who was present?"

"Alec Heath, Teddy Brenner and I."

"Mr. Brenner is now deceased, right?"

"Right."

"All right now, tell us what was said at the meeting about Mr. Parlier."

"Alec . . . that is Mr. Heath . . . said he had discovered facts about Mr. Parlier that made it impossible for him to continue at the network and also that he'd caught Parlier copying the company files on Sunday afternoon, the day before our meeting."

"Did he say what those 'facts' were that he'd discovered about Mr. Parlier?"

"Yes. He said he'd discovered Mr. Parlier had a criminal record."

"And this was said on Monday morning, the day after the Sunday Mr. Parlier was fired?"

"Yes."

"It was not two or three weeks later?"

"No sir, it was the day after Mr. Parlier was fired. Mr. Heath talked about catching Mr. Parlier copying the files 'yesterday afternoon' and said he'd fired him on the spot. It was definitely the day after he was fired."

"And in this same meeting Mr. Heath said that he had discovered Mr. Parlier's criminal record?"

"That's correct."

"That's all I have of this witness, Your Honor."

Aldrich had a brief, whispered conversation with Alec Heath and rose to cross-examine.

"Mr. James, how long have you known Mr. Parlier?"

"Oh, about ten to twelve years."

"You'd worked with him at ABC before you both came over to UBS, right?"

"Yes, that's right."

"And over that period of years you became his friend, isn't that correct?"

"No, no not really."

"Didn't you see each other socially?"

"No, only at network functions."

"And those occurred frequently?"

"Yes."

"And you cooperated in your work, isn't that correct?"

"Yes, that's certainly true."

"And your wives knew each other, right?"

"Yes, that's also correct."

"You and Mr. Parlier were not enemies, were you?"

"No."

"But even after all those years of association, you refuse to describe yourself as a friend?"

"Yes, that's right."

"Okay. Now, are you friends with Mr. Heath?"

"No."

"You don't like Mr. Heath, do you?"

"No."

"You lost your job at UBS because of Mr. Heath, didn't you?"

"He recommended that I be replaced."

"Did you feel that was justified?"

"No."

"I suppose that made you angry at Mr. Heath, isn't that correct?"

"Yes, it did."

"And, Mr. James, your date book doesn't show what was said at the April eleventh meeting, does it?"

"No, it doesn't."

"You didn't choose to write that down, did you?"

"No, I just generally list those present and sometimes the general subject matter of the meeting."

"And here your notes simply show 'Parlier firing,' right?"

"Yes, that's correct."

"You didn't write 'Parlier criminal record,' did you?"

"No, I didn't."

"Before April 11, 1983, did Mr. Parlier ever tell you he had a criminal record?"

"No."

"He kept that from you for the whole twelve-year period that you worked together, isn't that correct?"

"Well, he didn't tell me."

"And you didn't know?"

"No, I didn't know."

"That's all I have of this witness, Your Honor."

Aldrich had scored a few points, but nothing really damaging. Harry made a quick decision, once again, to leave well enough alone. "No further questions, Your Honor."

Next, Harry called Walter Solomon, a former partner in Price Waterhouse specializing in the television business and presently chief financial officer of NBC. Harry knew Solomon well and respected him, having represented his daughter five years earlier in a heavily contested divorce.

Solomon testified that he had examined Parlier's contract with UBS, the network's contracts with sponsors and agencies and its books and records on "High Rise," and that Parlier's percentage of the network's profits to date from this series would amount to five-point-three million dollars through the current season, but, of course, would continue so long as the series remained on the air. In Solomon's judgment, based on thirty years in the television business, the total value of Parlier's contract rights in "High Rise" was a minimum of ten million dollars.

Aldrich cross-examined Solomon briefly and gingerly. He brought out that his opinion was an estimate, that no one could really know accurately the amount of profits that would come from "High Rise" over the future years and that unexpected events, such as the death of one of the stars, might radically change the amount of money to be received. None of this really eliminated Solomon's ten million dollar estimate. Not if the jury wanted to buy it.

Again, Harry had no redirect examination. And when Solomon left the stand, Harry announced that the defense rested, both on the network's fraud claim and on Parlier's cross-complaint for the money due him under his contract.

Aldrich announced that he had at least one witness to call in support of his defense to Parlier's cross-complaint, but that having expected Harry to call additional witnesses, his next witness was scheduled to be in court first thing in the morning. Judge Hailey announced that court would be adjourned until ten A.M. the following day, a Thursday; and added that, since she was required to attend a three-day judicial conference in San Francisco, they would break for the day at lunchtime and there would be no session at all on Friday.

As Harry left the courtroom, anguish over Gail rushed in on him. He felt lucky to have made it through the afternoon without doing serious harm to the case, but now he wondered if he'd be able to do an effective job in the critical last phases of the trial, feeling the stress he did over Gail's leaving. At the moment, he felt absolutely miserable and unable to think of anything but Gail alone in a dismal London flat... waiting interminably for Robin Milgrim to call.

Reaching the front of the courthouse, he saw a gaunt man in a black suit standing on a stepladder surrounded by a small crowd.

The man held a cheap stopwatch in his outstretched hand.

"There is no God!" he shouted, facing the Music Center to the north.

Then, making precise military turns, he faced west, south and east, shouting his message in each direction.

Harry moved to the edge of the crowd.

"If there's a God, I give him one minute... sixty full seconds to strike me dead. If he can't do it, he ain't there. If he can't do it, we'll all know we've been had, that there is no God."

The man pushed the start button on his stopwatch and began calling out the seconds as they passed.

"Ten seconds. Where are you, God? How long can it take to strike this poor soul dead?

"Twenty seconds. He ain't done it yet. Pretty slow there, God.

"Thirty seconds." He began to do a little jig on the top of the stepladder. "He ain't gonna make it. He ain't gonna make it.

"Forty seconds." He pointed his stopwatch at the sky. "No one up there, my friends. No one up there.

"Fifty seconds. Not much time left. Kill me, God. Kill me fast or we'll all know the truth.

"Okay. That's it. Sixty seconds. One full minute, and I'm still alive.

"There is no God!" he trumpeted, turning to the north again.

Then the man repeated his message in each direction, folded his stepladder and moved away through the crowd.

It was a silly thing, and Harry couldn't explain it. But somehow he felt better—even felt the beginnings of a smile as he made his way to his car.

In the morning, a rainy Thursday, the bailiff called the court to order while some of the spectators were still hanging wet raincoats and stowing umbrellas. There was a scurry to find places as Judge Hailey took the bench.

"Remember, gentlemen, we'll break early today—at one o'clock—and we'll have no session tomorrow. I hope that causes no inconvenience."

Simultaneously, Harry and Aldrich assured the judge that it was fine.

"All right then, Mr. Aldrich, please call your next witness."

Aldrich called Neil Talbot to the stand. Harry looked knowingly at Matsuoka. They both knew Talbot would be the network's key witness on the creation of "High Rise." They knew Talbot would claim the series had been solely his idea.

Talbot, a network vice president for fifteen years, was Heath's chief henchman and constant companion. Harry thought that he had been somewhat tarnished in the jury's eyes by Parlier's testimony about the runaway teenager, but that he generally made a good impression and might just convince the jury that Parlier had made up the entire story.

A tall, stylish man in his early fifties, Talbot had wavy brown hair brushed back from his temples, prominent cheekbones and steady gray eyes. Looking tan and fit, he was dressed in soft English tweed and a subtly patterned Turnbull & Asser shirt. He moved with dignity to the stand and, from a leather pouch in his coat pocket, took out horn-rimmed half-glasses, which he placed at the end of his long, straight nose.

Talbot spoke quietly but with a deep, pleasant voice as Aldrich led him slowly through his background. He had worked in television for more than twenty years, first as a writer, then briefly as a producer and, finally, as a network executive primarily in the "creative" rather than financial end of the business. He described the numerous series and programs on which he had worked, sprinkling his testimony with humorous anecdotes about famous actors or story points in the network's best-known series. The jury was both interested and visibly impressed.

After the morning recess, Talbot told how "High Rise" came into being. As expected, he claimed the idea was entirely his. Convincingly, looking directly at the jury, he described in detail the very day it had occurred to him. He was, he said, in New York at the time, standing in his room at the Sherry Netherland Hotel. He was gazing out his window, looking at the General Motors building across the street and at the office workers taking lunch at the outdoor café in the plaza just below that building. That sight, he said, triggered the idea for a series based on life in a modern high-rise building, like the General Motors building itself . . . a series focusing on four girls, each working in a different office in the building.

Later that day, he had lunch with Lee Parlier and Teddy Brenner at the Côte Basque. He told them his new idea and they were highly enthusiastic. Writers were assigned to the project immediately, and it was quickly developed into a series for the coming season. The rest was history.

As Aldrich reached into his file for a document, Harry watched him with anger and frustration. Talbot's story about the moment of creation was not only highly effective but a complete surprise to

Harry, and, in his view of how to try a case, that should *never* happen. Unfortunately, in the pre-trial deposition Jay Kelly had taken early in the case, Kelly had not pressed Talbot sufficiently on the details of where, when and how he had created the idea. Now Harry would have to find a way to demonstrate that Talbot was lying, without the kind of careful, advance preparation upon which Harry typically relied.

Aldrich stepped to the witness stand and handed Talbot a copy of Parlier's memo of May 15, 1982. Talbot read it carefully and testified that this was the day of the lunch meeting at the Côte Basque, when he had presented the series idea, the same day on which the idea had come to him looking out the window of his hotel room.

"Then there is no question in your mind, Mr. Talbot, that you, not Mr. Parlier, had the original idea for 'High Rise' and that you, not Mr. Parlier, presented the idea at the May 15 meeting?"

Talbot looked directly at the jury again, peering over the top of his horn-rimmed glasses. "No question whatsoever, Mr. Aldrich," he said in a voice resounding with confidence and certainty.

"Your witness, counsel," said Aldrich, turning to Harry with a frigid smile. It was twelve-twenty. If the judge went until one, Harry had forty minutes to fill, with no effective cross-examination prepared. He needed time and needed it badly. He decided to try a bluff.

Smiling as he got to his feet, Harry tried to project to the jury the impression that he hadn't been hurt in the slightest by Talbot's testimony.

"Your Honor, I understood we were to break during the noon hour. If this is not a convenient time to stop, I'll be delighted to begin my cross-examination now." He rubbed his hands together as if he were prepared to destroy Talbot and relished the idea. He held his breath, awaiting the judge's reaction.

Judge Hailey looked over at the courtroom clock, then paused for a moment, considering the alternatives. "No, Mr. Cain, I see no point in starting, only to break for the next three days. We'll break now until Monday morning at ten o'clock and start your cross-examination then. Have a pleasant weekend, gentlemen."

Harry breathed an inward sigh of relief; and stuffing his papers hurriedly into a briefcase, rushed from the courtroom without a word

—220—

to anyone. Surprised at Harry's sudden departure, John Matsuoka raced after him, leaving their files scattered all over the counsel table. Matsuoka caught up to Harry in the corridor.

"Hey, you're in some hurry. We need to meet. Are you going back to the office?"

"No, John. I'm going to New York . . . and *fast*. I'll see you Monday."

*H*arry arrived in New York early Friday morning in the midst of a record blizzard. After checking into his hotel and showering, he hunched into his heavy Chesterfield coat and trudged through the falling snow, trying as best he could, in the limited time available, to check out Talbot's story—to find the facts that would help him overcome the favorable impression Talbot had made on the jury. It was a difficult, frustrating job, and one he wasn't sure he could complete before the New Yorkers he had to see dispersed for the weekend.

Nevertheless, by Saturday afternoon, having interviewed countless witnesses and called upon influential contacts to get him access to otherwise private records, Harry thought he had the key—the plan that could turn the case around still one more time.

In any event, by that time, there was little more he could do. The blizzard had stopped, and his work done, Harry went out to enjoy the city in its dazzling coat of white. The streets, blocked and free of traffic, were strangely silent. The sky was bright blue, the air crisp. The snow was piled high against the sides of the buildings, covering the litter, leaving everything clean. People were walking down Fifth Avenue on skis, while children threw snowballs and built igloos on the street corners. It was a New York Harry had never seen.

Breathing in the icy air, he crunched through the snow to Rockefeller Center. He stood at the rail above the ice rink, watching the skaters gliding to waltzes and carols, the massive brown-gray buildings rising behind them, their giant flags flapping and snapping in the winter wind.

After a few moments, feeling adventurous, Harry decided to walk all the way to the frozen East River. As he turned away from the rink, he bumped into a girl huddled into a red fox coat, the collar turned up over her ears. A beige muffler covered her face to the eyes . . . huge amber eyes.

"Carmel!"

"My God—Harry!"

Instinctively he pulled her to him, and she hugged back, rubbing her face against his with joy. Then she held him at arm's length.

"Harry, what are you doing here?"

"Business. But I get here often. How about you?"

"I live here now."

"You live here?"

She shivered. "Yes. Listen, would you like a cup of coffee? I'll tell you about it."

"I think I'd like more than that . . . I'm so excited to see you."

Carmel smiled; and hand in hand they moved through the crowd to the rink-side café, where they sat grinning at each other over a bottle of new Beaujolais.

Under her coat she wore a white silk blouse with a cashmere cardigan patterned in white, beige and camel. Her camel ski-pants were tucked into elegant suede boots of the same color. Her honey-blond hair, cut shorter than before, fell in soft curls around her splendid, high-cheekboned face. To Harry she looked like a delectable giant ice cream sundae . . . butterscotch with whipped cream.

After some laughter and preliminary small talk, Harry turned serious.

"You know, I felt like I was hit by a truck when I heard you were doing that at the Deauville."

"Doing *what*?"

"Letting Billy Frankenthal send you up to rooms."

"Who told you *that*?"

"Pat Tierny."

"Well, he's very wrong. I did work for Frankenthal, but strictly as a shill at the baccarat table, never a hooker. Even that made me feel sordid—you know, dressing up each night and pretending to be a player. I quit after a week."

Harry was suprised at the relief he felt. Reading it in his face, Carmel smiled.

"Do I get a question now?"

"Sure," he said.

"You're still with Nancy, aren't you?"

"Yeah."

"I knew you would be. Nobody new?"

He knew what she meant.

"No one," he said as he reached across and took her hand, looking into those overwhelming eyes. "I don't think I'm over *you*, Carmel. Maybe I won't ever be."

Carmel shuddered. The cold?

"Don't, Harry. Don't do that. We had our time together, our chance to make it. We didn't. I almost died, Harry. I wanted to or at least thought I did. One night, visiting home, I was about to drive right off the Mystic River Bridge. End it all. You know, the classic finish for the rejected lover. I sat there in the car, getting ready, for half an hour. But somehow, when it came time to jam my foot on the gas pedal, I didn't really want to do it.

"Vegas was bad, but not that bad. I had my painting. I'd started riding out into the desert—and I loved that. I had a couple of friends. Anyway, I just decided then and there that, as bad as the pain was— and it was still very bad—I wanted to live.

"So I flew back to Vegas and went on. I started some writing. Not bad really. I got a piece published in *Desert* magazine. I kept writing and riding and painting, and slowly I began to heal.

"Then one night I met this tall, serious man—Ben Taylor, a surgeon here in New York, out there for a medical convention, and everything changed."

"Married?"

Carmel grinned. "You sure know how to hurt a guy." Then the grin faded. "Yes, he's married, Harry, and I suppose, like you, he'll never leave her. But you know, I'm different now; I've got a better center of gravity. I enjoy him, really enjoy him, and I love him too."

"How often do you see him?"

"Oh, two, three times a week, sometimes more."

"Carmel, that's no life."

Suddenly the amber eyes flared with anger. "What more were you offering, Harry? An occasional picnic, an extra bang on the way home from court? Come on!"

Harry reached for her hand again. "You're right, Carmel. I'm sorry. But who said I'm fair when I care a lot?"

"Maybe you *cared* a lot, Harry. But even then it wasn't enough. And I was weaker then; I couldn't have made it. Maybe a few more months and I'd have gone off that bridge. But not now. Not with that sweet, bright, gentle man."

"Gentle?"

Again the eyes flared. "If you think 'gentle' means 'unexciting in bed' then you're an ignorant fool, and I don't think you are."

Now Harry grinned. "Okay, okay. I'm out of line. Go on, tell me about him."

And Carmel did, smiling again, laughing, telling Harry about her new man and their life, together and apart, as if Harry were an old, comfortable friend.

They finished the Beaujolais and strolled arm in arm up Fifth Avenue, delighting in the beauty of the silent, white day.

As they walked, Harry was swept away with his feeling for Carmel, for the magic day, for life in general. It was wildly exhilarating to be together again in the magic silence of that snow-covered city. It was as if they'd never been apart. He kept glancing over at that honey-colored hair, shining in the late afternoon sun. He could smell her fragrance, feel the warmth of her body pressed against his arm. He imagined her beside him again, arching her body, crying out with pleasure. He felt himself grow hard even as he walked.

As they reached the entrance to the Hotel Pierre at Sixty-first Street, he stopped. Taking Carmel by the shoulders, he looked directly, probingly, into her eyes, the way he used to, the dark, intense look she always said made her weak, yielding, "buttery in the knees."

His eyes never left hers, as he spoke. "This is where I'm staying, Carmel. Come on in. Let's be together again."

For just a moment the amber eyes glazed and then focused again. Carmel stepped back and took his hands from her shoulders. There was a long silence. Then she spoke, slowly and quietly.

"You'd really do that to me, wouldn't you? Really spoil everything I told you I've tried to build. And why? For what? Because you want to win . . . to beat Ben, a guy you don't even know? Or, worse still, is it just that you're horny and I'm available?

"Jesus, Harry, you plunge through life like a destructive child.

Don't you ever consider the impact of what you do on those you do it to? Don't you care? Listen, forget about your general behavior. What about me? What about your old friend Carmel. Would you really do that to *me?*"

She paused, taking another step back toward the corner. She looked at him in silence for a long time. Then she smiled. "Don't look so stricken, pal. You haven't lost it. You'd always tempt me. A year ago . . . six months ago, I'd have gone for it, blown it all, wallowing in the excitement of self-degradation. But not now. Oh boy, not now! I've got the man I want and the life I want. And as for you . . . well, it wouldn't really be honest to say 'the feeling is gone,' but I can sure as hell tell you 'never again.' I can say 'we're over' and mean it, Harry—and we are—Harry, over for good. So good luck, my friend. Enjoy yourself."

She turned and walked quickly across Sixty-first Street. Harry stood as if poleaxed. He watched her move on up the avenue, fading into the gathering twilight, moving away, out of his life.

Like an automaton, Harry lurched through the swinging door into the Pierre cocktail lounge. Reaching the bar, he ordered a vodka martini. He drank it quickly, ordered another and carried it to a dark table in the corner.

An hour later, as the lounge began to fill, Harry rose shakily and moved toward the elevators through the growing crowd at the bar. Only one man, an advertising executive in from Chicago, noticed that the dark, slim man in the Chesterfield had tears in his eyes.

On Monday morning, Harry had control again. He had to. This was the day that would make or break the case. He wore his favorite navy suit, his lucky rep tie. He looked fit and ready, even though one who knew him well would have noticed a grayness to the skin, a slight redness of the eye, a tension at the corners of the mouth. All day Sunday, flying across the country, he had tried to drown his feelings about Carmel with Stolichnaya martinis. By the time he had landed in Los Angeles, he thought he had it all in place.

Monday morning brought a headache; but coffee and aspirin brought relief, and with excitement at the result of his investigation, Harry was actually looking forward to the day.

When Judge Hailey took the bench, Talbot had already resumed the witness stand, looking relaxed and ready. Harry rose slowly, measuring him. The man was an impressive witness, no doubt about that. If Harry was unable to destroy his testimony, the best he could hope for was a compromise verdict that would do very little for Lee Parlier.

"Mr. Talbot, it is your testimony that you actually remember the very moment of creating the idea for 'High Rise'?"

"Yes sir, I do."

"And you got that idea by looking out of your hotel room window?"

"That's correct, sir. I looked out across Fifty-ninth Street at the General Motors building, the way the building rose up above that crowded plaza. I saw all those pretty girls in the plaza having coffee in the sunshine, and I thought, God, what a marvelous setting for a series."

"Mr. Talbot, isn't this something that just *might* have happened, that you are speculating about, not something that you actually remember?"

"No, Mr. Cain, it happens to be quite vivid in my memory. It was a very big day in my life."

"You were in your own room, sir, at the Sherry Netherland Hotel in New York?"

"Yes, that's right."

"Not someone else's room?"

Talbot showed mild impatience. "My *own* room, Mr. Cain."

"You're sure?"

"I'm quite sure, sir."

"And are you telling us you actually recall looking out that window . . . seeing the girls in that Fifty-ninth Street café . . . you *really* remember that?"

"I am telling you that, and I do remember. You asked me two questions here, Mr. Cain, but that's quite all right."

Harry smiled with self-deprecation. "I'm sorry, Mr. Talbot. . . . Now, what did you do after you got the idea for the series there in your hotel room?"

"I left the room and walked over to the Côte Basque for my lunch with Mr. Parlier and Mr. Brenner."

"And that would be May 15, 1982?"

"That's correct."

"Could it have been *after* May 15 . . . or even before?"

Talbot looked impatient again—he sighed, showing the jury he was a tolerant gentleman. "It was May 15, Mr. Cain, the day of the Brenner, Parlier lunch, not after, not before."

"When you were looking from your hotel room out onto the General Motors plaza, did you look through the window or did you open it up?"

"It was open, Mr. Cain. It was a beautiful spring day and the window was wide open."

"The people you looked down on in the General Motors plaza, were they colorfully dressed?"

"Yes, I remember looking at all those short skirts, with some sadness considering my age, Mr. Cain." This time, Talbot gave a wistful smile. Harry smiled back.

"You're talking about girls sitting in the General Motors plaza, on Fifth Avenue and Fifty-ninth Street, is that correct?"

"Yes, Mr. Cain . . . once again, that's what I mean."

Even the jury was beginning to stir restlessly at the repetitious nature of Harry's questions.

"And could you see the *top* of the General Motors building from your hotel room as well?"

"I can't remember. I know I leaned out the window to look up, but I'm not sure if I actually saw the very top."

"Mr. Talbot, did you have to lean out the window in order to see the Fifty-ninth Street plaza below the building where the girls were having their coffee?"

"No, I could see that just standing in the room looking out the window."

"And Mr. Talbot, there's no question in your mind that this is how and when you got the idea for the television series 'High Rise'?"

Talbot sighed again.

"None whatsoever, Mr. Cain, as I've told you now three times."

"And you're sure that was the same day as your lunch with Mr. Parlier and Mr. Brenner?"

Talbot was getting angry now. Harry thought that might be helpful, but the jury was impatient too, and even Judge Hailey looked displeased. Talbot responded as if speaking to a retarded child. "Mr. Cain, we've covered this ground again and again, but I'll do it once more for you. On May 15, just before my luncheon date with Parlier and Brenner at the Côte Basque, I looked out of my hotel room at the Sherry Netherland Hotel and saw the General Motors plaza. At that moment, Mr. Cain, that very moment, I hit on the idea for 'High Rise.' That's all I can say about it. Please don't ask me again. My answer will just be the same."

"That's all I have, Your Honor," said Harry, and returned to the counsel table.

"No questions," said Aldrich, pleased that Harry's manifestly ineffectual examination had only reinforced Talbot's story.

After conferring briefly with Heath, Aldrich announced that the network rested its defense against Parlier's cross-complaint for the money due under his contract. It was eleven-thirty A.M.

Harry rose and quietly addressed the judge. "Your Honor, I'm reluctant to delay these proceedings at all, but our next witness, who will testify in rebuttal, is flying in from out of the city and will not arrive until about one o'clock. May we take the noon recess early?"

Again Judge Hailey looked displeased. But she was a courteous, tolerant judge.

"All right, Mr. Cain, we'll reconvene at one-thirty."

Parlier followed Harry from the courtroom, visibly shaken. Harry cautioned him to hold any comments until they were out of the hearing of jury members. When they reached the elevators, Parlier could contain himself no longer. "Harry, look, I know you're great, but that cross-examination, I mean you got nothing at all. You did everything you've told me a good lawyer shouldn't do—just got Talbot to repeat and re-emphasize his story. That jury's gonna buy his story, damn it. I can tell. I was ready to believe it myself and I *know* it's a lie."

Harry smiled, putting his arm around Parlier's shoulders. "Lee, I don't pick television shows. Don't try this case."

"Huh?"

"Just wait a little. Maybe you'll be surprised." He excused himself, sending Parlier to have lunch with John Matsuoka.

Harry telephoned Clara to see about the arrangements to get his next witness safely to court. Then he bought an egg salad sandwich, and a carton of milk from the stand in the courthouse and sprawled on the grass in the civic center mall, planning his afternoon.

When court reconvened at one-thirty, Harry was huddled with a portly, middle-aged man in a gray three-piece suit who, from his nervous glances around the room, seemed very ill at ease.

"Proceed, Mr. Cain," the judge announced in a particularly stern tone, adding to the discomfort of the nervous little man.

"Our next witness is Mr. Albert Navarro," Harry announced, nodding to the newcomer.

Aldrich looked over at Heath, who shrugged. He looked at Talbot, who also indicated he had no idea who this witness might be.

After the witness was sworn and gave his name, he moved stiffly to the stand. As he sat down, he dropped his file, scattering papers across the courtroom floor. He looked terrified as the bailiff helped him gather them together.

Harry leaned over to Parlier. "Lee, this guy's really nervous. I'm gonna try a little something to make the jury feel sympathy for him instead of thinking he's lying. Usually it works, but you never know."

Harry rose and stood silently for a long moment. Then, smiling, he said, "I guess you feel a little nervous, Mr. Navarro?"

The witness seemed to relax a bit, glad to have it out in the open.

"Yes sir, yes I do, just a bit."

"First time in court?"

"Yes sir."

"Okay, let me know if it gets too bad." Harry grinned. Most of the jury smiled too, their sympathy going out to someone who honestly admitted his natural reaction to the strange and sometimes terrifying courtroom situation. Navarro, who seemed visibly more at ease, shyly smiled back.

"What's your occupation, Mr. Navarro?"

"I'm assistant manager at the Sherry Netherland Hotel in New York City."

"And how long have you held that position?"

"Seven years."

"And how long have you worked at the Sherry Netherland?"

"In any capacity?"

"Yes sir."

"Twenty years next month."

"You started as a room clerk and worked your way up, is that right?"

"That's correct."

"And have you brought with you the hotel occupancy records for the week of May 12, 1982?"

"Yes, I have."

"Consulting those records, sir, was Mr. Neil Talbot registered at the Sherry Netherland on May 15, 1982?"

Navarro looked at the familiar records, feeling even more at home. "He was."

"And, what was his room number?"

"Five-fifteen."

"How long was his stay in that room on that occasion?"

"He stayed from May 12 through May 16."

Harry motioned to the back of the courtroom where Clara and another secretary from his office were standing. They came forward with a six-foot cardboard tube.

"May I have just a moment, Your Honor, to unfurl an exhibit?"

"Certainly, Mr. Cain."

Harry took from the tube a six-foot-square diagram, and, with John and Clara helping, tacked it to the cork board near the witness stand. Harry paused and turned to the judge. "Your Honor, I'm sorry. This is my secretary, Clara Porter. I've already introduced Mr. Matsuoka." Clara smiled nervously at the judge and returned to her seat. Harry turned to the witness.

"Mr. Navarro, would you please come over here and look at this exhibit. Does it appear to be an accurate diagram of the fifth floor of the Sherry Netherland Hotel?"

Navarro got up and walked slowly over to the diagram, examining it carefully. "Yes sir, it does."

"And would you point out Fifth Avenue on the diagram."

"Yes sir, it's right here at the bottom of the chart."

"And Fifty-ninth Street?" Navarro pointed to the right side of the diagram.

"And Mr. Navarro, where is the General Motors Plaza in relation to this diagram?"

"Well, it's not shown on the diagram itself, but it's here on the right, across Fifty-ninth Street from the hotel." Again, he indicated the right side of the exhibit.

"Now, what is the space right here in the middle of the hotel?"

"Well, that's an air shaft, Mr. Cain, it runs the full length of the hotel."

"Okay now, Mr. Navarro, where is room 515?"

"Well, it's on the air shaft, sir, right here." Navarro, now beginning to enjoy himself, pointed to the middle of the chart.

"On the air shaft?" Harry asked loudly.

"Yes sir."

"It's not on Fifty-ninth Street or on Fifth Avenue near Fifty-ninth Street?"

"No sir."

"Are you familiar with room five fifteen, Mr. Navarro?"

"Oh yes sir, I've been in it many, many times."

"And did you check it again, Mr. Navarro, just before coming out here to testify?"

"Yes sir, I did."

"Does room five fifteen have any windows on Fifty-ninth Street or on Fifth Avenue?"

"No sir."

"What do you see from the windows of room five fifteen, Mr. Navarro?"

"Well, sir, you see the other side of the hotel across the air shaft."

"Is that all you see?"

"Yes sir."

"Can you see any part of the General Motors Plaza from room five fifteen?"

"No sir. That would be impossible. From room five fifteen you can only see the other side of our own building across the air shaft."

"That's all I have of Mr. Navarro, Your Honor. I would appreciate it if Mr. Navarro could be excused as soon as Mr. Aldrich's cross-examination is over. He has a four o'clock plane to catch back to New York."

Judge Hailey looked over at Aldrich, who was writing a note to Talbot. "Well, Mr. Cain, I can't cut off Mr. Aldrich's cross-examination, you know that. But Mr. Navarro can certainly be excused as soon as Mr. Aldrich is finished."

Now, Aldrich, Heath and Talbot began to confer at the counsel table, whispering with some agitation. Aldrich looked up. "May we have a moment, Your Honor?"

"Yes, Mr. Aldrich, you may."

The whispered conference continued for three or four minutes with Heath and Talbot doing what appeared to be most of the talking. Then Aldrich rose, "Your Honor, as a courtesy to Mr. Navarro and considering the information given me just now by my clients, no cross-examination is necessary."

Harry stood also. "May Mr. Navarro leave then, your Honor?"

"Yes, he may, Mr. Cain."

At Harry's nod, Navarro left the stand, shook hands with Harry and walked to the courtroom door. Clara rose to leave with him.

Harry turned back to the judge. "We recall Neil Talbot as an adverse witness, Your Honor." Talbot gave Aldrich a look of surprise and walked back to the witness stand.

Harry just looked at Talbot for several seconds, then he began. "Well, Mr. Talbot, you didn't see the General Motors Plaza from your hotel room, did you?"

"I guess not, but—"

"Could it have been someone else's room in the hotel that same day?"

Talbot paused as if in serious thought. He took off his glasses and rubbed the bridge of his nose. "You know something, Mr. Cain, I think you're right. Now that I think more about it, I think it was Alec Heath's suite at the Sherry. It's on the corner of Fifth Avenue and Fifty-ninth Street. That's where I looked out the window and got the idea for the series."

"And you were alone in Mr. Heath's suite, is that your testimony?"

"No, the more I think about it, the more I think... in fact, I'm sure Alec was there too."

"And so it was in Alec Heath's rooms at the Sherry Netherland, and in his presence, that you looked out on the General Motors Plaza and go the idea for 'High Rise,' is that correct?"

"Yes. That's where it was, not in my room, but Alec's, and he was there too."

"Mr. Heath was in the room with you, you're sure?"

"Yes I am."

"And this was still on May 15, you're still sure about that?"

"Definitely. I had the right day and the right hotel but the wrong room, and I had simply forgotten that Alec was there too."

"Okay, despite your earlier testimony, you're now sure that it was Alec Heath's suite, May 15 and that's where and when you got the idea for the series?"

"Absolutely, Mr. Cain. Alec was there, as I said; I looked out the window of his suite and got the idea. I told him the idea and he was thrilled with it. Then, that same day, I met with Parlier and Brenner and told them the same idea."

"Thank you. That's all." Harry turned away from the witness.

Aldrich indicated he had no questions of Talbot. Once again, Harry looked over at the UBS counsel table. "Now we'll call Alec Heath, Your Honor, also as an adverse witness."

Again, a surprised look passed between Heath and Aldrich. They had no idea what Harry was doing or where he was going with this line of questioning. Heath returned to the stand a different man, far from the confident, clear-eyed witness at the start of the case. He was in trouble with the jury and he was smart enough to know it.

"Mr. Heath, you just heard Mr. Talbot testify that you and he were in your corner suite at the Sherry on May 15, and that it was there that he got the idea for 'High Rise' and described it to you, right there on the spot, is that correct?"

"Yes, I heard that."

"Now Mr. Heath, I want you to think carefully about this answer ... not one word of that testimony was true, was it?"

Aldrich was on his feet at once, "Objection, argumentative."

"I'll rephrase the question, Your Honor."

"Now Mr. Heath, please tell me whether or not Mr. Talbot's testimony on the point was true."

"Yes, it was absolutely true."

"Absolutely true," Harry repeated in a louder tone. "You actually remember seeing Mr. Talbot looking out the window of your hotel suite on May 15 and coming up with the series idea?"

"Yes sir, I do."

"Well, you heard him testify earlier that it was in his own room, not yours, that he got the idea. You didn't correct the record at that time, did you?"

Heath smiled. "That's true, counselor, but I thought it made no difference at all whether it was in his room or mine. The point is he looked out at the GM building and got the idea. Then, later in the day, he told the idea to Parlier and Parlier stole it. It made no difference which room it was."

"But you're certain that all of this happened in your room, not his, is that correct?"

"Yes, counselor, I'm certain."

"And you're certain that this occurred on May 15, before the Parlier luncheon meeting, *and that you were present?*"

"Absolutely."

"That's all I have of Mr. Talbot, Your Honor. If Mr. Aldrich has no questions, may we have a five-minute recess?" Aldrich looked up and smiled calmly. "No questions, Your Honor." The judge rose to leave the bench, announcing a recess until three-fifteen. Harry leaned over to John Matsuoka, giving him hurried instructions. John rushed from the courtroom.

Five minutes later, the jury filed in and Judge Hailey took the bench, looking with puzzlement at Harry, who sat alone at the counsel table with no witness in the courtroom. "Mr. Cain, are you ready to proceed?"

"Yes, Your Honor."

"Well, then, please call your next witness."

"Your Honor, our next witness is on his way down from the cafeteria. Mr. Matsuoka should be arriving with him right this minute."

An unexpected hush fell over the courtroom. All eyes focused on the courtroom doors. Ten seconds later the doors swung open, and John Matsuoka re-entered the room accompanied by Albert Navarro, the Sherry Netherland's assistant manager. "We recall Albert Navarro, Your Honor," Harry boomed.

Aldrich was immediately on his feet shouting, "Your Honor, I gave up my cross-examination to permit this man to make a four o'clock plane. We're the victims of misrepresentation here, another trick by Mr. Cain. This is totally improper." Down came the gavel "Gentlemen, approach the bench please." Harry and Aldrich each moved forward to the judge, who looked at Harry, expecting an explanation.

Harry spoke quietly. "Your Honor, my understanding with Mr. Navarro was that my secretary would drive him to his plane if I didn't get word to him in the cafeteria by three-fifteen that I needed him further. On the outside chance that I might need him, he agreed to catch a later flight. Because of the rather surprising change in testimony by Mr. Talbot and by Mr. Heath just now, I did feel I needed Mr. Navarro again. Fortunately, I was just able to catch him. If Mr. Aldrich has further questions, he can certainly ask them now."

Aldrich started to speak, but Judge Hailey cut him off. "Mr. Aldrich, I see no valid objection to Mr. Navarro's being recalled. You may cross-examine him as long as you like. Now let's proceed."

Navarro stepped once again to the stand, this time with a shy smile to the jury. Harry moved to the corner of the jury box and spoke in a clear, firm tone, "Mr. Navarro, does Mr. Alec Heath maintain a suite at the Sherry Netherland?"

"Yes sir, number eleven-oh-two."

"And do you keep a record of when Mr. Heath is in residence at that suite?"

"Yes sir, we do."

"And on May 15, 1982, was Mr. Heath in residence at the Sherry?"

Navarro thumbed through his file and consulted a lined sheet. "No sir, he was not. Mr. Heath was in London from May 12 through May 16."

Aldrich was on his feet again. "Objection, Your Honor, hearsay. This witness can't know whether Mr. Heath was in London. How can his occupancy records show that?"

The judge looked at Harry, who smiled. "Let me just lay the foundation for that, Your Honor." The judge nodded.

"Mr. Navarro, did you bring any records with you other than occupancy records?"

"Yes sir, I brought the hotel telephone records for the period May 12 through May 17."

Harry walked to the witness stand and took a sheaf of telephone records from Navarro. "And are these the telephone records?"

"Yes sir, they are."

"And are they records kept in the ordinary course of business of the Sherry Netherland Hotel?"

"Yes sir."

"And do those records indicate the whereabouts of Mr. Heath during the period of May 12 through 15?"

"Yes sir, they do."

"What do they show in that regard?"

"Well, sir, they show that on May 13, 14 and 15 Mr. Talbot called Mr. Alec Heath in London person-to-person at the Connaught Hotel and that those calls were completed to Mr. Heath in London. They also show that Mr. Heath called Mr. Talbot at the Sherry Netherland from London on May 13 and 14 and twice on May 15. Mr. Heath also made three other calls from London on May 15, charging those calls to the phone in his suite at the Sherry Netherland."

"So you have two sets of records that show independently of each other that Mr. Heath was not in residence at the Sherry Netherland on May 15, 1982, is that correct?"

"Yes sir, that's correct."

"That's all. Thank you."

Aldrich, looking pale and tense, tried for several minutes of cross-examination to cast doubt on the accuracy of the hotel records and on Albert Navarro's memory of the hotel layout. He made no progress at all, and correctly sensing that the jury was sympathethic to Navarro, gave up the attempt.

Navarro was excused at three-forty-five. Not in time to make the four o'clock flight to New York, but well in time for the six o'clock. As he left the courtroom, Harry announced, "The defendant and cross-complainant rests, Your Honor."

Aldrich stood slowly, visibly shaken by the turn in the case. "Your Honor, may I approach the bench again?"

"Yes, certainly, Mr. Aldrich."

In a whispered conference, Aldrich tried unsuccessfully to gain a two weeks' continuance in which to gather rebuttal evidence. Failing that, he asked for five days. Judge Hailey refused even one day but agreed to end the proceedings early that day, with Aldrich to present any rebuttal testimony he had in the morning.

Two hours later, Harry arrived back at his office to find John Matsuoka telling two young associates what had happened in court. He was crowing that Harry had sprung a double trap that completely destroyed both Talbot and Heath. When Harry sat down at his desk, Clark brought a tortoise shell tray containing slices of crisp pippin apples, Harry's favorite Parmesan cheese and iced glasses of Trefethen Chardonnay.

Harry twirled an imaginary cigar and mimicking W. C. Fields, growled, "What you saw today, ladies and gentlemen, was the old invited alibi trick."

Then, sipping the cold wine, he explained. "If I had just clobbered Talbot with Navarro's testimony about room five fifteen being on the air shaft, he would probably have come up with some explanation I couldn't disprove, at least not in time. But I wanted to suggest a way out for him when he was in trouble and before he had time to make a plan, a way out that I knew wouldn't work at all, I thought he might just grab at it, like a drowning man grabs at a life preserver; and when Talbot heard that room five fifteen was on the air shaft, he was certainly a drowning man.

"Anyway, if I could lure him into saying it was Heath's room, not his, I could kill him twice, with a chance at getting Heath as well."

Harry's senior associate wasn't convinced. "But Harry, you'd already destroyed Heath, and you'd just smashed Talbot. What could Talbot possibly have said that would have saved him?"

"Well," Harry grinned, relaxing with the wine, "as far as Heath is concerned, you may be right that his letter to the FCC destroyed him with the jury. But that was days ago, and I needed something dramatic to hit him with at the end of the case. As to Talbot, he could have said today what he probably will come up with tomorrow, that he got the idea for the series a week earlier, *before Heath went to London*, while he was standing in Heath's suite looking out at the GM building. They were just confused about the dates.

"That story would have been tough to deal with. Navarro couldn't have helped me with it because his books simply wouldn't have foreclosed the possibility. Heath really was at the hotel a week earlier, and Talbot could really have been in his room then."

"But he can still say that," replied the senior associate. "He can still hit you with that one in the morning."

"Sure, but I don't think the jury will buy it now. They might buy one change in story from Talbot, but not two. If he was going to move the date from May 15 to a week earlier, he had to come up with that explanation right away. Once he tried to shift the place from his own room on the air shaft... to Heath's room, *keeping the same date*, he was lost. I just don't see the jury buying still another change in his story, although I guess he'll try it."

John put down his glass and took his turn. "What I don't fully understand, Harry, is why you didn't hold Navarro over until tomorrow morning so that his testimony could be the very last thing before argument. Wouldn't that have had much more impact on the jury?"

"You're absolutely right about that, John. But if I'd done that, Aldrich probably would have used the evening to check on Heath's whereabouts on May 15 and he would have had Talbot and Heath both change their stories before Navarro testified. They would have said that the idea came to Talbot in Heath's room before Heath went to England.

"Before Navarro told the jury where Alec Heath was on May 15, Talbot and Heath might have gotten away with another change. This way, changing their story another time *after* Navarro blew their second alibi out of the water will look very phony.

"Now, if you'll all excuse me, I've got about twenty calls to return before I prepare my final argument."

That night, at home, Harry told Nancy how the day had gone. She listened appreciatively to the way he had used Navarro to double-trap both Heath and Talbot. She seemed a different person from the angry lady who'd attacked him so bitterly, so passionately over his tactics in the Malone case and over his own infidelity, which Harry assumed was the real cause of the attack.

Yet there was still a reserve about Nancy, a distance he couldn't fully bridge. Apparently it had been there since she had been confronted by his affair with Carmel and faced up to the knowledge that there had been others in the past. Harry was virtually certain it was

Liz Watterson who had told her. He supposed it didn't matter *how* she knew, as long as she knew. He wasn't sure what that knowledge meant to their marriage in the long run. He wanted the problem to go away, wanted things to be just as they had been with Nancy—or at least as he had perceived them to be. But he knew that probably couldn't happen, that, for years, Nancy had been avoiding her own feelings and trying to hide a lot of pain and growing bitterness that had finally come out into the open and might never be fully put away. And what kind of man was he, he wondered, not to have seen the pain in his own wife? He shivered at the answer to *that* question.

The next day, as Harry had predicted, Aldrich put Talbot back on the stand to change his story still one more time. He had been tired yesterday, he said, confused about the date. The idea for the series, in fact, came to him in Alec Heath's suite, not his own. That part of his testimony had been correct. But it had been a few days before the meeting with Parlier on the fifteenth, before Heath left for London. He now realized that it was not the day of the Parlier-Brenner lunch, as he originally had remembered it. After all, this was years before the trial, and he had attended at least a thousand meetings in that period.

Harry's cross-examination was short and concise. Unlike his usual approach, his tone was angry. "Sir, when you had your deposition taken in this case in early 1984, you testified you got the idea for the series the very day of the Parlier meeting, that is May 15, 1982, looking out the window of your room at the GM building, isn't that correct?"

Aldrich was on his feet at once. "We'll stipulate that's what the deposition says, Your Honor."

"That's not the point, Your Honor. This witness might claim that the court reporter took his deposition testimony down wrong. This witness might claim *anything*. This witness—"

Down came the gavel. "Enough, Mr. Cain." Judge Hailey gave Harry a menacing look. "I will not tolerate this kind of colloquy, not from either of you. Mr. Aldrich, if what you made is an objection,

it is overruled. The question is proper and the witness may answer."
Talbot looked uncomfortable.

"Well, Mr. Talbot, is that what you said back in early 1984?"

"Yes. I was wrong about the date though."

"And about the room as well?"

"Yes. I was wrong about that as well."

"In other words, your recollection now, years later, is much better than it was back then, closer to the time the events occurred. Is that what you want the jury to believe?"

"Objection. Argumentative and mischaracterizes the evidence."

"Withdraw the question," snapped Harry.

"Now, Mr. Talbot, after you heard Mr. Navarro testify yesterday that you could not have seen the GM plaza from your room because it was on the air shaft, you changed the place where you claimed you got the idea for the series to Mr. Heath's room, is that correct?"

"Yes. He brought it back to mind."

"And you then claimed that Mr. Heath was there when you got the idea, isn't that right?"

"Yes sir, he was. I'd forgotten."

"Yes, so you told us. And after hearing Mr. Navarro and having your memory refreshed you still said yesterday, as you also said way back in 1982, that you got the idea for the series looking out of Alec Heath's hotel room on May 15, the very day of the meeting with Mr. Parlier, isn't that correct?"

"Yes, but I was wrong about that too."

"Yes, and now after you heard Mr. Navarro testify the second time that Mr. Heath was in England on that day, your testimony has now changed again, so now you say it happened the week before, is that right?"

"Right, and that's the truth."

"And will the story change a third time if Mr. Navarro testifies that Mr. Heath was in some other city that day also?"

Talbot looked with ill-concealed terror at the courtroom door as if he expected Navarro to come back still again.

Aldrich cut in before he answered. "Your Honor, that question, like this entire line of questioning, is argumentative and improper and—"

"I withdraw the question, Your Honor. That's all I have." Harry sat down. Aldrich started to speak again, thought better of it. He sat down also, conferring in whispers with Heath. Finally he rose, "No redirect, Your Honor. We'll recall Mr. Heath."

Heath looked haggard, nervous, as he walked stiffly to the stand one more time. Harry recalled the confident, vigorous Alex Heath who started off the plaintiff's case so many days ago. This man seemed ten years older.

Quickly Aldrich questioned Heath about his testimony of the preceeding day. Like Talbot, he'd been confused about the date. It was not the fifteenth, of course. He'd been in London on the fifteenth. It was the preceding week, probably the eleventh or the twelfth that Talbot had come up with the series idea in his room.

Then Aldrich touched briefly on the testimony of Alden James. Heath testified that, contrary to what James had said, he did not give Parlier's criminal record as the reason for firing him in the meeting with James and Teddy Brenner—the meeting that took place the day after Parlier was fired. What he gave as the reason, he claimed, was Parlier's Xeroxing the records. "No further questions," said Aldrich, returning to his seat.

Harry, who had been leaning back in his chair gazing at the ceiling during Heath's entire testimony, continued looking bored and drawled, "No questions, Your Honor."

Aldrich seemed surprised and perhaps relieved. He turned to the judge, "That ends our rebuttal testimony, Your Honor." It was eleven forty-five.

"Mr. Cain?"

Harry rose and faced the judge. "We have nothing further, Your Honor. Will we begin argument now or after the lunch break?"

"Actually, gentlemen, I'd like to take this afternoon to review your briefs and read some of the cases you've cited. Please be prepared to argue tomorrow morning. We'll stand adjourned until ten A.M."

As soon as they left the courtroom, Parlier wanted to know why Harry hadn't gone after Heath the way he'd gone after Talbot. "Well, Lee, I'm convinced the jury doesn't believe this change of story and that they do believe Alden James. Anything I could have asked Heath would have been mostly a rehash of points I'd already made with Talbot or points that could be better made in argument when Heath has no chance to explain. If I went after him now, I might have

—241—

given Heath another chance to give some explanation, maybe convince somebody on the jury.

"By saying 'No questions,' I told the jury 'I just don't buy this any more than you buy it, and we don't need any more time and questions to show that this guy is a fake.' It's a judgment call, Lee, and I made the call. That's what you pay me for."

Parlier threw his arm around Harry's shoulders. "You're the boss, Harry, you're in charge and you're doing great, just great. Whatever you say is *it!*"

Sure, Harry thought, excusing himself to go to the phone, so long as it works.

"A divorce? Christ! I didn't dream you were coming here about a divorce. I mean, you must know what a difficult situation that is for me."

May Nathan sat across from Harry, her hands folded primly in her lap, the lamp light casting soft shadows on her pale, serious face. She had called for a late appointment while Harry was still in court, leaving word that it was "important." With his closing argument already prepared and generally committed to memory, Harry felt he could make the time for her. After all, Alan Nathan was an old friend, and with Alan confined to a wheelchair, Harry hadn't been surprised that it was May who was coming in to see him about whatever the problem was.

Now, sitting quietly in Harry's office, the rest of the staff gone, May had told him the reason for her visit. Her eyes registered surprise and concern at Harry's reaction.

"What's so difficult about it, Harry? I don't understand."

"Well, May, for Christ's sake. Alan's my friend."

"And I'm not?"

"You both are, May. That's just the point. I can't go after Alan the way I should if I'm going to represent you properly. You need someone without that kind of restraint. Someone who can really get tough if that's what the case requires."

"I believe you can do it, Harry, or I wouldn't be here." She had

—242—

a look of determination and intensity he had never seen in her before.

The clock on Harry's desk softly chimed eight o'clock.

"Listen, Harry, the fact is I *need* this divorce. I want to marry another man...as soon as I can. I'm in love—can't really help myself about it. It's the most important thing in my life right now. Look, I've put aside some money over the years...Alan doesn't know...a little here, a little there. I've got seventy-five thousand dollars now, Harry, and it's yours if you'll take the case."

"Money's not the problem, May, it's how I feel about Alan. It's whether I can do an adequate job feeling as I do."

"I know you can, Harry. Listen, my friend doesn't like you at all, but he says you're far and away the best."

"Your friend?"

"The man I love, the one I'm going to marry...Robin Milgrim."

Harry sat forward, startled. "Robin Milgrim?"

"Sure. Why do you seem so surprised? Look, I know you had a case against him, he told me, and I know he's married. But there's nothing left between him and Diana, and he's not going to stay with her. He's going to marry me. I'm sure of it."

Harry knew he should cut this off, stop May from making any further disclosures about her relationship with Milgrim. He couldn't. He had to know.

"How long have you been seeing Milgrim?" he asked, trying to keep the anxiety from his voice, to sound clinical.

"Seeing him? Come on, Harry, we can't be mid-Victorian about this. I've been sleeping with Robin on and off for six months now. Here, London, other places. Alan likes him, you know. They've become great buddies." She paused, as if deciding something. "What you probably don't know is that Alan is Robin's best source of inside information about Alan's supposed friends." She took a sip of tea and smiled at Harry, waiting to see how he reacted to what she'd told him. He didn't believe her.

"Anyway," she went on, "it started getting serious in October when the four of us, Robin, Diana, Alan and I rented a villa together in Portofino. The trip exhausted Alan, and he knocks himself out every night with Seconal anyway. Well, Robin emptied two of Alan's pills in Diana's brandy. Half an hour later, she was out like a light, and Robin and I made it all night long. Sweet Jesus, it was wonderful!

—243—

We decided to do that every night, and we got away with it. By the time the trip was over, we were in love. I mean the whole bit... smoldering looks, little squeezes under the table, all of it. We were like two kids, but how great it was... and still is.

"You know what he calls me, Harry?" Something made Harry afraid to hear. "Princess," she continued, "that's what he calls me ... 'Princess.' It comes from a poem he wrote for me, 'The Moonlight Princess.' My God, what a romantic he is! Anyway, we're in love. He's going to leave Diana, and then, if I've gotten my divorce, we'll be married."

Harry gripped the arms of his chair until his knuckles whitened. "Does he know you're leaving Alan?" he asked, trying not to show his shock and anger.

"He knows I want to, but I doubt he expected me to make up my mind so quickly and actually move ahead like this. He'll really be surprised... and pleased."

"I'm sure of it," said Harry, trying to keep the bitter irony out of his voice.

May reached over, took one of Harry's hands in hers. "Then you'll take the case?" she said, giving him a vulnerable, pleading look. It was almost childlike, that look. Harry thought she must deploy it regularly in manipulating Alan. Well, she'd have met her match in Robin Milgrim. Harry stood up, releasing her hand.

"May, I'm a peculiar guy. Alan's my friend. I just can't do it. I couldn't do the kind of job you deserve."

"I'll take that gamble," she said. "You're better with one hand tied behind your back than anyone else I'll get. Besides, Alan would understand. He'd consent if I asked him. Please, Harry, please do it."

"No, May, it's not a matter of consent. I just can't do it. I'm sorry, but I just can't."

"You mean you *won't*," she said, her eyes growing colder.

"Well, perhaps you're right. But either way, you'll need someone else, and I'll be glad to refer you to someone good."

May stood and moved closer. The coldness was gone from her eyes, replaced by the same look of childish vulnerability. "You won't take *Alan's* case, will you?"

Harry reached for his jacket and moved toward the door. "No,

May, I *couldn't* do that, not after we had this talk. It wouldn't be ethical. Listen, I've got to leave now. I'm meeting Nancy and Gail for dinner."

"You won't say anything about what I've told you, will you?"

"Of course not, May. What you told me was a confidential communication like confession to a priest. I can't tell a soul . . . ever."

*T*he dimly lit, noisy room at Morton's always, inexplicably, made Harry feel comfortable and at ease. Maybe it was the people, mostly a film crowd, mostly friends. Tonight it was packed and between the music and the noisy conversation, he had to bend close to hear what Gail was saying.

"Dad, I don't understand why you're on such a rampage tonight about Robin, why, suddenly, you're so certain he's been lying to me."

Nancy sat forward, patting Harry's hand. "You do seem a bit obsessed with it tonight, darling. Although I must say," she said, looking over at Gail, "he's always told you he doubted Robin would ever leave Diana."

"I know he has, Mom, but I always thought he was just inferring that from what he knows of the situation . . . you know, Diana's money, position, all that. It's easy for someone looking on from the outside to think he'll never leave her. Well *I* knew he would, so it didn't matter so much. But tonight, Dad, you're totally different. You're really on a crusade. You didn't even eat your lime grilled chicken, and that's *really* not like you. I mean, it's as though Robin called tonight and told you he was conning me. He didn't, did he?" She smiled at Harry, and he felt a surge of pity . . . pity and anguish. He had to convince her what Milgram was really like, make her know what was really going on, but he simply could not tell her about May Nathan and what she'd said—could never violate the confidence, not even for Gail. It was tearing him apart.

"Of course he didn't call me. I've just been thinking about it so much and asking around about him. Everyone who knows the man says the same thing. He's charming and urbane but a philandering shit. And when I keep hearing that from everyone, from people who know him and know him well ... people I trust ... well, I've just *got* to make you see it." Harry's palm slammed down on the tablecloth.

"What are you doing, practicing your closing argument?" came a voice from over Harry's shoulder. Harry looked up to see Karen Lloyd, lovely as always, a natural sable coat draped over her black worsted pants suit. She brushed her long dark hair from her eyes, and Harry noticed that she wore a peculiar, determined expression—one that Harry had come to associate with impending trouble in their dealings. Having negotiated with Karen countless times, Harry respected her quick mind and natural cunning. He considered her a tough opponent, but he was as fond of her as he was of anyone in town.

With a smile, he rose to embrace her. Karen warmly greeted Nancy and Gail, who had worked on a *Time* cover story about her two years before. Bending closer, she asked Nancy, "If you've finished your dinner, may I join you for just a few moments? I've got something I should take up with Harry."

Nancy smiled, indicating an extra chair. "You sound serious. Do you need privacy?"

"No, not really," Karen said, gracefully sliding into the empty chair and shrugging off her fur. "Everyone will know about this by tomorrow."

"Everyone will know about what?" Harry said.

"Know that you turned down May Nathan's case."

"How do *you* know?" he said, surprised and irritated.

"Never mind that. You shouldn't have rejected her. It's not fair, not at all fair."

Harry put down his coffee cup, looking annoyed. "Hey, Karen, don't I even get to pick my own clients?"

"As a matter of fact, Harry, I don't think you do. You lawyers prattle on along all the time about how it's your duty to represent an unpopular defendant, to protect the hated, even the possibly guilty, from injustice. You've said it yourself. Am I right?"

"Sure, but that's got nothing to do with May Nathan."

"The hell it doesn't, pal. How can you justify representing a murderer you believe is guilty and, at the same time, reject May Nathan because you don't like her and you're a buddy of her husband. And while we're at it, when did you ever reject *a man*, because you didn't like *him*?"

"Karen, please, one question at a time. Firstly, I've rejected plenty of men who wanted to hire me. I could give you a list. Secondly, I didn't turn May down because I didn't like her or because I do like Alan. I turned her down because, being Alan's friend, I couldn't do a good job for May, while other lawyers can. She should get some other guy who'll go balls out to destroy Alan if he has to. I could never do that." He sat back and sipped his coffee.

Nancy, who had been listening quietly, leaned forward to be heard above the music and noise. "I think he's right, Karen. Isn't the issue whether May can get effective representation elsewhere? I mean, if *no one* would take her case, then maybe you'd be right—it would be Harry's duty to take it on himself. But with plenty of lawyers ready to take Alan on full bore, it seems to me that Harry's acting properly in refusing."

Karen grinned good-naturedly, spreading her arms in a gesture of surrender. "Okay, okay. I'm not taking on the whole family. I give up. Besides, it's really none of my business. Not that that's ever stopped me before." She rose, bending to kiss Nancy and Gail. Harry stood as she left the table, hugging her again . . . even more warmly.

"You know, Karen, your problem is you're afraid to speak your mind. You've got to lick that shyness." She laughed, full-throated and free, and moved away, across the room, toward the restaurant entrance.

Harry shrugged. "There you are, even at dinner it's a course of legal ethics." He reached for Nancy's hand. "Thanks for the help, Nance. I needed it. That Karen can hold her own with anyone."

Nancy smiled. "I meant what I said, Harry. I love Karen, but I really think you're right about what you did. Don't you think so, Gail?"

Gail had been sitting quietly as if not listening at all. Now she turned to Harry.

"Okay, Mr. Sphinx. Now I know the reason for tonight's mysterious crusade."

"What do you mean?" Harry asked.

"I mean you know all about Robin and May Nathan, don't you . . . you just found out tonight? Am I right?"

"You *know* about that?" asked Harry, stunned by what she had said.

"Know about *what?* What *about* May and Milgrim?" Nancy asked, not understanding and irritated to be left out.

Gail smiled. "Okay, Mom. They've had an affair. That's all. I know all about it, and it's nothing."

"It can't be nothing, Gail, and the fact that he tells one woman what he's doing with another leads me to think your father is right about him."

"Oh come on, Mother, it's just a fling, a physical thing. May's got no life with Alan Nathan, and Robin's got none with Diana. So . . . they got involved together. And isn't it better that he was candid about it than if he tried to deceive me?"

Harry longed to blurt out the things Milgrim *hadn't* told Gail, that her tender, romantic Robin called May as well as Gail (and probably a dozen others) "Princess" and pretended to have written the same poem for each of them, and that it wasn't just "a fling" for May any more than it was for Gail, that Milgrim had led each of them to believe he was leaving Diana to marry her. But Harry couldn't tell her those things. It would still have been unethical. Worse, it would have hurt Gail too much. He simply could not have inflicted that much pain on her, even if it had been ethically possible.

Harry sat there miserably while Nancy and Gail continued the discussion. He finished his coffee; and, finally, with a heavy heart, he led his two women, a protective arm around each of them, through the restaurant and out into the starry California night.

The next day was set aside for closing argument in the Parlier case—that dramatic phase of the trial in which a lawyer could capitalize on all the planning, all the skill invested over months or years, to grasp success; or, in a brief moment, could see the entire effort, and all the hopes and dreams that went with it, converted into a costly and humiliating waste.

The day was bright and clear. Harry could see the snow-covered mountains in the distance as the Bentley rolled along the freeway, its sun roof open, a tape of Sousa marches playing at high volume.

The morning sun reflected from hundreds of Civic Center windows; and the traffic, as if stimulated by the beauty of the day, avoided its normal herky-jerky pace and flowed evenly toward the downtown off-ramps.

Harry was ready. As always on important days, he arrived early at the courthouse and took the elevator to the ninth-floor cafeteria. Sipping coffee heavy with sugar, he gazed out over the sun-washed foothills of Chavez Ravine, going over his argument still one more time.

At twenty to nine he went down to Department 47, greeted the clerk and bailiff and spread his notes as well as pens and blank pads before him at the counsel table.

Moments later, Maynard Aldrich arrived trailed by Alec Heath and the rest of the UBS legal team carrying heavy briefcases. Harry wondered what good all that paper would do Aldrich at this stage of the case.

Judge Hailey took the bench, smoothing her hair and placing her notepad before her.

"Gentlemen, I've now reread your briefs and you may assume that I am familiar with your points of law and have read the cases you cite. Mr. Aldrich—as plaintiff you may begin."

The jury seemed interested, curious to see what would happen now, what the lawyers would say. Aldrich rose slowly, placing his notes squarely before him.

This was a case, he said, turning to face the jury, that involves three basic issues, fraud, breach of contract and the identity of the creator of "High Rise." The question of fraud depends on the credibility of the witnesses for both sides. It was never easy to determine who was telling the truth when two people told conflicting stories, and there were several guides the jury could follow. What, for example, was the character and background of the witness, what motive did the witness have to lie, which story was the more plausible in light of all the circumstances. Applying these tests, Aldrich argued, the story offered by Mr. Parlier must be rejected.

"Take character and background, for example," Aldrich urged as he moved to the railing of the jury box, hooking his thumbs in the vest pockets of his gray worsted suit. "A leopard doesn't change his spots. An old saying but one founded in common sense. Parlier is a convicted felon, a man who committed fraud...a crime based essentially on obtaining money or property by lying to others. I repeat," he shouted, *"by lying."*

He lowered his voice again. "Not the case with the witnesses called by the network. No black marks on the records of Mr. Heath or Mr. Talbot. On the contrary, both have led exemplary lives, had exemplary careers. So the first factor... perhaps the most important ... comes down heavily on the side of the network."

Aldrich moved back to the counsel table and continued, "The second factor comes out the same... who has the motive to lie? Very clearly, Mr. Parlier does. He stands to gain millions of dollars to which he is not entitled... far more than he obtained by the fraud for which he went to jail last time. But the witnesses for the network have nothing to gain by lying, no motive for departing from the truth. If Parlier got his entire ten million, it wouldn't cost Mr. Heath or Mr. Talbot one penny. It's the network's money, not theirs, so why should they commit perjury?"

"Finally," he said, clasping his hands behind his back, "the factor of probability also weighs heavily in favor of the network and against Parlier. It is not even denied that network television is a highly sensitive business and that a network could not tolerate as one of its top executives a convicted felon, an ex-con who'd served time for fraud."

Aldrich reviewed the expert testimony to this effect. "Is it not probable that this man... already convicted of lying for economic gain... concealed the essential fact of his criminal record in order to avoid losing this rich new job? Of course it is," said Aldrich, gesturing with his hands.

"Is it probable that such a man was hired for a top job at the network unless he *did* conceal the fact that he had such a record? Certainly not!" said Aldrich, bringing his fist down with force on the counsel table.

He paused, and Harry looked at the jury. They seemed alert, interested. Aldrich continued. "So, evaluating each of the factors that govern our decision as to which side is telling the truth, the balance comes down heavily... overwhelmingly... on the side of the network."

Aldrich put on metal-framed Ben Franklin glasses to consult his notes. Then, looking over at the jury, he launched into a detailed analysis of the evidence and the testimony of each witness, stressing primarily those elements favorable to the network's case on the issue of fraud, and glossing over the problem areas, like Heath's letter to the FCC and the testimony of Alden James. Harry guessed that Aldrich would deal with those problems in his closing argument, when Harry would have no chance to reply. Harry would have to anticipate the explanations Aldrich would offer and destroy them in his own argument.

Now Aldrich put down his notes and walked back to the jury box. "On the basis of all these facts, there is an overwhelming case that Mr. Parlier committed still one more fraud, that he did not disclose his criminal record to Mr. Heath, as he claims to have done. If so, and you *know* it's so, UBS is entitled to cancel the contract and owes Mr. Parlier nothing."

Harry heard the scratching of Judge Hailey's pen as she noted each of Aldrich's arguments.

Aldrich himself had paused again and was looking from juror to juror. "But even if you were to find that there was no fraud, UBS was still justified in firing Mr. Parlier and canceling the contract because Mr. Parlier committed a serious breach of his employment contract when he surreptitiously and fraudulently slipped into the office on a Sunday and engaged in the clandestine copying, indeed theft, of the contents of sensitive, secret documents. On that basis alone . . . even aside from any fraud . . . UBS owes Mr. Parlier nothing."

Next Aldrich went to the issue of "High Rise." Even if somehow the jury felt that there had been no fraud and no breach of contract by Parlier, if he was not the creater of "High Rise," his recovery was limited to approximately four hundred thousand dollars, that is, six hundred thousand dollars for the one year left on the contract when he was fired, less the two hundred thousand the evidence showed he earned elsewhere during that year. "Still a very large sum," said Aldrich, knowing it was much more than the jurors would ever see in their lifetimes. "And it's four hundred thousand dollars more than he deserves." He smiled, wrinkling his tiny eyes. "But that's all he gets if he hasn't convinced you he was the creator of 'High Rise.' And that is his burden, ladies and gentlemen, as the judge will tell you."

Aldrich looked up at the judge, whose expression was completely noncommittal. He then embarked on an analysis of the evidence concerning the creation of the series. He described Albert Navarro's testimony about the New York hotel as a "theatrical trick," one that really had no logical bearing on the issues. "Certainly," he argued, "Mr. Talbot and Mr. Heath were confused about the date Mr. Talbot got the series idea... confused by a few days. Not surprising after the passage of years. And"—he smiled—"obviously Mr. Talbot was confused about the place where the idea came to him. Again, not surprising after all this time."

"But the point," Aldrich urged, looking again from juror to juror, "was that, regardless of *where* it happened and whether it happened on the twelfth or the fifteenth of the month, it *did* happen. Talbot *did* create the idea for the series."

Again, Aldrich returned to his three factors to be used in deciding a conflict of fact. "Character? Well, here again, we had the word of a convicted felon, an ex-con convicted of lying against people with an umblemished record. Motive? Here again, we have the strongest motive to lie on Parlier's part. None on the part of Mr. Heath and Mr. Talbot. Probability? Here again, the circumstances all point to creation of the idea by Talbot, not by Parlier."

"Thus, you see," Aldrich told the jury, "you have two independent grounds for canceling the contract entirely, fraud and breach of contract, and either ground alone would be enough. And you have one additional ground on which Mr. Parlier would receive four hundred thousand dollars, a sum exorbitant and undeserved in itself. But there is absolutely no way consistent with fairness and justice that this man can be entitled to the outrageous sum of ten million dollars that, in his greed, he seeks to exact from my client. Thank you."

Aldrich returned to the counsel table. It was eleven-thirty A.M. The judge turned to Harry. "Would you like to begin now, Mr. Cain, or start fresh at one o'clock?"

"One o'clock would be better, Your Honor."

"Very well then, Mr. Cain. The court will stand in recess until one P.M."

Harry excused himself from Matsuoka and Parlier, bought a tuna sandwich and spent the lunch hour on a bench in the Civic Center Mall, where the splashing of the fountains helped him relax and collect his thoughts. Once again, he reviewed what he had to do that afternoon. Now he had to harvest all the seeds planted on cross-examination. Now he had to anticipate the arguments Aldrich would make when, as the plaintiff, he got the last word.

This was it, the payoff. All the months of hard work, all the planning, the tactics, the tension, all of it would be made worthwhile or rendered a waste of time, depending on his own performance in the afternoon session.

As one o'clock approached, Harry began his "psyching up." As he made his way back to court, he used tricks, symbols that he knew were childish but would work him into a state of emotional intensity. As boxers put it, he wanted to "come out smoking." It was silly perhaps; and he would have been embarrassed—mortified, if anyone knew what he did. But no one would. And it worked. As he entered the courthouse, he began to sing a college fight song silently to himself. "Round the stands in flaming crimson, Harvard banners fly." His stride quickened, his heels pounding down the courthouse hallway. "Cheer on cheer like volleyed thunder echoed to the skies." He thought of Gail as a small child, of her faith and love. To her, he was the best in the world . . . and so he was, so he must be. Wasn't he the "Sunset Bomber"? "See the crimson tide is turning, gaining more and more." He thought of how the network had killed his friend Teddy Brenner and felt anger fill him. Finally he thought of Maynard Aldrich, his small piggy eyes, that prissy little smile on his wide, bigoted face, of the gratuitous insults about Harry's "kind." Beat 'em. That's the only way. Be better, smarter and *win*. He walked still faster, his head high now, his eyes shining. "We'll fight, fight, fight and we'll win tonight. Fair Harvard forevermore." No pompous, second-rate Wall Street snob would beat him. Not today. Not ever. He was *ready!*

He stopped at the courtroom door, took a long, deep breath, let it slowly out and entered the room. He moved to the counsel table and gathered his notes together. He knew he'd never use them.

Almost immediately, Aldrich and his entourage arrived, as did Matsuoka, Parlier and Jay Kelly.

After all these years, Harry's hand still trembled as he held a paper cup of water. The jury filed in. Now they were looking expectantly at Harry. Judge Hailey took the bench. "Mr. Cain, you may proceed."

There was a long moment of silence. Harry used it for dramatic effect. He rose and slowly looked at the judge, then at the jury.

He began by outlining the issues. "Number one, fraud. Did Parlier commit fraud by concealing his criminal record from Alec Heath? Number two, breach of contract. Did Parlier violate his contract when he came in on Sunday to Xerox documents, and if so, was that breach so material that it permitted the network to cancel the contract and to take away all the benefits Parlier had earned? Number three, damages. What was due Parlier under the contract? This, in turn, depended on who created 'High Rise.'

Harry agreed with Aldrich that much of the outcome turned on who was believed. But he said that the display of character the jury saw with their own eyes in the courtroom was far more significant than the mistakes Lee Parlier made and paid for twenty years earlier.

Harry walked to the railing of the jury box and looked squarely into the eyes of one juror, then another, then a third. His initial nervousness was over as he moved into the rhythm and flow of his argument.

"And what did we see about character here in the courtroom? You saw it yourselves. So did I. We saw Alec Heath tell us he had no idea ... no idea that Lee Parlier had a criminal record until two weeks after Mr. Parlier was fired in April of 1983. Yet, we saw Mr. Heath's own letter to the FCC, written when Mr. Parlier was hired, way back in May of 1981, telling the FCC that Mr. Heath knew all about Mr. Parlier's criminal record.

"What explanation does Mr. Heath give us for this letter that destroys his own case? None. 'I never saw it before,' he says. But it's his own signature, and he told us clearly that he 'never'—that was his own word, 'never'—signed anything in blank, never signed anything unless he knew its contents, and this was a very short letter, six lines in all."

Now Harry was making eye contact with other jurors—one at a time, drawing, holding their attention.

"They'll probably claim the letter was somehow changed after Mr. Heath signed it, but there was no evidence of that, and you can be sure that, with all the network's money, they had the best experts in the world examining that letter. If they couldn't find it had been changed, then you know it wasn't changed. It was just the way it is now when Mr. Heath saw it, read it and signed it. He knew all about Mr. Parlier's record, just as he says in his letter. But, to save ten million dollars for the network, he claims he didn't know."

Harry lowered his voice to the point where the jurors strained to hear him.

"And it wasn't only the letter, although that would have been enough. Mr. Heath told us he only learned about Mr. Parlier's criminal record for the first time two weeks after he was fired, when the FCC sent Mr. Heath a copy of Mr. Parlier's application showing his record." Now the voice began to rise again. "Yet we know from the testimony of Mr. Alden James that, on the very next day after Mr. Parlier was fired, long before Mr. Heath could possibly have known about Mr. Parlier's criminal record, if Mr. Heath's story *were true*, Mr. Heath announced that Mr. Parlier was being fired because," Harry bellowed, *"because he had a criminal record."*

"Oh yes, here was Mr. Heath, announcing publicly a fact he asks us to believe he never even knew until two weeks later, a fact he wrote about to the FCC *a full year* before he says he knew it. No one," Harry said slowly and quietly to the jury, *"no one* could believe Mr. Heath's story about concealment of the criminal record. It was just impossible in light of his own letter and the testimony of Mr. James." Harry leaned closer to the jury, making eye contact once again.

"That evidence took any element of fraud right out of the case." Some jurors began to nod.

"Besides," Harry continued, "if Mr. Heath didn't know the application contained Mr. Parlier's criminal record, why did he order secrecy? Why did he give the order that he would personally handle the form rather than the compliance officer who handled every other form in the history of the company? Why did he order that no file copy be kept, as was done in every other case? Why?" His voice came up. *"You know why.* Your own common sense tells you why. He knew the form contained Mr. Parlier's criminal record. There is no other rational explanation."

Again Harry drew nods from the jury.

"And so Mr. Heath's letter to the FCC, showing clearly that he knew about Parlier's criminal record, just confirmed what was obvious from the other evidence. So, as I said, fraud is out of the case, because Mr. Heath knew all along about the fact that supposedly was concealed.

"But Mr. Heath told us here in court that he didn't know . . . told us, in effect, that Mr. Parlier should lose the ten milliion dollars he'd earned under the contract because Mr. Heath says he didn't know about the criminal record. What does that tell you about Mr. Heath . . . about his character?

"And there were other things Mr. Heath told us that didn't square with the facts. I'll get to them later. But certainly, on the issue of fraud, we know very clearly, who is telling the truth and who is not."

Harry turned and walked back to the counsel table, then spoke to the jurors from there.

"Now, Mr. Aldrich says Mr. Heath had no motive to depart from the truth. No motive? We're not children, Mr. Aldrich." He turned and stared at Aldrich, who tried his best to look bored. Then Harry returned his attention to the jury.

"Our common sense tells us that claim is nonsense. Heath is president of the network. How is the performance of a president measured? How is he graded? On one thing, ladies and gentlemen, one thing. And you know what it is . . . the net profits of the company. If Mr. Parlier gets the ten million he earned, it's a big chunk out of the profits of even a huge company like UBS. That ten million decrease in profits makes the president look not so good. Put a different way, the president looks a lot better if profits are ten million dollars higher. That's only common sense. So when Mr. Aldrich tells us he has no motive, we have to smile a little. Of course he had a motive!" Harry slammed his hand on the books stacked on the table before him.

"Now, just for a moment, let's contrast what we saw of Mr. Parlier in the courtroom, not twenty years ago, when he was a foolish ghetto kid, but right here before our eyes. Not once was he impeached, shown by some document or outside witness to have testified falsely or even incorrectly. Not once. Not in this entire trial. Can Mr. Heath say that? Or Mr. Talbot?" Harry turned to look hard at the two men, who seemed uncomfortable under his silent gaze. Then he turned again to the jury. "*Hardly.*" Two jurors chuckled, three others smiled— not a clear indication of anything yet, but a good sign.

Harry went on, moving back toward the jury box. "But there's one

example that tells you better than anything else the kind of witness
... the kind of man ... Mr. Parlier is today. You probably noticed it
yourselves. Mr. Heath testified that the network sign-in book showed
Mr. Parlier used a false name to get into the building on Sunday.
Mr. Aldrich crowed about that, made a big thing about it, made Mr.
Parlier look bad. But Mr. Heath also testified that the sign-in book
had been destroyed; that's the critical thing here, *the sign-in book
had been destroyed.*"

Harry looked knowingly at the jury. They were in this together.
"Now remember, Mr. Parlier heard that the book had been destroyed
before he testified. He knew the sign-in book was gone. With no
sign-in book, there was no way to prove whether or not he'd used a
false name.

"If Mr. Parlier was willing to fudge the truth to help his case, then
he had a clear opportunity to do it right there. He could have flatly
denied that he ever used a false name—could have been outraged
at the claim. After all, they had no way to prove it, since he knew
they couldn't come up with the sign-in book.

"But ladies and gentlemen, Mr. Parlier did not do that." Harry
looked again from juror to juror, always seeking eye contact. "Even
though he knew it would make him look bad, maybe hurt his case,
even though there would have been no possible way to contradict
him if he had lied, Mr. Parlier still told us the absolute truth. He
still said, 'I don't remember. Maybe I did use a false name. I didn't
want Mr. Heath to know I was there.'

"Think about it. Think about what that tells us about Mr. Parlier
and his character—telling us the truth even where it hurts his case
... even where he didn't have to." Harry took a step back looking at
the jury as a group. "When you see a witness do that, ladies and
gentlemen, you know you've got a witness you can believe. After
seeing that, you know that when he testifies that he did tell Heath
about his criminal record, it's true. You know that when he tells you
'High Rise' was his idea, it's true, even aside from the overwhelming
evidence that supports his testimony.

"So we have the contrast. On one hand, you have Alec Heath
and what you saw of his conduct with your own eyes. On the other
hand, you have Lee Parlier and what you saw of him on the stand,
again right before you.

"So Mr. Aldrich"—Harry turned again to stare at his opponent—"if you want to let the case turn on character, you've got a deal." There were more smiles from the jury as Harry walked back to the counsel table.

"But now, let's get back to our outline of the issues. We've got fraud out of the case. Clearly—without a doubt. The burden of proving fraud was on Mr. Heath and UBS and they haven't come near meeting that burden.

"In fact, it's so clear Mr. Heath knew all along about Mr. Parlier's criminal record that, if the burden were on Mr. Parlier to prove he *didn't* commit fraud, he's more than met that burden by overwhelming proof."

Harry paused, watching the jury. They were with him, he thought, at least to this point.

"So let's turn to the other way UBS hopes to get out of its contract. They say coming in on Sunday to Xerox documents was a breach of Mr. Parlier's contract, a breach so very serious that it justifies canceling his contract and making him lose all of his financial benefits.

"Well, let's take those one at a time. First, was it a breach at all? They've overlooked a couple of major points in claiming Mr. Parlier's conduct was a violation of the contract. Firstly, Mr. Parlier's copying was limited to only those documents necessary to show what he was entitled to receive under the contract . . . the agreements, memoranda and records that show he created the series and how much money he's entitled to from the series.

"It would be sheer madness . . . just lunacy . . . to say that his pay depends on how much the network receives from the series but that he's not entitled to know how much the network receives so he can compute what his pay is. That's crazy, and we can't presume that the contract was intended to be crazy.

"Mr. Heath tells us, in a vague way, that these were 'top secret' documents, deliberately not specifying what they were, other than those things Mr. Parlier told us he copied. But here again, the circumstances show that Mr. Heath is not being candid with us, that he's stretching things again."

Once again, Harry spun and looked directly at Heath, letting his gaze remain on the man until he fidgeted with discomfort. Turning again to the jury, Heath continued.

"You remember, I'm sure, Mr. Heath's testimony about what he said to Mr. Parlier on that Sunday and what he and Mr. Parlier said and did. Mr. Aldrich went through it in detail and so did I. But there was one significant thing that *wasn't* said and *wasn't* done. Mr. Heath, the president of the network, never even asked Mr. Parlier to give him back the copies of these supposedly 'top secret' papers. You can read Mr. Heath's testimony twenty times, over and over again, and you'll never find any request for Mr. Parlier to turn over the copies he'd already made.

"In fact, Mr. Parlier testified that he packed up the papers and took them with him right in front of Mr. Heath, and Mr. Heath never contradicted that testimony.

"So come on, Mr. Heath." Harry stretched out both arms toward the embarrassed network president. "Here's a man about to run out the door with the network's top secret documents and you, the head of the network, you don't even try to stop him. If the papers were really top secret, wouldn't you at least ask for them back?"

Two jurors in the top row smiled to each other. They'd seen *that* point by themselves, discussed it already. Harry put one hand in his pocket, rested the other on the rail of the jury box, leaning close to the front row jurors, as if confiding in them.

"Anyway, there's a second reason why there was no breach of contract in what Mr. Parlier did, even if the documents he copied had nothing to do with computing his pay, even if they really were 'top secret' documents.

"Mr. Parlier is a stockholder of UBS. As such, the judge will instruct you later, he is entitled to look at and copy all of the books and records of the company. A corporation is owned by its stockholders. It can't have secrets from them. As a stockholder he was completely entitled to know what was in those documents and to copy them. So there was no breach of contract by Mr. Parlier. None at all."

Now Harry began to pace in front of the jury box.

"But if there had been a breach—if there *had* been—the judge will instruct you that the breach would still not justify canceling the contract unless it was a material, fundamental breach of Mr. Parlier's vital duties under the agreement. That can hardly be said here. Here's a man who was hired to develop new programming for the network, and he did that job better than anyone in the world, making the network hundreds of millions of dollars.

"The things Mr. Parlier was hired to do, he did superbly. The network... those folks sitting over there"—he gestured toward them again—"they've reaped and retained the rich rewards of his services. Can the fact that he copied some records necessary to compute his pay possibly be a fundamental breach of his duties under the contract so significant that he should lose all of his contractual benefits? Not a chance.

"Again—Mr. Heath thought the copied documents were so insignificant, he didn't even ask for them back. But he wants to use them as an excuse to deprive Mr. Parlier of everything he earned by his hard work and imagination."

Harry stopped and looked directly at the jury.

"No, ladies and gentlemen, like the artificial claim of fraud, the claim that Mr. Parlier loses his contract benefits by reason of breach is out of the case.

"So we turn to what's due Mr. Parlier under the contract. Four hundred thousand dollars? That's a sum that common sense will tell you will barely cover his legal fees and expenses over all these years.

"Or ten million dollars? That's the sum Lee Parlier actually earned by giving the network a series worth many, many times that amount. The result depends, of course, on who had the idea for 'High Rise.' Was it Mr. Parlier, as he testified, or Mr. Talbot, as he and Mr. Heath claimed?"

Harry then slowly and carefully reviewed all the changes in testimony, the inconsistent stories told by Heath and Talbot and how they were utterly destroyed by Mr. Navarro from the Sherry Netherland Hotel. He explained to the jury how each time Heath and Talbot got caught with one phony story, they made up another, until finally there really was no way out... until finally they were stuck with a changed and rechanged version that *no one* would believe.

Now Harry turned once again to his opponents. "No, Mr. Heath. No, Mr. Talbot. We don't believe you. Our judgment and our experience... our common sense... tells us that your story—pardon me, your *stories*—are poppycock.

"Mr. Parlier had created other hit series. He told us he created 'High Rise.' Cross-examination didn't impeach that testimony at all. Not one bit. And he'd already passed the test of credibility when he voluntarily testified against his own interest on the issue of using a false name. No, we can see the truth here, as we can see it in this entire case."

Harry resumed his pacing before the jury, stopping from time to time to gesture for emphasis.

"Mr. Parlier was a proven, highly successful creator. Mr. Heath wanted that skill at UBS and was willing to promise a percentage of the network's profits to get it.

"But when they got 'High Rise' out of him, when it became clear that it was going to be one of the biggest hits of all time, if not the biggest, a hit that would make the network hundreds of millions of dollars, then they didn't need Mr. Parlier any more, and they certainly didn't want to pay him his share of those millions.

"So how do you get out of a contract? You claim fraud. That's how. It's easy. After all, Parlier's an ex-con. Who'll believe him? Who'll take his word against such distinguished men as Alec Heath and Neil Talbot? He'll have no chance at all and he'll probably be scared to sue. He won't want the public to know about his record.

"But they want added protection. So their lawyers come up with the theory that copying the figures was a breach of contract. Then they want even more protection. So Talbot suddenly remembers that he created 'High Rise' looking out the window of the Sherry Netherland Hotel at the General Motors building.

"Now, they think that even if Parlier has the guts to sue and a jury believes him, he gets nothing. Of course, there's no evidence that Neil Talbot ever *created* a series in his life. Yet he says he created this one, the best of all time, just looking out the window of his hotel room." Harry slammed the jury rail again. "Onto the air shaft!"

Again he heard snickers from the jury. He paused and then continued, smiling. "Well, I suppose I'm being unfair to Mr. Talbot. If there's one thing he proved in this courtroom, it's that he's creative." This time, several jurors openly laughed. All of them smiled.

Now Harry spoke quietly, moving his eyes from one juror to the next . . . keeping the essential contact—keeping them his. "Yes, Lee Parlier's an ex-con. Twenty years ago he made a bad mistake. He paid for it with two years of his life. He's been straight ever since, an honest, productive citizen. Do we prove here in this courtroom that Alec Heath was right when he predicted that an ex-con can't win? Do we take the money that was fairly earned by Mr. Parlier, through hard work, imagination and creativity, and give it to the network, because twenty years ago, as a kid, he was convicted of a crime?

"Do we leave Mr. Heath and his friends with Mr. Parlier's series as well as Mr. Parlier's money? Do we make Alec Heath a company hero for his conduct, his behavior in this case, by making Parlier forfeit the ten million he earned, a small part of the money the network will receive from that series?"

Now Harry's voice began to rise. "Do we do these things?" He paused—then the hand slammed down on the railing again. "We do not! Not if there's justice and fairness in this world.

"What we *do* is to send a message to Alec Heath and all the Alec Heaths of the world. That message says"—again Harry looked over at Heath—"you can't get away with it. We're not gonna let you get away with it. That's why we're here. To stop people like you. And stop you we will! That's the message to send. If you believe I'm right, then please—for justice, for truth—help me send that message. Thank you."

There was a long silence. Then Judge Hailey announced the afternoon recess. Parlier pounded Harry on the back. "Jesus, Harry, that was fantastic, utterly incredible. Now I see why you were so het up about my admitting I might have used the false name. Now I see a lot of things."

"Okay, Lee"—Harry smiled—"there'll be time for all that praise *if* and when we win. It's not over yet."

And it wasn't. Aldrich, as the plaintiff's counsel, had the last word. He came back after the recess, seemingly undaunted by anything that Harry had said. Harry was surprised at the emotion displayed by the usually stiff New Yorker. Gesturing with his glasses, pacing the floor, pointing a fleshy finger, Aldrich hammered away at Parlier's being an ex-con, a convicted liar and a man who continued to follow that pattern, even using a phony name to gain admission to the network offices.

Sneering, he accused Harry of using a "cute technicality" in claiming that Parlier was only exercising his rights "as a stockholder."

He strolled to the jury box, his tiny eyes blazing with the righteousness of his cause. "If Parlier *really* thought it was proper for him to copy those records, *really* thought that he had the right to do so as a shareholder, then why did he use the phony name? Why did he come in on Sunday? He wasn't in there as a 'stockholder' acting properly to exercise his rights. Not for a minute. He sneaked in using a phony name, on a Sunday and for purposes of blackmail and betrayal."

Not bad, Harry thought, wishing, as always, that he could have one more crack at the jury.

Next Aldrich turned to Heath's letter to the FCC arguing, as Harry had anticipated, that "like the name in the sign-in book, like everything Mr. Parlier did in the case, this letter was a fake." Heath could have been tricked into signing a letter he thought was something else, perhaps handed to him as part of a stack of other letters that he signed without realizing that this letter was among them, or the letter could have been altered by erasure or chemical means after Heath had signed it. "We may not have had time to discover the *exact* way it was done; but one way or another, this lifelong faker did it again."

Aldrich returned to the creation of "High Rise," arguing that it was easy for Harry to make fun of witnesses trying their best, many years after the fact, to remember the date of a meeting or in which of two hotel rooms it occurred. Most people would have the same problem.

He moved closer to the jury. "Can you remember what you did on a particular date three years ago? Can you remember what hotel room you had on your last vacation? I can't."

Aldrich argued that, contrary to what Harry had said, it was a sign of *truthfulness* that the network witnesses were incorrect and sometimes inconsistent as to the details. It was the man who concocted his story that got all the details straight, even after many years.

"And," he said, "we are only talking about details . . . the exact date . . . exact room, everybody who was present. The important thing has been ignored. Mr. Cain *wants* to ignore it," he shouted. "Whenever or wherever it happened, whether in room five fifteen or room eleven oh two, whether on May 12 or May 15, *it happened*. Neil Talbot, not Lee Parlier, created 'High Rise.'

"Parlier tried to take the credit for it, tried to gouge the network for ten million dollars to which he was not entitled, which, even if his story were true, would pay him for his time expended on 'High Rise' at a rate of better than one hundred thousand dollars an hour. Not bad, not bad at all," cried Aldrich.

Again he moved in close to the jury. "Can you earn one hundred thousand dollars an hour? Can I? Certainly not. Should Lee Parlier? Most certainly not."

He stood, hooking his thumbs in his vest pockets, looking from juror to juror. "The network is, after all, owned by shareholders. Most of them are little people . . . widows, retired people, who worked hard all their lives and who invested their life savings in the stock of UBS, thinking that it was a safe and solid investment.

"Should ten million dollars be taken from those hard-working people and handed over to a convicted swindler who did nothing to earn it?

"Once again, ladies and gentlemen, I say 'certainly not!' And I'm sure you'll agree. Thank you." Aldrich turned and, staring balefully over at Harry, returned to the counsel table.

Again the courtroom was silent for a moment. Then the judge spoke: "Thank you, ladies and gentlemen, we'll recess for the day at this point and reconvene at nine A.M. tomorrow, at which time I'll instruct the jury."

This time it was Aldrich who got congratulations. Talbot rushed to his side. "Maynard, you were splendid, absolutely splendid." Heath quietly shook Aldrich's hand, grasping the lawyer's shoulder with his left hand in a gesture of intimacy and gratitude that surprised Harry.

Heath and the other network people were telling each other that Aldrich had done it . . . turned the jury around, that it was at least two to one against a really big verdict and better than even money that there would be a verdict for UBS.

Parlier looked dejected, sure now he'd lost. John Matsuoka was trying gamely to encourage him, but even he seemed unsure. Maybe they were right, Harry thought. Aldrich's closing had been surprisingly effective, surprisingly colorful. Maybe they're right. He packed up and left.

*T*he next morning, the twenty-fifth day since the trial began, Judge Hailey instructed the jury. She spoke slowly, carefully, summarizing the law applicable to the case—how and when one party to a contract could cancel it for fraud or breach by the other party, what rights a shareholder had to examine corporate records, and various other rules the jury was to apply in arriving at their verdict.

The attention of each of the twelve jurors seemed riveted on the judge as she spoke. Most took notes. None looked at the lawyers or the parties for either side. Harry got no sense of what they were thinking. This being a civil case he needed nine of the twelve to win. But so did Aldrich. It could be close.

Finally, the instructions over, the jury retired and the waiting began. It was ten-fifteen.

Harry made some phone calls and returned to sit in the courtroom, editing the appellate brief in his Nevada case. Parlier and Matsuoka paced nervously in the hall. Aldrich, Talbot and Heath went upstairs for coffee.

By noon nothing had happened, and the bailiff led the jury to a private room in the courthouse cafeteria.

By one-thirty they were back in the jury room, and Harry was back at his courtroom vigil. Now, Matsuoka, Parlier and Kelly were sitting beside him, with Aldrich and his associates sitting across the aisle. Talbot and Heath had gone somewhere else. The two sides said nothing to each other—avoided even looking at each other.

By three nothing had happened. Harry was finding it hard to concentrate on his other brief. Talbot and Heath had returned to resume their pacing in the hall.

At four, Harry was starting to become concerned about the possibility of a hung jury, one that could not reach the nine votes necessary for a verdict for either side. If that happened, the case would have to be retried, and if he had to try this case again, Harry was sure Aldrich would gain an enormous advantage. Not only would the network be far better able than Parlier to afford the huge cost of a second trial, but Aldrich would know in advance about the FCC letter, about the layout of the Sherry Netherland, everything Harry was going to do. It would be a totally different, far tougher case. Harry didn't think he could win a retrial. He was far from sure he'd won this trial.

He left his courtroom seat and phoned the office, getting a long list of calls that somehow would have to be answered that evening. He asked to be transferred to one of his associates so he could get the results of a motion argued that morning. He opened the yellow pad he had with him ready to take notes. He looked up to see John Matsuoka gesturing wildly at the phone booth door. "Jury's coming in." He hung up and rushed back to the courtroom.

The jury was indeed filing in. Harry always tried to gauge a jury's feeling from their faces as they came back to the courtroom. This time, he could see nothing in their expressions, could attribute no real meaning to where or how they looked. This jury was an enigma. Aldrich and his associates rushed in to take their places at the counsel table. Heath moved to sit by Aldrich; and Parlier, the last to return, took his place beside Harry and Matsuoka. Jay Kelly returned to the spectators' section, looking drawn and tense.

Judge Hailey took the bench. Harry's heart was pounding. He rubbed his moist palms along the seams of his trousers. He was always tense before a verdict was announced. This time he wasn't sure he'd survive until he knew.

"Mr. Foreman, has the jury reached a verdict?"

The foreman rose, "We have, Your Honor."

"Please hand your verdict to the bailiff."

The deputy walked slowly to the jury box, received the paper from the jury foreman, walked over to the Judge, even more slowly, and handed her the paper.

It seemed an eternity. The courtroom was eerily silent as Judge Hailey read the paper to herself with a slightly puzzled expression. She hesitated, frowning, obviously concerned about something and debating her proper course.

Finally, she handed the paper to the bailiff.

"Please return the verdict to the jury foreman."

Raising an eyebrow, the deputy slowly walked the paper back to the jury box.

Harry's mouth was dry, his heart continuing to pound as though it would burst through his chest.

"Mr. Foreman, will you please read the verdict as written, and then I will ask you about it." The foreman reached into his coat pocket for his glasses and, with agonizing slowness, adjusted them on his nose and spread out the paper before him on the railing of the jury box.

He looked up at the judge and finally read the verdict. "We the jury find for the plaintiff"—an excited buzz swept the gallery as Harry's heart sank, a bitter, metallic taste filling his mouth.

Judge Hailey rapped for order.

"Mr. Foreman, will you begin again and read the entire verdict as written."

Again the foreman began to read. "We the jury find for the plaintiff ... in the sum of ten million dollars."

Harry looked up with surprise. What does that mean? The network was the "plaintiff," but the ten million figure was claimed by Parlier, not the network. The jury was confused.

"Mr. Foreman," the judge said, interrupting Harry's thoughts, "you referred to a verdict for 'the plaintiff,' but your award was ten million, the full amount claimed by the defendant and cross-complainant, Mr. Parlier. The 'plaintiff' was United Broadcasting System. Was your verdict intended to be for Mr. Parlier or for the network?"

The foreman looked embarrassed. He whispered quietly to the lady on his right and nodded to the other jurymen who nodded quickly back. To Harry, all these movements seemed in slow motion, as in a dream. The tension was unbearable. The foreman stood facing the judge once again. "Your Honor, I'm sorry, you're absolutely correct. The verdict was for Mr. Parlier in the sum of ten million dollars. I just wrote it down wrong."

Harry felt the weight of the tension lift. Slowly he broke into a wide grin. He'd done it again, won again, beaten the Maynard Aldriches of the world one more time. Out of the corner of his eye he saw Parlier and Matsuoka grinning too.

"We request that the jury be polled," said Aldrich, standing stiffly at the counsel table, his face ashen, a quaver in his voice.

"Of course, Mr. Aldrich," replied the judge. And the jurors were polled, each one asked if his decision was for the defendant and cross-complainant, Parlier, in the sum of ten million dollars. Ten of the twelve replied "yes." Two replied "no," one wanting a forty million verdict for Parlier, and the other a verdict for the network.

Harry, competitive as always, began to wonder how he had failed to win that twelfth juror.

Judge Hailey confirmed the verdict for Parlier, praised the jury for their attention and diligence, excused them and left the bench.

Aldrich, Heath and the network group quickly left the courtroom, strained and angry, bitter in their disappointment.

Jay Kelly rushed forward and wrapped Harry in a bear hug. "Fantastic! What a job! From beginning to end, Harry, you were superb. No one else could have done it." The moment Kelly released him, Harry was grasped by Parlier, who was crying with joy and the release of tension. John Matsuoka patted Parlier on the shoulder to tell him the jury was waiting to congratulate him. Parlier turned, and one by one shook hands with the eleven jurors who had voted with him and who were thrilled at the outcome and proud of the role they'd played. The twelfth juror, sour at the result, had quickly left. Almost every juror told Parlier he was in the right, but that his lawyer was wonderful, the brightest, the best in the world. Parlier said that he thought so too. Matsuoka quietly turned to Harry, his hand outstretched. "One fine job, Harry—really well done." This time Harry grabbed Matsuoka and pulled him close in an affectionate hug. "Thanks for the help, John. I couldn't have done it without you."

After ten more minutes of celebration, the jurors had gone and Parlier left with Matsuoka and Kelly to return to Harry's office.

Suddenly the courtroom was empty, silent. Harry was totally drained. Winning was sweet, especially beating Aldrich. But he was just beginning to feel inexplicably let down. He stuffed the last of his papers in his briefcase, and taking a last look at the room that had been the focal point of his existence for the past four weeks, he slowly went out the double swinging doors.

With the trial behind him, Harry had to face the balance of his life. Nothing could prevent the exultation he felt at reading the New York *Times*'s story with its references to "California's legendary Harry Cain" or *Variety*'s headline "Sunset Bomber Levels Net."

Still the high that followed the coverage faded quickly, and without the intense concentration required by the trial, the troublesome thoughts came back more frequently than Harry would have expected.

He still had his taxes and loans to pay, and even though his share of the *Parlier* fee would be over two million dollars, UBS had announced an appeal. They would have little chance of success, but the money would be held up for months.

Over the following weeks, other cases, other clients, helped to push these financial problems away. But these things were overshadowed by the loss of Carmel and his concern for Gail—his kid, his pal, his baby—who would soon be away from him permanently, trying, against the odds, to build her life in another country, around a man who cared nothing about her—a man Harry despised.

On the good side, Harry and Nancy seemed fully able to enjoy each other again. Nancy seemed to be finding a way to deal with her concerns about Gail and, for that matter, about her life with Harry. They'd resumed their rambling bedtime talks; and once again they could be playful with one another, have fun together. One night after Harry returned home from the office, they decided to go to the movies in Westwood. After sitting through a mediocre film, they strolled hand in hand through Westwood Village to La Salsa, where they wolfed down soft tacos loaded with cilantro and onions and washed down with chilled cerveza claro. They laughed together delightedly, as in between mouthfuls they took turns mimicking particularly bad lines from the film. For a moment at least, it was as if the question of other women or where their lives were going had never arisen.

One morning, almost a month after the trial, Harry read in the *Times* that Robin Milgrim "the well-known English journalist" was on assignment in Los Angeles covering the opening of Malcolm Ridley's new film.

Immediately, Harry felt a rush of anger. Milgrim and Ridley were a perfect combination. A minor British producer, Ridley attracted attention to his pictures by launching vicious attacks on American stars and directors, claiming it was his duty as a "filmmaker." He had learned that the more outrageously he attacked a famous American, the more space he'd get in the local press; and so he did it with increasing virulence and decreasing respect for the truth with each new picture he had ready for U.S. release.

Now Robin Milgrim was to cover his American tour as though he were some sort of crusading hero. Worried about Gail now that Milgrim was back in town, disgusted that the man was being treated like some kind of latter-day Walter Lippmann, Harry slammed the paper down on his desk.

Only the day before, Harry had heard that the construction on Maurice King's building in Gaynorville was completed. He had immediately arranged another meeting with King, an event to which he looked forward with relish. But reading about Milgrim took all the joy out of the prospect and left Harry in a growing state of anger and concern.

His attempt to work the balance of that morning was largely unsuccessful, and nothing served to improve his mood. He tried to draft some letters but found it hard to concentrate. It was almost noon. He thought he might as well go a little early to lunch.

As Harry was putting on his jacket, Clara handed him a letter that had been delivered by messenger, after the regular morning mail. It was on the stationery of Blaine & Burton, an old-line downtown firm.

Dear Mr. Cain:
This firm has been retained by Mr. and Mrs. Carl Malone in connection

—270—

with your claim to a $300,000 fee and in regard to your conduct in handling the recent trial in *Marriage of Malone.*

The Malones have reconciled, and both are determined to resist this exorbitant claim on your part and to exercise all appropriate remedies in respect of your appalling conduct during the trial, including compensatory and punitive damages for abuse of process and the intentional infliction of emotional distress.

I am authorized to tell you that, in order to avoid litigation over this matter, Mr. Malone will pay your out-of-pocket costs (billed in the amount of $8,750), plus a fee of $30,000, and will attempt to induce Mrs. Malone to waive her claim for damages against you and your firm.

Please let me hear from you immediately.

Very truly yours,
Morton Unger of
Blaine & Burton

Harry put the letter down, momentarily stunned. Nothing like this had ever happened to him before. Malone had been thrilled with his work, had sworn he'd never forget what Harry had done, had said... Harry jabbed at the intercom to reach John Matsuoka. "John, that bastard Carl Malone reconciled with his wife and they're trying to stiff us on the fee... probably doing the same thing to Cal Pierce. I want that fucker sued today!"

"Jesus, Harry, I can't believe it."

"Well, believe it. Listen, John, let's ask twenty-five percent of what we saved him, that's about fifteen million dollars. There are some cases that support that approach, and it's probably the reasonable value of our services anyway. Let the asshole worry about *that.*"

"Okay, Harry, it's an easy complaint to draw. I'll get it right out."

"Thanks, John. Get it served today if you can. Line up Skip Corrigan and tell him to use a stake-out to serve Malone if he has to. All Carl Malone understands is force. Let's show him some.

"Oh, and one other thing. When Malone's lawyer calls—after he gets served—tell him he won't need to subpoena that film of Mrs. Malone. I've still got it. It's relevant evidence of my conduct in the trial; and, by God, I'm going to show it... in open court this time, not in chambers. Let the son of a bitch think about that!"

Harry's tough talk didn't reflect what he was feeling. He was disappointed and hurt, disgusted with Malone but deeply wounded. He wanted the money... needed it, now that the Parlier fee would be held up. But more than that, he wanted the approval, the appreciation, even the love.

Now, on top of everything else, he had *this* shit to put up with.

He had been about to sign six checks to pay overdue bills before leaving the office. He slipped them in his desk drawer. They'd have to wait. He asked Clara to call the bank and request an extension and increase of his loan. Well, what the hell, he'd make it. He always had.

*T*he intercom buzzed. "Judge Strauss on line one, Mr. Cain."

"Judge *Leland* Strauss?" Leland Strauss was a retired federal judge who, after a distinguished career on the bench, had become a senior partner at Cavanaugh & Cutler, Maynard Aldrich's firm in New York.

"Shall I inquire?"

"No, I'll talk to him." The phone clicked. "Hello."

"Mr. Cain?"

"Yes."

"This is Leland Strauss, Mr. Cain . . . of Cavanaugh and Cutler."

"Yes, Judge, are you here in the city?"

"Yes, I am, Mr. Cain, till tomorrow. Before I go back to New York, I'd like the opportunity to meet with you for a few moments, if that's possible."

Harry sensed a settlement approach and thought how odd that it was coming from Judge Strauss, who had had nothing to do with the case.

"Certainly, Judge." Harry glanced at his appointment book. "How about four-thirty today? Would that be convenient?"

"Perfect, Mr. Cain. Can we meet some place away from your office? The matter's somewhat confidential."

Harry raised an eyebrow at that. Confidential? Why? What could be confidential about settlement talk? He kept his questions to himself. "Of course, Judge. Do you know Le Dome on Sunset, west of La Cienega?"

"No, but I'm sure my driver can find it. I'll see you there at four-thirty."

"Okay."

More curious than ever, Harry noted the meeting in his book. The intercom buzzed again.

"Mrs. Cain on line one. She says it's urgent."

"Okay, Clara. Thanks."

"Nance, what's up?"

"Harry, I've got some bad news." His heart began to pound. "Gail's miscarried. They've taken her to Cedar-Sinai. I'm on my way there now."

"Is she okay?"

"I think so. But I don't know. I just got a call from the manager of her apartment house. I'll meet you at the hospital."

"I'm leaving right now."

His heart in his throat, Harry grabbed his jacket and rushed out of his office. Shouting to Clara that he'd call, he sprinted for the elevator.

Nancy was waiting outside Gail's hospital room when Harry arrived, harried and out of breath, having fought the traffic, the hospital parking and the confusing geography of the massive institution.

Even called on an emergency with no advance warning, Nancy was immaculately attired, apparently serene. Harry knew she must have rushed, terrified, to the hospital just as he had. Yet in her gray Adolfo suit and white silk blouse, she seemed completely in control. At times like this, she could be amazing. With a comforting gesture, she took his hand.

"She's okay, Harry. The doctor's in there now. She hemorrhaged some, but they've got it under control."

Harry leaned against the corridor wall breathing heavily.

"Thank God for that. Is Milgrim here? He's in town, you know."

"I don't know. I doubt it. I haven't seen him at all."

The door to the room opened and a young doctor with thinning

brown hair and a wispy mustache emerged. He wore a white coat far too large in the shoulders, his stethoscope dangling from a bulging pocket.

"Mr. and Mrs. Cain?"

"Yes."

"I'm Dr. Lebwohl. Gail's gone through a lot, but she's going to be just fine. She's lost a good bit of blood, but we've replaced it, and she's out of any danger. She's a lucky girl though. If they hadn't found her in time, we probably would've lost her." He looked back and forth from Nancy to Harry. "You can go in now, but she's weak and a little depressed. So try not to tire her. Okay?"

"Sure, Doctor."

Harry and Nancy entered the room. Gail lay in a big white hospital bed, her head slightly elevated, an IV line inserted in the back of her wrist. She was pale, more pale than Harry had ever seen her. She gave them a wan smile; and as Harry bent over to kiss her, he could see that a tear had run down her cheek.

Nancy kissed her too and smoothed her hair, murmuring, "It's okay, sweetheart, it's okay."

Another tear ran down Gail's cheek. She spoke in a weak voice. "I wanted that baby so much. Did you hear? It was a boy."

Harry wondered what sadistic moron had given her that information. Nancy continued stroking Gail's hair, a tear starting down her cheek too.

Harry took Gail's free hand, patting it gently. "I know you wanted the baby, Gail—how hard this must be for you. But you're okay yourself. You can have other babies."

"He's right," Nancy added. "I checked with the doctor."

Gail made no reply, and they stood beside her bed momentarily silent.

"Does Milgrim know?" Harry suddenly asked.

"Yes, I think so," Gail said, in a small, dry voice. "Louise said she told him."

"Louise?"

"The manager of my apartment house."

"Oh." Harry moved to the window that faced west toward Beverly Hills and Bel Air. The lovely homes climbed gentle green slopes to a clear blue sky. Beyond them was the silver line of the ocean. But

—274—

Harry didn't see these things. Instead he saw another hospital room twenty-four years before—a tiny, premature baby fighting courageously for her life. Momentarily his eyes blurred with tears. He shook his head like a fighter trying to clear his mind after a stunning blow. He continued to stare out the window.

Finally, he spoke, his anger emerging.

"And the son of a bitch still isn't here?"

"Harry!"

"No, it's okay, Mom. We can talk about it. Robin told Louise he had an important interview, that he'd try to get by later before he left town."

"Sure," said Harry sarcastically, turning back to face them. "Sure he will."

"Now, that's enough." Nancy's voice had steel in it.

"Okay, okay, Nancy, I'll drop it. I'm sorry, Gail, you know how I feel about him."

"Yes, Dad, I sure do." Gail smiled weakly. She sat up on her elbows. "But you know how much I love him. I know he'd be here if he could. He's a busy guy and he's only got a couple of days to get this interview done before he goes back to London."

"Okay, Gail, I'll lay off . . . for now." Harry moved back to the bed and gently helped her lie back on the pillows.

They talked about how the miscarriage had started, how she had passed out and was found by the manager, who probably saved her life. After ten minutes, a brisk, elderly nurse told them they'd been with Gail long enough, that they should have a seat in the waiting room. Harry told Gail he had a meeting to make anyway and would be back later in the day. He and Nancy kissed her and left the room.

They walked together down the corridor. At the elevator, Nancy stopped and looked at him.

"Can't you stay a while?"

"I can't, Nance. I really have something important. We can't be with her anyway."

"You could be with me."

Harry flared. "Okay, Nance, I'll cancel my Goddamn meeting and we'll sit in the waiting room and talk to each other. Is that what you want?"

"No, no, forget it," she said, hurt evident in her voice.

"Look, I'm sorry. I'm really uptight about this. I shouldn't take it out on you."

"I understand, Harry. You go ahead. Will you come back later?"

"I'll try. I'll either meet you here or at home. Maybe we'll go out for dinner . . . Nance?"

"Yes."

"Can you believe that guy not showing up after Gail nearly dies from his kid."

"Well, maybe he really couldn't get here, Harry. It's possible."

"I suppose so, Nance. I suppose so."

Harry kissed her and stepped into the waiting elevator.

*F*ifteen minutes later Harry pulled the Bentley into the parking lot of Le Dome. Entering the restaurant, he was directed to Judge Strauss's table. The judge was sitting alone in the enclosed front patio overlooking a small garden and, beyond that, the colorful bustle of Sunset Boulevard. Strauss was a tiny man, in his late sixties, perfectly proportioned and immaculately groomed. His hair and mustache were silver and neatly trimmed. His face was handsome, patrician. He wore a three-piece suit of dark gray flannel with a silver-gray tie. On his lapel was a medal rosette that Harry thought might be the Légion d'Honneur. He rose and gave Harry a firm handshake.

"Mr. Cain, good of you to come. I ordered some of your excellent California Cabernet . . . a Jordan. I hope you'll join me."

"I will, Judge, gladly. It's one of my favorites."

The older man poured Harry a glass of the deep-red wine. Strauss swirled his own wine in the large balloon glass, sniffed at it and smiled.

"Good stuff. Complex and vigorous. Like you, Mr. Cain." Harry smiled. "That's really why I wanted to see you, and I'll come right to the point. Although it's arguable we shouldn't be discussing this at all with our Parlier appeal pending, I don't consider it improper. If you do, then speak up and we'll postpone this discussion."

Now Harry was completely puzzled. How could settlement discussions possibly be improper? Hearing no objection from Harry, Strauss continued.

"I followed your handling of the Parlier case very closely. Your work was superb beginning to end."

"Thank you. Coming from you, that's quite a compliment."

"No thanks needed. Just a fact. One professional to another. You already know that Cavanaugh's one of the oldest firms in the country. It enjoys as fine a reputation as any such institution anywhere. But even the greatest of institutions needs changes—an infusion of new blood, new ideas. I joined the firm three years ago; and along with a group of more... how can I put it?... 'progressive' partners, I've made some rather radical changes in the firm's attitudes and policies. It's a very big firm and very prosperous too, I must say. We've got an office in Washington and one in London. The point is we'd like one here in Los Angeles. With the growing economic strength of the Orient, Mr. Cain, this is the coming place, and Cavanaugh is going to be here." Judge Strauss stopped and sipped his wine.

"The problem is how to do it. We could try a merger with a large local firm. But that's difficult and complex... and extremely time-consuming. We could send out three or four of our own young partners and ten or eleven green associates. But that won't keep the clients happy. It won't attract new local business either. Not the kind we want... the major motion picture studios, for example. From what I've seen, they'll go only to a handful of special attorneys they consider the 'stars' in their field. That's how they're used to selecting actors and directors, and they select their lawyers the same way. So Cavanaugh needs a 'star.' Some outstanding local man who'll give us immediate standing, a realistic, forceful presence here. Could that man be you, Mr. Cain?"

Harry was floored. "Me? With all respect, Judge Strauss, you're fooling yourself. Your partners would never swallow that. Why, if people like Maynard Aldrich ever—"

"Oh, I've talked about this to Maynard and his bunch. They fought it, of course—wanted no part of it, as you guessed. But confidentially, the white shoe boys, like Maynard, no longer have the power to get their way. It's a new day at Cavanaugh, Mr. Cain. Now we've got brains and vigor, not just history and pedigree. I think you'd be perfect for us, and consider what we can do for you. A full-service, prestigious firm, a steady, high income, the ability to retire with security when you're ready, a fine office in New York, Washington and London—many, many advantages."

Harry took a sip of his wine and sat back reflecting on what the man had said. After a moment he replied.

"Well, I'm very flattered, Judge, but what you're suggesting would be such a radical change in my practice, in my way of life, and on the personal level, it certainly wouldn't be easy."

"Of course, those are all things you must consider. And that's all I ask you, Mr. Cain. Just consider the matter. As I say, there are *many* advantages. And I'm not so sure you'd even find it so difficult on the personal level. Oh, we're a stuffier bunch than you're probably used to. But you're not really a Hollywood type yourself, Mr. Cain. You were at Harvard after all; and you seem well mannered and quite gentlemanly. I would guess that, although frequently in the public eye, you're a rather discreet person, sound and balanced. Certainly your intelligence and skill are undeniable. I'm sure you'll fit in better than you might imagine."

"Well, thank you again, Judge. It's a very new idea for me, and if you have the time, I'd like to ask a few more questions. Firstly, I—"

At this point the maitre d' appeared beside their table. "Telephone, Mr. Cain. It's your office."

"Will you excuse me for a moment, Judge?"

"Certainly, Mr. Cain."

Harry rose and left the table. He made his way to the phone in the rear of the restaurant, called his office and found that they had tracked him down only to read him his messages before the office closed. There was nothing urgent.

Somewhat annoyed at the interruption, Harry took a shorter route back to his table, cutting through the circular bar that occupied the center of the restaurant. Although he was already framing the questions he would put to Judge Strauss, his attention was momentarily diverted by a couple on adjacent bar stools across the dimly lit room. They were locked in a long and passionate kiss, the man's hand high up on the girl's bare thigh. As Harry came through the room, the man disengaged himself and waved.

"Harry! Harry Cain! It's me, old sod . . . Robin Milgrim. Bloody well pissed, but still functioning." He nodded vaguely in the direction of the girl.

Harry moved closer. Milgrim was in a tan safari outfit. He was a man of medium height with wavy ginger hair and mustache and a much too pretty face. He was grinning broadly. The girl's platinum hair was done in a spikey punk style. Her pink blouse was open practically to her waist, her black micro-mini skirt hiked up almost to the same point. Very red lipstick was smeared widely around her overly full lips. Milgrim started off the bar stool to greet Harry, his right hand extended.

"How's my little pal Gail, old sod? Some kid you got there. Too bad about..."

Before Milgrim finished the sentence—before he got fully off the stool, Harry's right fist smashed into his face with all the force of Harry's rage. The blow shattered Milgrim's nose, making an ugly crunching sound, spraying the air with blood. With a hideous grunting noise, Milgrim fell backward off the stool. On the bar room floor, he clutched his nose and tried to get up, then slid back to his knees making little whimpering sounds, the blood pouring freely between his fingers onto his bush jacket.

Terrified, the girl backed away from Harry and began to scream hysterically. Suddenly the room filled with onlookers of all sorts—waiters, customers, busboys, and, oh, Christ, Harry thought, Army Acherd from *Daily Variety*.

The manager appeared and took Harry by the arm. "Look, Mr. Cain, you better come on back to my office and wait there. I'll help Mr. Milgrim. The police'll be here soon, so you go on ahead. We'll talk back there." He led Harry through the rows of onlookers that parted as he approached. Harry passed directly by Judge Strauss, who was staring in horror at the bloody man on the floor, the hysterically sobbing girl. The dapper little man looked pale and shrunken. Harry stopped for a moment, the manager still clinging to his arm.

"I'm sorry about this, Judge. Very sorry."

Strauss drew himself up and replied coldly, "So am I, Mr. Cain. More sorry than you can imagine."

*I*t took Harry two frustrating hours to deal with the police and the press and make his way back home.

Nancy met him at the door, which was unusual in itself. She smiled and said pleasantly, "Hi, what happened to you?"

Harry made martinis and told her, from the beginning, in detail. When he was done, she held him tight, cradling his head against her breast.

"You poor bastard. I don't blame you a bit. I would have done the same thing if I could. Life has been tough for you these days, hasn't it?" Harry smiled gratefully for her sympathy.

"And some of the time, I've made it even tougher, haven't I?" He looked up in surprise. "That's right. You heard me right. I'm not apologizing for it . . . just recognizing it." She paused, then went on. "Harry, you know I've been trying to sort things out about us for some time now . . . and, lately, I've been dealing with it better than I was for a while there. Today's scare over Gail made me do even more soul-searching. Some things became clearer for me. You've certainly not been the perfect husband, and we're not the perfect couple. But damn it, Harry, I love you very much, and what we've got, I suppose, is better than most people have.

"I can't pretend I like everything about us, Harry . . . or about you. I've been badly hurt in the past, and as I told you before, I foolishly kept it in, turned my attention, my anger in other directions. But it started coming out."

"I've noticed." He grinned.

"I guess you did. And it may come out again, believe me. From now on, I'm going to tell you how I feel about this. You may not like it, but that's what I'm going to do. Maybe it'll help. But you can help too, you know. You can grow up a little . . . you know what I mean?" She smiled, no malice in her eyes, and without waiting for Harry to reply, continued. "I'm a big girl, Harry, and a realist. I know that neither sex nor monogamy is everything and that what we've got together is good in many ways . . . well worth saving. Still, my love, it hurts . . . and, if it keeps happening, the hurt is going to make me more and more angry —

going to grow into something I won't be able to control much less ignore. All I can say now is I'll try to deal with the past and hope the future won't pose this problem. If it does, I'll try to deal with that too . . . if I can. But will you try too?"

"Sure, Nancy, of course I'll try. I don't want to hurt you—ever."

Harry loved Nancy—felt a deep emotional bond to her. He also liked and respected her. Certainly, he owed her a great deal. He knew these things, and as he promised to "try," he meant it. But having said the words, he wondered if he would ever succeed. Worse, he wondered what would really happen when some new and exciting woman appeared, offering the thrill of the quest, the risk, the high adventure, the pleasures of discovery. When that happened, would he even try?

Well, he'd do what he could.

He took Nancy's hand and brought it to his lips. "I love you, Nancy."

She looked at him tenderly. "I know. I know."

They had more martinis, danced for a time to George Shearing and then had dinner by candlelight. They laughed together, relaxed and enjoyed each other.

As he finished his coffee, Harry suddenly sat back and threw his napkin to the table.

"Damn it! I've got to drive out to the Grant house tonight. I completely forgot."

"Tonight, Harry? Why?"

"I'm sorry, Nance. They've sold the house. The buyers take possession tomorrow. I've been putting off going back there again, but if I don't pick up those books David left me, that's it, I'll lose 'em. And some of those are valuable books. Say, why don't you come with me. We'll take a bottle of champagne and kind of say goodbye to the place?"

Nancy paused, deep in thought, chewing on her lower lip. "I'll ride out with you, Harry, but I couldn't face going inside. Too many memories. Why don't you drop me at Barbra's place and pick me up when you're done?"

"Okay, Nance, I understand. Give Barbra a call. I'll grab a sweater, and we'll drive out right now. It won't take more than a couple of hours."

*T*hey drove out the coast highway, and Harry dropped Nancy at Barbra Streisand's Malibu ranch. He left her safely inside with Barbra and three friends, then drove on. It was close to midnight when he reached the top of David's private road.

There were no lights, but the house was bathed in moonlight that sparkled on the ocean beyond it.

Harry got out, unlocked the garage and pulled the car in. Then he closed the garage door. He had no reason for doing this. It just felt better. And David always liked it closed, felt the house looked "sloppy" with the garage door open.

As Harry turned his key in the front door, the gong sounded even louder than he remembered it. He found the light switch and the room had the same dramatic impact it always did. It took him back to so many times there, so many laughs and so many troubles.

He prowled the living room and went into the kitchen, where he found one last bottle of champagne on ice. He opened it and poured himself a glass.

He turned out the interior lights, opened the sliding glass door to the patio and went outside. The ocean was shimmering in the luminous moonlight, and Harry could see down the coast for miles, the tiny lights stretching in a great arc all the way to Palos Verdes.

Across the moon-washed patio Harry could see the suspended loops of heavy black chain over which David had fallen. He walked to the edge and looked down at the white foam breaking over the rocks far below. He tried not to think of David's head shattering on those jagged ridges of stone, his heavy body floating in the surf, flowing in, bumping, turning, drifting out.

Harry shook his head and sat on a deck chair in the moonlight. He recalled so many nights on that patio. He remembered David's early brilliance and unwavering confidence, long nights of drinking and talking about anything and everything, sharing the world, so exciting to all of them. Then the wildness, the cruelty and disillusion had come, and, finally, the anguish, the enormous crippling doubts, the tears—the death.

But there had been laughter too and so much sentiment. David, in his inevitable Hawaiian shirt, a drink in one hand, swaying to Mabel Mercer's "It Never Entered My Mind," singing with the record, "and order orange juice for one," a tear starting down his cheek. My poor friend, what were you remembering? . . . David sitting cross-legged on the deck while his friend, Manolo, his aged face like dark carved wood, played the guitar and softly sang of the war he had fought so long ago. "Madrid your tears of sorrow, Madrid your tears of sorrow, Madrid your tears of sorrow, Mamita, we will avenge you someday." . . . And the long, winding run through the moonlight, ten, twelve of them, racing down the path to the beach, diving cleanly through the phosphorescent surf—naked, drunk, so full of life, so charged with—

Harry's reverie was interrupted by the huge gong sounding through the house. A key had opened the front door.

He heard the door close softly, followed by footsteps in the entry hall coming in his direction. An instant later, the living room lights came on. Whoever it was remained momentarily screened from Harry's view by a huge palm.

The seconds seemed an eternity. Then Sonny Ball moved across the room. Obviously, he couldn't see Harry outside in the dark, but soon enough he'd wonder why the sliding glass door was open to the patio.

Harry was tense and, strangely, just a little scared. It began to dawn on him that Sonny must have had another key to the house all along, that Sonny could have come in the night of David's death—could even have killed him. But why?

Sonny, chic as always, in his soft brown tweed coat and designer jeans, moved across the room to the fireplace, his Gucci loafers making quick hard sounds on the oak floor. The blond curls fell softly over his forehead, as he bent to the hearth and began prying out first one oversized brick, then another.

Harry had always admired the way David set the giant bricks in a loose pattern without mortar. Now he began to understand why. In a short time, Sonny had lifted six bricks out and had an opening about two feet square. He seemed to be pulling at some kind of hinged metal top set in the floor beneath the bricks. It was giving him trouble, and Harry could hear him quietly muttering "shit" as he worked at whatever it was.

Then Harry heard a metallic bang as the hinged top fell back against the piled up bricks. Sonny reached in the opening and pulled out what looked like a plastic garbage bag, only white and much slimmer. It was full.

At that point, Harry's chair squeaked, making a noise that seemed thunderous. Sonny looked up and saw the open patio door. He moved quickly across the room, pulled the huge oriental sword from its scabbard on the wall and made for the patio.

"Okay, who's out there?" His voice was strained with fear, but the sword looked steady enough in his hands.

With a fluid movement, faster than Harry would have expected, Sonny reached for the wall switch, flooding the patio with light and moved swiftly outside, the two-handed sword held in the attack position like a samurai warrior.

The sword dropped a bit when Sonny saw who it was. But only a bit. It still looked very big and very dangerous. "Harry, what the hell are you doing out here?" Sonny started to smile. Then he saw too much knowledge in Harry's face, and his own expression changed, hardened, the blue eyes glinting like steel chips.

"You know, don't you, Harry? Oh yeah. I can tell." Now Harry *did* know, where before he'd only suspected. It began to drum in his head, Sonny killed David. Holy Christ! Sonny killed David.

"I had to do it, Harry. He was gonna blackmail me. Besides he tried to choke me. That giant queen would have torn my head off."

"So you pushed him?"

"A long way, Harry." Sonny smiled a sort of strange smile. It was more like a snear, his lips pulled back, making a big slice across his face.

Harry began to stall. Somehow he instinctively felt he had to keep Sonny talking. "Why'd you come back?"

"Half a million bucks worth of coke, pal. That pays a lot of rent. I lost my job, remember?"

"I never figured you for a heavy user, Sonny."

"Oh yeah? Why do you think the studio dropped me? You think it was because of that silly skid row movie case? Shit no! Yank could've lived with the rumor I was AC/DC, especially after we won. But doing drugs? Not Yank. Not Mr. America. Hired a hotshot detective out of New York. Followed me two days—trying to catch me with coke, not cock. Finally, got stills of me sitting by my pool, snorting, strung out—got 'em from right over the side wall of my house. Yank invited me to his office. He had huge four-by-six-foot blowups all over the room—you know, straw up my nose, eyes bugging out, that kind of thing. I took one look and agreed to his terms. But I didn't know how tough it would be living without that big bread coming in. I had no idea how addicted I'd gotten to money. No idea."

"But why did you keep the stuff here at David's?"

"You gotta be kidding, counselor. It's not my stuff. It's his. Who the fuck do you think was supplying half of Hollywood? That great artistic cocksucker, David Grant."

"You shoved him off the edge for the cocaine?"

"Shit, Harry, use your head. I just took it out of his fireplace this minute. Why would I wait all these months if that's what I killed him for? Besides, I was winning Oscars then. I had my work, for life I thought, making those very big bucks." Ball paused, the sword still pointed at Harry.

"It was old-fashioned blackmail really. We were out here on the patio. He was bombed out of his mind—kept pushing me to act in that pretentious piece of shit he wanted to make with the German dyke."

"You mean *Medea 1990?*"

"Yeah, that's right. I said 'no way.' He said if I felt that way, I could Goddamn well buy my coke at Thrifty Drugstore from then on. That was no big deal. But then he got nastier. Said he'd give the *Enquirer* a story about what gay movie star was keeping a teenage male model.

"One thing led to another, and he got mean as hell. He started grabbing me, first my shoulders, then my throat. That big fucker was gonna throttle me, I swear, and so I just shoved as hard as I could, and then . . . he was just gone. That's all, just gone."

"Jesus Christ."

"You are fucking articulate tonight, counselor." The sneer returned. "Listen," Sonny went on, "I gotta take off now. So do you." He paused. "I'll make you a deal. Instead of slicing you up, I'll let you jump—just like David—only maybe you'll live."

Christ, Harry thought, the crazy bastard really means it. He felt a moment of fear that was overcome with surging anger. Grabbing the champagne bottle by the top, he moved toward Sonny.

Ball took one step back and, with an easy side arm motion, pulled the sword back, so that he could cut Harry in half if he came on. "I studied *kendo*, Harry. I know this weapon. I'll take your head off if you come one step closer. Now put the bottle down!"

Harry felt the fear again. Sonny looked deadly. Harry stopped, then backed up, placing the bottle on the table. He calculated his chances. If he jumped off the patio, he'd probably get killed, certainly maimed. If he didn't, Sonny would kill him anyway. Why leave a witness?

"Look, Sonny" Harry spread out his arms—"you don't need me to jump. You don't need to run. It was self-defense. He tried to choke you, for Christ sake, you'll..."

"Eat it, Harry, you've conned me enough already. Self-defense, shit! This time, it'll all come out... everything. Who's gonna believe me—the queer who fooled the world—so romantic the girls creamed in their jeans—until they found out I was a junky queen all along, especially one who didn't come forward and tell the story right away, who lied to the cops, who probably killed David over dope or jealousy or both? 'You know those fags.' Come on, Harry. That's what the cops will think. That's what the jury will think. I'm not taking any chance on that kind of justice—not when I like Acapulco so much." He grinned for a moment, then turned serious again.

"All right, don't fuck with me any more. I want you to go over the side right now. If not, I'll kill you. It's the same to me. So *move!*"

Sonny stepped toward Harry, the huge two-handed sword drawn up over his head ready to strike downward, splitting Harry in two from his head on down.

Harry backed up slowly—a step at a time, his mind racing. This lunatic was really going to kill him. He'd be gone—finished—no more Harry Cain. What would the papers say? "Prominent attorney leaps to death?" Front page? Surely. Christ, he'd miss being Harry Cain. But then he'd never know. He wouldn't exist. The sun would come up in the morning on a world without him. In ten years— hell, in *one* year, no one would even remember. Oh, maybe Nancy would still feel some pain—and Gail, of course. She'd smile now and then at some memory. But, soon there'd be nothing—no evidence that a man named Harry Cain had ever walked the earth. He felt another surge of anger and determination—determination to live.

As Sonny Ball slowly closed the distance between them, Harry remembered something he'd seen in a movie. He had to keep Ball talking. Continuing to step backward, Harry put up one hand, "Hang on, Sonny," he said, "how do I know that, if I jump—if I miss the rocks and live, you won't climb down and kill me on the beach?"

As he said this, Harry looked right at Ball and then just for a second let his eyes flicker to the fireplace behind them. Ball caught the glance and his eyes shifted for just a second. Then he concentrated again on Harry. He kept nervously licking his lips; and, when he spoke, his voice was flat and deadly.

"You don't know, counselor. But if you don't jump, I'll butterfly you right now." He took another step toward Harry, who retreated toward the ledge and then stopped again.

"Sonny, for God's sake, why don't you just tie me up. Take me with you as a hostage." His heart was pounding out of his chest. He could feel the razor-sharp cutting edge of the huge sword driving down through his collarbone, shearing through his ribs, his lungs, cleaving him in two.

Again he shifted his eyes to a spot behind Sonny and quickly back to meet the man's stare, as Sonny started just the beginning of a turn, but checked himself. The sword dropped just a bit; and, this time, there was uncertainty in his eyes. He was worried.

Sonny moved toward Harry, pulling the sword up high again, ready to swing it downward in a killing stroke. Harry stepped back again until he felt his heel against one of the short redwood posts that bordered the patio and held the single heavy chain that served David, inadequately, as a fence.

Then Harry stopped and Sonny moved in, faster now, doing a fancy kind of Oriental shuffle, sword raised high in an attack position. Harry tried to focus on a point just over Sonny's shoulder. He widened his eyes and, as Sonny came within striking distance, Harry screamed, "Okay, Sergeant, take him now."

Sonny couldn't resist. He turned quickly to look, as Harry pushed off the redwood post and drove his shoulder into Sonny's gut, pistoning his legs to increase the impact, the way he'd learned in high school, as a hopelessly outweighed free safety.

Harry's momentum sent Sonny gasping and reeling backward across the patio and into the living room, Harry clinging to his midsection. The sword dropped from Sonny's grip, bouncing across the living room floor and coming to rest some twenty feet away. Harry clamped his arm around Sonny's neck in a brutal chokehold, squeezing, crushing, venting his rage . . . until Sonny went limp and began to sob.

Harry's grip slackened. He took his arm from around the man's neck and slowly got to his feet, still shaking. Gradually, Sonny lifted his face. Tears were streaming down his cheeks. Beckoning Harry to come nearer, he struggled to speak, his voice a hoarse, croaking whisper. Harry bent closer, straining to make out the words.

Suddenly, with no sign of warning, Sonny lurched away in a crashing leap for the sword. Reaching out in desperation, Harry managed to catch Sonny's foot and, stumbling behind him, was able to hold on with both hands.

Actors! Harry thought as he struggled to keep his grip. Grunting with the effort, Sonny aimed vicious kicks at Harry's fingers and reached out, straining toward the sword which still lay a good ten feet from his outstretched fingers.

Then, Sonny's loafer came off. Finding himself free, he scuttled toward the weapon, with a scrambling, spiderlike crawl. For an instant, Harry looked in bewilderment at the empty shoe in his hand, irrelevantly noting the Hunting World label stitched inside. Then, dropping the shoe, he took two huge strides and launched himself up and over Sonny, in a desperate, headlong dive for the sword.

He fell short and landed heavily on Sonny's back, driving him to the floor, forcing the air from his lungs. Without pausing, Harry rolled away, throwing himself toward the sword.

As he heard Sonny scrabbling along the floor behind him, Harry's fingers closed at last on the heavily braided hilt. He jumped to his feet, clutching the weapon and stepping back away from Sonny, who was still in a crouch on the floor.

After a moment, Sonny got slowly to his feet, shaking his head, breathing heavily. He looked at Harry, then around the room. He reminded Harry of a tired, angry bull—pic'd, wounded, still dangerous.

Then Harry saw him spot the champagne bottle resting on a nearby table. In one quick movement, Sonny swept it up and shattered it on the table's edge, the bottle's jagged neck still clutched in his fist. Then, gathering speed as he moved, Sonny ran at Harry, his arm outstretched before him, the razor sharp glass aimed at Harry's face.

Harry's eyes were wide, his jaw tightly clenched. He saw the scene as if in slow motion. He stepped backward, away from Sonny's charge, away from the vicious weapon coming straight at him.

As in a dream, Harry pulled the large sword back, far back, on his right side. Momentarily, he wondered if he could really kill this man. Horrified, he imagined what it would be like to drive that enormous blade into another human, slicing through flesh, smashing through bone, ripping him open, destroying him. But was there a choice?

As Sonny's momentum closed the distance between them, Harry began to swing the sword forward in a wicked side-arm arc. Still Sonny came on, and Harry saw the cruel shards of glass rushing toward his eyes. If only there was some way to hurt Sonny, stop him, without... There was no more time to think. Turning his wrists, Harry drove the dull flat of the weapon into Sonny's side with all the force of his body.

Sonny screamed, a horrified, strangled cry from somewhere deep in his throat. The sword shattered with a *thwak*, and the huge blade clattered to the ground, leaving only the hilt in Harry's tightly clenched hands.

Sonny staggered, dropping his weapon, clutching his side. He slumped to the ground, moaning. No blood was visible.

Harry smashed the jagged bottleneck with his heel and stood with the sword hilt in both hands, watching Sonny writhing on the ground, making sure he would give no more trouble. There was no need.

Sonny, his ribs badly broken, was permanently out of the combat. Harry picked up the blade, his hands shaking, his shirt soaked with sweat. He turned the bent blade over in his hands examining its thin, hollow form.

Good Christ, it was only a prop... a tin copy, a fucking prop. David had a prop on his wall all those years.

Two hours later a very tired Harry left the sheriff's Malibu substation and drove to Barbra Streisand's. After describing his adventure to Nancy, Barbra and her excited guests, he and Nancy started the long drive home.

The first gray hint of dawn outlined the hills and vaguely illuminated the surf, as they headed down the coast highway and turned up into the winding canyon that was the beginning of Sunset Boulevard.

"Can you beat David trying to palm off a hollow piece of tin as the Shogun's sword? Probably thought I'd never take it out of that fancy scabbard."

"That's twice he did that to you, Harry. You don't think that green rag on the floor of your den really belonged to the Shah of Iran, do you?" Harry had taken a somewhat worn oriental rug instead of a large fee the very first time he had done legal work for David Grant.

"Well, I guess that was David. Fool everyone, always, and hope it works twenty percent of the time."

"But pushing cocaine, Harry. Why?"

"Money, I guess. David needed tons of it. You don't attract young Italian boys without a suite at the Hassler, a limousine and a yacht at Santo Stefano—not the kind of boys David wanted."

"Okay, but Harry, he was making good money from his work. Why did he need to push coke?"

"Not really the money you'd think, Nance. Sure his name was big. But it was three years since he'd done a picture. The last one was a disaster. Then he had that fight with Mike Ovitz—wouldn't take Mike's advice. After that, he tried it without an agent. There was always lots of talk, you know, Redford and Eastwood, and all that; but the fact is he couldn't seem to get any project going, and it was getting worse. Probably the money just ran out and the coke was all he could think of.

"He had a dozen friends like Sonny who used it a lot and had the money to pay for it. So David, with that terrible combination of insane boldness and bad judgment, just fucked up his whole life."

"Maybe he went out at the right time?"

"Yeah, maybe. Maybe he didn't resist too much when Sonny pushed."

They drove on, through the Palisades, down past the old polo field, then up again into the suburban park of Brentwood.

"You know," Harry broke the silence, "he's got one hell of a defense case."

"Who, Sonny?"

"Sure. David outweighed him nearly a hundred pounds, and he was always a mean drunk." Harry warmed to his theme. "In a rage, he comes for Sonny, gets those big hands on Sonny's throat. Sonny tries to get away, spins around so David's momentum is carrying him toward the ledge. Sonny pushes David away from him, not trying for the cliff—certainly not trying to kill, just trying to get this maniac killer away from him, and then, as he said, suddenly David is 'just gone.' Christ, any jury would have reasonable doubt about that."

"Why didn't he come forward with the story; why did he lie to the police?"

"Easy. Turn your disadvantage into an advantage. He's a homosexual masquerading as straight because his work demanded it. It's common sense. What would happen to his box office appeal, to his rich contract at Consolidated Studios, if the story came out? Gone the next day, that's what. And what kind of treatment could a gay in his position expect from the police, press or the public?

"No, he could only keep his work, his position, his life, by keeping silent, keeping out of the whole thing. Besides, David was already dead. Telling the true story wasn't gonna bring him back."

Driving with his left hand, Harry began to gesture with his right, as if making a closing argument in court.

"Of course he was wrong to lie, ladies and gentlemen of the jury, but you can understand why he did it. And, certainly, it's no indication that he intended to kill David Grant or pushed him other than in self-defense."

"What about the cocaine, counselor?"

"Well, he can't lie about it, because they'd crucify him with my testimony; but he can use that disadvantage too. Try David, make David a 'dirty rat pusher.' He was older, more sophisticated, the most persuasive man in the world. He got Sonny involved when he was young. Like he got a hundred other susceptible kids hooked. They couldn't help themselves. He deserved to die."

"Kids? Sonny was forty. I don't believe that for a minute. Neither do you."

"Hey. We don't have to believe our theory of defense. We're not the jury, thank God. Besides, I'm a witness. I couldn't try this case even if Sonny wanted me to."

"He probably will. He tries to kill you, but he'll still want your skill. But tell me, Clarence Darrow, how does he get around the attack on you tonight?"

"That's tough, but he can still do it. He knew the sword was a prop. He never would have forced me to jump, not really. He just wanted to scare me so much I'd be glad to let him tie me up so he could get away. At the last minute he was gonna do just that. There was never any intention to hurt me."

"I don't think you believe that either."

"I don't know. Maybe. Anyway, who knows *what* to believe about human conduct under stress. Take me. I'm a nonviolent guy if ever there was one. As of this morning, would anyone have believed I'd be in *two* soon-to-be-notorious brawls in the space of a few hours? I sure wouldn't have; but then lots of us may have a much greater capacity for violence than we'd ever dream."

"I suppose so."

Once again, they lapsed into silence.

The morning light gave the UCLA buildings a soft rose color. A few more cars were on the road now, winding beside them along the lush gardens of Bel Air.

"Harry?"

"Yeah."

"I love you." She moved over and put her head on his shoulder. Harry looked down at that face, the face that had been there, all those times, through all those years.

He put his arm around her. "I love you too, Nance. You're really all I can count on, all I can trust. You're all I've really got."

"No, Harry, you've got your work, that big complex, dramatic sport, the world-class law game. You've got that, Harry, and it's more than I could ever be to you—more than *any* woman could be. It's really your life." There was no bitterness in this, just a tender smile.

"Well, my work's not more to me than you, Nance, and it's not really 'my life,' but it *is* an important part of it. That's for sure."

"Well, thank God you've got it, Harry. Thank God you do."

*H*arry loved the sound of rain. The drops beating on his office windows, the cars swishing by on Sunset, made him relax. He liked the look too. The rain-washed hills gave him a happy, contented feeling, the trees especially green and the colors of the roofs brightened by the water.

Today was different too... special. A meeting he'd pictured for months was about to take place. Harry was excited, keyed up for the outcome of his plan, the last act of the Maurice King drama.

"Mr. Brody is here, Mr. Cain."

"Okay, send him in." Ben Brody's bulk filled the door. He swung his wet raincoat on the rack, took a cup of steaming coffee from Harry's secretary and sat on Harry's couch. "Why did you set up the meeting with King, Harry? You want to talk sale? He's so pissed at you, I doubt he'll pay anything right now."

"You mean because of the brick shaving?"

"Goddamn right because of the brick shaving. You fucked him out of his cute plan. I loved it, Harry. You kept him from stealing my building. I'll have to sell it; but, thanks to you, I'll get a fair price, even though the market isn't really great just now."

"I think you'll get much more than a fair price, Ben. Just keep quiet for the next few minutes."

"What do you mean?"

"I mean I want you to say nothing at this meeting but 'hello,' okay?"

"Okay, Harry, but Christ I wish I knew what you were doing."

The phone rang. "Mr. King is here, Mr. Cain."

"Send him in."

Maurice King made his customary theatrical entrance. Shedding his white ankle-length trench coat, he was immaculately dressed in a gray silk suit with gray alligator shoes and a gray silk tie. His slim attaché case was the same gray alligator.

From the start he was pompous and irritable. "Look, Cain, I came because you said it was urgent and would save me a million dollars. I was a fool to do it, especially in the rain. Now what's on your mind?"

"Well, Mr. King, it concerns Ben's property and yours."

"Look, I made you an offer and you turned it down. Don't expect much more, even if you did get out of moving the building. I know Brody's gotta sell, and, although I shouldn't, I'll still buy. For ninety thousand in cash . . . maybe even a hundred thousand. Certainly no more."

"Mr. King, you know that building is worth three hundred thousand or more."

"Not to me, Cain, not to me. I may not have the leverage I had before, but I don't need it any more. You won't find many buyers in that area and none for cash . . . and if you keep on hassling me, I won't buy it either."

"I don't think we'll take your deal, Mr. King, I—"

King broke in. "Well then, you've got a lot of nerve getting me over here. You could have said this on the phone." He reached for his briefcase and stood, ready to walk out. "And don't bother me again about this. Find yourself another buyer, Brody. Your shyster here just cost you a sale." He moved toward the door.

"Just a minute, Mr. King. That's not why I asked you here. It seems you've put your new building on Mr. Brody's property. It's not finished, but the walls are up, and that's where they are."

King stopped and turned to face Harry.

"What? That's nonsense!"

"No sir, it's not nonsense. Here's our surveyor's report. Not a big encroachment, I'll grant you. But enough. More than an inch."

Brody looked on in amazement as King took and thumbed through the report that supported Harry's claim. Then he looked over at Harry—still angry but with a hint of uncertainty in his eyes. "This can't be, Cain. It can't be. When you shaved that inch off Brody's building to get him off my property, we built right up against Brody's wall. We can't be over the property line, because we're exactly up against his building." The old confidence and disdain returned. "You got a plumber for a surveyor, counselor. *That's* your problem."

"No, Mr. King, it's *your* problem. You see, we didn't shave just an inch off Ben's building. We shaved more than two inches, took Ben's wall back more than an inch from your property line. When you built your walls right up against Ben's building, you put them an inch or more on his property. That makes you a trespasser, Mr. King, a trespasser." Ben Brody's face broke into the biggest grin of his life. Now he saw it all.

King was thunderstruck. Harry went on. "Now, Mr. King, we want you to move that building immediately. Either move it or demolish it, but get it off my client's property."

King slumped like a fighter on the ropes, but he was a fighter, nonetheless. He sat down again. "Very cute, Cain, but we'll do just what you did, we'll shave an inch. So it'll cost us ten thousand dollars. You can forget us moving the building. It won't happen, and we won't pay you anything either."

"Well, that's pretty slick, Mr. King, but it won't work. You can shave brick, okay? But you know you just can't shave concrete; and that's what you built your walls with, Mr. King, concrete. Not only that, with those two buildings side-by-side, there's no room to shave anything."

King was white now, burning with silent anger. Harry looked over at Brody. He was ecstatic. Harry winked. "So, Mr. King, we want that building moved. Unless, of course, you're ready to, uh, buy Mr. Brody's property?"

"You mean that inch?"

"No, I mean the whole property."

"All right, Cain, how much?"

"Five hundred thousand dollars, cash."

"What? You cheap shyster. I'll disbar you, I'll break you first."

Harry grinned. "That makes it five twenty-five, Mr. King."

King stood up again, grabbing his briefcase, and glared down at Harry. "Don't give me that crap, Cain. I know how to deal with you, and when I get through with you, you'll wish you'd never pulled a stunt like that." He reached for the long white raincoat and headed for the door.

"Mr. King." The man paused at the quiet tone and looked back. "Yes?"

"That makes it five fifty. Goodbye, Mr. King."

When King left, Ben strolled across the room and gave Harry a bear hug. "You son of a bitch, you brilliant, fucking, devious son of a bitch. I never knew you shaved two inches instead of one."

"I didn't want you to know. A court might have held you were estopped if you knew... that's a legal theory that could have beaten us."

"What'll he do now?"

"Oh, I guess his lawyer will call tomorrow. He'll offer two hundred or two fifty. We'll hold firm at five fifty for a day or two. He'll panic, and we'll get four hundred thousand easy. Listen, his building is worth millions and we've got him by the *pelotas*."

"Jesus, Harry, that's fantastic, I mean it's the greatest maneuver of all time. I can never thank you for what you've done."

Harry looked down at the street now lit by neon lights and still wet in the rain. He answered softly, "I didn't do it for you, Ben, I did it for me. To win, Ben, just to win."

When Ben Brody left, Clara brought Harry a copy of the *Times* with a front-page article circled in red pencil. Headed "Prominent Lawyer Strikes Columnist," it detailed the events at Le Dome and quoted the District Attorney as saying that the facts were being reviewed and a decision would soon be made as to whether charges would be filed.

Harry sighed. He was sure they would never file and Milgrim would never sue. After all, if he did, the whole story would come out in the press, and no jury would likely bring in a plaintiff's verdict on these facts. Still, as much as Harry loved publicity, this kind didn't help. He looked through his mail and was dictating a reply when Clara announced a call from Leland Strauss.

"Good morning, Judge. I'm really sorry about yesterday. I certainly understand how you must feel."

"I'm sorry too, Mr. Cain, but for a different reason. I made a hasty judgment, condemning you in my mind as a barroom brawler. Last night, at a dinner, Aaron Fernbach filled me in on the facts about your daughter and Milgrim. That man's quite a fan of yours, you know—quite an advocate of your cause."

"How the devil did Aaron know about Gail and Milgrim?"

"I have no idea, Mr. Cain. I imagine he has sources of information that would surprise us both. What I do know is that, under these circumstances, one cannot really blame you, and that nothing that occurred negates our offer to have you join our firm."

"Oh? I hadn't realized it was actually an offer."

"Absolutely, Mr. Cain. Cavanaugh and Cutler would be prepared to have you head our Los Angeles office with a partnership share as large as any in the firm, as large even as my own and that's large." He laughed lightly. "I hope you'll give it due consideration and let us know as soon as you can."

Harry paused. Putting the receiver down for a moment, he leaned back in the soft-gray chair and took a deep breath.

"Mr. Cain?" came the faint voice from the receiver.

Harry picked it up again. "I don't really need more time, Mr. Strauss. It's a very flattering offer, but I'm really a loner—a renegade. I'm too old to change. I could never fit happily in an organization like yours—as advantageous as it might be. I don't mean any of this unkindly. I like you and admire your firm. It's just that . . . it's just that I don't really *want* to do it. What I *want* to do is just to keep on as I am."

There was a long pause.

"Well, I'm very sorry to hear that, of course, Mr. Cain. Is there anything that would change your mind? I mean, on the West Coast, we'd even consider calling the firm Cavanaugh, Cutler and Cain . . . if that would make the difference."

"Well, I must say that has a nice ring to it, Judge. But it really wouldn't change things. I want to thank you again however. You've really been most gracious."

"You're very welcome, Mr. Cain. I understand." Another pause. "Well, goodbye then. I certainly enjoyed meeting you."

"Thank you again, Judge, and goodbye."

Harry sat back and smiled. He looked slowly around the lovely, quiet room and out the window at the traffic swishing by in the rain. Then he rose and, shrugging on his coat, found himself whistling.

*T*aking a chair at Gail's bedside, Harry looked out at the hills, dark green and wet with rain. Gail was propped up in bed, wearing a pink sweatshirt that said in red lettering, "Life Is One Fucking Thing After Another." Her sleeves were pushed up to her elbows. Her color was good and Harry was amazed at her youthful powers of recuperation.

He saw the *Times* on her bedside table. "You read about me and Milgrim?"

"Yes."

"Gail, honey, I'm very sorry. Please forgive me."

He expected anger, maybe tears. Amazingly, she grinned and reached out her arms for a hug. He moved over and held her closely.

"You're not sore? You don't despise your crazy old man?"

She patted his back. "Oh Daddy. How could I be sore at *that*. You hit him because you love me and you thought he abused me ... which he had. How could anyone but an idiot despise you for that?"

"Well, I'm afraid I messed him up a bit, Gail, and—"

"Hey. He was much too pretty anyway. It'll do him good to realize he can't always get away with anything he wants in life. No, on balance, it might be a good thing. It may teach him a lesson. It certainly made you feel better; and who knows, maybe what happened will give me some new insight too." He looked up, pleased and surprised.

"Now, no promises," she said, seeing his expression. "I'm still *very* involved with Robin. But I *am* reassessing things, and who knows? Anyway, let's forget it for now. Tell me how the Ben Brody thing came out."

Harry sat back in his chair. He explained his strategy and described the final meeting with Maurice King to his enthralled daughter. When he finished, Gail beamed at him with such pride that Harry wanted to cry.

"Dad, that's just brilliant. Cunning and devious, but incredibly brilliant. Mr. Brody must be terribly grateful for what you did for him. I mean, you saved his life."

Harry sat back and thought about that for a moment. "You know, Gail, Brody said something like that too. But the thing is, I didn't really do it for Brody. I did it for *me*. I did it to win."

Gail smiled. "So what, Dad? So what? You say that like it's some kind of terrible crime. Listen, I know it's supposed to be the other way around, but can I give you the benefit of my own limited experience?"

"Sure, kid."

"Well, I haven't lived that long, but from what I've seen so far, ninety percent of the good deeds in life are done for selfish reasons. You think a brain surgeon is motivated by feelings of humanity? Not from what I've seen. Mostly it's ego. Money too, of course, but mostly ego. Maybe ten percent of it is concern for that poor guy on the operating table. But that doesn't make the surgery any less valuable or any less a good or even great act.

"I've known lots of doctors. They don't go through years of vicious competition in college and med school and then the ordeal of internship for the love of mankind. Believe me. They want to be honored and revered, make money, attract women, all of the rest that goes with being a doctor. So what? They do good things. They do *great* things, every day. Who cares why?

"And it's not just doctors or lawyers, its everyone who does good. The man who builds a new wing on the orphans' home, what does he really want? To see his name up there on that big new building, to receive homage at board meetings and at the country club. Besides, it's deductible. His reasons are no good at all. But he helps a lot of kids.

"Who acts just to help his fellow man, really? Politicians? Not a chance. I've seen enough of them, God knows, working for the magazine. They're probably the worst bunch of all so far as motive is concerned. Why sponsor a good bill? Why work and fight for it, even to the point of jeopardizing your health? What are the reasons? To get re-elected, to exercise power, to feel good—like a hero, to be thought of as a statesman, to go down in history, to make your kids proud, to appeal to a good-looking woman . . . a million selfish reasons. You know what's in last place? To help those poor folks back home. But the new law may still do great things for those folks, change their lives, bring them happiness or health. The *reason* the senator got the bill through doesn't really count.

"You know, Dad, T. S. Eliot wrote that the 'greatest treason' was 'to do the right thing for the wrong reason.' To me, that's utter bullshit—just theatrical posturing. If Eliot really meant that—and I doubt he did—he had damn little common sense. From what I've seen, the 'right' things we do in life are nearly always done for the 'wrong' reason; and, if a person's hunger to satisfy his ego were ever taken away, not a thing of importance would ever get done in this world. No medical discoveries. No great pictures. No pyramids. Not even cathedrals." She grinned. "Damn it, Dad, you worry too much."

Harry was amazed and somehow touched at her perception. He moved closer and hugged her again. This time, he did cry. They both cried and held each other, until the same starchy nurse came in and suggested, once again, that he'd been there long enough.

*H*arry pulled out of the hospital garage and, turning right, then left, joined the stream of traffic heading north on La Cienega. It was still raining and the *tick-tack* of his windshield wipers added to the other comforting sounds of the rain.

As he drove, Harry wondered again at Gail's youthful insight. Did he really know her? Had he really known any other person? Not his father—a child's view—seeing love, tenderness, wisdom—none of the fears, the aching loneliness that must have been there. Not even Nancy. Not really.

Multicolored lights and garish signs swam at Harry through the haze and spray sent out by the other cars. It crossed his mind that he was on a planet careening through dark and limitless space with all those others—millions of them, each enclosed in his own separate car, his own separate life, veering alone across the universe. I'll never really know them, Harry thought. Not one of them.

He came to a stop at Sunset and La Cienega and looked across the street, half expecting to see Carmel there, as on that first day almost a year ago. He felt a sharp pang. Christ, he missed her sometimes. What a year. Not only Carmel, but David, Gail, Sonny Ball. Jesus.

He turned right into Sunset, surrounded by mist and neon and the sounds of the rain and the other cars. He began to feel good... even happy. He was alive, and he was going home.

He pulled up to the next light with a skid. On the corner a tall, dark-haired girl stood under a Vuitton umbrella. She wore a fitted tweed jacket over a white silk blouse. Beige twill pants tucked into knee high boots accentuated her long shapely legs.

As her eyes met Harry's, she tentatively lifted her thumb as if totally unaccustomed to doing so. She was obviously not a hooker. Too chic even for an actress. A model? Perhaps, but how strange to be thumbing a ride. Whatever her career, she was certainly one of the most striking women he had ever seen.

It flashed through his mind that, only the day before, he'd told Nancy he'd "try." Had his "effort" lasted just one day? Even *he* had expected more of himself than that. Still, this did seem an unusual situation.

The light changed, and Harry made a fast decision. He pulled around the corner and opened the door. The girl moved to the car and slipped in beside him like a big cat. She had spectacular cheek-bones and a wide, sensuous mouth. Although her eyes were a startling shade of green, they were almond-shaped and huge, suggesting a trace of Malaysian or Balinese.

"Where you headed?"

"Anywhere really, I just got out of a car—left a man I've lived with for eight years. I just need some quiet and sympathy... and you did look safe."

"Oh, I am. Listen, I know a Japanese Inn where we can sit by the fire and watch the rain fall on the city."

"Where's that, Kyoto?"

"No, Hollywood. Way up in the hills."

"Okay with me. I'm Alla. Let's go."

Harry pulled the Bentley away from the curb and turned toward Hollywood, switching on the stereo as he moved back into the wet flow of the traffic. He grinned at her like a kid with a new toy. Oh well, he thought, I'll go home later.